A Dime a Dozen

MINDY STARNS CLARK

HARVEST HOUSE™ PUBLISHERS

EUGENE, OREGON

Cover by Terry Dugan Design, Minneapolis, Minnesota

Cover photo courtesy of Richard Weisser and smokyphotos.com

A DIME A DOZEN

Copyright © 2003 by Mindy Starns Clark
Published by Harvest House Publishers
Eugene, Oregon 97402

ISBN 0-7369-0995-8 (pbk.)

Printed in the United States of America

For my daughter Lauren...
When God gave me you, He gave me the sunshine
to hold in my arms. You are so kind, so gifted,
and so beautiful inside and out.
I love you!

Acknowledgments

Many, many special thanks:

To my husband, John Clark, J.D., C.P.A., for being a writer's dream come true. With your advising, editing, brainstorming, insight, child care, support, and love, you are making every step of this magical journey a true joy. Honey, I couldn't do any of it without you!

To my editor, Kim Moore, of Harvest House Publishers: Kim, you exemplify God's grace in all that you do.

To Kay Justus, for coming through for me in ways too numerous to count: You are my PCAW, always.

To my father, Robert M. Starns, M.D., for excellent medical advice and information.

To my brilliant readers Jackie Starns and Shari Weber.

To all of those who filled in the gaps of my knowledge: Daniel Bailey, Cecilia Baldini, Charles and Kay Buchanan, Ariane A. Chavez-Luviano, Alice Clark, Emily Clark, James B. Hedrick, Wells and Frieda Justus, C.J. and Melissa Martin, Dave Snyder, Adam Sullivan, David Sullivan, the owners of Old Pressley SM, and the friendly, helpful staff at the Hendersonville, NC, Visitors Center.

To everyone who went to my website (www.mindystarnsclark.com) and entered my Name-the-Charity contest, especially the winners Barbara Pistache, David Tinker, and Kim Colley.

To the great minds at CWG, DorothyL, and MMA, for advice and support.

Thanks to all of you!

Indeed, the very hairs of your head are all numbered. Don't be afraid; you are worth more than many sparrows.

LUKE 12:7

One

I'd never been part of a sting before. Sure, I'd blown the whistle on some defrauders in the past, and I had seen more than one person arrested because of felonious deeds I had brought to light. But this time was different. This time the crime was still in the process of being committed. Worse than that, most of the people at this party were involved.

I stood near French doors that led to the patio, holding a soda in my hand and looking out through the glass at the pool sparkling in the cool March afternoon. Behind the pool was a small lawn dotted here and there with ornamental groupings of shrubbery and plants, all surrounded by a high, thick hedge. I knew that a team of cops was on the other side of that hedge, ready to enter from every direction as soon as I gave the signal.

"Callie, would you like a hamburger? Maybe a hot dog?"

My hostess appeared in front of me bearing a platter of raw meat shaped into patties, and I assumed she was on her way back outside to the grill. My eyes focused on the marbled beef, and then back at her expectant face. She was the very picture of charm and hospitality. Oh, and theft.

"No, thank you," I said, forcing a smile. "I'm fine."

I opened the door to let her out since her hands were full, and music poured into the house, compliments of the large speakers mounted under the eaves outside.

"You should come on out," she urged loudly as she handed the platter off to her husband, Skipper. "It's a gorgeous day."

"In a while, perhaps," I said as I let the door fall shut between us. She turned her attention to a group of guests near the pool, and as she worked the crowd I thought, *You don't want me to go outside, Winnie. The last thing you want me to do is go outside.*

I glanced at my watch, wondering how much longer this would take. The police had instructed me to wait until all of the elements had fallen into place, and so far that hadn't happened. The tension was getting to me, so I set my glass on a nearby countertop and made my way through the small crowd in the kitchen to the upstairs bathroom. I needed to be alone, to catch my breath, to make a call.

Once I was locked inside, I pulled out my cell phone and dialed the number of the police captain. He knew it was me and that I couldn't say much on my end for fear of being overheard.

"Looks like things are moving along as expected," he said.

"Yes."

"Have they brought out the hamburgers yet?"

"Oh, yes. Everything's in full swing."

He chuckled into the phone.

"I hope they're enjoying it while they can," he said.

"They seem to be."

"We're all set on our end. Soon as the guy shows up, we'll call you."

"I'll be ready."

"You found the garage?" he asked.

"Yep."

"Empty?"

"Except for the boxes in the freezer."

"Perfect. Simply perfect. Hang in there, kid. We're on the home-stretch."

I hung up the phone and slid it into my pocket, wondering if all would go off as planned once they called me back. There were so many elements coming into play here, and it was important that they close in at the moment when we could nab the greatest number of guilty parties. I shook my head, marveling at the situation I now found myself in. This wasn't how I usually spent my Saturday afternoons!

As the Director of Research for the J.O.S.H.U.A. Foundation, my job was to investigate charitable organizations in order to verify their suitability for a grant. I had come here to get a closer look at Dinner Time, a food bank and soup kitchen for the homeless in a suburb of San Francisco. I had gone "undercover" by posing as a volunteer to get a good look at the organization from the inside. Almost immediately, however, I realized there was something stinky in the sauce. Dinner Time may have been providing food to the homeless, but it was also providing a handy second income to its founders and many of its employees by way of food donations that were ending up in places other than on Dinner Time's tables.

Even this party was an appalling, blatant display of theft, and, according to my source, they had similar such events every few months. From the chips and hamburgers to the condiments, most of the food being consumed here today had actually been donated to the charity, intended for the poor. Instead, our hosts had simply loaded many of the boxes into their cars and driven the food home for this impromptu party. Any minute now a local food supplier would show up and collect his share of the take, which was waiting for him in the garage. Unbeknownst to any of them, however, much of the donated food this time was marked, from the codes printed on the bottom of the mustard bottles to the labels on the frozen steaks in the freezer.

A knock on the bathroom door startled me from my thoughts.

"Just a minute," I called, and then I washed my hands in the sink and glanced at my reflection in the mirror. My own image still surprised me sometimes, since four months before I had gone from having long hair to short, from wearing my hair in a tight chignon at the back of my neck to having just enough length to frame my face and touch at my collar. I liked the new look, both because of the years it seemed to take from my features and in the way it worked with my usual attire of suits and dresses. I'd spent this week in more casual clothes, however, and today was no exception. I had on jeans and a lightly knit tan shirt, and I felt I looked the part I was playing—that of a woman interested in some simple volunteer work at the local soup kitchen. Little did they know that I was something much more threatening: an investigator with a mission to ferret out the bad guys in the nonprofit world and bring them all to justice!

I opened the bathroom door and found a familiar face waiting to get in, a fellow volunteer named Clement Jackson.

"Oh, hey, Callie," he said, "I didn't realize that was you in there."

"No problem."

I moved out of the way so that he could pass me and go into the bathroom. As he closed the door behind him, I made my way back downstairs to the kitchen.

Clement was such a dear man, a tireless worker who served full time at the food bank for a salary so low I didn't know how he managed to make ends meet. He wasn't aware that I knew his salary rate or anything about him beyond facts he had mentioned to me in casual conversation. He had told me about his lovely wife of 36 years, his five grown children, his eight grandchildren. But the scope of my investigation had included all of the employees and volunteers of Dinner Time, so I also knew his address, his work record, and much more. In the end, he had turned out to be one of only three people connected to the center who apparently weren't involved in the theft of the food.

I was so glad, because it confirmed what I had felt to be true about him all week, that he was a wonderful person with a true heart for charity. His personal side mission was to collect and distribute free used books to all of the children who came to the food bank and, whenever he had time, to sit and read to them and encourage them to read more for themselves.

"Reading can get you through some mighty tough spots," I had heard him say more than once this week. "Even if your feet can't always go somewhere else, your mind sure can." Poor Clement was going to be stunned when this sting came together, for he believed most people were motivated by the same altruism and good faith he himself possessed.

"Callie, can I get you something to drink?"

This time, Winnie's husband, Skipper, was playing the host, walking toward me with a newly filled ice bucket.

"No, thanks," I replied. "My drink's right over here."

As if to prove it, I walked to the spot where I had left my soda, picked it up, and swirled the liquid. Skipper's very presence made me so nervous I didn't dare speak for fear I would begin to babble. Unfortunately, he persisted.

"How about a little ice then," he said, using the tongs to load my drink with ice. Holding my tongue, I watched as he clunked ice cubes into the glass that I held in front of me.

"So what do you think of our weather here in California?" he asked. "Winnie said you just recently moved here, right?"

Actually, I hadn't told her that. What I had said was that I had never lived in California *before*, implying, I guess, that I lived here now. It was the kind of half-truth that going undercover necessitated and the very reason I hated playing a role. As a Christian, lying was hard for me to rationalize, even when the ends seemed to justify the means.

"It's certainly a beautiful day today!" I said, glancing toward the window. I was desperately trying to think of some other sort of socially acceptable patter when I was saved by the bell—or the ring, to be exact, because Skipper's cell phone began ringing from his hip pocket.

With a smile, he thrust the ice bucket at me, extricated the phone, and turned it on.

"Skipper here," he said amiably, winking at me as he did so.

Clutching the ice in front of me, I took a step back, wondering if I could seize the moment and get away before his conversation was finished. Unfortunately, it seemed to last all of about 15 seconds. He said, "Yep. Okay. See ya," and then hung up the phone.

"You'll excuse me, won't you, Callie?" he asked smoothly, slipping the phone back into his pocket.

"Of course."

I held the ice bucket toward him, but he didn't take it.

"Um, could you take that ice out to Winnie?" he asked. "I need to get something from the garage."

He turned and walked down the hall without waiting for a reply. I stood frozen, trying to decide how to get the ice "out to Winnie" without taking a step outside myself. Suddenly my own phone began ringing. I took the opportunity to pass the ice off to someone else, asking a nearby man to please take it out to our hostess as I had a phone call.

"Yes?" I asked into the receiver once I was able to step away from the crowd and into the empty dining room.

"Our guy just turned into the driveway," the captain told me. "Give it about two minutes and then take a peek at the garage."

"Okay."

I hung up the phone, glanced at my watch, and waited, my heart suddenly pounding in my chest. For an absurd moment, I wondered if there was any hidden firepower here, if perhaps Skipper and Winnie kept a Colt .45 tucked in the nearest flowerpot or something. Just because their crimes of theft were of a nonviolent nature didn't mean they didn't know how to defend themselves when push came to shove. As it was about to.

At one minute, forty-three seconds, I heard my name called from the other room. I looked through the doorway to see Clement just coming down the stairs on the other side of the kitchen. Clement, who could be in the line of fire if things went down in a nasty way. Clement, who was heading toward me with a genial smile, eager to start a chat just when it was time for me to move.

"I need a favor!" I said urgently, walking forward to meet him. "I can't find my contact lens. I'm afraid it came out in the bathroom. Do you think you could go back up and look for me? Check all over the floor, the sink, you know."

"Well, I'll try, Callie," he said, nodding his head, the tightly-curled gray hair a sharp contrast to his brown skin. "But my eyesight's not so good myself. Come up and we'll look for it together."

I glanced at my watch. Two and a half minutes.

"You go on up," I said. "I'll be there in just a bit."

"Okay."

"And, listen, if you can't find it, at least stay there and guard the door until I get there. I don't want someone else stepping on it and breaking it."

"All right."

He dutifully trudged back up the stairs as I slipped from the kitchen, walking toward the long side hall Skipper had gone down less than three minutes before. I reached the door of the garage at the end, put my hand on the knob, and turned it.

The door swung open to reveal Skipper and another man lifting boxes into the open trunk of a black Cadillac. Both men looked up to see me, their faces about as guilty as two boys caught dipping their fingers in the peanut butter.

In a way, that's exactly what they were doing.

The men recovered quickly. Both put the boxes into the trunk, but the man I didn't know turned and stepped away where I couldn't see his face. Skipper, on the other hand, took a step toward me, putting on a wide, fake smile.

"Can I help you, Callie?" he asked.

"I'm sorry," I said. "I was looking for some more soda. Maybe root beer?"

"There's nothing like that out here," he replied. "Try the pantry, off the kitchen."

"Okay, thanks," I said, returning his fake smile before stepping back out of the garage and pulling the door shut.

I turned on my heel and walked up the hall with my heart pounding loudly in my head. Despite the chatter and confusion around me, I made straight for the French doors, opened them, and stepped outside. This was my signal to the police who were in hiding on the other side of the hedge, watching the party, waiting to pounce. Once on the patio, I simply kept walking through the loud music, heading around the pool and toward the backyard.

"Callie, can I help you with something?" I heard Winnie call after me.

Suddenly, before I could reply, there were shouts and screams and the sight of at least 20 police officers descending on the partygoers on the patio. I heard the words "freeze" and "raid" and "you have the right to remain silent." Once I finally turned around and looked at the scene, all I could do was pray that Clement was safe, that the cops had apprehended the men in the garage before anyone could do anything stupid.

I waited at the back of the yard until I saw the captain come to the kitchen door and give the "all clear" signal to the cops outside. Breathing a great big sigh of relief, I headed back toward the house, allowing myself to be herded into the corner of the patio where they were sorting everyone out. Counting heads, I realized they had managed to nab almost every single person who was on the list of those who had either stolen food or accepted food they knew was stolen. The cops didn't single me out but merely pointed me in the direction of the innocent parties, the few standing near the garden shed who hadn't the slightest idea what was going on.

Eventually, Clement was sent out from the house to join us. I gave him a big hug, certainly much bigger than our seemingly casual acquaintance would allow. Obviously shaken, he hugged me back even tighter.

When the police told us we were free to leave, I thought it would be best to stick with Clement, perhaps even offer to take him home. He accepted that offer, sitting in a sort of daze in the passenger seat of my rental car as I gently tried to explain all that he had just seen.

By the time we reached his house, he was still quite shaken. He invited me inside and I accepted, eager to see him safely delivered into the arms of his wife.

She wasn't home, however, so I insisted that he call one of his children, perhaps Trey, since I knew he lived right down the street and could be here in a matter of minutes. While we waited, I heated some water on the stove for tea and essentially made myself at home in the kitchen. The house was small but tidy, and everything was easy to find in the neatly organized cabinets. As the water began to bubble on the stove, Clement took a seat at the table, silent, looking every bit of his 59 years. As I was setting his tea in front of him, Trey burst through the door, concern evident on his face.

"Pop?"

Short but muscular, with his father's coffee-colored skin and deep brown eyes, Trey was dressed in jeans and a T-shirt, both of which were covered with spatters of blue.

"We were painting the baby's room," he added, sounding breathless, looking from me to his father. "What's going on?"

Clement didn't answer, so I introduced myself and tried to explain the situation as best I could. The place where Clement worked, I said, had been busted for fraud and theft. Clement was in the clear, but he had been fairly traumatized by the whole event.

"And who are you, exactly?" Trey asked, looking at me as if this were all my fault. In a way, it was.

"My name is Callie Webber," I said, carrying over two more cups of tea and taking a seat at the table. "I'm a private investigator."

Clement turned toward me, his face suddenly registering disbelief rather than shock.

"You're a *what?*" he asked.

"A private investigator."

"Since when?"

"Since I was old enough to get certified in the state of Virginia," I said. "I'm also a lawyer. I work for the J.O.S.H.U.A. Foundation out of Washington, DC."

Clement shook his head, as if to shake off the confusion. Before he could launch into more questions, I continued.

"I live in Maryland now," I explained, "and I just came to California to investigate Dinner Time on behalf of my employer. Dinner Time had requested a grant, and it's my job to verify eligibility."

"You don't even live here?" Clement asked me, still incredulous. "You mean you've been pretending all week?"

"I'm sorry, Clement," I said. "Sometimes that's the only way I can really see what's going on."

Trey slid into the seat across from me, ignoring the tea I had put there for him.

"So what happened today?" he asked. "I'm still confused."

"In the course of the investigation of Dinner Time, I uncovered fraud, theft, tax evasion, distribution of stolen property, you name it. I took that information to the police, only to learn that they already knew about it and that they were very close to making some arrests. We worked together on a sting operation, and today we caught most of the guilty parties red-handed."

"I can't believe they were stealing food," Clement said, shaking his head sadly.

"I always told you there was something slick about that Skipper person," Trey said to his father. "'Skipper and Winnie,' good grief. Sounds like a pair of Barbie dolls."

"Will Dinner Time have to close down?" Clement asked.

"Probably," I answered. "Even if someone were to try to keep the place up and running, I doubt it will be able to stay open for very long. Between the bad publicity and the incarcerated principals, I think it'll soon fold. I'm sorry."

"I'm sorry too," Clement said. "I'm sorry I was so blind, so stupid."

Trey put a reassuring hand on his father's arm.

"C'mon, Pop," he said. "You couldn't know. You were just doing your job."

"Oh, yeah, my job," Clement said. "Guess I'm out of a job now."

"We'll find you something," Trey said. "Maybe Tanisha can get you on over at the grocery store."

"I liked working at a nonprofit," Clement said, shaking his head. "I liked feeling that my efforts were making just a little difference in the world."

I reached into my pocket, grasping the familiar square of paper there. I pulled it out and set it on the table in front of me, still folded in half.

"I'd like to talk to you about that," I said. "And I'm glad Trey is here, because this would involve him too."

Both men looked at me, their faces somber.

"In the course of my investigation," I continued, "I had to check into everybody's background. Including yours, Clement. Your life story paints a picture of a good man, a steady reliable worker who knows the value of a dollar."

"That's my dad," Trey said suspiciously. "But what are you getting at?"

"Well, I've watched you this week reading to the children down at the food bank, Clement. I've heard you talk about the benefits of reading, of being read to. I want you to think about starting a charity of your own. Something that lets you go around and give away books and have regular reading times with homeless children."

"Like a bookmobile?" Clement asked.

"Perhaps," I said. "Or maybe you could get some space in the recreation center or a homeless shelter or another food bank. Somewhere that you could set up a little reading corner filled with books and beanbag chairs and stuffed animals. It's not hard to get people to donate children's books to a charity. You could provide reading times, give the books to the children who seem to want them, encourage their parents to read with them…"

I let my voice trail off, seeing that a spark was lighting up behind Clement's eyes.

"What do I have to do with this?" Trey asked.

"Your father told me that you're an accountant," I said. "Maybe you can help him get started and then keep the books for him."

"Well, yeah, I could do that."

"And I understand your sister is a graphic artist? Maybe she could put together some brochures and promotional materials. You'd be surprised how many resources are available, usually right at your own fingertips."

I looked at Trey and then at Clement, surprised to see the fire quickly fading from the older man's eyes.

"As good as our intentions may be," he said, shaking his head, "There's one thing standing in the way. I can't afford it."

I smiled, fingering the square of paper in front of me.

"Well, then let me take it a step further," I said. "My job allows me a certain amount of leeway with small monetary grants. What would you think if I gave you a check to get started? You could get yourself incorporated as a nonprofit, file for federal tax exemption, and cover your basic start-up costs. Once you've got that tax exemption, I would encourage you to fill out a grant application from the J.O.S.H.U.A. Foundation for a much larger amount of money. We believe strongly in what you could accomplish, Clement, and we would like to have some small part in furthering your efforts."

I sat back, thinking that in the two and a half years I had worked for the foundation, this was the first time I had to talk someone into taking our money!

"Still, I don't see how it would work," Trey said. "He'd need at least a thousand dollars just to get set up."

"How does five thousand sound?" I asked, unfolding the check and handing it to them. It was already made out to Clement Jackson, who picked it up and studied it as if it were a ticket to somewhere important. "And, like I said, once you've got that tax exemption and your policies and procedures in place, you can apply to us for more. I have a feeling we'll be very generous as long as you can show you've got a good business plan."

The two men looked at each other and grinned, and not for the first time I wished my boss, Tom, the philanthropist behind all J.O.S.H.U.A. grants, could be here to witness their joy. Tom was half a world away right now, and though later I would recount this entire scene for him over the phone, it still made me sad that he wasn't here experiencing it for himself.

Then again, he never was. Tom always donated anonymously through the foundation and then enjoyed the moment of presentation vicariously through me. I was happy to recreate every word, every detail, but I had never understood why he chose to remain so removed from the whole process.

Of course, he and I talked frequently during every investigation, and in fact it was the time we spent on the phone that had allowed us to become friends and then eventually something much more than friends. Four months ago, after several years of a phone-only relationship, Tom and I had finally been able to meet face-to-face.

At the time, he had been out of the country for his work, but he had surprised me by flying back to the States and showing up at my home. We had spent exactly 12 hours together—12 amazing hours that I had relived again and again in my memories ever since—and then he had to leave, returning to Singapore and the urgent business that awaited him.

Now, four months later, Tom was still in Singapore, though his business there was quickly drawing to a close and soon he would be coming home for good. His home was in California and mine was in Maryland, but our plan was to meet somewhere between the two in exactly seven days at some quiet place where we would finally, finally be able to spend some real quality time together—time getting to know each other even better, time exploring the possibilities of a relationship that had gone from friendship to something much more in the space of one 12-hour visit. I was already counting the minutes until we could be together again, knowing that once he returned, a new chapter in my life would begin in earnest. Tom was handling the logistics of our reunion, and my primary concern was to wrap up my next investigation by the following Sunday, because I didn't want work or anything else to detract from the time we were going to spend together.

Clement spoke, snapping me out of my thoughts and back to the moment at hand.

"I've been praying for something like this for quite a while," he was saying, looking at his son, and I realized there were tears in his eyes. "For so long," he repeated, blinking. "I didn't think the Lord was hearing me. But He was. Because He sent me an angel."

I held up one hand to stop him, emotion surging in my heart as well.

"Now, don't—"

"I'm not kidding, girl. You *are* an angel. A very generous angel."

"So you'll take the money and start your own charity?" I asked.

"Oh, thank You, Lord," he said, grinning up toward the ceiling. Then he looked back at me. "Yes, Callie. Yes. Most *definitely* yes."

Two

After directing Trey and Clement to some resources that might be helpful in their new venture, I bid them farewell and then spent several hours down at the police station, giving my full statement about the arrests and the events that had led up to them. Once I was finished, I found a Saturday night service in a church near my hotel and was able to slip into the back just a few minutes late. I would have preferred to go to church in the morning, but I was at the mercy of an early flight and the fact that I needed to get all the way across the country and on to my next destination before nightfall.

Fortunately, the service ended up being a rousing one with an amazing choir and a good back-to-the-basics, Bible-thumping, foot-stomping pastor. The sermons I got back home were usually much more sedate and cerebral, and though that was usually my preference, sometimes it felt good to get out and enjoy other styles of worship. I was still humming one of the more spirited praise songs as I drifted off to sleep back at my hotel.

I was at the airport bright and early the following morning, ready to move on to my next assignment. It was going to be a long day. Even with a 7:00 departure, I wouldn't reach Asheville, North Carolina, until nearly 5:00 in the evening, and from there I still had to rent a car and drive another hour and a half into the Blue Ridge Mountains. I was grateful for that interval, though, because I would need it to prepare myself for the challenging emotional voyage that lay ahead. Hopefully, by the time I reached the small mountain community of Greenbriar, North Carolina, I would feel ready to be there.

After checking my suitcases, I found the gate for my flight and chose an empty seat near a window, looking absently at the airplanes parked just outside. From where I sat, I could see airport personnel loading luggage from a metal cart into what looked like a 727. Lulled by their repetitive movements, I thought about the trip ahead and my own personal connection to the people involved.

This journey was not going to be a typical venture by any means. On paper, of course, it looked simple enough. Much like what I had discussed today with Clement, this was a situation where the J.O.S.H.U.A. Foundation had provided start-up money for a new nonprofit several years ago, and now that they were fully up and running, I was going back to approve a much larger grant. Of course, it was all relative: Unlike Clement and his $5000 check, this agency had started with a grant of $200,000, and now they were in line to get $1,000,000. That initial $200,000 check had been one of the first grants I had ever given out as an employee of the foundation. It wasn't the money that had me concerned now, however. It was the people involved: The agency was run by none other than my former in-laws, Dean and Natalie Webber.

The parents of my late husband, Bryan.

Not that I wasn't eager to visit them. The Webbers were delightful people, not stereotypical in-laws at all. I had known them since I was a teenager, had liked them from the moment we met, and a part of me was so excited about this trip that my heart quickened at the thought of it. On the other hand, I hadn't seen them in two years. Though the Webbers and I had kept in touch, it was much easier to maintain the relationship via e-mail and Christmas cards than it was standing there, face-to-face, and acknowledging that the very person who linked us together was no longer with us at all.

To make matters more complicated, this would be the first time since Bryan died that I was going back to our vacation house, the little mountain cabin where we always stayed whenever we went to Greenbriar to visit his family. Bryan and I had lived and worked in Virginia, and when he died in a boating accident four years before, I had sold our home there and moved away to Maryland's Eastern Shore. But I had never let go of the cabin in the North Carolina mountains; instead, I had simply turned it over to a local management company and let them handle it for me as a vacation rental. The income from the rental more than covered the upkeep and small mortgage, and I think in the back of my mind my hope was that one day I could start going there again myself occasionally to spend time with old friends and family in my beloved mountains. I felt I might be ready to return now, but the situation still brought with it a bit of apprehension. What if I were overestimating how far I had come in my own grieving process? At least I wouldn't be alone in all of this; my friend and coworker Harriet would be joining me to do the financial side of the investigation.

And I was eager for the investigative part of this visit, because I felt certain that the Webbers' charity would check out beautifully. I always enjoyed giving away the biggest grants, the ones for a million dollars, but that it might go to people I loved made it even more thrilling. I couldn't wait to see what they had accomplished since we gave them the original grant. What had started as a simple memorial fund in honor of their son had since evolved into the well-known and well-respected nonprofit agency, Migrant Outreach Resource Enterprises, or MORE, a charity that served the needs of the migrant fruit pickers who flooded their region every year at harvesttime.

As far as my own feelings were concerned, perhaps the best thing I had going for me at this point was the fact that my boss, Tom, was so supportive of this trip—both the professional aspect and the personal. Long before Tom and I were anything more than simply boss and employee, he was aware of my connection here and my in-laws' desire to start a nonprofit in Bryan's honor. When Tom heard that their little memorial fund had grown to nearly $25,000 on its own, he was the one who told me to encourage the Webbers to get a state license, file for nonprofit status, and then apply to us for some serious start-up money. They had done just that, and the original trip two years ago when I had come here, examined their plans, and given them the J.O.S.H.U.A. grant was a bittersweet time of memories and tears. This visit, by contrast, would hopefully be much more upbeat and extensive. I was going to Greenbriar for a full investigation of MORE. This new grant would allow them to expand their nonprofit and take it to an even higher level. And since it was a follow-up grant to an earlier approval, I would be able to conduct the investigation with the knowledge and cooperation of everyone involved. That was going to be a welcome relief to my usual methods of discreet inquiry, and a marked contrast to the week I had just spent undercover.

Of course, once my relationship with Tom had evolved into the personal arena, the most amazing part to me was that he continued to be supportive of my relationship with my former in-laws. The fact that he was now authorizing me to go to Greenbriar with the goal of approving them for a million dollars for their charity truly showed the kind of man he was. When I thought of Tom's character, I thought of integrity, compassion, generosity—and not just generosity with his money, but generosity with his heart as well. In short, Tom was willing to make room for my married past in our new relationship. That, as much as anything, had contributed significantly to my own healing process.

Closing my eyes, I remembered back four months before to the first and last time Tom and I had been together. After having a tele-phone-only relationship for so long, that moment of seeing each other face-to-face had taken on such importance that there was almost no way it could ever have lived up to either of our expecta-tions.

And yet it had. In every way it had, and more. It began the after-noon when I went out for a canoe ride on the branch of the Chesa-peake Bay that ran behind my house on Maryland's Eastern Shore. A difficult investigation had landed me in the hospital for a few days, and though I was home by then, it was my first time back out in the canoe, back out on the water. With my trusty Maltese, Sal, in the bow of the vessel, I had used the opportunity of the late afternoon paddle to clear my head, to pray, and to close up some loose ends in my mind. Then my cell phone rang in my pocket, and I answered it, glad to find that it was Tom. My face had broken into a smile, thinking that in the entire world, his was the only voice I had felt like hearing right then on the other end of the line. I thought he was calling me from Singapore.

We had talked for a bit, his voice etched with concern for my injuries. I hadn't wanted to worry him, so I hadn't told him how hurt I had been or that I had spent time in the hospital. But, in following up with his contacts about my investigation, Tom had found out anyway. Thinking that his call was merely an attempt to fuss at me for not being completely honest with him—and, of course, to make sure I was okay—it never crossed my mind that he had flown back to the States the moment he had heard about my injuries, and that, in fact, he was calling me from my very own property!

Floating with the current, I had slowly rounded that final bend toward home, and in the gathering darkness saw that someone was standing on my dock. I thought back to that moment now, the memory of it as alive and real as if it had happened yesterday.

Distracted, I asked Tom to hold on while I brought the boat in, telling him I needed both hands free. I carefully set the phone in my lap and paddled quickly, guiding the canoe toward the landing.

At first I thought it was my friend Kirby standing there waiting for me. But as I drew closer, I realized that it wasn't Kirby after all. This man was just as handsome, but he was taller, with dark hair and broad shoulders.

"Hang on another minute, Tom," I said, picking up the phone and speaking into it. "I'm just home, and somebody's here at the dock."

I set the phone by my feet, coasted in, and then climbed from the boat, pulling it onto the shore. As I tied off the rope, Sal jumped out and ran to the man, sniffing at the cuffs of his tailored slacks.

"Can I help you?" I asked, grabbing the phone from the bottom of the canoe and holding it at my side.

The man didn't reply for a moment, but when he did, it was to say my name, his tone deep and instantly familiar.

"Callie," he said, looking down at my phone and then back at my face. "It's me."

It wasn't until that moment that I noticed the cell phone in his hand as well. He pressed the button to disconnect it, and then he took a step toward me on the dock. As he did, I saw that on the front of his suit jacket, peeking out from under his coat, was a big red mum—the sign Tom and I had already agreed to use for identifying each other in a crowd.

I gasped, air rushing to fill my lungs. Tom stepped toward me again, but I backed away.

"You're in Singapore," I said, shaking my head, trying to align reality with what I was seeing and hearing. I held my phone to my ear, but the line had been disconnected. As I fumbled to turn it off, tears sprang unexpectedly into my eyes.

"No, I'm not. I needed to be here with you," he replied gently. "Business in Singapore can wait."

I swallowed hard, my heart pounding, my voice caught somewhere in my throat. I didn't trust myself to speak, didn't trust myself to do anything but stand there and gaze at him, trying to match the voice of the man I knew so well with this handsome stranger. Finally, I dropped my phone onto the grass and took a tentative step toward him.

That's all he needed. A smile teasing at his lips, he crossed the wooden slats of the dock, walking until he stood on the grass in front of me. He reached out and put one warm hand on my arm. I looked up at him, searching for the person I knew inside, thinking that even if I didn't recognize his face, the man behind those beautiful eyes was already my very best friend in the world. I smiled, and then I whispered his name.

"Tom."

He studied my eyes as well, and then he whispered back to me.

"Callie."

After a long pause, we both finally grinned—and then we laughed out loud! We threw our arms around each other, laughing, holding on to each other in a hug that lasted a long, long time. Somehow, it hadn't seemed right yet to share a kiss. But I would remember that hug for the rest of my life. That hug was the transition for me between a fantasy voice on the other end of a distant telephone line and a true flesh and blood man I really could hold on to, who really did exist.

After that, it hadn't mattered what we did next. We were together, finally, and that's what was important. Looking back, that entire evening was a blur. At some point, Tom had knelt down to retrieve my phone and get acquainted with Sal, and then we had gone inside my house, where we built a fire and shared some tea and started talking, the way we always talked but in person this time. Tom had asked me to recount my entire investigation, particularly the part when I had been kidnapped at gunpoint and then later nearly killed. He seemed devastated for my sake that I'd had to cut my long hair off to get loose from an underwater trap. But he couldn't stop gazing at me or remarking at how different I looked from my photos and from the one other time he had glimpsed me in person.

"I know you're probably sad about losing your long hair, but I think this new style suits you perfectly," he pronounced finally. "In fact, I would venture to say that you are even more beautiful now than you were before."

At that moment, we weren't sitting that far apart on the couch, and I thought then that he might kiss me. But he merely held my gaze, his smoldering look telling me there was much going on under the surface, far beyond a simple conversation in front of a crackling fire.

Around midnight we raided my kitchen, suddenly ravenous, making an impromptu dinner of leftovers that we ate at the table while Sal nosed around outside in the dark. Through the entire night, conversation flowed as effortlessly as if we had always done this, as if there were nothing strange at all about Callie and Tom sitting together and chatting and laughing and even occasionally holding hands. There was no nervousness, either, or even a moment of feeling uncomfortable. We grew punchy but not tired, and I came to recognize certain gestures of his that I thought I might already be quite fond of. The hand that chopped at the air when he wanted to make a point. The way he tipped his head to one side when he was teasing.

Truth be told, if I had suddenly looked up and found myself in Oz, I wouldn't have been surprised. The night was that magical, that ethereal, that far removed from any experience I had ever had.

In person, Tom was everything I had ever imagined and more. Handsome in a way that made my heart pound. Sweet and funny and smart—and surprisingly genteel in his manners, much like the men I had grown up with in Virginia. When I finally commented on that, he reminded me that he was a Louisiana boy, born and bred, and that in Louisiana gentlemen also did things like holding out chairs and opening doors for ladies. Goodness, I thought I might swoon!

Best of all was deep in the night when, back in front of the fire, Tom shared his testimony with me, how he had come to know the Lord at a youth rally at the age of 21, and how nothing had ever been the same since. His grasp of the Scriptures seemed to be knowledgeable and true, and as he talked I could tell that he was a man of deep faith.

I was happy to learn his last name, which was Bennett, but there was still a lot he wouldn't really discuss regarding the work he did beyond the J.O.S.H.U.A. Foundation. I knew he dealt a lot with the government and that much of his work was classified, but it still confused me, for I didn't even know the name of his company, and when I asked, he simply put a finger to my lips and told me he wasn't free to talk about it. I let it go and decided that that and other answers would come in time. At least he was here. He was real.

He was wonderful.

As the sun came up, we pulled on our coats and walked down to my dock, a sudden quiet descending upon us in the early morning chill. He had to go, had to head back to Singapore and the work that would keep him there for several more months. I thought my heart would burst with the conflicting emotions I was feeling: an absolute elation and yet also an utter sadness. He seemed to feel the same.

"I have to leave," he said mournfully, slipping his hand into mine. We were side by side at the edge of the water, looking out at the gentle flow of the morning tide. He still hadn't kissed me, and my mouth nearly ached with the desires of my heart.

"There're two things I want to do before I go," he said softly. I looked at him, pulse pounding. "First, I think we should pray together."

Emotion surged through me. How blessed I was to have fallen for a man of faith! In a way, I had always felt that prayer was one of the most intimate things a couple could do. Now here he was, asking to join hands with me in the presence of the Lord.

I nodded and he turned toward me, taking both of my hands in his. Then we bowed our heads, and he spoke softly on our behalf.

"Lord," he prayed, "we thank You for this precious time together. I thank You for Callie, for her gentle spirit, for the work she does, for the love and kindness that radiates from her like a light. Father, I ask that You will keep Your loving hand on both of us as we go our separate ways, and, if it be Your will, to bring us back together again in Your timing. Give me a safe flight, Lord, and continue to provide healing for Callie's wounds in the days ahead. Thank You for the gift of Your presence and the death and resurrection of Your Son. In all of these things, we give thanks. In Jesus' name, amen."

"Amen," I echoed.

Still holding hands, we stood there and looked into each others eyes.

"Why," he asked softly, "is getting in that car and driving back to the airport one of the hardest things I've ever had to do?"

I didn't answer right away but merely looked at him. Finally, I spoke.

"You know why," I said, my heart thudding with my own boldness. He squeezed my hands, nodding slowly.

"Yeah," he said. "I know why."

In the distance, I could hear the muted trill of an early morning fishing trawler. Closer by was the sound of water lapping at the dock, of Sal scuttering through the leaves at our feet.

"What's the second thing?" I asked.

"What?"

"You said there were two things you wanted to do before you go. What's the second thing?"

I knew what it was. I knew it as surely as I knew this man was standing here in front of me.

"To kiss you," he said. "May I?"

Unable to speak, I simply nodded.

Our lips met slowly, sweetly, and then we were joined in a deep, long kiss that seemed to go on forever. My mind was transported away to some other place, to some other time, to some point where conscious thought and reason no longer existed. Behind my closed eyes flashed colors and lights and images too unreal to find focus. Kissing Tom was like going to the very limits of a place I hadn't ever gone before, like perching on the end of a high dive or holding to the edge of a cliff.

When the kiss ended, I pressed myself against him, wishing the world would simply stop and we could get off together and steal away more time, more time, more time.

"Ah, Callie," he whispered, his lips at my ear. "I…"

I thought he was going to say "I love you." Maybe he wanted to, maybe he was. But instead, after a long pause, he pulled away just a few inches and said, "I…I have to go."

Tears filled my eyes, and though my heart still clung to him, with my arms I released him. He could see me crying, and he wiped away a tear from my cheek. When I looked up at him, I saw there were tears in his eyes as well.

"This time will fly," he said wistfully. "I promise."

I nodded, swallowing hard. Holding on to his arm, I walked with him to his car.

"Have we caused a scandal, do you think?" he asked, pulling out the keys to his rental. "Theoretically, I did spend the night."

I shook my head.

"If I lived in town, absolutely," I said. "But out here, no one sees anything. It's all very private."

He nodded.

"Then I guess it would be okay for me to kiss you again," he said.

There, beside the car, he swept me into his arms and gave me another kiss that would blaze into my mind, another kiss that I would relive again and again as I thought about him and that whole magical night in the months ahead.

As he drove away into the morning mist, I thought I could very well die right at that moment and find heaven no more perfect than what I was feeling here on earth.

Now, as I sat at the airport on my way to the Smoky Mountains of North Carolina, I knew that in seven days he would be with me again.

I knew this would be the longest seven days of my life.

My cell phone rang, startling me from my thoughts. As I pressed the button to answer it, I hoped it was Tom.

"Callie Webber," I said.

"Did I wake you?"

It *was* Tom, his voice deep and familiar, his tone intimate despite the fact that he was thousands of miles away in Singapore. I smiled, feeling myself relax at the very thought of him on the other end of the line.

"Nope," I said. "I'm at the airport, waiting for my flight to North Carolina. I'm so glad you called."

"I'm glad I was able to reach you before you left. I tried calling this morning—well, last night where you are—but we've had more trouble with the line. This is the first time I've been able to get through all day."

"That's all right," I said. "I was gone most of the evening. Once I got back to the hotel, I went straight to bed."

"Big night out on the town?" he teased.

"Oh, sure," I replied. "Three hours at the police station followed by two hours of church. I ought to be ashamed of myself."

He laughed.

"Ah, yes, the police station. So tell me all about the big sting."

Picking up my carry-on, I stood and walked to an empty area where I could talk without being overheard. Tom and I always talked at the conclusion of a case, and he liked to hear every detail. This time was no exception.

"The whole event went off like clockwork," I said softly, launching into the tale of the party and all that had taken place there. I told Tom about everything, ending with my conversation back at Clement's house and my presentation of the check from the foundation. "I wish you could've seen Clement's face when he saw that money. He told me that he'd been praying for something like that for almost twenty years."

"So once again you've been instrumental in providing an answer to prayer."

"It's *your* money, Tom."

"That's why we make the perfect team, Callie."

I smiled, playing with the strap of my watch. We did make a good team, in every sense of the word.

"Only seven more days," he said softly, as though he could read my mind.

"I know."

I held the phone close, glad he couldn't hear the beat of my heart across the phone line.

"Are you okay about going to North Carolina?" he asked. "Any worries?"

"Maybe just a few," I told him. "A part of me can't wait to see the Webbers again. Another part of me would like to jump on a plane heading in the opposite direction."

He sighed.

"In that case, you might end up here in Singapore. I like the sound of that."

"Hey, listen, if you weren't coming home in exactly one week, I just might do it."

I bit my lip. More than once in the past few months I had entertained the notion of simply popping up in Singapore and surprising him the same way he had surprised me last fall by showing up at my house, out of the blue, when I thought he was thousands of miles away. But that was impractical, not to mention expensive, and I knew that his job there was keeping him much too busy to do anything more than work and sleep. That was another reason that he was looking forward to our reunion: He hoped to spend at least a week, maybe two, simply relaxing with me and recovering from the grind of the last four months.

"Well, at least you're *flying* to North Carolina," he said. "I talked to Harriet yesterday, and she was getting ready to *drive* there. I told her she was nuts."

"You shouldn't have said that," I scolded, laughing. "She's scared to death of airplanes, you know."

"Yeah, she told me. Let's just hope I don't ever need to send her overseas. I'd hate to see her have to paddle her way to an assignment!"

I noticed some activity near my gate and saw that my flight had begun boarding. I stood, grabbed my carry-on, and told Tom I needed to get moving.

"All right," he said. "I hope it goes smoothly for you back there in the coach section."

He was just teasing, but I knew he hated the fact I wouldn't fly first class when I was on business for the foundation. That was one perk I wasn't willing to accept no matter how much he insisted.

"Why, thank you, Tom," I said sweetly. "I will."

We talked a minute more and then said our goodbyes, and as I stood in line to get on the plane, I tried to focus my mind away from Tom and onto my next investigation—one which just happened to involve my late husband's parents in the very town where he and I had met and fallen in love.

Whatever was in store for me there, I prayed that God would provide the strength for me to handle it.

Three

My final flight reached Asheville a few minutes after 5:00 P.M., providing a gorgeous view of the Smoky Mountains as we came in for a landing. The airport was as low-key and simple to navigate as I remembered, and I easily retrieved my bags and handled the details of my car rental. An hour and a half of driving later, I passed the sign welcoming me to Greenbriar.

The town looked exactly as I remembered it. Coming around the curve and down the hill, I could see rooftops peeking through the trees and, beyond that, the glimmer of the sun setting on Greenbriar Lake in the distance. I took a deep breath as I continued to drive. In an odd way, coming here almost felt like coming home. This place was in my blood, as much a part of me as the color of my eyes or the sound of my voice. It owned a piece of my heart.

I thought back to the first time I had come here. I was a nine-year-old kid ready for a week at Camp Greenbriar, the local Christian summer camp that covered 300 acres of wooded lakefront property. I had loved it so much that I continued to return as a camper every summer through age fifteen. When I turned sixteen, I started coming back as a junior counselor. To me, summer would always mean the sparkling lake, the shadowy blue mountains, the intoxicating smell of dirt and moss and pine.

Anticipating that smell, I rolled down my window and inhaled deeply. Knowing I was almost to the Webbers' house, I slowed as I passed the big Cornerstone Community Church, which had a giant sign out front announcing "Free Concert Tonight!" by a Christian rock group. Though, according to the sign, the concert didn't begin for another hour, the parking lot in front of the church was already filled to overflowing.

Just past the church, I made a left turn into the Webbers' long, winding driveway. As their house came into view through the trees, I had to blink away sudden, sentimental tears. I had been afraid I might feel anxious or depressed once I got here, but the opposite was true. As I pulled to a stop and looked up at the house and then out at the lake behind it, I was flooded with a calm sense of peace and contentment.

After the long flight and then the drive, my legs were stiff as I climbed from the car. I had brought along some Ghirardelli chocolates from San Francisco as a small gift, so I grabbed the box from the backseat, shut the door, and started up the walk. I was a bit concerned about the number of cars parked in the driveway. The Webbers had said they would be having "a few people" over so that I could meet the directors of the different migrant programs MORE was affiliated with. But this looked like more than a few, and I wished suddenly that I had asked them to hold off on all of this until tomorrow. We should've reserved tonight for a private reunion for the three of us, not a public gathering with 50 of their closest friends and associates.

Holding my breath, I knocked on the door and tried to decide what the Webbers were to me now anyway. With Bryan gone, were they still my in-laws or were they my "former" in-laws? When the door opened and I was face-to-face with Bryan's mom and dad, I knew there was nothing former about it. These people were still my family.

"Callie!" Natalie cried, her arms flying open. "Honey, I'm so glad you're here."

We hugged, holding on for a long, long time. I didn't realize until that moment how much I had missed her. Once we pulled apart, Dean was there for a hug as well.

Finally, I stepped back and looked at them, thinking that in two years they hadn't seemed to age a bit. As always, Dean sported trim gray hair and just the slightest paunch under a tailored shirt and sweater-vest. Natalie, with her silver bob and genial face, looked almost like an older, female version of Bryan.

"You look beautiful, my dear," she pronounced, reaching up to touch the back of my short hair. "Elegant as ever, and this hairdo is perfect for you."

Thanking her for the compliment, I gave her the chocolates and stepped inside. As Dean closed the door behind me, I could hear voices and music coming from the other rooms, and I quickly realized this wasn't just a small welcoming reception, but an out-and-out party.

"I'm so sorry," Natalie said softly, leaning toward me, "but this thing has escalated out of control. Some of the cousins found out you were coming and spread the word among the family, and before I knew it, the house was completely filled with relatives who insisted on being here when you arrived. They even brought food, and it looks like they're here for the duration."

"That's all right," I said, feeling butterflies fill my stomach. "It'll be nice to see them."

We stepped into the parlor, and before I could blink, I was assaulted by the loving hugs of cousins and aunts and uncles and two of Bryan's brothers and their wives and children. For a moment, I hesitated, wondering if I was strong enough for this after all.

After the hugging and kissing, I realized the room was decorated with balloons and streamers and a big banner over the hearth that said "Welcome Back, Callie! We Love You!"

Overwhelmed, I accepted a glass of iced tea someone thrust into my hand. Then I sought out a stool at the kitchen counter and sat, wishing suddenly that I could withdraw from the confusion surrounding me. One by one, relatives exclaimed about how much younger I looked with shorter hair, how great it was to have me here, how much they had missed seeing me. Someone asked how I had been, and before I could answer, someone else asked how my flight was. Women set out food and children ran through the room grabbing at streamers, and the best I could manage was to take a deep breath and remind myself that this was family. *Enjoy the moment, Callie. These are people who love you.*

In the corner I could see Bryan's Uncle Rob about to light up a cigar, and I predicted that his wife would catch him at the first puff of smoke and shoo him out the door. Sure enough, she was just chasing him outside when Natalie started sending everyone else into the backyard, asking the women to take the food they had brought and set it up on the picnic tables for an impromptu covered-dish buffet. It was nearly dark, but someone flipped a switch, and suddenly the deck and yard were awash in glowing yellow lights.

After washing my hands at the sink, I busied myself with putting ice in cups, slowly relaxing enough to enjoy the conversations that ebbed and flowed around me. It was touching, I had to admit, that so many of Bryan's relatives had wanted to see me when I came. Perhaps, this was easier after all. We could get the social part out of the way this first night, leaving me free to get more work done as the week progressed.

Once all of the relatives were outside, things quieted down a bit, and I was able to focus on my goal here, which was to evaluate the Webber's charity for a grant. I thought about Dean and Natalie Webber and how they had come to be involved with helping migrants in the first place.

The area in North Carolina where they lived was known as "apple country," and its rolling hills were dotted with apple orchards both large and small. In fact, there were so many orchards there that at harvesttime there weren't enough local workers to handle the job of picking all the fruit. That's why every July and August migrant workers would flood the region, coming north from Texas and Mexico and staying until the harvest was finished at the end of October.

Basically, the system worked well for everyone concerned. Picking apples was a labor-intensive process, and the window of opportunity for getting the apples off the trees and into storage was actually quite small. The migrants showed up when they were needed, worked inexpensively, and left when they were finished. Also, they were excellent pickers, highly skilled and careful with the fruit.

Of course, as well as the situation worked, some problems were inevitable. The housing of all of those migrants was a challenge, as were the child care and education of their children. A number of government programs had sprung up in recent years to treat some of these issues, but there were still needs that weren't being met, and the goal of the Webbers' organization was to fill in some of the gaps.

Back when Bryan was just a child, the migrants who came to their area lived in fairly deplorable conditions—usually in tents or in their cars along the creek near one of the bigger orchards. A huge migrant camp sprang up there every year, and even as a kid riding past in the family car, Bryan had been appalled at their living conditions. With no running water, no sewage disposal, and no real shelter, it seemed to him to be the worst kind of existence. When he was much older and studying architecture at college, his senior thesis had involved designing low-cost, functional housing for migrant workers.

When Bryan passed away, his parents chose to honor his memory by establishing a memorial fund. Keeping in mind the concern their son had always had for the migrants, Dean and Natalie had decided to take a closer look at the different migrant-related charities in the area and choose one where they could make a donation in Bryan's honor. The more they saw and learned, however, the more they felt compelled to go beyond a simple donation. Dean, in particular, was a "big picture" person, and he could see that there was a need there for one overriding agency to facilitate the operations of the other, smaller agencies. Natalie possessed her own unique set of talents that related to the cause, since she had worked in facilities management for the local community college and knew a thing or two about coordinating different entities under one larger heading. At the same time, I was just starting out with the J.O.S.H.U.A. Foundation, and it was almost as though the Lord were putting together pieces of a big puzzle. As I was learning the ropes in my new job with the foundation, Dean and Natalie both retired from their jobs and began their second, much less highly paid careers as executive director and volunteer coordinator of this new agency.

When I approved the first grant, all they had was their nonprofit status, some solid ideas of where they wanted to go, and an excellent business plan to get them there. Now I was excited to see how their ideas had translated into reality. Knowing them, I had a feeling the place was going to be everything they had hoped it would be, and more.

Tonight's party had originally been planned as a way for me to meet the directors of some of the local migrant-related charities that MORE helped to support. Now, Natalie took my arm and began to introduce them to me.

First was Karen Weatherby, a soft-spoken woman about my age, perhaps a few years older, dressed in a simple, faded cotton dress and slip-on flats, her hair pulled back from her face by a beaded headband. Karen was the director of a local education program for migrant children called Go the Distance Learning Center. Though Karen seemed shy, her face lit up and her voice grew stronger as she spoke about her program and the children it served. Karen gave me her card so that we could arrange to meet later this week. She said she was eager for me to see her program in action.

With her was a fellow in jeans and a flannel shirt, cute in a boyish way, though he had to be at least 35, with brown curly hair and dimples. He introduced himself as Danny Stanford.

"Danny works for Go the Distance as a volunteer," Karen explained. "He's our orchard liaison."

"Really? What is that?"

"Oh, it sounds more important than it is," Danny said. "I just keep the lines of communication open between the school, the parents, and all the orchards in the area. If somebody has a problem or a question, I hook folks up and smooth things over. I guess you'd say I'm a facilitator."

"You must have a lot of connections," I said, "to do a job like that."

"Well, actually, it's kind of the opposite. I just moved here two months ago. The fact that I don't have any connections at all probably helps, because then nobody thinks I'm playing favorites."

He grinned and winked at Karen, and by her shy blush I guessed that there might be something more between them than simple friendship.

"So what do you do when you're not volunteering at Go the Distance?" I asked.

He took a sip of iced tea and smiled.

"I work over at Tinsdale Orchards," he said. "I started out as general farm help, but lately I've been training on the forklift."

He went on to talk about the different jobs on the orchard, and I found the whole subject of growing apples fascinating. Clearly, there was much more to it than simply planting trees in a row and then picking the fruit when it was ripe! I sipped my own tea and listened as he talked about scabs and grafts and frost watches.

"I could give you a tour sometime, if you'd like," he said, and Karen nodded enthusiastically.

"You really should tour the orchard, Callie," she added. "It might give you a feel for what the migrants' work entails. And Danny can explain the ways the migrants are essential to the whole process."

I agreed that a tour of an apple orchard might actually be the perfect way to begin my investigation, and we made tentative plans for me to meet Danny at Tinsdale Orchards the next afternoon.

"While you're out there," another man said, "be sure to stop by Su Casa and say hello. Their facility is up behind the orchard."

"Su Casa?"

"A nonprofit organization that builds dormitories for the migrant workers. My father runs it."

The man introduced himself as Butch Hooper, owner of Hooper Construction. He was a big man with a booming voice, genial if a bit intimidating.

"My company works a lot with the Webbers too," he added. "In fact, we built the MORE facility."

"Is Hooper Construction a nonprofit?" I asked.

"Not intentionally," he said, laughing.

Dean joined our conversation, putting one hand on the man's shoulder.

"Don't let Butch kid you, Callie," Dean said. "He has a very successful construction company. But he always gives a big price break whenever he does work for us or one of our charities."

After chatting for a few more minutes, Dean led me around and introduced me to the rest of the people who were there, including the director of services for the migrant clinic and the coordinator of the local Head Start program. All in all, it was an impressive bunch, and I felt honored to be there in my own capacity. All of these migrant-related charities were connected to the Webbers' charity, MORE. Hopefully, my investigation here would benefit them all.

We eventually went outside and helped ourselves to the impromptu buffet. As I ate I talked with one person after another, and soon I realized I really had been able to relax. It was good to see everyone and to catch up on all of the family news. One by one, the charity directors finished eating and took their leave, and eventually I realized that all we were left with was family.

Since it was a school night, those who had children departed right after dinner, and once they were gone things quieted down considerably. As I sat on the porch and took in the smells and sounds of a night in North Carolina, I was hit with a wave of familiarity so raw and so fresh that I might as well have been nine years old again and sitting on the front steps of my cabin at camp. As fireflies blinked in the darkness and gentle waves lapped at the dock, I closed my eyes and went back into the past, wondering how I could've survived a full two years without coming here to this place that was like my second home.

As vividly as if it were yesterday, I could recall the first year I returned to Camp Greenbriar as a junior counselor, the year I turned 16. Like me, many of the counselors came from other states, but the camp also employed plenty of local teens—including one particularly cute fellow named Bryan Webber. During the afternoon sessions, Bryan was in charge of canoes and I was a swimming instructor, and soon our long hours at the lake together began to blossom into a romance. Among other things, Bryan loved to talk about his big family, his five brothers and sisters, and the new home they were building on the lake, not too far from the camp.

I couldn't believe I was at that home now, remembering back to the first time Bryan had brought me here to see it one day during our free period. The camp was close enough that we could've walked up the dirt road to get here, but there were always nosy hangers-on, and somehow this was just supposed to be between the two of us. We had come by canoe instead.

The house was merely framed out at that point, a cement foundation with intermittent boards outlining where the walls would go. I could still picture him once we were here, going from "room" to "room," describing to me how it was going to look. Even at the age of 16, Bryan already knew he wanted to be an architect when he grew up, and he had an enthusiastic way of describing images and ideas as if they were already a reality. At one point, I gazed up at him as he was talking animatedly about post-and-beam construction, and I thought to myself, *I'm going to marry him some day.*

And, eventually, I did.

Now I was back at that house, where Dean and Natalie Webber still lived even though all of their other kids were now grown with families and houses of their own. Nearby Camp Greenbriar was surely the same little unassuming place it had always been. At this time of year, it would be all closed up, but I hoped to be able to stroll around the grounds while I was in town. At the very least, I thought I might be able to borrow the Webbers' canoe and paddle past.

"Beautiful night, isn't it?" Dean asked, startling me from my thoughts.

"Like no other place on earth," I replied, grinning.

I gestured toward the seat next to me and he sat, exhaling slowly as he did.

"Well, you certainly got a heck of a homecoming. Leave it to the whole Webber 'army' to welcome you in such a big way."

"It was good to see everyone."

We talked about specific relatives—who was off at college, who was working where, who had been ill or had gotten married. I was pleased to learn that Bryan's sister in Ohio was pregnant again, sorry to hear that his aunt had had a stroke.

Changing the subject, Dean asked how things were going with me, and I told him the truth, that my job kept me very busy, but that I had made some good friends around my new home and that I was happy.

"We hear from your parents now and then," he said. "They worry about you."

"You probably haven't talked to them in the last few months," I said. "I went home for Christmas, and we had real time of healing and bonding. We've made great strides. I don't think they're so worried anymore."

"That's good to hear."

"What about coming here?" Dean asked. "Was this difficult for you?"

I looked at him, at his kind face, and then I looked away.

"I was a bit worried," I said honestly. "But seeing you and Natalie is worth—"

I couldn't finish the sentence because I began to choke up, much to my surprise. It wasn't that I was sad, really, just overwhelmed with emotion. I swallowed hard, glad no one else was near us at the moment to see two tears spill down my cheeks.

Perhaps not knowing what else to do, Dean reached out and took my hand in his, squeezing it firmly. When he spoke, his voice was also full of emotion.

"You don't even need to explain," he said, letting go of my hand. "We feel the same way too."

Fortunately, Bryan's first cousin, Ken Webber, chose that moment to come over and talk to Dean about a computer issue at the office. Ken was the family computer whiz, the go-to guy for almost any technical issue that came up. Because he did some consulting for MORE, he and I would probably be working together a bit later in the week as I did the research for the grant.

While they talked I went around the yard picking up cups that had been discarded by the kids and crushed on the ground. Out near the back of the yard along the woods it was dark away from the lights, but the cups were white, so it was easy to spot them in the grass. I had found about ten when I heard a rustling sound beyond the woodpile, and I looked up, surprised to see a man running past through the trees.

"Hey!" I called, but he didn't stop or even glance my way. He disappeared into the darkness, and for a moment I wondered if I had seen anything at all or if it had just been an illusion.

Goose bumps dotting my arms, I clutched the cups to my chest and quickly walked back to the deck, telling Dean and Ken what I had just witnessed. From the brief glimpse I'd had, I described the person as a young male, dressed in dark clothes and wearing a baseball cap. Beyond that, I hadn't noticed any specific details.

Dean seemed concerned, but Ken was a bit more relaxed.

"Was he running toward the church or away from it?" he asked.

"Away. He was kind of angling toward the lake."

Ken nodded, the yellow lights bouncing off the circles of his wire-framed glasses.

"Probably a teenager who stayed too late at the concert and had to get home before curfew," he said.

"Home where?" I asked. "In a cave? There's nothing out that way but woods and water."

"Oh, no," Dean corrected me. "They've put in a whole subdivision off of Marshall Road, about a quarter mile back from here as the crow flies."

"You're kidding," I said, finding the trash bag and dumping in the cups. "I didn't realize that."

"Yeah, it's a fairly pricey neighborhood. Especially the lots that are along the lakefront."

I said I would have to drive through there and take a look, which led Ken to say that I might see more from out on the water, which led Dean to remind me that I was welcome to use the canoe any time I wanted to go for a paddle. Soon we were talking about canoeing and the lake, and I had forgotten all about the man I had seen in the woods.

Eventually I went inside, and when I got to the kitchen, I found Natalie there by herself, standing at the sink and staring absently at the window. Because it was dark outside, the glass had become like a mirror, with her own reflection looking back at her.

"Natalie?"

She turned to me, startled, and I realized that her face was flushed, her eyes a bit red.

"Callie," she said, reaching up to wipe her eyes. "I'm sorry. I was lost in thought."

"Are you okay?"

She nodded.

"I was just thinking that even with all of the family around, there's still one person missing. There's still one person who ought to be here and isn't."

I knew she was speaking of Bryan, and suddenly it hit me that the thought of my coming here had been as unsettling for her as it had been for me. In an odd way, I found that comforting. I wasn't the only one who knew there could be setbacks in the grieving process.

"It's still hard for you," I said softly.

"I have good days and bad," she replied, glancing at me, embarrassed. "But I don't have to tell *you* that." We shared a sad smile, bonded in a way that neither of us would've chosen. "And anyway," she said firmly, crossing the room toward me, "we've got a lot of work to do this week. Dean and I are so excited about this new grant, we can't tell you."

"I'm anxious to see the program," I said. "From what I hear, you've really done some amazing things."

"It's been so rewarding," she said. "The Lord has definitely blessed our efforts."

Natalie told me more about the charity and the things they had been able to accomplish. We talked about the grant approval process, and I explained that though I would be needing different documents and peppering them with questions, I wouldn't really be taking up any large chunks of their time. I simply needed a space to work on-site, access to the agency's files and records, and a private area where I could talk to employees and use the phone. Beyond that, it was merely a matter of going through the process step-by-step.

"In general," I said, "I have ten criteria that I use for judging a nonprofit. I start with the first one and work my way through, examining finances, procedures, programs, and much more as I go."

I went on to explain that the agency would be approved for a grant only if they scored well on every single criterion. With an amount as large as the one we were dealing with here—and despite the fact that I knew them personally—the investigation would have to be painstaking and extensive and fully documented.

"We wouldn't have it any other way," Natalie said. "I believe you'll find the organization to be more than worthy in the end."

"Good," I said as I crossed to the sink and filled a cup with water. In the distance, I could hear the lonely sound of a siren, though I couldn't tell by listening if it was a fire truck or a police car. "I also need to meet with some of the migrants while I'm here," I said, ignoring the sound. "It would be good to have an interview with at least one of them for my report."

Dean had come walking in at that moment, and he paused next to Natalie.

"Wrong time of year for that," he said. "The migrants left in November, and they won't be back until July."

I turned around, leaning back against the sink.

"Oh, that's right," I said, wondering if there might be contact information for some of them, so that at the very least I could conduct some interviews over the phone.

"Actually," Natalie added, looking at Dean, "Callie could talk to Luisa Morales."

Dean sighed as he went to the freezer, opened it, and took out an ice tray.

"Luisa Morales?" I asked.

"She's a migrant who's been coming here for years," Dean said. "This year, unfortunately, once harvest was over she stayed put."

"Why is that unfortunate?"

"Well, I don't mean to sound callous. She's a very nice woman, and she's certainly welcome to stay here in Greenbriar. It's just that—"

Dean cracked the ice tray and several cubes shot out onto the floor. As he picked them up and tossed them into the sink, Natalie finished his answer for him.

"It's just that she's had a bit of trouble," Natalie said. "Her husband left her last fall, and now she's alone with her two kids, trying to figure out what to do next. In the meantime, there have been a few...problems."

"Problems?"

"Some vandalism," Dean said. "Somebody spray painted her drive-way, and another time she had some things stolen out of her car. It seems like bad luck just sort of follows her around."

"Our hearts go out to her, of course," Natalie added, "but she just won't accept the fact that her husband is gone. She is living here in limbo, and it's especially difficult for her because her family and support system moved away when harvest was over. We've done what we can, both through the agency and on our own, and our church helps her out a lot too. But I'm afraid she's sort of stuck waiting for a man who left her high and dry and isn't coming back. It's very sad."

"How involved is she with MORE?" I asked, hearing in the distance the sound of more sirens joining with the first. "Has she benefited from your programs?"

"Oh, she's benefited plenty," Dean said. "We even gave her a staff position last fall, working in our main office. In fact, she caused some problems there that we'll need to talk with you about, since they will probably come up in your investigation."

"Anything that might put a hitch in the approval process?"

"No, nothing like that," Dean replied, though I thought I could detect a hint of concern in his voice. "But I'm sure you'll need to make note in your report of the problems she caused. It's a long story. Once you hear it, you'll understand why I get so exasperated with her."

The sounds of the sirens had become unmistakably close. We looked at each other in alarm and then put everything down and headed outside to see the rest of the family already gathered in a clump at the end of the driveway. As we walked to where they stood, I thought I could detect the acrid smell of smoke in the air. Through the woods we could clearly see the flashing red-and-blue lights of the police cars.

"That's the church," Natalie said, one hand to her mouth. "They were having that big concert tonight."

"The man," I whispered, remembering the shadowy figure I had seen running through the woods.

"Oh, Lord," Dean added, "just don't let anyone be hurt."

Four

Everyone wanted to get over there and see what was going on, so rather than walk or run we decided to drive. Quickly, the group dispersed into three cars—mine, Dean's, and Natalie's. I backed out of the driveway, let them both pull ahead, and then I brought up the rear.

I followed Natalie's minivan to the church parking lot, where a large crowd of teenagers was standing around, blocking traffic and watching the police activity. Natalie parked her van on the grass, so I followed suit and got out to see what was going on.

Apparently, though thick smoke lingered in the air, there hadn't been a fire. Word was that no one had been injured. Instead, it was a prank: Someone had set off a bunch of stink bombs in somebody else's car.

Teenagers!

As the news spread of what had caused such a commotion, there were plenty of chuckles and accusations flying between the young people milling around in the parking lot. I was afraid this little stunt had interrupted the rock concert, but apparently the deed had been done as the concert drew to a close—in other words, just before people began pouring out of the building.

Feeling certain that the man I had seen running through the woods was somehow connected, I went straight to an officer and told him what I had seen. The cop I spoke to took down the description I provided, but he didn't seem very concerned that I couldn't give a lot of details. After taking my name and contact information, he thanked me for my help and turned his attention to crowd control.

Also helping were church officials, who seemed to have sprung into action fairly quickly. Men in orange reflective vests put themselves into position and began directing traffic out of the place and onto the highway. Though no one knew who was responsible for the stink bombs, the police seemed to be letting people leave anyway, I assumed because the nature of the crime was fairly benign. I stood among the fringes with Ken Webber's sons, Jake and Rick, who had both been inside at the concert. They couldn't decide which was more exciting: the concert itself or the commotion in the parking lot afterward. I listened to them talk, thinking how refreshing it was to hear two teenage boys expound on the spiritual aspects of rock and rap. To hear them tell it, the biggest irony of the whole thing was that they had spent almost two hours inside listening to songs about peace and love, only to come outside and find that someone had done something so disruptive and hateful.

By the time the crowd had dwindled down to the last 15 people or so, most of the Webbers had left as well. One by one, they hugged me goodbye and said they hoped to see me again during the week, and then they headed off to their own homes. Dean and Natalie were busy talking to the police, and I decided to wait for them. I found a bench near the sidewalk and sat, simply enjoying the unusually warm night air, turning my mind from the confusion at hand to think about the investigation that lay ahead of me.

With Tom due to come back from Singapore in exactly seven days, I hoped that everything would go as smoothly as clockwork so I could wrap this case up by next Saturday and be ready for his arrival on Sunday. I still didn't know the details of his visit, nor where we were meeting, but Tom was handling most of the details, and all he had told me was to count on taking a little time off and to leave the rest to him. He hadn't said how much time we would be spending together, nor where, exactly, but just to be on the safe side, I had already arranged for Lindsey, the girl back home who cared for my dog, Sal, to plan on having her for an extra week.

Thinking of Tom, I felt a wave of yearning to see him, and that, in turn, made me feel relieved. That I could sit here, in the town where Bryan and I had first met and fallen in love, and yet find my mind and my hopes focused on Tom was a very positive sign. *Time does heal wounds, even wounds as deep and scarring as mine.*

Natalie called to me, interrupting my thoughts, and I looked up to see her waving from where she stood next to the car that had been the cause of all the ruckus. It was an old beat-up Toyota with one shattered window, and as I came closer I could smell the stench of the stink bombs that had been set off inside. Most of the smoke had dissipated by now, but the odor remained, and it was awful.

"Callie," she said, "I'm going to be a little while longer. If you want to head back to the house, just take the bedroom at the end of the hall on the left, the one with its own bathroom."

"Is everything okay?"

"Well, to be on the safe side, Luisa and the kids are going to spend the night at the pastor's house, so I'm going to help them get settled over there. Even if they wanted to go home, I don't think their car is driveable with this terrible odor anyway, not to mention all that broken glass."

I tilted my head, wondering if I had heard her correctly.

"Luisa?" I asked. "The car with the stink bombs belongs to Luisa Morales? The migrant you were telling me about, the one with all the problems?"

Natalie nodded her head tiredly.

"After all that's been going on lately, she wanted to give her kids a break, so she brought them to the free concert. Figures, doesn't it? While they were inside enjoying the music, someone was out here breaking into their car and throwing in stink bombs."

"That's terrible."

"Yes, well, why don't you go ahead and get on back to the house, take your stuff in, maybe change into pajamas or more comfortable clothes. If you're still up when I get back, we can sit and chat."

"Sure," I said. "Take your time."

As I turned to leave, I saw Dean across the parking lot, talking to a Hispanic woman who was, no doubt, the migrant worker in question. Luisa appeared to be in her early thirties and quite attractive. Beside her stood what I assumed were her two kids: an adorable girl of about six and a sullen teenage boy of perhaps fourteen or fifteen.

I got in the car and was just sliding my key into the ignition when I heard another commotion outside. Startled, I rolled down my window to see what was going on, and immediately I realized that someone was yelling. I got out of the car and spotted a police officer waving both arms from the back of the church property, calling for an ambulance.

I joined the others in running to where the officer stood near to the woods. At his feet was a man who lay crumpled in a heap on the ground. While another cop told everyone to stay back, and several people turned away, I got as close as I could, peering at the scene in front of me.

The person on the ground was hurt, but from the jerking motions in his legs he obviously wasn't dead. To my eye it looked as if he had been stabbed in the stomach, for there was a dark circle of blood on his crisp London Fog jacket, and he clutched at his abdomen as he writhed on the ground. Judging from the amount of blood that surrounded him, he had been here for a while, though back here in the dark it had taken this long for someone to spot him.

"Sir!" barked the officer as he knelt down, one hand on the man's shoulder. "Help is on the way. Can you tell me who did this to you?"

The man tried to speak, but only gurgles came from his throat.

"Who did this to you, sir?" the officer demanded.

The man gasped and whispered one word.

"What?" the cop said, leaning closer. "Jim? Jim's? Jim's what?"

The man tried to speak again, but blood bubbled over his lips and down his chin, and his head fell back with one last spasm.

Then he was still.

The cop grabbed the man's wrist and felt for a pulse while we all held our collective breaths.

"He's dead," the cop pronounced finally, setting the lifeless limb back on the ground even as the siren from the approaching ambulance could be heard in the distance. Two of the women started crying, and the men shuffled and coughed and looked everywhere but at the man on the ground in front of them. I had seen dead bodies before—including that of my own husband, whom I cradled in my arms moments after his death—but standing there I realized that this was the first time I had actually witnessed someone in the act of dying, someone making the shift from "living" to "dead."

It was a bit of a shock.

"Who is he?" someone asked, and I was surprised to see that no one in the small crowd seemed to know.

"Maybe he's with the band," Dean said.

"No, they're all loaded up and gone," a man in an orange safety vest replied.

"Did anyone see him earlier?" the cop asked. "Maybe in the parking lot or at the concert?"

Everyone shook their heads, mute, as if stunned by what we had all just witnessed. Looking around, I was glad to find that the migrant woman, Luisa, was herding her children away from the scene. I wondered how much the kids had seen, particularly the little girl, and my heart went out to them. Death was hard enough for adults; it didn't need to be witnessed by children.

The next hour was a blur of more police cars, tons of cops, and lots of official business. Since the man I had seen running earlier might be pertinent here, I was forced to wait around and periodically answer the same questions over and over again. While Dean and Natalie talked to the police and helped Luisa with the children, I sat on the bench where I had sat earlier, listening to all that was being said around me. I learned that the victim had no ID on his person and that there were no unclaimed vehicles remaining in the parking lot. None of the police recognized the corpse, and for a small town that was saying a lot. Obviously, the dead man hadn't been a citizen of Greenbriar or any of the neighboring environs.

The detective in charge of the case was a woman in her fifties with waist-length straight black hair that she wore pulled into a ponytail.

She had the high cheekbones and smooth skin of an American Indian, and eventually she introduced herself to me as June Sweetwater.

At her request we drove to the Webbers' house, where she had me recreate my encounter with the man in the woods. Though neither she nor her men could find footprints or any other evidence that someone had been there, she seemed to feel that the person had been running away from the church and toward the new neighborhood that backed up to the woods from the other side. As I listened, she spoke into her radio and dispatched a few units to comb the streets there and canvass the houses, despite the late hour.

I was finally freed from police questioning with the promise that I would remain local and available to the investigation for the next few days, should the need arise. I agreed, feeling regretful that even if they were able to round up some suspects, my encounter had been too dark and too brief to allow me to be able to pick out from a police lineup the man I had seen.

As I walked into the Webbers' house, I could feel my eyelids growing heavy, the toll of jet lag and a very long evening. Numbly, I cleaned up from the party, and I was just putting out the last bag of trash when Dean and Natalie arrived home. Though they seemed wired up and eager to rehash all that had taken place, I was simply too weary to do anything but hug them goodnight and head off to bed, promising we could talk in the morning.

Slipping under the covers in the guest room, I thought again about what it had been like to watch a person die. *We're all in the same boat. We're all a breath away from death, with no way to know when it will be our turn, so we better be right with God.*

Thinking about that, I felt the Lord stirring me to renew my commitment to Him. I climbed out from under the covers, put my pillow on the floor, and knelt there on it, my hands clasped together, leaning against the bed. As tired as I was, I felt led to pray for the salvation of the people on my prayer list who hadn't accepted Christ as their personal Savior. I always kept a running list of names and frequently prayed that each of them would somehow find their way to God—or that God might use me in some way to touch their hearts for Him.

Tonight, my words were fervent, my mood urgent. Time was of the essence. The death tonight had reminded me of that.

Once I was back in bed, I thought about what the events of the evening might mean to the J.O.S.H.U.A. grant. Though this stranger's murder would definitely involve some of my time because I was a potential witness, I didn't think it should have any real impact on my investigation. After all, there was no correlation between the murdered man and the agency I had come here to approve. Feeling settled about it, I turned on my side and went to sleep. Deep in the night, I dreamed of ghosts running through trees, calling my name and whispering something I couldn't quite hear.

Five

After a difficult night, I awoke at 7:30, feeling achy and apprehensive. I quickly showered, dressed, and got ready for the day. It was just a little after 8:00 by the time I emerged from the bedroom and walked down the hall to find Dean and Natalie at the kitchen table, finishing their breakfast.

"Callie, good morning," Natalie said, looking pretty tired herself. "I wish I had known you were up. You had a phone call a little while ago from someone with the foundation. He sounded like a very nice man."

It had to have been Tom, since the only other people who worked for the foundation were women. Leave it to him to identify himself as merely being "with" the foundation, rather than saying he was my boss, or even more importantly, that he was the man whose money we all worked so hard to give away!

"Was his name Tom?" I asked.

"Tom, yes," Natalie answered. "He was calling from overseas, and he said to tell you he was headed out somewhere and he would call you in the morning."

"His morning or our morning?"

"Oh, why, his morning, I suppose. Our night."

I looked at my watch and did a quick calculation; after four months, I had gotten used to the time difference. It was 8:15 A.M. here, which meant it was 9:15 P.M. in Singapore. I'd probably hear from him around 7:00 or 8:00 tonight, which would be tomorrow morning for him. I missed him so much, I hated to go that long without talking to him—especially after the emotional turmoil of the night before.

I excused myself for a minute, thinking I could call him before he left. Back in my bedroom I sat on the bed, got out my cell phone, and dialed the familiar numbers.

As I listened to the connection go through, I could just picture Tom after a long, hard day, eyes closed, head leaning back in some anonymous limo, driving through the Singapore night toward another meeting with yet another power broker where he would count the minutes until he could go back to his hotel suite and go to bed. I hated to burden him with the news of what had happened here, but I needed to share it with him, needed the comfort of his soothing voice.

The call went through, but when Tom first answered, I thought perhaps I had the wrong number. Instead of the calm quiet I had been expecting, I was greeted by a cacaphony of noise and music.

"Hello?" I said loudly.

"Hello?" he replied.

"No phones tonight!" I heard a sultry female voice say. "You promised."

"Tom?" I asked.

"Callie? I'm sorry. I can hardly hear you."

"Where are you?"

"It's a dinner party. Just a little celebration."

"C'mon, Tom," the woman said. "Let's get some laksa."

"It's probably not the best time for me to talk," he said. "Was there anything specific?"

"Uh, no," I said, biting my lip. I wished I could see through the phone right then, to see him and the woman to whom the velvet voice belonged. "What's laksa?" I asked.

"Coconut soup. They're just bringing it out now."

"If you don't hang up, I'm hanging up for you," the woman said. "Come on, it's time for Nonya, not work."

"Look, why don't you call me when you get home?" I said, trying not to sound irritated.

"I'll try," he replied. "But I think it's going to be a long night."

"Who's Nonya?"

"Nonya?"

"The woman."

He laughed.

"Nonya is a type of food, Callie. Like Szeshzuan or Creole. Nonya's a mix of Chinese and Malay food. It's pretty good."

"Oh."

Despite the culinary information, I was acutely aware he hadn't answered the real question, which was *who is that woman?*

"I have to run. I'll call you later."

With the woman's giggle as the final note, Tom's phone was turned off. I sat, stumped, replaying the conversation in my mind.

I wasn't really a jealous person by nature, but right now my heart was pounding. I stood and paced in the bedroom, confused and upset.

I needed some air. Without pausing to think, I walked quickly up the hall and through the living room so as not to go directly past the Webbers.

"Callie?" Natalie called.

"I have to get something out of my car," I replied. Then I let myself out the front door and closed it softly behind me.

My heart was still hammering as I walked to my car. I opened the passenger door, sat in the seat, and closed my eyes. I forced my breathing back to normal and told myself to calm down. Tom was thousands of miles away. There was nothing I could do *here* to change the situation—whatever it was—over there. And what was it, anyway? Probably something completely innocent.

Eventually, the pounding in my heart subsided. I realized that my reaction was exaggerated, that I was just worked up from all that had been happening here. *If only he weren't quite so far away.*

If only I didn't care quite so much.

That was it, really, I told myself as I finally stood and closed the car door. Leaning back against it, I looked out at the lake, sparkling in the early morning sun. Here I was at the home of my late husband's parents, in the very place where Bryan and I had first fallen in love—and yet I was consumed with thoughts of Tom. That, more than anything, told me my heart and mind were turned fully toward the future and no longer just dwelling in the past. That was a good thing, I reminded myself. Growth is good. Even when it hurts, growth is good.

I walked back toward the house, telling myself that there was a logical explanation. And even if there wasn't, I realized, neither one of us had ever made any promises.

When I got back to the kitchen, neither Dean nor Natalie seemed to sense that anything was amiss. I was determined to put Tom out of my mind until such time as he decided to call me back and explain what had been going on. For now, I would focus on the moment. I was very good at compartmentalizing my feelings when I needed to. I'd had lots of practice at tucking away the hurt and getting on with the business at hand.

"There's a plate for you in the microwave," Natalie said. "Just press the 'Start' button if you want to heat it up."

I did as she directed, and a minute later I pulled out a steaming plate of scrambled eggs, bacon, and grits. It looked wonderful, though it was a slight departure from my usual breakfast of poached eggs and dry toast.

When I sat at the table, Dean handed me the local newspaper, where a report of the murder was featured front and center under the headline "Murder in Greenbriar," with the subheading, "Identity Sought for Victim of Stabbing." I skimmed the article and learned nothing new, though I was glad to see that in my tiny part of the drama I was referred to merely as a "local witness," rather than by name. There was a sidebar with a description of the man who was killed, where he was listed as a white male with black hair and brown eyes, 5'11" tall, 182 pounds. They also included my limited description of the person seen in the woods: a young male wearing dark clothes and a baseball cap.

The three of us talked about the whole event, each from our own perspective. As a deacon at the church, Dean's main concern was with practical issues like church liability and safety. Natalie seemed more worried about Luisa, wondering if the murder was somehow tied in with the stink bombs found in the car.

I hadn't considered that, but now as I thought about it, I realized that the stink bombs and the murder might be connected, probably with the former serving as a diversion for the latter, though I didn't know enough about the woman's situation to have an opinion on whether her car had been targeted specifically or if it had just been a coincidence.

"I'm telling you, this poor woman seems to draw trouble," Dean said, pushing away from the table and standing. He carried his dishes to the sink, rinsed them, and set them in the dishwasher. "She's really a good soul, but her life is a mess. She's already taken up far too much of our time."

He excused himself to get ready for work.

"Up until last night," Natalie added as he left the room, "the few odd things that happened to her really have been minor. Spray paint in her driveway, the occasional slashed tire, stolen laundry from her car. But if that man's murder had anything to do with Luisa directly, then the nature of whatever is going on with her has definitely taken a turn."

"What have the police done for her prior to last night?" I asked, taking a bite of my grits and savoring the perfect blend of taste and texture. Somehow, cooking grits was never an art I had perfected.

"Not a lot," Natalie answered. "Like I said, until last night these things weren't really serious enough to warrant much attention."

"Do you think it could be because she's Mexican?" I asked. "Perhaps there's some anti-Mexican sentiment in town."

"I don't think so. There are other Mexican Americans who have settled here, and they haven't had any problems. Looking at the big picture, it does seem as if Luisa's being harassed."

"Does she have any enemies?"

"None that she can think of."

"What about the teenage son? Maybe he's involved in a gang or something and Luisa just doesn't know it. Maybe these acts are meant to be against him."

"Callie, as far as I know, there aren't any gangs in Greenbriar. Besides, a few of the early incidents pointed directly to Luisa. Work-related stuff, you know."

"Yes, you started to tell me about that last night."

Natalie stirred cream into her coffee, quiet for a moment. I let the silence sit there between us as she gathered her thoughts.

"I'm telling you because I'd rather you hear it straight from me than from some government official. And it's definitely going to come up in your investigation."

I felt an uneasy flutter in my stomach.

"What is it?" I asked. "You said she worked for MORE, right?"

"Yes," she sighed heavily. "Every summer, when the migrants first arrive, we offer free testing for any of the workers who would rather do something other than pick fruit. Then we match up those who tested well with local seasonal jobs."

"And you offered Luisa a position in your own company?"

"She has a full high school education," Natalie replied, nodding, "and she tested well for secretarial work. So we gave her a data entry position, and she did such a good job that eventually we promoted her to the position of database technician."

"What went wrong?" I asked.

She shook her head sadly and looked out the window at a beautiful azalea bush outside that appeared to be just on the verge of blooming.

"When you work with migrants," she said finally, "there are a lot of county, state, and federal regulations you have to follow. Basically, we have to keep records of everything we do and every migrant we serve."

"It's not unusual for a social service agency to track their population."

"No, but it means a lot of paperwork and a lot of data entry."

"Okay."

"That's the database Luisa worked on, the record of our migrants and all the services we provided for them."

"So Luisa worked on the database," I said, dabbing at my mouth with my napkin. "Did she mess it up?"

"No, she was very good at her job. Things went along fine for a while. The problems didn't start until her husband disappeared last fall." Natalie took a sip of coffee and then swallowed. "The first incident was terrible, though with all Luisa was going through, I didn't blame her for being distracted."

"What happened?"

"What happened is that she left an entire stack of confidential files and records from our office sitting in a chair at the local laundromat. Someone found them and turned them into the police, who weren't sure what they were and handed them over to the County Migrant Bureau. The bureau eventually returned the records to us, but not before citing us for a number of confidentiality violations."

"Yikes!"

"Tell me about it. Even though Luisa had been in that laundromat the night before, she swore up and down she hadn't brought any paperwork with her, that in fact she never took paperwork out of the office."

"Did you believe her?"

Natalie shrugged.

"I don't know. She certainly seemed sincere. Dean and I decided that perhaps she had grabbed the papers by accident without realizing it. We agreed to give her one more chance."

"And?"

"And less than a week later she accidentally did something to the computer that erased large portions of data from our database."

"Oh, no! How did she do that?"

Natalie shook her head.

"She doesn't know. Again, she swore she didn't do it, that it wasn't her. But there was no one else it could've been."

"Oh, Natalie, that's terrible. Wasn't there a backup of the system?"

"There was supposed to be. But the backup discs were blank. It was obvious that Luisa hadn't been doing the backups all along, though, again, she swore that she had."

"What did you do?"

"We had to let her go. We had no choice. It was almost the end of the year by then and time for us to start submitting our records to the proper agencies. Unfortunately, we didn't have many records to submit. As you can imagine, we missed a lot of deadlines, which meant we were in a lot of trouble. In the end, we had to hire someone else to go around and collect data from the local orchards, plus we had to load information back into the computer from the hard copies we had of some of our records, all in an attempt to reconstruct the database."

"Did you pull it off?"

"We managed to squeak by without losing our license," Natalie said. "Though we were cited for poor record keeping. And now we have a bit of a black eye with the County Migrant Bureau. Frankly, I don't blame them. These problems made us look very inept indeed."

I folded up my napkin and set it beside my plate.

"You were right to tell me," I said, nodding. "This would've come out further down the line anyway."

"Oh, I know. I'm still willing to take some of the blame since we were ultimately responsible, but Dean fully blames Luisa. He feels she let her personal problems affect her work."

Looking almost relieved that her story was out on the table, Natalie thanked me for my understanding and said she hoped this wouldn't have any impact on the grant. She finished her coffee and began loading dishes in the dishwasher. I tried to help, but she shooed me away, saying she would be dressed and ready to head to the office in about ten minutes if I wanted to ride in with her.

I went down the hall to my room, feeling very disheartened about Natalie's revelations. Though it wouldn't disqualify them for the grant, it was going to affect it somewhat, because one of my criteria was that a place have a good reputation.

Still, at least I had the explanation behind the problem. Now we needed to see if there was anything else MORE could do to improve relations with the agency that held them in such contempt. I would also need to examine the policies and procedures that had allowed such a breach of database security.

Packing didn't take long at all because I had only brought in one small bag from the car. As I had explained to Dean and Natalie when we were first planning this trip, I didn't think it was appropriate for me to spend the entire week enjoying the hospitality of the very people I was investigating, even if they were my former in-laws. Fortunately, they understood and had suggested a lovely bed-and-breakfast in town. I had surprised them both by revealing my intention to spend the remainder of the trip in my vacation home. I felt ready to face old memories, and it seemed a bit silly to get a hotel room in town when I owned a perfectly good house up on the mountain. I had already arranged for my stay with the management company. All that remained was to drop by there and pick up the keys.

For now I gathered my things, double-checked the creases on the bedspread, and then walked back up the hall to join Natalie for the drive to the office. Despite the trauma of the night before and the bad news of the morning, I was still excited to do what I had come here to do.

Natalie emerged from her bedroom wearing a sharp navy jacket and skirt, her makeup subtle, her hair just so. I was glad I had chosen to dress up a bit myself in a light cashmere jacket and a pair of tweed slacks.

"Are we ready?" Natalie asked, gathering her purse and keys.

"Yes," I said, and I *was* ready. I was eager, in fact, to put all of these problems aside for now and go to see the MORE building and the legacy my husband had left behind.

Six

As Natalie drove, she and I talked about the events of last night before the murder. She was still concerned about my welcoming party and apologetic that it had gotten out of control and turned into a spontaneous Webber family reunion.

"Please don't think anything more about it," I said. "I would've preferred a more subtle greeting, perhaps, but once things got underway, I thought it was great. I was very touched to realize everyone wanted to see me again."

"You're still family, Callie," she said. "You always will be, you know, even when you find someone else and get married, settle down, have kids. We want you to think of us that way always."

I was surprised by her comment and felt my face flush. She didn't seem uncomfortable with what she had said, however, and even looked as though she wanted to continue the line of conversation. But I really wasn't comfortable going there with her, especially not if she were to ask if I was dating again or if there was someone special in my life yet. I had a hard enough time talking about these things to my friends; I really didn't think I could handle such a conversation with Bryan's mother!

"So tell me more about yesterday's bean dip," I said quickly, trying to change the subject. "Was that your recipe?"

She was easily distracted, and we managed to talk food the rest of the way to the office. As we turned into the parking lot of the muted brick building with crisp white trim, I couldn't help thinking that the last time I was in town, all they had were blueprints and an empty lot. Now, the facility was up and running, thanks in part to the original $200,000 grant the J.O.S.H.U.A. Foundation had given them.

And it was a lovely place—not huge by any means, but functional and very tastefully done. We parked in front and stepped into the lobby area, and I immediately noticed the large brass plaque that hung in the center of the facing wall. Subtle lighting from a ceiling fixture illuminated the plaque that simply said "This building is dedicated in loving memory of Bryan Davis Webber." Under his name were his birth and death dates, and under that was inscribed Matthew 5:8: *Blessed are the pure in heart, for they will see God.*

"That's lovely," I said, feeling a lump in my throat.

Dean and Natalie gave me a tour of the building, which included a reception area and separate offices for accounting, records, human resources, fund-raising, and public relations. In the very back of the building were a row of what they called "start-up offices." There, for a very low fee, any migrant-related service agency could rent, on a monthly basis, one room with a desk, computer, phone, fax, etc. as they attempted to establish themselves. Working out of the MORE facility gave them access to a fully functional office with a receptionist and a very professional atmosphere. Once they were fully up and running, they would have sufficient resources to move into their own space. Dean said that at any one time, about half the offices were kept in use, and that more than one successful agency had been launched that way.

We ended the tour in the conference room. I sat at the big table and let them present their organization to me in its best possible light. Once they had showed me their full program, they brought out information on each of the agencies that came under the MORE "umbrella." The needs these agencies met included migrant housing, education, child care, medical care, and more. It was all very dazzling, and I was especially pleased to see complete records for every company on the roster. Once the information was all laid out in front of me, I felt glad that my friend and coworker Harriet was on her way to town to help with the financial side of the investigation. This job certainly was too big for one person!

When they were finished with their presentation, I commended them for their efforts in building this amazing operation, and then we talked about what it would take to get the company through the grant approval process for the million dollars.

"As I've said before," I told them, "I have ten criteria that I have to apply to MORE. If we can show that you pass on every single count, then I can recommend that you get the money."

"Are these criteria financial?" Dean asked.

"Only some," I replied, and I went on to name them as Dean and Natalie both leaned forward, listening intently.

"A good nonprofit agency," I began, counting off on my fingers, "serves a worthwhile cause; adequately fulfills its mission statement, showing fruit for its labors; plans and spends wisely; pays salaries and benefits on a par with nonprofit industry standards; follows standards of responsible and ethical fund-raising; has an independent board that accepts responsibility for activities; is well rated by outside reporting sources; has a good reputation among its peers; believes in full financial disclosure; and has its books audited annually by an independent auditor and receives a clean audit opinion."

"That's a pretty tough list," Natalie said.

"Think you'll pass?" I asked.

Dean winked at Natalie before answering me confidently. "We wouldn't have applied for the grant if we didn't."

The three of us worked together in the conference room the rest of the morning, and in that time I was able to familiarize myself with their bookkeeping system and their policies and procedures, and to obtain much of the paperwork I would need to do the job. I expected Harriet to arrive late in the day, and in the morning I would bring her here to the office and get her set up with the books to begin her own audit.

Harriet would be handling two of the criteria for me fully, including "believes in full financial disclosure" and "has books audited annually by an independent auditor and receives a clean audit opinion." She would also help with a third, "pays salaries and benefits on a par with nonprofit industry standards," because it was her job to ferret out all of the "extras" that working for this company provided. Often, the benefits were a gray area to which we gave a lot of attention. Of course, here things were a little different, since I believed unequivocally in the Webbers' integrity. But we still had to go through the full process and sign off on every detail.

Just by seeing on paper all that they had accomplished with their charity, I had already checked off the first criteria. I knew they served a worthwhile cause. This week I would spend time looking into their fund-raising efforts, their rankings, their reputation, and their board of directors. The main part of my time, however, would be spent checking to see how they fulfilled their mission statement, and if they were planning and spending wisely, as I felt certain they were. Of course, I would also have to assess the effect of the problems that arose when Luisa Morales had worked here.

Feeling well organized by noon, I took Natalie up on her offer of lunch. Dean excused himself to catch up with some paperwork, so Natalie and I left the office without him and drove up the street to one of my old favorites, Auntie's Country Kitchen.

According to the sign next to the hostess stand, today's specials included a variety of meat-and-starch-type dishes—meatloaf and mashed potatoes, pot roast with rice and gravy—all with sides of biscuits and collard greens and applesauce. In other words, good old Southern home cooking! Inhaling the wonderful aromas coming from inside, I could feel my appetite quickly springing to life.

We sat in a booth next to the window and perused the menu. The restaurant was an unpretentious place, with a small vase of plastic flowers at the center of every Formica-topped table. Natalie pushed our vase to one side, reminding me to save room for the fruit pies that were the restaurant owner's specialty.

Before we had a chance to order, however, Dean entered the restaurant and walked quickly to our table.

"Dean!" Natalie said happily upon spotting him. "I'm so glad you decided to join—"

Seeing the expression on his face, she cut herself off in mid-sentence.

"What is it?" she asked. "What's wrong?"

"There's been a new incident. With Luisa."

"Is she all right?" Natalie asked.

"She and the kids are fine," Dean said. "But someone just tried to burn down their trailer."

Seven

Dean explained further as the three of us drove toward the trailer in question. Apparently, Luisa had brought her car to the auto shop just a while ago to have the window repaired where the person had broken the glass to throw in the stink bombs. Because it was going to take some time before it was ready, the tow truck driver had given her a ride home. When they got there, the trailer was on fire.

"The guy from the auto shop said they managed to put it out before it did any real damage," Dean said. "But he sounded pretty shaken up, and I could hear Luisa crying in the background."

Dean added that the man had wanted to call the police, but Luisa insisted that he phone Dean and Natalie first.

"Why you and not the police?" I asked.

"I don't know," Dean said, "I think Luisa has lost faith that the cops can help her at all. They didn't treat the stink bomb incident very seriously last night; at least, not until the poor stabbing victim was found."

"Yeah, but come on," I said. "There's a big difference between a stink bomb and a house fire. Especially now that there's been a murder."

Natalie shook her head sadly.

"Poor Luisa," she said. "Her troubles never seem to end."

The three of us were quiet for a while as Dean continued to drive. The closer we got to downtown Greenbriar, the more I felt an odd sort of déjà vu. I had come into Greenbriar from a different direction yesterday, so this was the first time I had been to the downtown area in several years.

The names on the stores may have changed, but the old structures with their lovely ornate cornices were the same. Narrow buildings lined both sides of the street for several blocks, most of them with little shops downstairs and what I assumed were mostly converted apartments upstairs. Fortunately, there seemed to be some effort to keep the area attractive and viable, despite the draw of the giant Wal-Mart I had passed on the outskirts of town. A new row of trees grew from brick-lined circles spaced along the sidewalks, interspersed with wooden benches and old-fashioned coach-type lampposts. The street had always been a little too narrow for the passage of cars and parking on both sides, but now it looked as though they had widened the lanes and built public parking lots along the back sides of the buildings.

At the main intersection, Dean made a left turn and then followed the highway out of town where it snaked alongside a creek. It was a gorgeous spring day, and many of the trees and plants we passed were alive with early blossoms of pink and white and purple. Of course, between the breaks in the trees on all sides were the Smoky Mountains, vivid shadowy peaks topped by white tufts of clouds. Reluctantly, I forced my mind away from the beautiful scenery and back to the task at hand.

"Can I ask you a question?" I said. "After all the harm this woman did to your agency, why are the two of you still so involved with her?"

Natalie sighed deeply before answering.

"She really doesn't have anyone else," she said. "And besides whatever has happened with her in the past, it is still our charity's mission to help migrants."

"It seems to me you go more than the extra mile."

"That's what it takes sometimes," Natalie said. "And our hearts really do go out to her. She's a very sweet woman."

"How does she know the fire was intentional?" I asked. "I mean, it could've been electrical or something."

"From the smell," Dean replied as he slowed and put on his turn signal. "The man from the auto shop said it smelled like someone had doused the side of the trailer with gasoline."

Dean turned onto a gravel drive that dipped down and ended abruptly at a tangled mess of bushes and kudzu vines. He pulled in next to a tow truck, and we got out and walked toward the trailer, a tiny blue-and-white aluminum capsule that was even smaller than I had expected. It sat at a slight angle in tall weeds, perched next to the creek, and one end was stained black. The smell of gasoline was still prevalent, though there were no containers nearby except for an empty bucket.

Dean stepped onto the upside-down milk crate that served as a front stoop and was about to knock on the door when a man called out from the far side of the trailer.

"We're over here," he said.

We walked around the corner toward the voice to find Luisa sitting at a rickety picnic table under a tree, crying. Pacing nearby was a man in an oil-stained work uniform, looking decidedly uncomfortable.

Natalie went to Luisa and hugged her while the man stopped pacing and explained what had happened. Apparently, they had seen the fire before they even turned into the driveway. Once they got out of the truck, they tried dousing the flames with water from the creek, but with only one bucket it was a losing battle. Finally, he remembered the truck's fire extinguisher, so he retrieved it and sprayed the fire until it went out.

"This whole trailer woulda probably burned down if we hadn't got here when we did," he said in a thick mountain accent. "She's all upset, but I tol' her she's lucky. At least the fire didn't burn all the way through to the inside."

While they continued talking, I walked back around the trailer to look at the big blackened mess, and I saw he was correct. It appeared to have burned down to the insulation, but not beyond.

"Look, I know the police are probably gonna wanna talk to me, but it's takin' too long for them to get here," the man was saying as he walked to the tow truck. He opened the passenger door and began digging through the glove compartment. "If I don't get back to the garage right now, I'm gonna lose my job. Tell 'em to call me if they need me, would ya? I'll be there 'til four. Her car'll be ready by then anyway."

He handed Dean what looked like a business card, and then he climbed up into the truck, gave us a wave, and drove away.

Dean and I walked back to the other side of the trailer where Natalie was still comforting Luisa. They looked up when we appeared, and Natalie introduced me as her daughter-in-law, Callie Webber. I said hello and quietly took a seat on a nearby tree stump. Dean found a spot at the table to sit, and then we all waited as Luisa wiped her eyes and pulled herself together.

"I can't take it anymore," she said finally, stifling more sobs. "Thank the good Lord at least the children are not here to see this."

"Where are the children?" Natalie asked, her brow wrinkled.

"At Go the Distance. I called and checked on them. Karen said they're fine."

I cleared my throat and then spoke.

"Do you mind if I look around a bit?" I asked.

"Go ahead," Luisa mumbled, barely noticing as I rose and walked away. As she recounted her version of what had happened, I studied the situation, careful not to disturb anything since this was a crime scene. I couldn't get around the back of the trailer because it was covered with more kudzu, a stubborn plant prominent in the Southeast that sometimes grew so quickly and heartily that it was able to cover almost anything in its path—including old house trailers. I thought that in a better moment I ought to warn Luisa to cut down the vines before they completely took over. For now, I went around the other way and tried to see if I could find any clues to the fire. No one had asked for my help here, but it wouldn't hurt to take a look.

Years ago my investigating mentor, Eli Gold, had taught me the basics of arson detection. As if I could hear his voice in my head directing me, I examined the side of the trailer and the grass underneath for any evidence that might have been left behind.

And, actually, there was a lot. At first I didn't quite understand what I was seeing, but as I played with some scenarios in my head, it began to make sense. To me, it looked as if someone had indeed doused the side of the trailer and the ground under that side with gasoline or some other similar incendiary agent. Then from there they had poured a line of the liquid out about 15 feet for their own protection when lighting the fire. It hadn't worked, however, because there were half-burned matches every few feet along the line. The best I could figure was that the grass was so wet—and the line of liquid poured so thin—that the matches wouldn't stay lit. The fire would travel a few feet and then fizzle out. The arsonist would obviously try again, a bit closer this time, but the same thing happened twice more. The last few matches were a mere five feet or so from the trailer, and I guessed at that point the arsonist hadn't wanted to risk being any closer when lighting the fire.

I supposed that explained why the ignition source actually responsible for the fire wasn't matches at all but a road flare. A small, blackened piece of it remained, half hidden in the burned grass at the point of origin. I could only assume that the flare had been lit and then tossed into the gasoline from a safe distance, finally doing the job of starting the main fire.

That led me to think that the arsonist had probably come here by car or truck rather than on foot, since he—or possibly she, I guess—must've grabbed the flare from the vehicle when it became obvious the matches weren't going to work. The ground was muddy from recent rains, so I looked for telltale tire tracks. Unfortunately, the driveway was rutted by numerous imprints, and I doubted this crime would warrant enough police manpower to analyze those tracks in the hunt for suspects.

As for witnesses, I walked to the road to scope out any nearby houses, but there were none. This stretch of highway was lined on one side by woods and the other side by the creek. I knew the road was dotted with other houses and trailers along the way, but none were close enough to be of any use.

I stood at the top of the driveway and looked down at the scene, trying to form a mental picture of the perpetrator. To me, this seemed like a careful, methodical display of aggression. This person—or people—had wanted to make it clear that this fire was no accident. After all, they had left everything behind except the gasoline can.

I walked back around to the group at the picnic table, and I could see that Luisa's eyes were still red, but she seemed to have stopped crying.

"Excuse me," I said, interrupting them to address Luisa directly, "but can you honestly say that you can't name a single person in this town who has a problem with you? Some kind of grudge? Some reason to want you to suffer?"

Luisa blew her nose before looking up at me.

"I don't know that they want me suffer, necessarily," she said. "They just want me to go away."

"That's one of the first things they did to her," Natalie explained. "They spray painted those very words, 'GO AWAY,' right on the driveway."

"But I won't go away until my husband comes back," Luisa said, her face threatening to crumple into tears once again.

"Your husband left you?" I asked.

"No," Luisa said, sniffling. "He didn't *leave*. He would never leave us. Something happened to him. And we are going to stay here until we find out what that was and where he is!"

Her declarations brought on a fresh wave of sobs.

"Enrique was always a good man, a family man," Dean said to me. "It was a surprise to all of us when he disappeared."

"I've been trying to find him for over four months," Luisa cried. "But the police, they do nothing. They said they are conducting a missing persons search, but I don't believe them. Maybe they sent out one or two pictures, but that was all. They think he is a deadbeat. They think he is off to greener pastures without me or the children to hold him back."

"Did he take any of his things when he left?" I asked as gently as I could.

"He didn't leave!" Luisa cried. "Of course he didn't take anything. Enrique was at the orchard, picking apples. Mr. Pete sent him off to prune some trees in the high block, and he simply never came back."

"The high block?"

"Sometimes orchards are divided into sections," Dean explained. "Over at Tinsdale Orchards, they call the very top field the high block. It's the last section of apple trees before the property line."

"Was there a search?" I asked. "Maybe he fell down an old well or something. Maybe …" I cleared my throat. "Maybe a wild animal got him."

"They considered all of that," Dean said. "When Enrique still hadn't shown up the next morning, the foreman organized a search. He had every one of his employees combing the entire place. Later, the police came out and did the same thing. But there was no trace of him, no evidence of foul play, no sign of a struggle."

"Then the letter showed up," Natalie added.

"The letter?" I asked.

Luisa looked up at the sky and took a deep breath.

"I got a letter in the mail about a week after he disappeared, post-marked from New York City. It said 'I'm sorry but I don't love you anymore, and so I had to go. Goodbye.'"

"Does your husband have any ties to New York City?"

"None at all. I think the farthest north he's ever been is Virginia."

"Do you think there could be another woman involved?" I asked.

"No," Luisa replied calmly. "There is no other woman. The letter was not even from Enrique."

"How do you know?"

"First of all, it was typed. He does not know how to use a type-writer. Secondly, it was written in perfect English. Enrique speaks English well enough, but he can't write in it. I mean, I suppose he could try, but he would never spell the words correctly. English letters don't follow the same rules as in Spanish. He writes only in Spanish."

I thought about that, a letter sent from a city where the man had no ties, typed, in English. Whether the letter was completely fraud-ulent and written without his knowledge, or written for him on his behalf, at the very least it proved that someone else had to have been involved here.

"Do you have the letter?" I asked.

"No, I gave it to the police. Big mistake. Instead of using it as a clue to find him, they decided it was proof he had left of his own free will. Case closed. I still go to the police station every week, and ask, 'What are you doing to find my husband?' They tell me they are looking. But I know they do not even try."

"What about the person or people who started this fire? Could they have kidnapped him or something?"

"If he is kidnapped, then why? Where is the note? What are the ransom demands? Where is my husband?"

We let that question settle as we sat, lost in thought. I felt sorry for Luisa and her children, but as an outsider looking in, I didn't think the situation was as hopeless as it seemed. Now that there had been a murder, especially, I felt certain the police would revisit Luisa's situation with more careful attention. In the meantime, I didn't see what purpose it served for her and her children to remain in Greenbriar, where they were obviously in danger themselves. I said as much, though from Dean's and Natalie's expressions, I could tell that this was a conversation the three of them had had before.

Sure enough, Luisa sat up straight, her fists clinched, her shoulders high.

"I am not leaving this town," she declared, pounding her fist on the table, "until I find my husband."

"Then perhaps you have some relatives living somewhere else," I said, "who can take care of your children until then."

Luisa's firmness seemed to waver just a bit.

"Relatives?" she asked.

"Someone attacked your car and your home, Luisa," I said firmly, leaning toward her across the table. "It's no longer petty vandalism. The stakes are too high now. And you can't ignore the fact that there has been a murder."

Luisa was quiet for a moment, and finally she nodded.

"We saw that man die," she whispered. "But I didn't think it had anything to do with me. With us."

"It probably didn't," I said. "But just in case, don't you think you're better safe than sorry?"

She chewed on her bottom lip.

"I will call my sister in Texas," she said, blinking as two tears trailed down her face. "Perhaps she will let the children come and stay with her."

Dean exhaled loudly, patting Luisa on the arm.

"Now you're talking," he said. "We'll even pay for the tickets to get them there, if you need."

The police arrived at that moment, so while the three of them talked about the logistics of sending away the kids, I walked over to meet the officers who had pulled into the driveway. The way I saw it, this case didn't begin with today's fire or even with last night's murder.

It started last fall, the day this woman's husband disappeared.

Eight

~

Talking with the uniformed officers who responded to the call, I was disappointed to learn that June Sweetwater, the detective in charge of the murder investigation, wouldn't be coming. When I suggested that perhaps she should, they told me she was in Asheville at the medical examiner's office and wouldn't be back for several hours. In any event, they said, since this was a fire, the fire marshall was on his way and he would be the one to investigate. Detective Sweetwater would be fully apprised of the situation when she returned.

Sure enough, the fire marshall showed up a few minutes later and began taking some digital photos of the scene for the records. While he worked, he fired off questions to Luisa about what had happened. The cops took notes, and Dean gave them the business card of the tow truck driver to corroborate Luisa's story. I mostly hovered around the fringes, watching and listening.

It seemed to me that everyone grasped the gravity of the situation and its possible connection to last night's murder. The cops were obviously familiar with Luisa's plight and the missing persons search for her husband, though they didn't seem convinced that the fire was related in any way to his disappearance. One cop actually wondered aloud if perhaps the person who started the fire *was* her husband, now back from wherever he had been hiding and ready to make trouble. Though Dean spoke out in the man's defense, I had to admit I had been wondering the same thing as well.

Once the fire marshall collected all of the half-burnt matches and the discarded auto flare, the men wrapped up their questioning and thanked us for our cooperation, telling Luisa she could come down to the police station anytime after noon tomorrow to pick up a copy of the report if she needed one for insurance purposes.

She began to express her worries about money after they were gone. The cost of repairing the fire damage hadn't occurred to her before now, and she was afraid that the kind-hearted local who had loaned her the trailer would hold her responsible for the expense. From what I could gather, the trailer belonged to Butch Hooper, the big man with the booming voice I had met at my welcoming party. Dean assured Luisa that Butch undoubtedly had insurance on it, since he was in the construction business and owned a number of rental properties. What Dean didn't add was that the whole trailer couldn't be worth more than a few hundred dollars at best anyway.

As we prepared to leave, it crossed my mind that concepts like insurance and mortgages and home values were probably so far removed from Luisa's life as an itinerant migrant picker that she might not even understand how they worked. What would it feel like, I wondered, to have no home, to own nothing more than what could be carried around from job to job in your car? I had a feeling it was that very mobility that had probably complicated the search for the missing husband. There weren't many ways to trace a man who owned no property nor had any assets.

Dean and Natalie and I were starving by the time we left, but with so much happening, we didn't want to take the time to go back to Auntie's Country Kitchen for a full meal. Instead, we stopped at a fast-food restaurant on our way back to town and had a quick late lunch. Over hamburgers we talked about Luisa.

Though I felt sorry for her and her children, my own personal concern was more for how her troubles were affecting the Webbers—and the impact that all of this had had on MORE. Though Luisa no longer worked there, the "black eye" that Natalie had spoken of still remained with the county—and would until a full understanding of the situation was reached.

The sequence of events was a bit confusing, and so I asked them to go back and clarify it for me. Natalie reiterated the whole story. According to her, Luisa and Enrique Morales had come to Greenbriar last July with their two children, moving into the migrant family dorms as they did every year during harvest. Enrique had gone to work picking apples for Tinsdale Orchards, and Luisa had taken a job at MORE. Things were fine until November, near the end of harvest, when the husband disappeared, seemingly without a trace. Subsequently, Luisa had the two big mess-ups at work where she left confidential papers in the laundromat and then wiped out portions of the database. She lost her job, and then she and the kids moved from the seasonal migrant dormitories into the trailer where they lived now. Soon after they moved in, they found the words "GO AWAY" spray painted on the driveway. Since then, several times Luisa had found herself the target of some menacing act—a slashed tire, last night's stink bombs, today's fire—all apparently meant to harass her into leaving town. Luisa took in laundry to provide for her family, but last week she had lost one of her best clients when their neatly washed-and-folded clothes were stolen from the back seat of her car.

My eyes widened.

"A criminal act," I said, "that led to the loss of employment? You understand, don't you, what this means?"

They both looked at me blankly.

"All of the things that have happened to her—but particularly the stolen laundry—actually support her claim that she wasn't responsible for the problems at your agency. I mean, think about it. What better way is there to get a person to leave town than to make them lose their job?"

Dean and Natalie looked at each other and then back at me.

"You think someone really did those things intentionally so that Luisa would get fired?"

"It fits the pattern. I haven't got a clue why someone would want her to leave town so badly, but I think it started back then, and now I feel strongly that she was telling you the truth about what happened. I think it wasn't her own carelessness, but some sort of deliberate, malicious act by someone else."

"What about the murder?" Dean asked. "Surely that was something more serious than simply trying to get her to leave town."

"True," I said. I still wasn't sure what to think about the murder. But, as a part of my own J.O.S.H.U.A. grant investigation, I knew I would have to find out if there was a connection between it and MORE.

As Dean and Natalie talked, it soon became obvious that there was an additional issue here. For someone to steal files or tinker with the computer, they would need actual, physical access to those things. And who had access, I asked, except the employees of MORE?

"Oh, Callie," Natalie said, sitting back in her seat. "I had never considered that before."

"The last thing we need," Dean said, frowning, "is someone inside the company who's willing to sabotage our work and our reputation simply to get at one particular person. Perhaps you're right, Callie. Perhaps the situation needs to be revisited in a new light."

"If I were you," I agreed, "I would make a list of every person who was working for you when that all happened. Then you need to go through the list together, maybe ask some discreet questions, and see if you can't narrow things down a bit. At some point, I think you need to produce a list of suspects, and you need to bring that information to the police."

Their faces seemed to register many emotions, but primarily disappointment. I had been involved in many corporate investigations where a trusted employee turned out to be a bad seed, so I knew that look well.

"If you'd like," I added, trying to soften the blow, "I could poke around a bit on the computer and see if I can turn up any traces of Enrique Morales. Finding the missing husband seems like a logical step, since none of this started happening until he disappeared."

"You could do that?" Natalie asked, her eyes hopeful.

"I could try. A lot of the databases I subscribe to for my job can also be used for missing persons searches. Back when I worked for Eli, I used to run missing persons cases all the time."

"How hard is it to find someone?" Dean asked.

"You never know until you try," I replied. "I've turned up people in ten minutes, and I've had one or two that I never found. At the very least, I think this would probably be worth looking into, because it relates to my grant investigation in a peripheral sort of way."

"Whatever you can do, Callie," Natalie said, "we would appreciate it."

Dean nodded in agreement.

In light of that, as we finished eating I had them tell me everything they knew about Enrique—his life history, his hobbies, his education level, whatever they could think of. Apparently, the man came to Greenbriar for harvest every year and had been doing so for as long as they could remember. He never took their employment testing, because he dropped out of school somewhere in the elementary grades and didn't think he was suited for anything but farm labor. Despite his limited education, however, Enrique was a good man, a devoted father, and always calm and even-tempered.

"According to Luisa," Natalie said, "His biggest fault is his indecisiveness. Where she tends to act first and think later, she says he's often frozen in indecision, seeing every side of every issue until it renders him almost motionless."

As for hobbies or side interests, Enrique had none that Dean or Natalie knew of. Migrants rarely did, they said, considering their income level and lack of free time. Enrique was an especially hard worker, but he lived hand-to-mouth, as was the only way most of them could.

Once the Webbers finished telling me all they could recall, Dean admitted that the description didn't really fit a man who would abandon his family. Perhaps, he said, Luisa had been right, and Enrique hadn't left of his own free will after all.

As Dean paid for lunch, I stood anxiously by the door, shifting my weight from one foot to the other. I had come to Greenbriar feeling certain I would easily move through the grant approval process. But now the complicating factors were becoming too big. From Luisa's troubles and Enrique's disappearance to the murder of an unidentified man, it was looking more and more like this million-dollar grant was indefinitely on hold. I didn't share this with the Webbers, and I wished it wasn't true, but the investigator in me was waking up, certain that I had to act and figure things out before my beloved in-laws were inevitably drawn deeper into this mess.

Nine

We retrieved my car from the Webbers' house and then went back to the office, where I set up my computer in the conference room. So much was happening around me that I knew I had to step back and get a good perspective on things. I decided it might help to call Eli.

Eli Gold was one of my dearest and oldest friends, the man who taught me everything I knew about investigating. He was retired now and living in Florida, but we had worked together in Virginia for years, and I still found myself consulting with him from time to time when I needed to reason things out on a difficult case.

I dialed his number and felt a surge of relief when he answered the phone. We usually chatted for a while before we got down to business, but this time he was on his way out the door.

"I can give you five minutes, doll," he said with his characteristic bluntness. "Stella's meeting me at the yogurt stand on Third and Peters, and if I'm late my mocha chocolate chip ice cream will melt."

"I'll make it fast then," I said, grinning at the image of Stella waiting for Eli, a dripping cone in each hand. "I've got a case that was supposed to be fairly straightforward, but it's growing more complicated by the hour. Things have begun to intertwine in some very confusing ways."

"Play it out for me," he said. "I'm gonna put you on speakerphone while I put my socks and shoes on."

I heard a few clicks and then his voice, farther away, telling me to go ahead.

"All right," I said. "I'm in North Carolina, and I'm here to investigate a nonprofit called Migrant Outreach Resource Enterprises or MORE for short."

"Why does that sound familiar?"

"It's run by my former in-laws, Dean and Natalie Webber."

"Ah…" he said musically. "That's right."

"Anyway, we're considering them for a big grant, and I'm trying to do a charity investigation."

"Which you could do in your sleep, I might add."

"Yes, well, good thing I'm not sleeping on this job, because I've already got a murder, a missing person, and some company sabotage."

"Sounds to me like MORE isn't gonna be getting more money."

"At least not until I can straighten out this mess."

I went on to give him an overview of all that had happened thus far. As we pondered the facts of the case, I decided to break it down into three parts: find out what happened to Enrique, find out who was terrorizing Luisa, and continue with the parts of the charity investigation that weren't affected by these irregularities.

"You can probably kill a bunch of birds with one stone here. You might have an interview with someone about your charity investigation, and it turns out they know a little something about the missing man or the vandalism. You know the drill, Callie. Go about your job and keep your eyes and ears open."

"You make it sound so simple."

"It is simple. One step at a time, is all. You can do this, girly. I have absolute faith in you."

"I'm glad one of us does."

The phone clicked and then his voice sounded closer.

"All right, hon," he said, "Stella awaits. Gotta fly for now."

I thanked him for listening and hung up the phone, feeling encouraged.

I decided I would begin with a computer search for Enrique Morales, ask for some more information from Dean and Natalie, and finally set up some appointments for the peripheral charities so that I could go out and, as Eli said, keep my eyes and ears open.

Ten

From their records, Dean got me Enrique's full name, date of birth, and social security number. With that as a starting point, I would attempt to track the man down, though his itinerant status was going to make this missing persons search a bit more difficult than the average case.

I said a quick prayer before I began, and then I kept my eyes closed to try to clear my mind of all distractions except the pursuit of this missing man.

If some physical trouble had befallen him—an abduction, an accident, an animal attack—then the investigation would require the examination of physical evidence, something that could no longer be done because so much time had passed. If that were the case, then I would need to talk to the police to see if I could get a look at their records of the investigation after the original disappearance.

If, however, Enrique had left of his own accord, then chances were that somewhere, somehow in the months since then, he had done something that had left a record. That was the hope I was going on now and the type of thing that I would spend the next hour looking for. Though it was quite possible for someone to slip under the radar, it at least deserved a try.

First, I went down the standard avenues of computer searching, using Enrique's information to scan various databases. One by one I checked telephone records, marriages, divorces, bankruptcies, property records, and other court-related filings. A few Enrique Moraleses did show up here and there, but once I weeded them out by age or social security number, my man was nowhere to be found.

Considering Enrique's migrant status, it didn't surprise me that he hadn't exactly left behind a paper trail either before or after his disappearance. I sat back in my chair and thought hard, trying to picture the life of a migrant and how it differed from a mainstream American. For a migrant there would be no real estate transactions, no credit reports, probably no bank accounts. There was a possibility that his name would pop up in the public assistance databases—things like welfare, unemployment, and food stamps. Unfortunately, those records weren't available to private investigators, not even through LexisNexis or any of the other subscription services I maintained. Of course, the police had probably already gone down these roads, using official avenues to see if Enrique was sitting back somewhere collecting assistance checks or if he had been arrested.

For now, I went online and did a search for "migrant services," and I was amazed at the number of programs that popped up for migrants needing help across the country. From health care and dental visits to education, there were many nonprofit groups and government agencies that seemed to be involved with serving migrants in one way or another.

I was intrigued with a certain type of place, many of which appeared under the category of "travel assistance." Apparently, there were migrant welcome centers of sorts along many of the picking routes, where vouchers were given out to qualifying migrants for inexpensive hotel stays, meals, and gasoline. "Getting you through the night and back on the road" was one place's slogan. Thinking that Enrique might have availed himself of something like that, I borrowed a map from the office and did a concurrent search for such places along the highways he could have taken as he left the area, particularly the ones between here and New York City.

I tried calling a few of the places, but after several disconnected phone lines, I realized they were most likely seasonal in nature and wouldn't be up and running year-round. Trying to come at the information another way, I went back into several of my paid databases and with a lot of clicking was eventually able to find my way to a database of a place called the Office of Local and Rural Health. It had data on food, hotel, and medical vouchers given out to migrants for most of the states I wanted to check. The names 'Enrique and Luisa Morales' names popped up a number of times, but when I limited the search to those dates on or after last November 11, the search came up empty.

As expected, everything I'd tried had come up empty.

Disappointed, I logged off of the computer and went to find Dean and Natalie, who were sitting in Dean's office, hunched together over a legal pad covered with scribbles.

"No luck," I announced quietly after I shut the door behind me. "At least to the computer and the types of records I have access to, this man does not exist after November 11."

"We're not doing very well, either," Natalie said. "We made a list of the people who were working here then, and there's not a single person on it that we would suspect of stealing files or sabotaging the database."

I took a seat across from them and suggested they bounce their thoughts off of me.

"Well," Dean said, "it helps to understand that our work is very seasonal in nature. Because the bulk of the picking is finished by the end of October, most of the migrants are gone by then. At the bigger orchards, a few migrants are paid to stick around and close out the job, but by and large our staff here drops significantly before the first of November."

"Okay."

"The records were left in the laundromat on November 17. At that time, we had eight employees. The data was erased on November 23, and by then we were down to five employees, not counting Luisa."

Natalie handed me the list of names.

"Two of those people can be counted out automatically. One of them was at a convention in Florida at the time, and the other was in the hospital having gallbladder surgery. That leaves three people, three women, on the list of possible suspects."

"What about the one at the convention?" I asked. "That could've been faked."

"She was the keynote speaker for the night of the twenty-third."

"All right, then she's in the clear," I said, smiling.

"Callie, I have to be honest," Natalie said. "I absolutely cannot imagine any of those three women having anything to do with this. They are old and dear friends, members of our church, and lovely women all. I just refuse to believe that any of them would've done something so malicious."

We talked about the possibility of some other person letting themselves into the building with an unauthorized key, perhaps a former employee or someone's family member.

"They might get into the building," Dean said, "but that wouldn't allow them to get into the database. I'm not very computer savvy myself, but I know we've got some protections in place."

I nodded, thinking.

"Who's in charge of database security?" I asked. "Are they one of the names on this list?"

"Ellen Mack is our database administrator," Natalie said, "but she's the one who was having her gallbladder out when it happened."

"Ken set up the system," Dean said. "He knows how the security is put together."

"Let's call him. I have some questions."

While Dean got his nephew on the phone, Natalie and I went to the break room area and started a fresh pot of coffee. As it brewed, I had her walk me down to the database administrator's office and introduce us. Ellen Mack was brusque but friendly, in her forties, and wearing a gray skirt and sensible brown shoes. She was obviously a technical person because her office was littered with equipment, including a motherboard that was spread open on her desk like a patient in surgery.

We spoke for just a minute or two and then excused ourselves, leaving her to her computer and her PalmPilot and all of her other high-tech tools.

Back at the break room, Natalie poured herself and Dean some coffee and I made myself a cup of hot tea. Then we returned to Dean's office, where he put Ken on speakerphone. Ken explained to us the security levels that would need to be penetrated in order to accomplish such a big loss of data.

He said there were four levels of password protection, and each level was accessible to fewer people than the level before. At the tightest level, only two people knew the passwords, which were changed regularly.

"You always want two people to know that final password," Ken said, "just in case something happens to one of them."

"Who would those two people be?" I asked.

"The database administrator and the database technician."

I looked at Natalie, who said, "Ellen Mack and Luisa Morales."

I nodded.

"And Ellen was in the hospital at the time," I said. "No wonder you thought Luisa did it."

"Whenever you have passwords," Ken added, "there's always the chance that somebody will get stupid and write theirs down. But when we set up the system, I made it very clear *never* to do that. Once the disaster happened, if y'all recall, Uncle Dean and Aunt Natalie, we questioned both women extensively, and they both swore they had never written down any passwords."

"Is there any way to override the passwords?" I asked.

"Sure," Ken replied. "If you know what you're doing, I guess you could reinstall the operating system and wipe out the entire database. But that's not how this was done. In this case, large chunks of data were simply erased, and the only way to get that kind of access is through passwords."

"So somebody's lying?"

"It looks that way."

We thanked him for his help and wrapped up the call.

"What next?" Natalie asked me as Dean hung up the phone.

"I'm not sure," I replied, even though I already had several ideas in mind. "For now, why don't the two of you interview Ellen Mack about those passwords one more time, just to make sure there's not any question of her having written them down somewhere or told them to someone. For all we know, she mumbled them out as she was going under anesthesia for her gallbladder operation."

They smiled grimly but agreed it wouldn't hurt to revisit the situation one more time.

"I've got some things to take care of," I said. "But I'll be in touch later."

Back in the conference room, I packed up my computer and briefcase. The next stop for me was the police station. I needed to talk to them, to see what they had done, what they knew.

Before I left the office, however, I asked Dean how I could reach Danny Stanford, the man from Tinsdale Orchards whom I had met at the party last night. Danny and I had tentatively agreed to a tour of the orchard this afternoon at 5:00, but I thought it best to postpone it until the next day, if possible. With all that had happened, the tour had an added interest for me, since I wanted to see the area of the orchard where Enrique supposedly disappeared, the "high block."

Dean suggested that I call Karen Weatherby, the woman I had met at the party who was the head of Go the Distance Learning Center. I did just that, and she gave me Danny's cell phone number.

"I'm sure he won't mind putting it off," she said. "They're unsealing a room this week, and the timing on that is always kind of tricky."

"Unsealing a room? What's that?"

She explained that although the apples were all picked in the fall, many of them were stored in special rooms where they remained fresh until they could be shipped throughout the year.

"Didn't you ever wonder how you could buy apples year-round, even though they only grow in the fall?"

"I never thought about it," I said. "I guess I figured they brought them up from South America or something."

"Nope," she replied. "Not at all. They have special rooms that keep the apples fresh. It's kind of hard to explain, but it has to do with the temperature and oxygen levels."

"Interesting," I said. "I hope Danny will show that to me on my tour."

Before we hung up, we made plans for me to visit her facility the next day as well. Despite the questions that now hung over my investigation like a black, roiling cloud, I needed to press onward in other areas of the case, and that included learning more about the different organizations that MORE supported.

Using the number Karen had given me, I called Danny from the car and told him simply that I had been held up. He said it was no problem, that whatever time I wanted to swing by tomorrow would be fine.

Eleven

I drove on to the police station, which was downtown and near the post office. At the main desk I asked for June Sweetwater, and they told me she had stepped out but would be back in about 15 minutes.

Actually, I realized, that was probably good. I still needed to pick up the keys to my cabin from the Skytop Vacation Rentals office. As much as I had been dreading this particular errand in the past few weeks, I couldn't imagine how I had almost forgotten to do it at all in the confusion of the day.

The place was only a few blocks away, so I decided to walk. Fortunately, once I got there, I didn't recognize a single person in the rental office. That made it much simpler for me, because I didn't have to face any of those young-widow-whose-husband-died-a-tragic-death pity looks I had received when I first signed up with the place. To these strangers, my house was just another rental unit.

It did strike me funny that I had to sign some paperwork before I could be given the keys to my own home, but then I supposed that was just as well. Better they be too careful than not careful enough. As I walked back outside, I slipped the keys into my pocket, thinking about the cabin and all of the bittersweet memories that it held, trusting that God would provide each little bit of strength as I needed it.

From there, I slowed down a bit and enjoyed the stroll back to the police station. I looked around as I walked, reorienting myself to the charming little downtown.

Greenbriar had grown a bit in the last few years, with a new high school stadium marking one end of town and a big, glowing Wal-Mart on the other. When I first started coming to Camp Greenbriar, the town always seemed fairly superfluous; the campground, after all, had everything we needed. But at least once during camp every year we were bussed into the sleepy downtown of Greenbriar and set loose for several hours of free time. My friends and I usually made a beeline for the Indian shop, where we strung turquoise necklaces and bought beaded keychains for souvenirs. From there we would hit the drugstore, which had an old-fashioned soda counter and a good-looking clerk named P.J., who made up our orders and ignored our preteen giggles.

Finally, we would end our time at the Carolina Gem Museum, a small volunteer-run facility that featured rows and rows of glass cases with real gems inside—diamonds and emeralds and rubies—that had been dug from the dirt of the Smoky Mountains nearby. The highlight of the museum for us was the "panning" area in the back, where for a dollar you'd get a scoop of dirt from a real mine and a screen-bottomed pan. By dipping the pan in a trough of running water, the dirt would rinse away and you might be left with a few rough gems of your own to keep. I still had a little bottle at my mother's house that held some of the miniscule rubies I had panned for myself.

Smiling at memories of being young and silly, I paused and tried to recall where each of those places had been. From what I could see now, the Indian shop and the gem mine were both long gone, though the drugstore was still there. On a whim, I peeked inside but was dismayed to see that the soda counter had been replaced by an aisle of depilatories, a rack of tabloids, and a shelf filled with Chia Pets.

As I walked the rest of the block, I decided that Greenbriar's attempts at downtown renewal seemed to be working beyond just new trees and lampposts and benches. There was a funky coffeehouse on one corner and a nice-looking independent bookstore across from it. Signs in several windows advertised an upcoming wine and cheese tasting, and apparently there was live music on Friday nights at "Sparky's," a corner bar and restaurant that seemed to be rather busy for a Monday afternoon. As I reached the police station parking lot, I wondered if things perked up even more on the weekends. So many small-town downtowns were disappearing these days with the advent of superstores and shopping malls. It looked as though Greenbriar might be an exception to the rule.

At the main desk I asked again for June Sweetwater, and this time she appeared through a doorway and invited me back to her office. I followed behind her, noting that today her ponytail had been woven into a thick, heavy braid which swung at her waist like a pendulum.

Her desk was at the back of a large room, separated from the others by a low partition. She pulled up a chair for me next to the desk, and I started to ask if we could speak somewhere privately. Looking around, however, I realized we were the only ones in the room at the moment, so I sat.

"How can I help you today?" she asked.

I wasn't quite sure. I had a lot of questions I hoped she might answer, but no good reason to convince her to do so except the truth. I decided to explain my situation fully in the hope she would be willing to bring me just a little bit into the loop.

"First of all," I said, "I need to explain to you who I am and why I'm in town."

"I thought you were the Webbers' daughter-in-law."

"I am, but I've also come here in an official capacity."

I hesitated, knowing I might put her instantly on her guard by throwing out my qualifications of "attorney" and "private investigator." Instead, I told her simply that I was the director of research for a nonprofit foundation, and that my task here was to "inspect" and "audit" the Webbers' agency with the intention of approving them for a large grant.

"I have to examine policies and procedures, finances, things like that, as well as look at more esoteric issues like effectiveness, reputation, results. I'm sure you understand."

"I think so."

"In any event, some things have come to light in my invest—"

I cleared my throat.

"—in my audit," I continued, "that have me a bit concerned, and I'm hoping perhaps you and I can share some information."

She leaned back in her seat and crossed her legs.

"Who do you work for exactly?" she asked.

"It's called the J.O.S.H.U.A. Foundation," I replied, reaching into my bag for a business card and then handing it over. "We are a national foundation based in Washington, DC."

"Hey, I know who y'all are," she said, studying my card, her face lighting up. "Your foundation gave a van to the Greater Nashville Honor Guard."

"What?"

"Just a few months ago, over in Tennessee. You gave a brand-new van to a veterans group so they could go around and serve as an honor guard at funerals."

I nodded, smiling as I recalled that particular assignment fondly.

"How did you know that?" I asked.

"The story is legend among the veterans around here. My dad's in an honor guard unit too, and he loves to tell the tale of how this woman from the J.O.S.H.U.A. Foundation showed up after a funeral one day and told the men there was a new van waiting for them at the car dealership."

"I was that woman."

"You're kidding."

Grinning, I relaxed and listened to her expound on the story, how on the day we gave the men the van they drove around Nashville for hours, stopping at the homes of every member of their group to show it off, gaining passengers and blaring out patriotic tunes all along the way. That had been a fun grant to present and a little out of the ordinary, since we had actually ended up awarding them with more money than they had requested so that they could have a new vehicle instead of a delapitated old used one.

By the time the detective finished relating the story, she was visibly more relaxed, and I thought, thankfully, *What goes around comes around.* Our good deed somewhere else was going to help us out here in a completely different way.

"So tell me what you need to know today and why," she said warmly, setting my card on the desk in front of her and squaring it with the blotter. "I'll see what I can do."

"Thank you."

With a silent prayer, I delved ahead, focusing on my investigation. Methodically, I explained the two work-related incidents that happened with Luisa Morales last fall, about the files that had been left in the laundromat and then the breach of security on the wiped-out database.

"We now have reason to suspect," I continued, "that in fact Luisa didn't do those things herself, but that someone else did them to her. If that is the case, then I've got a problem. Simply put, I can't approve a grant for the agency until all of this is settled."

"I understand your position," she said, "and it's unfortunate. But what does that have to do with us?"

"Last night, a man was killed in the same location and about the same time that stink bombs were set off in Luisa Morales' car. I know you must suspect that those two incidents are connected. I just need you to shed some light on the whole situation, and also on the ongoing missing persons investigation for Luisa's husband. The missing husband, in fact, seems to be a key issue here, since this all seems to have started with his disappearance. If I could find out what happened to him, then I might be able to search out the person who set Luisa up to lose her job. Once I've done that, the Webbers can take care of the employee problem and I can give them their grant."

June nodded, tilting forward until her elbows rested squarely on her desk.

"I have to admit," she said, "until the murder last night, we weren't very convinced that Enrique Morales didn't just walk off that orchard and thumb a ride out of town on the nearest highway."

"I know," I said. "It was an easy conclusion to jump to. Can you tell me what has been done in the missing persons search?"

She reached into a lateral file holder and pulled out a manila file. She flipped through pages, skimming the information.

"No arrests, no hits running his fingerprints, no information from the scene or from interviews. No sign of a struggle, no sign of anything. Last person to see him was the foreman of Tinsdale Orchards, Pete Gibson, who sent Morales off to a back field at the orchard to do some pruning. That's about it."

In other words, they didn't know anything more than I did.

"Did anyone ever run a search of public assistance databases?"

She continued to flip through the file.

"Yes," she said, reading. "Looks like the wife is enrolled in a few programs, but there's nothing on record for the husband."

"What about the letter from New York that showed up soon after he disappeared?"

She closed the file and put it away.

"After the events of last night, we've reexamined our position and have sent that letter off to be analyzed. But I can show you a photocopy, if you like."

She reached over to the bulletin board next to her desk and took down and handed me the infamous New York City letter that was supposedly sent from Enrique to Luisa shortly after he disappeared. Sure enough, it was intelligently worded and perfectly spelled and punctuated. As Luisa had said, there was no way a man who couldn't write in English could've written that.

"Do you sense a connection between his disappearance and the man who was murdered last night?" I asked, handing the paper back to her.

"Oh, there's a definite connection," she said. "I'm sorry that I can't elaborate."

I looked at her, trying to read her face.

"Enrique Morales wasn't the man who was stabbed, was he?"

"No, absolutely not."

I decided to take another guess.

"Fingerprints," I tried. "Please tell me you didn't find Enrique Morales' fingerprints on the murder weapon."

"We didn't find a murder weapon," she replied. "But you're correct in guessing that fingerprints are significant to this case. Though not in the way you might expect."

I was dying to know what she wasn't telling me. I tried to reverse my line of thinking, and after a moment, my eyes widened in surprise.

"The letter," I said. "The letter that was supposedly written by Enrique and sent to Louisa from New York—"

"Yes?"

"Don't tell me the man who was stabbed had some connection to that letter. Fingerprints, maybe?"

Just from her expression, I could tell I had guessed correctly. She tacked the paper back on the board.

"You're very clever, Mrs. Webber," she said. "The dead man's fingerprints were all over that letter. Have you ever considered a career in law enforcement?"

"My father and brother are both cops," I said, feeling guilty I hadn't told her I was a PI. "I guess it runs in the family."

"I suppose so."

"Can you tell me what you know about the dead man," I asked, "other than the fact that his fingerprints were on that letter?"

She shook her head.

"With no ID and no vehicle, we still don't know who he is. He's a John Doe for us right now, and no one is exactly stepping forward to claim the body, despite the fact that he was wearing expensive clothes and a diamond-encrusted watch."

"You've searched nationally?" I asked.

"Of course," she replied, sounding vaguely offended. "We're doing everything we can to ID the man. We've got him up on a national crime database, so if anyone runs an official search for a man with his stats, his info will pop up. So far, no one's come looking, and his fingerprints have had no match except to that letter."

"So what will you do next?" I asked, hoping she didn't think me too pushy.

"We're pursuing several avenues," she replied, and at my entreating expression, she lowered her voice and elaborated just a bit. "For example, apparently the man's shoes were custom made by an expensive leather crafter. We've been in contact with the manufacturer, and hopefully we'll be able to trace him out that way."

"That's good news," I said. "Thank you for sharing it with me."

"No problem."

"What about the diamond watch?" I asked. "I guess that rules out robbery as a motive for the stabbing."

"Not necessarily," she said, shaking her head. "It's a Bohgan Ghia watch."

At my blank stare, she explained.

"It has an unusual clasp, one that's very hard to open unless you know exactly what you're doing. From what I understand, the corpse had scrape marks all over his wrist. So someone tried their hardest but must've finally given up."

"Well, at least that gives you another expensive item to try and trace through the manufacturer."

"Yep, we're working on it. It also links the dead man back to the Morales case in another way, since the person who tried to remove the watch also left some prints on a stink bomb in the car, one that didn't go off."

"I knew there had to be a connection! So the person who set off the stink bombs was also the person who committed the murder?"

"Just going by fingerprints, it sure looks that way."

I was about to ask another question when several people came walking into the room. Instantly, June Sweetwater sat up straight, her expression closed off, and I knew this free exchange of information had come to an end. I stood and shook her hand, thanking her for her help and reiterating how sorry I was that I hadn't gotten a better look at the man I spied running through the woods.

"Nevertheless," she said, "I do hope you're being cautious. You're our only witness at this point, Mrs. Webber."

"Witness? Of the guy I saw running through the woods? I've already told you I didn't see much of anything."

"Doesn't matter," she replied. "If the perp thinks you can ID him, then you could be in for some trouble."

Twelve

With that comforting thought, I left the police station and climbed into my car. It hadn't crossed my mind that I might be in danger. Hopefully, the detective was overstating the situation.

Before starting the car, I dialed the Webbers to touch base with them. They invited me to dinner, but I told them I wanted to get up to the cabin and get settled in before it got too dark. They made sure I had all of their phone numbers—home, office, and cell—and then I told them I would see them in the morning. I told Natalie about my appointment at Go the Distance, and she said she would line up some more meetings for me the next day so I could visit some of the other charities they supported.

On my way out of town, I stopped for a few quick groceries, and then I decided to take the long way around to the cabin. The sky probably wouldn't be dark for another hour, and I thought it wouldn't hurt to check out some of the charities I would be visiting before I actually went there. More importantly, if I went the long way, I would also go right past Tinsdale Orchards. Though I would see the orchard tomorrow on my tour with Danny Stanford, I still wanted to check it out on my own.

Most of Greenbriar was merely hilly, a series of pleasant mounds clustered with neighborhoods, schools, downtown, and the lake area. Near the lake, however, was a road that headed steeply up what people called "the mountain," though I wasn't sure if, technically, it was high enough to be a real mountain. Certainly, it was much higher than the rest of the town, and the road meandered all the way up to the top. Dotted all along the way were hillside homes nestled privately among the trees—some incredibly beautiful and expensive and others not much more than trailers set up on cinderblocks. My cabin was near the top, on the side that faced the lake. A short way beyond there, the hill crested and then the road started back down the other side. I knew that the Tinsdales owned most of the land all the way down. Apple trees lined the road, and, near the bottom, was the gorgeous Tinsdale mansion.

Today I would be coming at the orchard from below it, as I was circling around the long way to drive up the back side of the mountain. The same highway Dean had driven to get to Luisa's trailer would eventually lead me to the orchard, where I would turn off and begin my ascent.

First, however, I watched the mailboxes for the address of Go the Distance Learning Center. I knew it was along here somewhere, and, sure enough, I passed it only a few blocks out of town, on my right. I slowed as I drove past, to see what looked like a weathered old house that had been converted to a small business.

The building was a white two-story with a sagging gray front porch and a handicap ramp leading to a side entrance. Hanging over the door was a sign that said "Go the Distance Learning Center," and in each of the many panes of the front windows were construction-paper apples in faded reds, yellows, and greens. From what Karen Weatherby had told me at the Webbers' party, the place offered an internet-based educational program for the migrant children, and it ran from kindergarten all the way through twelfth grade. I wasn't quite sure how it worked, but I was interested in paying her a visit and learning more about it.

The creek played hide-and-seek with the road as I drove out of town, the shallow, shimmery water tumbling over and between flat, gray rocks of all sizes. As I caught glimpses of the creek through the trees, I was reminded of the time at Camp Greenbriar when the arts and crafts instructor took a bunch of us campers to another branch of this same creek and told us to choose our favorite rock, one in which we could "see" something within the stone. I didn't know what she was talking about, so I just picked the smoothest, most symmetrical, most pleasing one I could find. Back at the camp art room, we were given tempera paints and told to paint our "vision" onto the rocks' smooth surfaces. Only then did I realize that most of the kids had chosen rocks that were shaped like things—animals, flowers, food. While the boy on one side of me painted his rock like a banana, and a girl on the other made hers into a frog, I turned mine over and over in my hand, wondering what I could do with an oblong oval rock. Finally, at the ten-minute warning, I covered it in dark green paint, dotted it with wiggly stripes of lighter green, and said that it was a watermelon.

Smiling at the memory, I realized suddenly that I was nearly at the scene of the trailer fire earlier today. Sure enough, just a few miles out of town, I passed Luisa's forlorn little trailer in the weeds beside the creek. In the last light of day, the place seemed so small and so vulnerable, and I made a mental note to find out whether or not Luisa's sister in Texas would be taking the children. Given all that was going on, I thought it important for them to go somewhere safe.

Beyond the trailer was an area where the trees thinned out and the creek widened. There, among the kudzu and the thick underbrush, was where the old migrant camp used to spring up every year, the place that always upset Bryan as he rode past. Now, thanks in part to MORE, there were official migrant dormitories further up the mountain, which I hoped to get a look at later this week.

It wasn't long before I reached the orchard with its rows and rows of lush, gnarled apple trees. As I rounded a curve, a beautiful antebellum home appeared in the distance, complete with tall white pillars and a sweeping front lawn. The Tinsdale mansion.

I didn't know anything about the family that owned the place, but I had always loved driving past the gracious home and its surrounding orchards. Tinsdale Orchards was one of the biggest fruit-producers in the county, and Dean had told me that they provided generous support for many of the migrant-related charities in the area.

I turned at the Tinsdale Orchards sign, drove past the house, and then switched the car into a lower gear as the road began to climb. Though the way slanted steadily upward, the orchard was laid out in tiers, almost like wide steps that slowly worked their way up the mountain. It was interesting to me how the apple trees were so varied in their stages of growth, and that I could tell the difference between the older, more mature trees and the ones just starting out.

As I drove I thought about Harriet, who had a serious fear of heights. It hadn't occurred to me until now, but I wondered if perhaps this drive up to my cabin might be too much for her, particularly on a day-to-day basis. That would be a shame, since I had been planning on having her stay at the cabin with me this week. I supposed I would let her decide, and if she was too frightened, we would just have to get her a room in town.

I, on the other hand, was loving every moment of the drive, from the reddish-purple sky overhead to the lush valley below that I kept glimpsing between breaks in the trees.

Near the end of the orchard, I passed a small building with a sign out front that said "Su Casa," and I remembered Butch Hooper, telling me this was the charity his father ran. I hoped to get in there to see it this week as well.

The apple trees ended a short way behind the Su Casa building, and I wondered if that were the end of the Tinsdale property. More importantly, was this the high block where Enrique Morales disappeared?

Beyond the apple trees were thick woods, a gravel road, and then more, even thicker forest. At that point, the mountain crested, and as I followed the road up and over the top, the sight in front of me took my breath away. Through a wide gap in the trees I could see the gorgeous Smokies in all of their varying shades of blue. Less than a half a mile down the other side, I came to my own property. It was just twilight, and as I turned into the driveway, my headlights swept across the front of the little A-frame house.

My cabin.

I felt excited to be here, not sad, and that was a relief. Climbing from the car, I pulled out the keys and walked up the steps and across the front porch to the door.

Stepping inside, the first thing that struck me was that the house had been stripped of all of our personal items. I vaguely remembered someone doing that for me, though I couldn't recall if it had been the Webbers or the Realtor. I did remember sending the Realtor a check for several thousand dollars to make the place more desirable as a rental unit. I asked her to replace our garage-sale furniture with nicer stuff and add more beds. She had done a good job, I decided now as I walked around. There was nothing fancy about it, but it was tasteful. And without any of our photos on the wall or our clothes in the drawers, this really did look like some anonymous vacation home, complete with a living room and kitchen area, bathroom, back room, and a loft. Nothing personal about it.

The living room held a big, cozy couch and chairs with an entertainment center at one end and a little breakfast nook with a skylight overhead at the other. The kitchen area was small and fit between the breakfast nook and the bathroom. Stairs led to the loft, and I headed up to peek at the queen-sized bed and chest of drawers that it now housed, trying not to picture Bryan and me up here together, cozy under the covers on an old twin mattress on the floor. We had been so young and so in love that most of the time we were oblivious to everything but each other.

Back downstairs I checked out the back room, which had been converted from our game room—complete with Ping-Pong table, shelves of board games, and a sagging orange couch—to another bedroom, with a chest of drawers and two double beds with blue chenille covers.

I crossed the room to push back the floor-to-ceiling vertical blinds and then opened the sliding glass door and stepped through onto the deck. I walked to the edge of the deck and looked out at the view, which even in near-darkness was so beautiful that my breath caught in my throat again. What a vista! In the distance, purple-and-blue peaks of the Smokies reached up to touch the darkening sky. From where I stood, the ground dropped off to a series of rolling, heavily treed hills. Far down at the bottom, between the trees, it was too dark to catch glimpses of Greenbriar Lake, but I knew it was there. Truly, I had forgotten just how gorgeous the panorama was from up here.

My phone rang in my pocket, and my heart quickened at the thought that it might be Tom. I had managed to put the incident from this morning out of my mind—the party, the giggling woman—though now that he was calling the memory sprang forward, unbidden, and the anxious feelings that went with it rushed into place as well.

Unfortunately, it wasn't Tom after all. It was my trusty friend and coworker Harriet, who was driving here from Washington, DC, and was calling to tell me that she wasn't going to make it in tonight. She was running late and had already checked into a hotel outside of Hickory.

"I'll get up 'fore the rooster crows," she said, "saddle up ol' Bessie, and probably be there by nine or ten in the morning."

"Uh, Harriet," I said, "you're not really coming here by horseback, are you?" Where Harriet was concerned, nothing she ever did surprised me.

"Sure I am, darlin'. I got myself a wild mustang. A wild *Ford* Mustang!"

After she finished cackling at her own joke, I gave her directions to the main office and agreed to meet her there in the morning. In a way, I was relieved she wasn't coming right away so that I could have this one night to myself.

Once I had unloaded the car and put away the groceries, I decided to call my mother and let her know I had made it here okay. She and I had spoken just prior to my trip to California, and she knew I was on my way to Greenbriar after that, but I thought it wouldn't hurt to touch base with her now that I was here. I was really trying to get better about keeping my folks connected with my life.

As it turned out, my mother wasn't even home. My dad answered the phone, and I could hear the sounds of a televised basketball game in the background. According to him, Mom was at her Monday night sewing circle and should be home anytime.

"Who's playing?" I asked and listened as he named the teams and described the game thus far. I hadn't really been following basketball this year, but it was his passion, so I let him talk.

The conversation eventually moved back around to me and the purpose for my call. I told my dad that I was on a new assignment, though I didn't say where and he didn't think to ask. I knew the subject of Greenbriar would inevitably lead to the subject of Bryan, which always led to the subject of his death. It was easier not to go there at all.

"So how are things with everyone?" I asked.

"Oh, fine," he said, still sounding a little distracted by the game. "Your brother's got a new girlfriend. She's very nice and kinda quiet."

"Quiet? That's a change from the last one."

I could hear some shuffling in the background, and then the noise level dropped.

"There. Commercial's on. Yeah, that last one, she never stopped talking, did she? Never shut up. Drove me crazy. This one, the silence is kinda nice."

We chatted for a while about Michael and the new girl, but the whole time I kept thinking about Tom and what my father's opinion would be of him. My parents had never mentioned the subject of my dating again, and I wasn't even certain how they felt about it. Surely they didn't expect me to remain alone forever.

My mother would probably love the idea and fall for Tom instantly. My father, on the other hand, might resist it at first, regardless of whether he liked Tom or not. Once he warmed up to the idea of my dating, however, I had a feeling he still might be slightly scandalized by the whole boss/employee angle, despite the fact that Tom and I didn't really work together.

No matter how my father might react to my dating someone, I knew I would need to start paving the way soon for the possibility of it, rather than springing things on him full blown once Tom and I got more serious.

"I've been thinking," I said casually, "that I might start going out a bit myself."

My dad was quiet for a moment.

"That's good, Callie," he said finally. "You still got time on that clock of yours to give me some grandchildren."

"Oh, thanks, Dad."

"Just don't let your dates come pick you up at your house."

"Why?"

"The dog!" he said, surprising me so much that I had to laugh.

"What's wrong with my dog? Sal's sweet."

"Yeah, but she's just a little powder puff. You wanna attract a man? You need to get a real dog, like a German Shepherd or a Lab."

The conversation led off that way, and I gladly followed along. The first bit of groundwork had been laid with no harm done.

When the game came back on, I told Dad to let Mom know I had called and that I would try her again later in the week. We said our goodbyes, and then I hung up the phone.

Feeling antsy, I decided to put together a light dinner for myself. I had bought some chicken breasts at the store, so I stir-fried the chicken with some broccoli and soy sauce before turning my attention toward making a fruit salad. As I was cutting up an apple, I thought about how funny it was that I always craved apples whenever I found myself surrounded by orchards.

Thinking of my conversation with my father, I decided I should call Tom myself. It would be around 8:00 A.M. where he was. Despite my earlier hurt and confusion, I was eager to talk to him. I felt a need to hear his voice, to ground myself in the reality of our connection. I quickly ate my supper and then washed my dishes, dried my hands, and settled down on the couch.

He answered on the first ring.

"Callie?" he said, the voice that always brought everything sharply into focus. "I'm so glad you called."

"Hi," I said calmly, not knowing what kind of tone to take.

"So how are things going?"

I hesitated, wondering if he really didn't know what this morning's phone call had done to me. I didn't answer, trying hard to phrase the obvious question. "Did you have a date last night?" sounded so juvenile, but "I thought we were going steady" was even worse. Finally I just decided the truth might be the best option.

"Things are not going well."

"What's wrong? Your voice sounds weird."

I took a deep breath, pinching my lips together.

"I've been wondering if I misread our situation, Tom, if I made certain assumptions that weren't true."

"Assumptions?"

"About us. About our relationship."

That seemed to quiet him for a moment.

"Last night," he said finally, as if the memory was just coming back to him. "The phone call at the party."

"Yeah," I replied, trying not to sound nervous. "The phone call at the party."

I felt the pressure of tears at the back of my eyes, and I stood and began pacing, thinking a little activity might fend the tears off. I realized I was actually afraid to hear what he had to say.

"What can I tell you, Callie? I'm sure it sounded bad, but the situation was completely innocent."

"That's just the thing, Tom. Did it need to be innocent? Was it supposed to be innocent?"

"What do you mean?"

"I mean, we've never declared anything. We've never made any promises. If you had a date last night, who am I to say you were breaking any rules? We've never made any rules."

My comments seemed to bring him up short. He was quiet for a while, and I didn't speak just to fill the silence but instead let it sit there between us. Finally, his voice came back to me, soft and thoughtful.

"Maybe you're right," he said. "Maybe we never made anything official. I suppose I thought the rules were implied. I guess I made my own rules, Callie. Because I've been here for four months, and I've been true to you every single minute of every single day."

I was so touched by what he'd said that I sat back on the couch and let the tears spring unbidden into my eyes.

"You have?" I whispered. "You've been faithful?"

"Of course I have," he said. "Haven't you?"

"Yes," I said, my laugh catching in a sob. "But then this morning, and that woman…"

"That woman was a pain in the neck," he said. "But she was the sister of an important associate, so I put up with her for as long as I could."

"Was she pretty?"

"I guess," he said. "But she wasn't *you*."

"Ah, Tom," I whispered.

"To be honest," he said, "I think she was making a play for me. Maybe I'm a little slow on the uptake. But as soon as she started trying to hand-feed me a piece of Pulau chicken, I figured out what was going on and extricated myself from the situation."

"How can men be so dense?" I asked. "I could hear it in her voice from halfway across the world."

"Yeah, well, I've had my head buried in a computer for four months," he replied. "I'm out of practice."

"Good," I said. "From now on, though, just practice with me, okay?"

"You've got yourself a deal."

Feeling so much more at peace, I didn't even want to talk about the problems that I was having here with the investigation. As the conversation turned that way, I said simply that it was complicated but I was too tired to go into it right now.

"Fair enough," he said. "I need to get back to work anyway. Just tell me, are you at the house? Your cabin, I mean?"

"Yes. I got here a little while ago."

"Was it difficult to go inside?"

"No," I said firmly. "It's changed, new furniture and stuff. It doesn't even look the same. This isn't difficult at all."

"I'm so glad."

In the silence that followed, I thought perhaps, in a way, my coming here to this house, to this town, was tougher on Tom than it was on me.

"Hey, Tom?"

"Yeah?"

"This visit isn't…" I hesitated, not knowing how to put it. "I'm not… I haven't been spending my time here constantly in mourning."

"You haven't?"

"No. There are a lot of good memories, of course. But the person that's most on my mind—the one I keep wanting to tell things to and show things to—is *you*. I miss you."

He was silent for a moment.

"Thanks for telling me that, Callie," he said finally, exhaling slowly. "You didn't have to. But it means a lot to me that you did."

Thirteen

*

Feeling so much better after our phone call, I decided I was too full of energy to retire for the night. My mind went to Luisa and the questions I wanted to ask her, and it occurred to me that I might be able to catch her in town right now.

She had told me earlier that she had no phone but that she spent her evenings at the laundromat doing other people's laundry for pay. By the time I finished dinner, it was nearly nine o'clock, but I decided to drive into town and see if I could find her there. I had a feeling she might still be distraught enough from this afternoon's fire to welcome a shoulder to cry on and a sympathetic ear.

I changed into jeans and a light sweater before putting together a small basket of laundry. Looking in the phone book, I saw that Greenbriar had two laundromats, so I scribbled down the addresses of both, loaded the car with my dirty laundry, and headed down the mountain toward town.

Once there, I easily found the first laundromat, a tidy, art-deco-looking establishment with glass block walls and swing music playing loudly from a sound system. The place was empty except for an attendant, so I drove on and sought out the other one, which turned out to be a much more likely candidate for where Luisa probably spent her evenings, placed as it was between a Mexican restaurant and a little Spanish church. It was in a strip of shops near a row of run-down apartment houses, and each of the signs on the wall was printed once in English and once in Spanish. Several Mexican children were playing with an empty laundry cart in the parking lot.

I parked in front and carried my laundry inside, spotting Luisa at a table with a mountain of clean clothes in front of her.

"Hello again," she said as she saw me. "Callie, is it?"

"Yes. How's it going?"

"A little better," she said softly, looking almost embarrassed. "I've had worse days, I suppose."

"Well, I'm glad you're here," I said. "I hate doing laundry alone."

"Ha," she said tiredly. "Laundry is my life."

Knowing we would have a less self-conscious conversation if it seemed as though I were here for a reason, I set down my things and began to put my load into a washer. Before I got very far, Luisa spoke again.

"Excuse me, but that washer tends to eat clothes," she said.

I looked at her, and she was gesturing toward another machine.

"Try that one instead."

"Thank you," I said effusively, moving my load to the other washer. "I hate when machines do that."

"It completely ruined a sweater of mine," she said. "I think there is something wrong with the—what do you call it? The thing in the middle. The aggravator."

"The agitator?"

"Yes. Agitator. It sucks things in underneath and gets them all tangled."

"Thanks for telling me."

I poured detergent into the machine, closed the lid, and put quarters in the slot.

"You do laundry here a lot?" I asked as I slid in the tray and the machine kicked to life.

"Every night," she replied. "I can do yours too, anytime you want. Pickup and delivery included if you're not too far out of town. Cash only."

It took me a minute to realize she was asking me for work.

"Oh, sure, next time, definitely," I said. "Tonight, I'll do it myself. I don't have anything else going on."

I offered to help her fold the clothes on the table in front of her, but she declined, so I took a seat along the wall. As I did, I realized her daughter was quietly coloring in a corner. That was too bad, because I had a feeling Luisa wouldn't really want to talk about all of the vandalism in front of the child.

"Is that your daughter?" I asked. "She's adorable."

"Yes, that is Adriana."

"Don't you have a son too?" I asked. "Where is he?"

She rolled her eyes.

"He is fifteen," she said, as if that answered my question. "I will not know where he is until he walks into the trailer at one minute before his curfew."

"Mommy caught Pepe smoking last month," the little girl suddenly volunteered from the corner.

"Adriana!" the mother scolded.

"Well, he was! He got grounded for a week and everything!"

I smiled at the little girl, a small beauty with straight black hair and big saucer eyes.

"Smoking's yucky, isn't it?" I asked her.

"I learned a song in school," she said. "Wanna hear it?"

"Sure."

She stood and began singing a ditty about "No no to smoking, no no to drugs," complete with hand motions. The tune was catchy, the motions cute. When she was finished, I applauded and then asked about her school.

"I go to school on the internet!" she said proudly.

"It is a special plan for migrant children," Luisa added. She went on to explain that her children took part in a wonderful program that allowed them to keep up with their studies here in North Carolina, even though the credits they were earning applied to their home school in Texas.

"Is that Go the Distance?" I asked.

"Yes. My children are at Go the Distance Learning Center almost every day."

"So you really like it?" I asked, settling back in my chair.

"Oh, yes. It is so hard during the picking season when the kids have to keep switching schools," she said. "They used to lose a lot of credits, but now they do not, because no matter where we travel they are still basically going to the same school. We love it."

"Are there many students there?" I asked.

"At this time of year, no," Luisa said, her face clouding over. "My children are the only ones. I mean, technically, they should be back home at their own school by now. Mrs. Weatherby is letting them stay so she can test out the new curriculum."

"We can't go home until our daddy comes back," Adriana announced gravely.

Luisa looked at me, the pain in her eyes still very fresh. I wondered what the children thought of their father's disappearance, especially Pepe. A 15-year-old boy with an absentee father had to be a fairly confused creature. I wondered if there was any chance he had started today's fire, perhaps with the same matches he'd used when smoking.

"Hey, didn't I see you with a coloring book?" I asked the little girl, hoping to distract her. "Why don't you color a special picture just for me?"

"Sure! Do you like horses or dogs?"

"Hmm...I love them both. Why don't you surprise me?"

"Okay!"

She ran to the corner and picked up her coloring book and began flipping through the pages, totally engrossed in her assignment.

"So Callie," Luisa said, "tell me about yourself. Your husband is dead, no?"

I jerked back as if struck.

"Y-yes," I stammered, startled by her bluntness.

"Mrs. Webber, she misses him a lot. She talks about him to me."

"She does?"

"She says he was very talented, even as a boy. When his brothers and sisters were still scribbling stick figures, he was drawing houses to scale."

I smiled.

"That sounds like Bryan, yes. He studied to be an architect. He was very smart, very talented."

"Mrs. Webber talks about you, too. She says that when her son died, his beautiful wife ran away to the sea and lost herself inside of her pain."

I swallowed hard, thinking of those early days, wondering how Natalie had known to put it quite that way. Yes, I had been lost in the pain of it all. But eventually, I had found my way out. I was still finding my way out, a little more each day.

"I'm sorry," Luisa added softly. "I'm not trying to pry. But I know that pain. If I did not have two children I have to be strong for, I would be lost too."

I didn't know how to reply, so I stood, peeked into my washer, closed the lid, and sat back down.

"Mrs. Webber said your husband, he had a heart for the migrants."

"Yes, he did." Eager to get off the subject of my late husband, I turned the conversation back to my informal interview. "He was especially interested in migrant housing. Have you ever used migrant housing programs, or have you always been in the trailer?"

"No, we usually stay in the migrant family dorms. But when the season ended last year, I had nowhere to go, so Mr. Butch let me and the kids move into his trailer."

"Mr. Butch?"

"Butch Hooper. He owns Hooper Construction. I do his laundry in exchange for rent."

"Sounds like a good arrangement."

"He is a nice man. Very kind to a woman like me."

I looked at the attractive Luisa, thinking that for some men, it wouldn't be hard to be kind to a woman like her.

"Does he know about the fire yet?" I asked softly, so Adriana wouldn't overhear.

Luisa nodded, glancing at her daughter and lowering her voice.

"He has insurance, like Mr. Webber said. It is not a problem."

"So what are the dorms like?"

"They are nice. Small, but warm and dry. And at least we could all be together as a family."

She went on to talk about the dorms for a while, and from there I moved the conversation to some of the other migrant services in the area.

"Anyway," she said finally, "I am all finished here now. It was nice talking to you. It helped to pass the time."

I was surprised to realize she had made it all the way through the laundry pile. Everything was neatly folded into baskets.

Reluctant to see her go, I had no choice but to help carry the baskets to her car and load them into the back seat. There was still a vague stink bomb odor, though the window had now been replaced. I said goodbye to Adriana as she presented me with the picture she had colored just for me.

"It's got a horse *and* a dog!" she said happily, her wide smile warming my heart. Looking at her, I had a hard time believing that a loving father could walk away from a smile like that.

Once they were gone, I was eager for my own load to finish so that I could get back to my house and go to bed. After I moved my clothes to the dryer, I left the load tumbling and walked over to the little Mexican restaurant next door, where I bought a diet soda.

Then I came back to the laundromat and drank it sitting in a hard plastic chair, watching my laundry tumble around and around through the little window in the dryer, wondering how it would feel to be all alone with no money, no home, two children, and an absentee husband.

Fourteen

After a good night's sleep, I was awake bright and early the next morning. The sky was cloudless and clear, so I ate my breakfast out on the deck, enjoying the glow of the sunrise despite the early morning chill. Once it was fully light, I could see the lake at the bottom of the mountain, the view as pretty as a postcard from way up here.

The seclusion of this house reminded me of my place on the Chesapeake. Nestled deep in the trees along the banks of the river, my Maryland home was my sanctuary, my favorite place to be alone, to commune with nature and with God. Of course, recognizing that I had allowed myself to become a little *too* secluded, in the last few months I had made an effort to get more involved at my church and to make more friends in the community. But the truth remained that nothing made me happier after a busy church social or a friendly lunch in town than to come back to the peace and quiet of my isolated little dwelling.

This cabin had always offered the same sort of attraction, though not for me alone, but for me and Bryan together. We had bought it on a whim from an older couple the Webbers knew who were retiring and moving to Florida. They hadn't wanted much for the place despite the incredible view, and Bryan's practical architect's nature knew a good deal when he saw one. Truthfully, Bryan had been more gung ho about buying the house than I had been, because it was far up from the lake and I really preferred to be closer to the water. Once we owned it, however, I quickly changed my mind. It was easy enough to drive down and have lake access from his parents' house, and there was a lot to be said for getting off alone up here where no one bothered us and we were free to enjoy each other in the privacy of our mountaintop retreat.

Thinking of those early times here together led me to think of how much had happened to me since Bryan passed away. Sometimes when I looked back, it felt almost as though it was a different life back then, as though I had been a different person. And, in a way, I had been. I was much more innocent then, more trusting of what life had to offer me and what the future held in store. Now I knew that nothing was ever guaranteed, except maybe that part about "till death do us part."

I cleared away my dishes and brought them inside, thinking that despite the pain I had gone through, how blessed I was that God had chosen to send someone else into my life now, someone also good and kind and smart and funny and handsome. When I compared Bryan with Tom, I could see they were such very different people, and yet there was something about them that was the same. A goodness. A decency. A way of treating me gently and respectfully. In high school, most of the girls I knew saw "love" in their boyfriends' possessiveness or in the dramatics of their breakups and reunions.

I had never been like that. To me, if you loved someone, there was no need for jealousy or drama, just simple decency. Arguments? They were necessary and unavoidable, of course, but they were meant for solving problems, not creating new ones. Bryan was the first boy I had ever met who seemed to think like me, who valued our getting along with each other and our having fun together above emotion and histrionics.

Tom, of course, might be a different sort once we spent more time together, but thus far he and I had never had anything beyond petty disagreements, so I really didn't know. Certainly, he possessed a passion, bubbling under the surface, that spoke volumes. As I thought about that passion, about the intensity of his gaze and the firmness of his hands on my back as he held me to him, I felt a delicious shiver run through me, like a stirring of something that had long been asleep. Knowing it was too soon to go there, too soon to think beyond the confines of our current relationship, I forced my mind onto the tasks at hand. I quickly dressed for the day, styled my hair, and put on my makeup. There was so much that needed to be accomplished, and I was glad to be getting an early start. As I walked to my car, I could hear someone whistling a tune to themselves nearby, and it reminded me that I wasn't alone up here—and that there were probably a lot more houses now than there were when Bryan and I first bought the place. As I backed out of my driveway and onto the road, I spied the whistler in my rearview mirror: Walking down the road was an older man, tall and lanky with white hair and a gnarled old walking stick. I thought how lucky he was to have these gorgeous mountains for hiking.

I drove down the mountain the shorter way, on the road that would come out by the lake. As the view appeared and disappeared among the trees, I reviewed the events of the previous day, rolling around in my mind the problem of the erased database at MORE. Perhaps I was grasping at straws, but I just kept wondering if the database administrator, Ellen Mack, was being completely truthful about not having written down the passwords to the system. If I hadn't seen this happen so many times in the past, I might not be so suspicious, but in my experience, serious breaches of security could often be traced back to one careless worker who scribbled down passwords and taped them to the inside of their drawer or something. With someone savvy like Ellen, the placement might be a little less obvious, but I still had a hunch they were hidden in her office somewhere. She may have been having her gallbladder taken out the night the hard drive was erased, but that didn't mean she hadn't played a part in this drama simply through carelessness.

To that end, I had been hatching a plan all morning that would let me see whether that was the case here or not. When I reached a straight part of the road, I dug out my phone and dialed Ken Webber.

It was early, but I knew someone would be awake since it was a school day and the boys were probably getting ready to go to the bus.

Fortunately, Ken answered the phone sounding chipper, as usual.

"Hey, it's Callie," I said. "You got a second?"

"Sure. What's up?"

"I have a question for you. If Dean wanted you to change the very tightest-level password on the MORE system, what would you need in order to do that?"

"Just the passwords that are in place now. Those would let me in, then I could change whatever you want."

"Could you do it remotely?"

"Sure. I'm set up for running diagnostics for them that way."

That was good news. I asked him if he would be available to change the password in about an hour, and then I told him that I would call back. I also asked him not to say anything about this to anyone in the meantime.

Once I reached the bottom of the mountain, I dialed the Webbers and was glad to find them still at home. Yes, Dean said, they had a camcorder I could borrow, and yes, if I needed the keys to get into MORE early, that was fine with them, just come on by.

"What time does Ellen go to the office in the morning?" I asked.

Dean wasn't sure, but he thought she went in around 8:30 or 9:00, the same as everyone else. It was 7:45 right now, so I would have to hurry.

After stopping by the Webbers' house to get the keys and the camera, I let myself into the MORE building at exactly 7:57 A.M. Though the office wasn't supposed to open until 8:30, there was always a chance of some early bird popping in and catching me.

I set about my task as quickly as I could, first by going straight to the conference room, putting my stuff down, and getting the camcorder out of its case. I played with it for a moment, figuring out the controls, and then I gripped it and headed down the hallway to Ellen's office. So far, so good, as I was still the only person in the building.

First, I did a cursory search of all of the logical hiding places in her office—drawers, cabinets, even the notepad in her computer. As expected, I came up with nothing, so finally I turned my attentions to the camcorder.

Placement was going to be an issue since the camera was so bulky, and I found myself wishing for one of the tiny pin cameras I kept in my investigation kit at home. Still, this didn't need to be concealed for long. I peeked and poked around her office and finally found a spot sort of behind and beside the trash can, under a counter opposite her computer. I tucked the camera in there, turned it on and let it film for a minute, and then rewound and watched what I had done. The view cut off too low, but after fiddling a bit more I finally got the camera tilted correctly to film the entire desk area.

Unfortunately, pressing the Record button also caused a bright red light to come on at the front of the camera. In desperation, I taped a small piece of paper over the little light so that it couldn't be seen.

I left the camera in place but turned it off for now. Standing in the doorway, I tried to see things as she would see them, and I was convinced that she would never notice the hidden camcorder unless she bent directly down to look under the counter.

I heard some noises from the front of the building, so I ducked out of Ellen's office and made my way back to the conference room. Now it was just a matter of waiting for her to come in for the day and of getting Dean and Natalie to go along with what I needed for them to do.

In the meantime, I got my papers organized on the conference table. For a moment I looked longingly at all of the information Dean and Natalie had so diligently handed over to me the morning before. What if we couldn't find the company mole? Would I really have to look my in-laws in the eye and tell them their grant request had been denied?

My thoughts were interrupted by their appearance. They looked grim, as if they had been thinking the same thing I had. I gave them both a hug and told them not to lose hope. I still had a few tricks up my sleeve.

Ellen Mack showed up for work just as I finished explaining the plan to the Webbers. We gave her a moment to get settled, and then, as I had instructed, Natalie walked with me down to Ellen's office.

"Good morning!" the woman sang out when she saw us in the doorway.

"Good morning," Natalie replied, her smile fake and her shoulders stiff. I could tell she wasn't used to deception and that it made her very uncomfortable. Nevertheless, she told Ellen that I was verifying security measures this morning and that we needed the current passwords that would get us all the way into the system.

"Certainly," the woman replied, jotting them down on a piece of paper from memory.

"And prior to this, you've never written down the passwords or told them to anyone?" I asked as she handed the paper to Natalie.

"Never," she said confidently. "That would be careless."

Natalie thanked her for her help, and as she moved to block Ellen's view and pointed to something on the computer screen, asking a question, I quickly reached down and hit the Record button on the camera, hoping Ellen wouldn't notice the slight humming sound it made as it kicked to life.

Once that was done, Natalie and I left Ellen and went into Natalie's office, where I called Ken on my cell phone. I gave him the current passwords and asked him to change the one at the tightest security level. I held on as he did so, and once he had confirmed for us that it had been changed, I asked him to hold on.

I had Natalie call Ellen on the office phone.

"Ellen, it's Natalie," she said stiffly. "I'm sorry, but I can't get this last password to go through. Would you please double-check it?"

She was quiet for a moment and then said, "Okay, thanks."

I smiled encouragingly as she hung up the phone.

"She's going to try it herself and call back," she said.

About two minutes passed as Ken waited on the other end of the line, and in that time I could only hope that Ellen wouldn't do anything that would cause her to discover the camera. When the phone finally rang, it made us both jump.

"Yes?" Natalie asked, and then she listened, nodding. "Yes, all right then. Okay. Goodbye."

She hung up the phone and nodded at me.

"That was Ellen," she said. "She can't get the password to go through either."

"All right, Ken," I said into the phone. "Change it back to what it was."

He did that as we waited, and when he was finished I thanked him for his help and hung up.

"Call her back," I said to Natalie, "and ask her to come down here and try it on your computer. It should work now."

She did that, and then I walked out of the office, passing a flustered Ellen Mack in the hallway, headed in the opposite direction.

I went directly to Ellen's office, reached under the counter for the camera, and pulled it out. Hiding it as best I could in my jacket, I walked straight to the bathroom and shut and locked the door.

"Please, please, please," I whispered as I rewound the tape. Once it stopped, I pressed Play and then Fast Forward.

It didn't take long to see that my plan may have worked. At first, the camera was blocked by my legs, then the film showed Natalie and me walking out and Ellen sitting at her computer screen. The camera filmed her back for a while, then I zipped ahead to where she answered the phone, hung up, and typed into the computer.

I watched as she obviously grew frustrated with the system that wouldn't let her in. Then, in a piece of filming more talented and more telling than the finest Hollywood director's best work, I watched with a mixture of pride and shock as Ellen reached into her purse, took out her PalmPilot, and typed something into it. A moment later, she went back to her computer keyboard and typed something into there as well.

Bingo.

True to her word, Ellen Mack didn't have a hidden place where she kept the passwords scribbled down for easy reference. That had been my suspicion and the reason for my filming.

No, Ellen Mack was more high tech than that, and she had been telling the truth. She didn't write the passwords down.

That would be careless.

Instead, she simply entered them into her PalmPilot.

Fifteen

At first, Dean and Natalie were devastated by what I showed them on the tape, but then I explained how, in a way, this was actually good news.

"Think about it," I said. "Now that we know there was a way for someone to figure out the passwords, we don't have to limit our suspects just to employees. It could've been anyone who was able to get their hands on Ellen's PalmPilot—which greatly widens the circle."

"Why is that good news?" Dean asked. "That leads to even more suspects."

"True," I replied. "But now we know it could've been Ellen's husband or a friend or maybe even the cleaning crew. It doesn't necessarily have to have been someone on staff here. See, before, my hands were tied. If I knew for a fact that somebody on your staff intentionally wiped out your database, then there was no way I could approve you for a grant until your procedures were reworked and tested. But now that we know it wasn't necessarily someone on staff, it looks more like this was someone after Luisa, not your agency. Of course, it's troubling that they were able to get to the passwords, but that can be dealt with."

"So what should we do about Ellen?" Natalie asked.

"See if you can get her to confess on her own. No one likes to think their employers spied on them, but your goal here is to close the security breach. Get her to come in here and ask her, straight out, if she puts her passwords into her Palm Pilot. Don't even mention that you caught her on video, though certainly you can imply that you have some kind of proof. If she's as honest as you say she is, she'll own up to it."

"Then what?"

Through the window behind Dean's shoulder, I saw a bright red convertible pull into the parking lot.

"Then you need to write her up. The woman should have known better."

My voice trailed off as the door to the convertible opened and a woman climbed out, bright red curls piled on the top of her head. I grinned.

Harriet.

"Excuse me a minute, guys," I said, standing. "I believe my friend has finally arrived."

I stepped outside before Harriet reached the front door. We hugged, and I told her how very, very glad I was that she had made it.

"What a cute little town!" she exclaimed. "I think I must've died and gone to Mayberry."

"How was your trip?"

"Fine, just fine." She turned toward the car. "See, I told you I rented a Mustang. Isn't it a hoot? I've had the top off most of the way."

"What was wrong with your car?"

"Honey, if I've got to drive all the way to North Carolina, you can bet I'm not doing it in my little clunker. This was business!"

"Well, I've got plenty of work waiting for you, so at least you can justify the rental on your expense report."

I held the door open for her as she stepped into the building. The Webbers came into the foyer to meet her, and then we all gave her the tour. Finally, Harriet and I ended in the conference room, where the Webbers left us alone with the admonishment to Harriet to make herself at home and please don't hesitate to ask if there was anything she needed.

Natalie pulled the door shut behind her as Harriet plopped into a seat at the table.

"What lovely people!" she exclaimed. "When you said we'd be working with your in-laws, I was picturing the absolute worst. But they're so nice."

"I've been very fortunate," I said. "On the other hand, as nice as they may be, this is a tough job, very big. I hope you didn't wear yourself out on the drive, because I'm really counting on you."

"And when," she asked, fluffing her hair with well-manicured fingers, "have I ever let you down?"

"Never," I replied, grinning. "Now let's get to work."

I reached for the papers to begin orienting her to the case, but before I could even speak, she held up one hand.

"Gossip first, then work," she said. "I have big—and I do mean *big*—news."

"Come on, Harriet, you know it's wrong to gossip."

"Okay, well if you don't want to hear about what Mr. T-O-M has been doing over there in Singapore…"

"Tom?" I asked, my heart skipping a beat. "What about him?"

"Well," she said, lowering her voice and leaning forward. "First of all, I finally learned his last name."

I swallowed, feeling guilty, since of course I had known his last name myself for quite a while.

"It's Tom Bennett," she announced proudly.

If she only knew, I thought, the number of times I had written out *Callie Bennett* or *Callie Webber Bennett* or, best yet, *Mrs. Tom Bennett!*

"I also know what he looks like," she said.

"You do?"

"Yes. I have it on good authority that he is very tall and very, very handsome. Just as we suspected."

I nodded, my mind racing. I simply had to tell her about Tom and me and our relationship and our one night together. It was now or never.

"Harriet—"

"Wait," she said. "There's more. He's romantically involved with someone."

"He is?" I managed to squeak out.

"Yes. See, my cousin's former college roommate works for the Raffles Hotel in Singapore, and she's in on all of the who's who of society. Now, I know Tom tries to keep his work completely separate from the J.O.S.H.U.A. Foundation, but apparently over there the secret kind of got out. At least some people know that Tom is more than just a rich guy with a pretty face. The rumor has it that he's a philanthropist who likes to donate anonymously through a foundation."

"That's our Tom."

"Well, anyway, my friend was at a party the other night, and she saw our mysterious philanthropist with none other than a former beauty contestant."

"What?"

"Some six-foot blonde who used to be Miss Denmark or Miss Sweden or something. Her brother is like some biggy wig in some company in Singapore. Anyway, this beauty queen was all over Tom like a wet washcloth."

I felt the air seeping from my lungs.

"She was?"

"But here's the best part. She made a play for him, and he turned her down flat! He said, and I quote, 'You're a lovely lady, but I'm sorry, I'm involved with someone back home in the States.'"

My knees grew weak, and I gripped the table as I sat. Not only was he being faithful to me, he was up against formidable temptation!

"How did your friend know what Tom said?"

"Because the poor beauty queen ended up sobbing her eyes out in the bathroom. My friend gave her a sympathetic ear and a shoulder to cry on, and then she helped the woman put herself back together again."

I tried to feel sorry for the woman, but, truly, I didn't. Tom had turned down Miss Sweden for me!

Heart soaring, I knew it was time to tell Harriet about me and Tom. I just hoped she wouldn't be too furious with me for not sharing it sooner. Gathering my nerve, I moved my chair closer and looked her square in the eye.

"I have to tell you something," I said. "When Tom said he was involved with someone back in the States…"

"Yeah?"

"He was talking about me."

Studying her face for a reaction, I was surprised to see not anger or happiness there—but pity!

"Oh, hon," she said, patting my arm, "I know you two are phone buddies and all, but don't kid yourself. Tom's a very sophisticated man. I feel certain it's got to be some movie star. Maybe a politician or a CEO of some big corporation."

I sat back, bemused.

"Are you saying I'm not good enough for him?" I asked.

She shook her head vigorously.

"No, of course not!" she replied. "I'm just saying he travels in different circles than you do, sweetie. I know he's fond of you, but I hate to see you think his feelings go any deeper than that."

I wasn't sure whether to laugh or be insulted. After fully 30 seconds of silence, I finally decided to leave it alone for now. Perhaps I would tell her more later, when she was finished trying to let me down easy.

For now, I just wanted to get off alone somewhere and burst out laughing. Tom turned down Miss Sweden for *me!*

With renewed energy, I got Harriet involved in the work she needed to do, showing her all of the records and giving her a clear list of the criteria I needed for her to cover. Because I didn't want to scare her off, I didn't tell her about the problems that had popped up, especially the dead body. I knew she'd hear about all of that sooner or later, but I thought it might be good to let her get a running start first. As Eli and I had discussed on the phone when we were talking through this case, I still needed to go on with the investigation of MORE as if nothing had changed.

Mainly, I told her I needed a good, clear picture of how MORE's finances were run, a review of previous audits, and a solid summary of salary and benefits for every single employee in the place, including the Webbers. She seemed ready to get to work, and if I was talking a little too fast or acting a bit too happy, she didn't seem to notice.

I had some appointments I needed to keep all over town. I told Harriet I might be tied up most of the day, but I would check in with her later via phone. As I drove away, I turned the radio as high as it would go and sang happily along with it. I may not have been a movie star or a politician or a CEO. But I certainly traveled in the right circle for Tom.

Our own little circle of two.

Sixteen

My first appointment was scheduled for 11:00 A.M., and I arrived a little bit early. I considered calling Tom to kill time, but it was midnight in Singapore, and I thought he might not appreciate being awakened in the middle of the night just to chat!

Instead, I pulled out my map of the county and made sure I had marked the locations of the charities I was scheduled to visit. I had planned out a sort of circular route that would let me get to all of them without much doubling back, and I was starting at the farthest point, which was a migrant day care center. The place wasn't open this time of year, but I was able to tour the facility and meet with the woman who ran it.

From there, I stopped at a dental clinic that accepted migrant vouchers for service, and I particularly liked the main dentist. He told me that on the weekends he was a stand-up comedian in Charlotte, and from the jokes he was throwing around in the office, I could believe it. I just hoped he wasn't that funny when people were in his chair, their mouths full of dental implements.

Next, I visited a Head Start branch, which looked like an elaborate kindergarten. To my surprise, it was fairly full even at this time of year, and the woman explained that their population ebbed and flowed, but that it was by far the most crowded during harvest season.

The next charity on my list was Su Casa, the group Butch Hooper was affiliated with. I was particularly interested in this charity, because they provided migrant housing. As I drove there, I felt a twinge of sadness that Bryan wasn't with me. I could well remember the long nights he spent on his senior thesis in architecture, studying the problem of migrant housing and working to design some good solutions.

Fortunately, Su Casa was located up near the top of the mountain, so I was able to stop at my cabin first and grab something to eat. It was nearly 2:00 P.M., and I was starving! Since my appointment wasn't until 2:30, I took the time to make myself a big salad that I ate out on the deck in the sun. It was supposed to rain later in the week, but for now the weather couldn't be more beautiful.

I reached Su Casa quickly and easily, since it was just over the top of the mountain and a little bit down the other side. Turning into the parking lot, I pulled in beside an old Impala that had a bobble-headed Chihuahua in the back window. As I got out and walked toward the building, I reminded myself of the goal of each of these visits, which was to meet the principals, to find out their impressions of MORE, and to see if they were fulfilling their own mission statements, showing fruits for their labors.

Speaking of mission statements, I saw that Su Casa had theirs framed and hung on the wall beside the front door, hand lettered in a delicate script, the borders decorated with watercolor apples. *This agency will provide safe, clean, comfortable housing for migrant fruit pickers to be used on a seasonal, temporary basis.* Declaring their mission so boldly right up front certainly made a good first impression.

"You must be Callie Webber!" a voice drawled loudly from across the room.

Startled, I turned to see a woman rushing toward me, arms outstretched.

"I'm so happy to meet you. My name is Trinksie, and we're just tickled pink that you're here!"

She threw her arms around me in a generous hug. Before I could hug her back, she let me go, the release so unexpected and swift that I nearly fell backwards.

"I've just heard such nice things about you!" she exclaimed, already halfway back across the room, her wide hips jiggling as she went. "You'll just have to meet everybody and tell us all about yourself! How do you like the area? You're related to the Webbers, aren't you?"

"Yes, I'm—"

"Butch! Get out here! We got company!"

A young man peeked through a doorway, his face and neck so long and thin he seemed almost reptilian. The shaved head only added to the illusion.

"Snake!" Trinksie said. "Where's Butch?"

"He's gettin' something outta the back room."

"Well, come on out here yourself and say hello to Mrs. Webber. It is 'Mrs.,' isn't it?"

"Yes."

The young man stepped closer and offered me a damp handshake, his eyes looking down at the floor.

"Nice to meetcha," he said, and in the tone and pattern of his speech, I realized that he was mentally handicapped.

"Nice to meet you too," I replied, bending down a bit so I could catch his gaze. "Did I hear her call you Snake?"

"That's my nickname," he said, meeting my eyes and nodding rapidly. "C-c-cause I'm slick and slithery, and I look just like a snake."

"My son the snake!" Trinksie cried. "'Ceptin' he don't shed his skin, and his tail don't rattle when he gets all riled!"

They both laughed at what I had a feeling was a familiar joke, and then Snake reached for a leather thong that hung from a belt loop on his hip. At the end of the tied-off strip of leather were about eight small decorative beads.

"I'll rattle once I get more beads," he said earnestly, shaking the leather so that the beads clicked against each other. I was about to comment when another man entered the room, a fellow so tall and wide he nearly filled the doorway. I remembered him as Butch Hooper, from the party.

"Well, hello again," he boomed in a voice that matched his size. "Did you have any trouble finding the place?"

"No, not at all," I said, shaking his hand. "I have a little cabin just over the top of the mountain."

"Oh, yeah? Then you and my dad must be neighbors."

"Did you move here, Callie?" Trinksie asked. "I thought you were just visitin'."

"I keep it on the market as a rental unit," I said. "Through Skytop."

"The little A-frame?" she cried. "That's an adorable house."

"Quite a view from there," Butch added. "My father is just a few doors down. But where are our manners? Callie, would you like some coffee? Tea?"

"Tea would be nice, thank you."

Trinksie sprang into action and made us some tea while Butch gave me a tour of the small building. Basically, it had the main office area, a tiny kitchen, a bathroom, some storage space filled with boxes and tools, and then another small, windowless room tucked in the very back, with a desk and a chair.

"That's my dad's office," Butch said as he shut the door and we walked to the front. "He's retired from Hooper Construction, but keeping the books for Su Casa gives him something to do. He always comes in later in the day, answers the phones, does a little paperwork."

"Mr. Zeb is a sweetheart," Trinksie said, handing me a cup of hot tea. Then she added in a whisper: "So is Mr. Butch here. He's been such a help to all of us."

"Now, Trinksie, don't flatter me," Butch said. "We're all proud of what we've accomplished with this agency. But it's definitely a group effort. Callie, we'll be happy to answer any questions or show you anything you need to see."

"Actually," I said, "I do have some questions for you, and at some point this week I'd love to see an example of the migrant housing."

"Of course," he replied. "The dorms are still closed up for the winter, but I can take you over to one, let you in."

"Oh, I can just peek in the windows," I said, "if you'll tell me where to find them."

He gave me directions to several, and then we sat at a desk and simply chatted for a few minutes. As Snake tended to janitorial-type duties, Trinksie returned to her own desk, where she was sorting, folding, and stuffing envelopes for some kind of mailer. Butch explained that Trinksie had started a few months ago as a fund-raising consultant, but things had worked out so well that she stayed on as a full-time employee.

"I've always been good at bringing in the bucks," she said proudly, "but self-employment is for the birds. I tried to start up a nonprofit consulting business, but I didn't do very well. I'd rather represent just one company and bring home a steady paycheck."

"P-plus we get to build things here," Snake added, though I hadn't realized he was listening.

"Snake loves it when the dorms go up," Trinksie said.

"They're just nothing and then, boom, there's something!" Snake said excitedly.

"The dorms go up when the different groups come in," Butch explained, "sort of like Habitat for Humanity. We might spend months drumming up volunteers, gathering materials, lining up the equipment, procuring the land, all of that type of thing. But when a group comes in and gets to work, these places go up in a matter of days. It's something amazing to see, I'll tell you."

"Almost like an Amish barn raisin' or something," Trinksie added.

"It sounds exciting," I said.

"Oh, it is," Butch said. "We get people building these dormitories who've never even held a hammer. Teenagers. Housewives. Suit-and-tie types. You name it. Next thing you know, they're up there in a hard hat straddling a main joist and hammering away."

As he described the way their program worked, I thought about the end results of an effort like this. On paper, the migrants were the ones who benefited from the program, because the dormitories were built for them, after all. But there were other, less tangible benefits here as well, since most volunteers were also getting as they were giving, getting things like self-esteem, new skills, and a sense of community.

We talked about funding for the program, and Butch was very forthcoming with the mechanics of their operation. Money for the migrant housing came from a variety of sources, including government programs and private donations. Much of the labor was free, of course, provided by church groups and civic clubs and other bands of volunteers. His father collected only a small salary, since his work here was part time, and Butch donated his efforts entirely, since he served mainly in an advisory capacity and only stopped in occasionally to read the mail or see how things were going.

"We're a small operation," Butch said, "but I think we serve a vital purpose."

I asked about MORE and how it fit into the picture. I was pleased to hear Butch describe how very much they depended on Dean and Natalie's company for many services, like payroll and volunteer recruitment—not to mention public relations and representation with the county, as well as handling all the paperwork related to the migrants. That was a variation on the same thing I had heard all day from each of the places I had visited.

After talking with them for a while, I said I needed to get on to my next appointment. I thanked all of them for their time and told them I would be in touch if I had any other questions. As I was leaving, Butch opened the door for me and I nearly walked into someone. I took a step back, realizing it was an older gentleman—the same fellow, in fact, whom I passed on the road this morning on my way down the mountain. Now he wore a khaki hat over his shock of white hair, and he was no longer carrying the walking stick.

"Howdy," he said, nodding at me as he stepped inside. "Didn't mean to knock into ya."

"Callie, this is my father," Butch said. "Zebulon Hooper."

"How do you do?" I said. "We passed each other on the road earlier."

"Yes, I think we must be neighbors," he replied, pulling off his hat, his handshake weathered but very firm. "Nice to meet you. Please call me Zeb."

The man was as tall as his son, though not nearly so broad. And where Butch was healthy and robust and energetic, his father seemed, most of all, kind of tired.

"Mr. Zeb likes to spend his afternoons in here, after we've all gone for the day and it's nice and quiet," Trinksie said.

"Well, Trinksie," Zeb said, shaking his head and winking toward me, "no one ever accused you of being quiet."

Butch and I laughed, Snake grinned, and Trinksie kind of squealed.

"Mr. Zeb!" she cried. "You just hush! Kin I help it if I like to chitter chatter?"

They were still teasing each other and laughing when I finally extricated myself from the group and headed for my car. Mentally, I was exhausted, but I still had to visit Go the Distance Learning Center before my tour of the orchard with Danny Stanford. I started up the car and drove on down the mountain, trying to focus. There was still so much to cover in this investigation, and I wanted to do a good job.

But I also couldn't deny that much of my mind was preoccupied with the countdown to Tom's arrival on Sunday, which was tick-tick-ticking in the back of my head like a timer.

Seventeen

After all the talk and laughter of the Su Casa office, the silence of Go the Distance was a peaceful alternative. The building appeared to be empty when I first stepped inside, and then I was startled by a soft tap on my shoulder from behind.

"Whoa!" I said, spinning around and flashing a smile. "I didn't see you!"

"Sorry," said Karen Weatherby, the program director I had met at the Webbers' party two nights before. "I tend to sneak up on people."

We shook hands, and I thanked her for taking the time to talk with me and show me her facility.

"Oh, I'm thrilled to," she said, and when she smiled I realized she was quite attractive. I found myself mentally giving her a makeover: lose the headband, work in a few highlights, add a bit more color to her clothing, and she might even be a bit of a knockout. Of course, ever since the transformation of my own new hairstyle, I had to resist the urge to fix up everybody else's as well!

"Why don't we start with an overview and then a tour?" she said. "Then we can talk in the back."

"Sure."

She started by explaining that Go the Distance was not a school but an "education facilitation center" for migrant children. Most of the kids who traveled during the picking season with their parents were at a real disadvantage when it came to school, she said, because every move meant starting over in a new place with new requirements and a new curriculum. Consequently, migrant teens had a drastically high dropout rate, and children in the lower grades sometimes ended up being taught the same things over and over at each new school they attended as they moved with the harvest. Still others faced huge gaps in their education from subjects they missed completely.

"These kids are already enrolled in their home schools in Texas or Florida," Karen said, gesturing for me to follow her as we walked through several large, sunny rooms with tables in the middle and shelves of books along the wall, "so the goal of our program is to let them keep 'attending' their home schools even when they're on the road."

"Interesting."

"Fortunately, the internet has given us a way to provide continuity in education," she said, opening the door to a computer lab with about 20 PCs and half as many printers. "The kids go from place to place as their parents follow the picking season, but instead of their having to start over at a new school each time, they simply go to the nearest Go the Distance Learning Center and pick up right where they left off. The goal is to provide them with one single school curriculum that follows them wherever they go."

"You mean there's more than just this one?" I asked.

"There will be," she replied. "Right now the program is in its infancy. But if we can secure the funding, we can put satellite offices all along the main migrant routes. We do have a mobile unit, but I'd rather see some permanent structures go in wherever possible."

The whole operation was very impressive, and she said that if I stuck around for a while, I could observe the kids actually using the program. Today their schedule was a little mixed up and they would be coming in for a few hours this afternoon.

"Currently, the only students I have enrolled are Pepe and Adriana Morales," she said. "And they really should be back at school in Texas by now. But they've had some family problems that have kept them in town, so I let them continue with the program."

"Yes, I've met Luisa."

"In a way, having them here has been very helpful to me. They're good kids, and working with them has given me the opportunity to familiarize myself with the entire curriculum."

"Do they come every day?"

"Pretty much five days a week," she replied, glancing at her watch. "Though lately their schedule has been a bit erratic."

I commented on the big old building, saying that there was something very warm and welcoming about it.

"I agree," she said, smiling. "It is pleasant here, despite the sagging floors and the creaking stairs."

"Was it a house at some point?" I asked.

"It still is, upstairs," she replied. "In fact, right now I'm using it as an apartment."

"Wow," I said. "That's pretty handy. All you have to do is walk downstairs and you're at work."

"It gets a bit claustrophobic sometimes," she admitted, "but, yes, it is convenient."

"What does your husband do?" I asked, wondering if there was a Mr. Weatherby and how he felt about sharing his home with a school.

"No husband," she replied quickly. "I'm divorced."

Once my tour was complete, Karen led me down a narrow hallway to a bright and sunny room at the far end. Judging by the buckets of safety scissors, the tub of glitter, and the multicolored splatters of paint that had dried on the hard wooden table, I decided this must be the art room.

"I was just assembling some packets when you got here," she said, gesturing toward a pile of oversized plastic containers against the wall. "I hope you don't mind if I work as we talk."

"Not at all. Can I help?"

"Sure. I just finished the planets. We can do the number tree."

She carried one of the boxes to the table and set it down, pulling out a manila folder from inside that held a brown tree trunk cut from construction paper and about 20 orange, yellow, and red leaves with simple addition facts printed on them.

"You just go down the line, taking one of each," she said as she made a row of piles on the table. "At the end, stuff it all in a manila envelope and put the envelope in the box. We do that over and over again until we've used up all the pieces."

"You don't want to actually assemble the trees?"

"No, that's for the students to do. See, the lesson plans sometimes combine a craft with learning facts. When they get to the number tree lesson plan, they have to assemble it themselves in a certain order. It's just another way to help them learn their addition."

Following Karen's example, I went down the piles on the table and began the process of assembling and stuffing. We chatted as we worked, and Karen had nothing but good things to say about MORE.

"If they didn't have that nonprofit start-up program," she said, "I doubt I would be in business today. Beyond providing me with a cheap place to get myself established, Dean and Natalie have also given me an enormous amount of support and advice. I owe them everything."

I was glad to hear what she had to say. She was my last charity of the day, and this final interview was as glowing and positive as the rest had been.

We continued to work as we talked, finishing the trees and moving on to the animal alphabet. Karen asked me about my job, and though I didn't feel like getting specific, I told her that basically the J.O.S.H.U.A. Foundation supported many different kinds of charities.

"In fact," I said, "I just spent last week researching a soup kitchen and food bank for the homeless in California." I didn't add that I had investigated them, worked with the police to set up a sting, and watched them all get arrested!

Talk of work eventually moved on to talk of the Smoky Mountains and all that there was to do here.

"I know your slate is full this week," Karen said, "but I hope you'll get a chance to hike the mountains or pan for gems or tour the Biltmore House or something."

"Actually," I said, "I do hope to do a little hiking, and I'm particularly interested in canoeing on Greenbriar Lake."

At the very thought of canoeing, my hands physically ached for the feel of a paddle. I needed to get out on the water soon and paddle all of my cares and worries and concerns away!

Just then, we heard noises from the front hall, and Luisa and her two children entered the room.

"Mrs. Weatherby!" Adriana cried, throwing herself at Karen, who bent down to the child's level to accept her hug.

"I found a beautiful flower!" Adriana said, offering up a handful of half-crushed peonies.

"Are those for me?" Karen asked softly. "Because you know purple is my favorite color."

"Then they're for you!" Adriana cried happily.

The two of them went off in search of a vase while Luisa directed her son to sit in the nearest chair.

"Hello," Luisa said with a weary smile. "How are you today?"

"I'm fine," I replied. "Right now, I'm putting together the animal alphabet."

"Adriana did that one a few months ago. There is still a 'J for Jackrabbit' hanging over her bed."

"I don't believe I've met your son," I said, smiling toward the sullen teen.

"This is Federico," Luisa said, gesturing toward her son. "'Pepe,' for short. Pepe, this is Mrs. Webber. She is a friend."

He barely acknowledged me with a nod before turning to stare out of the window again. I wondered what was going on with them, if she had been able to make plans for the children to go to Texas and stay with her sister, but I didn't know if I should ask in front of the boy.

"Pepe and Adriana are going to take a trip," Luisa said, as though reading my mind. "They're going to visit their cousins back home."

"Really?" I said, giving her a significant glance. "When are they leaving?"

"My brother just finished up a job in Tennessee," Luisa said. "He's coming by to get them any day now, and then they will drive down together."

"Oh, that's great," I said, hoping the man would come soon and that they would be safe until then. The boy didn't even acknowledge my comments with a glance, so I spoke directly to him. "Hey, Pepe, maybe you could help me out here. All you have to do is go down the line, take one of each, and put them in an envelope."

Without speaking, he slowly rose from his chair and shuffled over to the table, sighing as if it all required a Herculean effort on his part. Looking embarrassed at her son's impertinence, Luisa excused herself for a moment and left the room.

"It gets kind of tedious," I said chattily as we worked, though he didn't reply. I tried to think of some common ground we could find, some point of conversation. Racking my brain, I pictured the only other kid near his age I interacted with on a regular basis, a young friend I had made during an investigation last fall named Carlos. Carlos was now 13, and most of our e-mails revolved around elaborate discussions of video games.

"I can't do this for long," Pepe said finally as he inched his way down the row. "I'm supposed to meet my math tutor online at five o'clock."

"That's pretty cool," I said, "going to school online."

"Yeah, it's all right," he replied.

"So do you ever go online and pretend you're doing schoolwork," I asked, thinking of Carlos, "but really you're playing Time Warrior Challenge?"

He looked at me suspiciously.

"No," he said.

"Dragon Search Five is good too," I said.

He shrugged and said, "Nah, Time Warrior Challenge is the best. If you can get to the third level, there's a secret passageway that gets you around the Door of No Entry."

"I have a shortcut for that," I said. "Shift F8 gives you the Golden Key without having to go down the passageway at all."

"No way!" he said loudly.

"Yes, way," I said. "But it doesn't work unless you already have the Silver Sword."

"I always have the sword by then. I pick it up on level two, when I go around the herdmaster."

Pepe grew more animated as we talked, and I silently thanked the Lord for sending one teenage boy into my life to help me get through to another. We continued to talk as we worked, throwing around terms like "health points" and "transport packs" and "food replenishment."

"So how do you know about all this stuff?" he asked finally. "You're kinda old to be playing video games."

"Not really," I laughed. "I have a friend who goes online and finds out all the cheats and shortcuts for me."

"For real?"

"Yeah. Don't you and your buddies trade tips like that?"

He slid a stack of animal cutouts into an envelope, his shoulders suddenly sloping downward.

"Not really," he said. "My buddies don't have computers, so they wouldn't really know what I was talking about."

In a flash, I found myself staring reality in the face. Of course his buddies didn't have computers.

They were migrant children.

"That's a drag," I said. "I guess you're lucky to go to school here, then."

"Yeah, it's okay," he said. "Although I'd rather go home to Texas and go back to school there. I miss my friends."

There followed an awkward silence, and my heart ached for the boy as I thought of his missing father and these three lives in limbo.

"Anyway, Mrs. Weatherby lets me earn video game time," he said. "If I get an A on my spelling test, then I get a full hour of Time Warrior Challenge. But I wish I could play more."

"I've got a computer up at my cabin," I said, describing where I was staying. "You're welcome to come and play anytime this week before you go to Texas."

"Really?"

"Sure," I said. "If it's okay with your mother."

"That would be awesome."

"Or if you go into the game here, let me know and I can go on there and meet you online. That's what I do with my friend Carlos. In fact, maybe I could hook the two of you up that way. You can do tournament play, even with you here and him in Pennsylvania."

"Cool."

Pepe was animatedly recounting his highest-scoring game when Karen and Luisa came back into the room. They both seemed a bit surprised by Pepe's demeanor, and I realized he probably played the sullen teen most of the time these days.

"Next time," I told him, ignoring their surprised faces, "try holding the F9 key when you reach level twelve."

"You've been to level *twelve?*" he yelled. "No *way!*"

"Pepe!" Luisa reprimanded, thinking the boy was being rude.

"Way," I said, hoping his enthusiasm wouldn't dim. "If you do that, you get to go into the fourth dimension."

"Oh, man," he cried, "do you know any other good tricks?"

"Hmm. Not off the top of my head."

"Then I gotta go study my spelling!"

"Good idea."

"Do you mind?" he asked me, gesturing toward the piles that still remained on the table in front of us.

"Not at all," I said. "Go ahead. Learn those spelling words. Just don't be late for your math tutor!"

He ran out of the room and his mother and teacher stared at me, their mouths open.

"Video games," I said, grinning widely. "The universal language."

Eighteen

As the two children settled into their studies, Luisa went about cleaning the building. I realized that she and Karen must have some sort of special arrangement, like housekeeping services in exchange for some extra education time for the kids. Karen had excused herself to handle a computer problem, so I finished up the last of the packets for her and then went in search of her to tell her I needed to run. My tour of the orchard was scheduled to start in 20 minutes.

"Callie," Karen said as I walked into the computer room, "I'm sorry. I didn't mean to abandon you back there. We have a printer jam."

"That's fine," I replied. "But I need to get going."

"Are you sure you can't stick around and observe the kids at work?"

I glanced at my watch.

"Well, maybe for just a few minutes. I'm supposed to tour the orchard at five."

"Good. You can just watch them, ask them questions, or whatever," Karen said, gesturing toward the two children, who were sitting, absorbed, in front of computers.

As Karen turned her attention back to the malfunctioning printer, I walked over to Adriana, who was playing a game that looked kind of like Pac-Man. Upon closer inspection, however, I saw that the munching creature was eating a series of numbers. The top of the screen said "Factors of Ten" and Adriana was clicking on each number that didn't end in a zero. When she clicked, the little monster came over and gobbled up the number.

"What happens if you click on the twenty?" I asked.

"I won't—that's a factor of ten," she said, absorbed in her game.

"Right. But what if you get it wrong?"

"Then it makes me start all over again."

"What if you get them all right?"

"Watch," she said. One by one, she clicked on the numbers that weren't factors of ten: 18, 7, 42. When she clicked on the last number, the little creature ran over, ate it up, and then exploded into a screen full of fireworks while a triumphant tune played in the background.

"That's great!" I said. "Do you always get it right?"

"No, ten's the easiest," she said. "And five, I guess, and two. But some are really hard. Seven and eight are tough."

She babbled on about the game as a new screen came up, this time headed "Factors of Three." She started playing again, and I crossed over to Pepe to watch him work. He seemed to sense my presence, because he turned to look at me, pulling the headphones from his ears.

"Sorry to interrupt," I said. "What are you working on?"

"Right now, history," he replied, rolling his eyes. "I had to put away my spelling to write a report on Egyptian pharaohs. Like that has anything to do with me and my life at all."

The screen in front of him featured a website with photos of sphinxes and tombs. Next to the keyboard, I could see that he had scribbled a page of notes about the subject.

He asked Karen a question about the history unit, and as I listened I began to understand her function. Though she wasn't their teacher, she was in charge of their course of study, and it seemed as though it was up to her to give tests, grade papers, and clarify instructions.

"I know you need to go, Callie," Karen said to me, brushing off her hands as she closed the lid to the printer. "I'll walk you out."

I told the children goodbye and walked with Karen back to the entranceway.

"Hey, Mrs. Webber!" Pepe called. "I'll talk to my mom about coming over, okay?"

"Okay," I called back. "I'll look forward to it."

At the door Karen spoke softly.

"This is the most animated I've seen Pepe in a long time," she said. "You seem to have a real way about you."

I thought of her own personality and how her natural reticence became a calm sort of centeredness that was attractive to Adriana. Different traits drew out different children, I supposed, and a woman like Karen offered a gentle spirit I knew most kids would find appealing.

"Thanks," I said. "So do you."

We shook hands, and I was struck with the thought that if I lived here, she and I would probably become friends.

"You enjoy your tour of the orchard," she said. "Danny's new there, but he's really catching on. You'll find it all very interesting, I'm sure."

"Oh, I know I will," I replied. "Thanks for suggesting it."

I thought about Karen and Danny, wondering again if they were a couple. They had seemed friendly enough at the Webbers' party.

"Hey," I said, "would you like to come on the tour with me, by any chance?"

To my surprise Karen's demeanor immediately changed. She stiffened, and her face flushed bright red.

"No, I don't think so," she said, taking a step back. "Danny can show you around by himself. I'm sure you'll be fine."

"Uh, okay," I said, wondering about her odd reaction. "Well, thanks again for your help."

"You're welcome," she said. "It was my pleasure."

As I stepped out and she shut the door behind me, I saw that her face had tightened into an expression I simply couldn't read. I wondered what on earth that was all about, and if I had somehow said something wrong.

I reviewed our final conversation in my mind as I walked toward the car. I finally decided her odd reaction must have something to do with either Danny or the orchard. Either way, I didn't have time to worry about it now. I had more important things going on—not the least of which was a visit to Tinsdale Orchards, the place where Enrique Morales had last been seen alive.

Nineteen

I turned into the orchard at 5:05 P.M. Hoping Danny wasn't a stickler for punctuality, I slowed significantly as I drove up the long and winding driveway, past the big house, and up the hill to the group of buildings that was there. Once I reached the parking lot, I saw that this wasn't some small-time apple farm. This was big business.

"I thought I heard a car out here," Danny said, coming around the corner with a smile. "I've been listening for you."

We shook hands as I apologized for being a few minutes late.

"No problem," he said. "Usually, the orchard is deserted by this time of day, but tonight a lot of the workers are on overtime. They're trying to pack up the last of the apples to make room for the ones that'll be coming out of storage in the morning."

Do you have time to do this now? I could always come back later in the week."

"Oh, no, I'm fine," he said. "Really, I'm just hanging out to help monitor the room as it equalizes. We got a new fan in there, and we're not sure how it's going to affect the timing."

"Okay."

He gestured toward the side of the building.

"Come on," he said. We'll use the cart."

He led me around the corner to a waiting golf cart, albeit one that had been modified for farm use. I made a joke about my backswing as I climbed into the passenger seat. He laughed, slipping behind the wheel and starting it up.

"Before we begin the official tour," I said. "I'd like to ask a favor."

"Sure. What's up?"

"I wonder if you'd mind taking me to the high block."

"The high block? Way up there? I can show you trees like those right here."

"Actually," I said, "I want to go up there because that's the place where Enrique Morales supposedly disappeared."

He studied me oddly for a moment.

"You're not one of those thrill-seeker types, are you?" he asked. "Like, a crime junkie?"

"A crime junkie?"

"Sure, every crime scene has them. You know, people who hang around and put flowers on the ground and cry for people they never met."

"No," I said. "My request is purely logical. The Webbers are friends with Luisa, and they've asked me to look into her husband's disappearance."

"Well, okay," he said. "But it's been a long time since it happened. I don't think you'll find anything."

He put the cart in gear and followed a paved path that ran uphill between rows of trees.

"I'm not sure of all the details," he said over the sound of the motor, "but it was my understanding that this guy skipped town. Didn't he send his wife a 'Dear John' letter or something?"

"Yes, but that letter is highly suspect," I said. "It's doubtful it actually came from him. They think foul play was involved."

Danny turned from the paved path onto a dirt one, and we bounced along potholes and ruts, still climbing upward. Eventually, we got to the highest tier of cleared land, and then Danny swung the cart around and pulled to a stop.

"Well, for what it's worth," he said, "this is the high block."

We got out of the cart, and I watched as he pointed out the perimeters of this section of the orchard. In front of us, the boundary stretched to the end of the tier, just to where the ground dropped by about ten feet. To our left and behind us, the block was bordered by dense woods thick with kudzu, and to our right, it was lined by the road that went down the mountain. The little Su Casa building, which sat nestled against the side of the hill, was in the next tier down.

"I didn't realize that building was on Tinsdale property," I said.

"Oh, sure, orchards donate space all the time. The McKinney Orchards gave an even bigger piece of their land for one of the migrant dormitories."

"Interesting."

"Anyway, as you can see," Danny said, "there's not much to look at up here."

"Did you help with the search?" I asked, walking back toward the woods.

"No, I didn't move here until a month or two after it happened. But people still talk about it. It's like this big mystery. 'What happened to the migrant man?' I say he took a powder on the wife and kids and is living the high life down on some beach in Mexico."

"Oh, yeah," I replied sarcastically. "Those migrants sure live the high life there."

We reached the end of the property, and I stared up at the deep, dense woods.

"I'm sure they searched up in here," I said. "Though it couldn't have been easy."

"They did two searches, didn't they?" Danny asked. "The orchard workers first and then the next day the cops? Neither search turned up anything."

I wondered if it would be worth returning to this place alone, later, and digging around a bit in the brush. After all this time, there probably wouldn't be any clues remaining, like torn clothing or bodily tissues. But I kept feeling there must be a well or a hole or some fissure in the earth that had simply swallowed Enrique up. For all we knew, his bones were mere yards away from us, hidden by soil or kudzu.

"Well," I said, turning around, "I guess you were right. There really isn't much to see here. Except, of course, that gorgeous view."

We walked together back to the cart, looking at the mountains in the distance topped with cloudy cotton puffs.

"So why did the Webbers ask you to look into this? Are you, like, a cop or something?"

"No," I said, hesitating. I never liked to play up my private investigator qualifications because they usually put people on their guard. "I'm not a cop, just a very detail-minded person. I came here to help out with some of their migrant programs, and they thought I might be able to come up with an angle no one had thought of before."

He was about to ask me another question when static burst from the walkie-talkie clipped to his belt.

"Danny, you there?" a voice crackled.

Danny pulled the walkie-talkie loose, held it up to his mouth, and spoke.

"This is Danny. Go ahead."

"The tractor broke down again. I need you come and get me. I'm down by the house."

"I'm on my way."

Danny clipped the walkie-talkie back onto his belt and gave me an apologetic smile.

"We gotta go give the foreman a lift. Then we can officially start your tour. Are we done here?"

"Sure," I said, climbing into the cart. "Thanks for showing it to me anyway."

"You're welcome. Hang on."

He put the cart in gear, and we sped back down the dirt path at top speed. The ride was actually quite fun, with a few dips that left my stomach in my throat. By the time we got down to the bottom of the hill, the beautiful Tinsdale home was plainly in view. Danny slowed and turned onto the long driveway that led up to the house.

Up close, the place was still impressively large, but it held signs of wear I hadn't noticed from the road. Weathered paint. A rotted window frame. Weeds in dried-up flower beds. The orchard was thriving with activity, but I had to wonder why the mansion was in such disrepair. Lack of money? General neglect? It didn't make any sense.

Alongside the house, in the middle of the driveway, sat a huge green John Deere tractor. Nearby, a man was leaning against a wall, and when he saw us coming, he held up his hand. Danny pulled to a stop near him and got out of the driver's seat to climb into the back. As the man sauntered toward us in jeans and dirt-covered boots, he thought the foreman looked vaguely familiar, as though I had seen him somewhere before. With a dark tan, weathered features, and sun-bleached hair, he was a picture of the rugged outdoorsy type. As he climbed in behind the wheel, Danny introduced him as the foreman, Pete Gibson. I had been planning to speak with him soon and get more information about Enrique's last day, so I was happy to make his acquaintance.

"Pete, this is Callie Webber," Danny continued. "Dean Webber's daughter-in-law. She's here learning about the migrants, and Karen suggested we give her a tour of the orchard. I was just gonna show her around."

Pete looked at me for a long moment, the expression on his face unreadable.

"Karen suggested it, huh?" he said finally.

"Yes," I said. "I've been doing some research on the different migrant charities in the area, so I'm interested in how they all come together."

He studied me for a moment, working his jaw.

"Well, I think we can give you an idea," he said finally. "Danny, how's SR3 doing?"

"It's at thirteen percent."

"Then I guess it won't be ready till tomorrow. That gives us plenty of time for a tour. Sure, we'll give you a nice tour."

He turned forward, put the cart in gear, and took off up the driveway. Somehow, I had the feeling that Pete had now become my self-appointed tour guide, though he didn't seem very happy about it.

"You know anything about apple growing?" he asked me loudly over the noise of the wind rushing past. He was driving much faster than Danny had, and I held tightly to the rail.

"Not a thing," I said.

Making a sharp turn to the right, he headed down toward the lowest field, the one with what looked like the youngest, smallest trees. Pete slowed the vehicle and began talking in mostly scientific terms about the variety of growing methods the orchard employed. He pointed out the distance between the tree trunks, telling me that the close proximity was a new approach, something they hadn't done before.

"You'll see the older trees in the middle block," he said. "They're much farther apart than these will be. These will grow up so close together they'll almost be more like apple bushes than apple trees. It's a new method we're trying, but it's supposed to be very land-use effective."

He continued to talk about width and height and separation, and I finally realized this was going to be a much more thorough tour than I had bargained for. I glanced back at Danny, who rolled his eyes.

Pete was onto the subject of the bees they brought in annually for pollination when I stopped listening and decided simply to look around and enjoy the drive. At least, the more he spoke, the more my eyes were being opened to the complexities of growing apples. I also hadn't realized what a cooperative effort was involved, as several different sections of the orchard had been given over to the University of North Carolina for research and testing.

"It's a very symbiotic relationship," Pete said. "We provide the land and the trees, they do the research, and we all benefit from the knowledge."

Once we had made the rounds of the trees, Pete drove us back up to the compound of buildings and slowly pulled through the open center aisle of an equipment shed. Looking around at the big machines housed there, I felt positively dwarfed on both sides.

Pete drove out the other end of the shed before pulling to a stop beside the door of one of the bigger buildings.

"Now I'll show you the storage," Pete said. "Danny, you can check the Orstat while we're here."

"Sure," Danny said, giving me a wink as he walked away.

"Karen said something about a controlled atmosphere?" I asked.

"Yeah," Pete replied. "Here, I'll show you."

He pulled open the door of the building and we stepped inside. As we did, I was hit by a thickly sweet apple smell, as if the air were filled with a concentrated apple perfume. We found ourselves in a long corridor lined with odd-looking doors on each side.

"When the apples are first picked, the ones we don't ship out right away get put into this building," Pete said. "At the beginning of harvest, these are all just a bunch of big empty rooms. But after we fill a room with apple bins, we seal it up airtight, lower the temperature, remove most of the oxygen, and pump in nitrogen."

"Really."

"Once we've controlled the atmosphere of the room," Pete continued, "the apples stop ripening. They're kind of like in suspended animation. Then, later in the year, when it's time to ship more apples, we unseal the room, which means we bring the temperature back up a little, pump out the nitrogen, and bring in oxygen. At that point, the apples are at nearly the same level of ripeness as they were when we first picked them. That's how you get fresh-tasting apples year-round."

"Fascinating. What's an Orstat?"

"It's a tool we use to check the air quality of the room. It lets us remove an air sample and then test it for the right chemical balance."

"Kind of like using a chemical kit to check for chlorine in a pool?"

"Exactly. See, we've got fans going that pump out the nitrogen and bring in the oxygen. But we can't open the sealed door until the room gets up to twenty-one percent oxygen, or it wouldn't be safe for the workers to go inside. Once we get the right atmosphere, we break the seal on the door, and then the men start unloading and packing the apples."

"Fascinating," I said.

"This is the room we'll be opening tomorrow morning," Pete said, pointing to a nearby door with a tiny porthole-like window in it. "Storage room number three, or SR3 for short. If you look through this little window, you'll see that the room's completely full. It holds twenty thousand bushels."

"Wow! That's a lot of apples."

"We've got eight rooms that size in this building alone," Pete said. "That's one hundred sixty thousand bushels—just under this roof."

I peeked in the doors of several of the sealed rooms, and I could see wooden apple crates, one on top of the other, stacked within a few feet of the high ceilings.

"Let's head outside," Pete said when he saw me pinching my nose. "The smell will get to you after a while. That's the ethylene gas the apples give off."

Feeling a little punch-drunk, I followed him back to the golf cart. Danny came out a moment later.

"The air mix in SR3 is rising fast," he said to Pete, looking worried. "A lot faster than usual. It's already up to fifteen percent."

"Probably because of the new fan," Pete replied. "That's okay. That's good. Excellent, actually. Don't worry, Danny. It won't hurt the apples to bring the room up quickly."

"If you say so."

I thought we were going to get back in the golf cart, but Pete took my elbow and guided me in the other direction on foot.

"Danny, if you wanna work on the tractor," Pete said, gesturing toward the cart, "I can finish the lady's tour myself."

"Okay," Danny replied, looking hesitant and a bit disappointed. Nevertheless, he gave me a handshake and a dimpled smile before jumping back into the golf cart and driving off.

"Nice guy, but this is all still kind of new to him," Pete said once Danny was out of earshot. "I hardly think he's qualified to give a tour."

"I don't know," I said in Danny's defense. "Karen Weatherby seems happy with him as the orchard liaison."

Pete snickered.

"Sure, that's just a bunch of glad-handing. Danny's great with people. It's the *apples* I worry about."

He directed me toward the nearest building, and as we walked I stole a few glances at his strong profile. I could almost swear I knew him from somewhere. I tried to picture him younger, but it wasn't until I noticed the small tattoo of a rose on the back of his hand that it hit me: Pete was *P.J.*, the boy who used to serve me ice cream sodas at the drugstore in town!

"Hey, I know you!" I cried, grinning in spite of myself. "Didn't you go by the name 'P.J.'?"

"Excuse me?"

"I used to come to Camp Greenbriar when I was a kid. You worked at the drugstore in town, didn't you?"

"Yeah, a lifetime ago," he said.

"I went there every summer! Isn't that funny? I *knew* you looked familiar. You're P.J., the soda jerk."

"Yeah," he said, rolling his eyes, "emphasis on jerk."

"No, please, all the girls used to think you were so cute. We'd all order the most complicated thing on the menu just to watch you make it."

He studied me for a moment, the stern exterior finally cracking the slightest bit into a smile.

"The giggling girls from Camp Greenbriar," he said finally, shaking his head. "Y'all made me a nervous wreck."

"Oh, but you were so handsome and so worldly. That tattoo—that was just so…so shocking to us. We were absolutely enthralled by everything about you."

He glanced down at his hand and grinned.

"At the age of seventeen, I made the great mistake of falling in love with a girl named Rose," he said. "She stayed with me exactly one week after I'd branded myself for life."

"Oh, no."

"Now from what I hear she's got four kids and lives in Raleigh with a man half her height and twice her age."

"Serves her right, I guess."

We smiled at each other, bonding over this interesting coincidence. Maybe he wasn't such a tough guy after all.

"You gotta be at least eight or nine years younger than I am," he said. "So when I was nineteen and slinging ice cream sundaes, that means you were one of those ten-year-old prepubescent nightmares who drove me nuts?"

"Guilty as charged."

"I'm sorry I don't remember you specifically," he said, studying my face. "But the summers were long. We got girls like you in there week in, week out for three months. From the attention they gave me, you would've thought I was the Fonz or something."

"Oh, but you were, Pete. To us, you were."

He grinned, looking up at the sky.

"Ah, the bad ol' days," he said. "That was back before my mom married Lowell."

"Lowell?"

"Lowell Tinsdale, the man who owns this orchard. He's my step-father."

"Oh," I said. "I didn't realize that."

He looked at me suspiciously.

"Yeah, right. Well, he's a good guy. I was well on my way to being a street-tough hood, but Lowell brought me here, put me to work, and set me straight right fast. In a way, the orchard saved my life."

"And now you're the foreman."

"Now I run the whole joint. But I learned this business, as they say, from the dirt up. There's not one single job at this orchard that some-body does now that I didn't do myself at some point along the way."

"You must be a very empathetic boss then."

"Not really," he said. "If anything, I'm way too tough on everybody. If they complain, I say, 'Hey, if I could do it, you can too.'"

We continued on the tour, much more relaxed than before. Eventually, I shared with Pete that my husband was Bryan Webber, the Webbers' son who was killed. Pete had heard of the incident, of course, but he said he had never known Bryan very well.

Now his focus was fully back on the apple business, and he showed and told me much more about apples than I really needed to know. Mainly, I had just wanted to see the place, to get an idea of what it must feel like to work there, and see if I could gather any information about Enrique. Instead, I was shown the inner workings of all of the buildings one after the other. We saw the room where the bruised and battered apples were separated out for cider, tanks where the apples were cleaned, conveyor belts where they were sorted by size. After a while, it became one big jumble of conveyor belts and workers in shower caps and hundreds upon hundreds of apples. There were so many apples already being processed, in fact, that I wondered where they were going to put the ones coming out of the storage room.

At one point, Pete got word over the walkie-talkie that the SR3 was now at 21 percent and ready to unseal. I was hoping that might cut the tour short, but he simply gave the go-ahead for his men to handle it and continued on with me.

Surrendering to the process, I followed along, watching as dusty, dull-colored apples rolled on a conveyor belt that carried them under a sort of liquid shower. As they continued on the other side, I could see that they were now beautiful, shiny, and red.

"Is that some special kind of cleaner?" I asked Pete over the noise of the machines.

"No, they've already been cleaned back there. This is like a shellac."

"Shellac?"

He nodded.

"Most people want to buy their apples shiny, so growers have to pass them through an edible shellac to give them that glow."

"That's odd," I said.

"I know, but the grocery stores won't buy them from us if we don't do it. So we have no choice."

Still surprised by that thought, I was glad when we made it through the last building and went outside. I glanced at my watch, wondering how Harriet had made out at MORE.

"I thought farmers' hours started early and ended early," I said.

"We're all working overtime tonight," he replied, "'cause we gotta clear the way for the apples coming out of storage."

Together we headed toward the parking lot.

"Tell me about the people who pick the apples," I said as we walked. "I mean, you've got a lot of folks working here now, but they aren't migrants, are they?"

He shook his head.

"No. These are the locals that work here year-round. They do the packing and the orchard maintenance but not the picking. The migrants will do that when they get here in July or August."

"How many migrants do you use?"

"Well, when the season first starts, we need about ninety workers. After a few weeks, that drops down to about seventy, then later to about twenty, then those last twenty dwindle down to none."

"You had a bit of trouble with one of the migrants this year," I said. "Enrique Morales?"

Pete nodded.

"Yeah, that was very sad. I woulda never pegged him as the kind of guy to go off and abandon his wife and kids."

"From what I understand," I said, "he didn't necessarily abandon them. Something might've happened to him that was outside of his control."

Pete looked at me, eyes squinting.

"You've been talking to Luisa, haven't you?"

I nodded.

"The poor girl. She just doesn't want to face facts. But I can tell you this: We mounted a search of this entire orchard, and I mean we combed it good. If something funny had happened to him here, we would've seen something or heard something."

"Did anyone look in the woods above the high block?"

"Are you kidding? We went up to the dirt road behind the woods, formed a line of about fifty people, side-by-side, and then we just moved forward, slowly, in a giant sweep. Through the woods, across the fields, and all the way down to the creek. There was not an inch of this place that someone didn't check."

"It sounds very thorough."

"Well, the cops came back and did the same thing the next morning, and they didn't find anything either."

I opened my mouth to ask him another question when I was distracted by a beat-up old pickup pulling into the parking lot. Behind the wheel was the white-haired Zebulon Hooper, the man I had seen on the road this morning and then met up with again at Su Casa.

"Howdy, Pete!" he said, waving out the window.

"Zeb?" Pete asked. "What are you doing here?"

"Pickin' up a bin of apples. Should I back up to the loading dock?"

"No, just turn it around right here and you'll be fine."

We both watched Zeb turn his truck around, and when he shut off the engine, Pete called out to him.

"Now, what are you gonna do with an entire bin of apples, Zeb? You going into the pie-making business or something?"

"Nah, I'm buying cider apples. Thought I'd try my hand at a batch of apple wine."

Pete laughed as Zeb climbed down from the cab.

"Well, hello again," Zeb said, noticing me. "I guess I'm just gonna keep running into you all day."

"I guess so."

Pete's walkie-talkie crackled at his hip. He grabbed it and pushed the button.

"This is Pete," he said.

"Uh, Pete? This is Sam. I think you need to get to SR3 right away."

"You got the room unsealed okay?"

"Yeah."

"Then what's the problem?"

"Uh...well...I think maybe you'd better call the police."

Zeb and I looked at each other, eyes wide.

"The police?" Pete barked, already walking away from us and toward the storage room. "Why?"

"Kind of hard to explain," the voice said, and I could hear it because I was following after him. "Down in one of the crates of apples?"

"Yeah?"

"Looks like we got ourselves a—"

The walkie-talkie crackled. By now, Pete was running, and, therefore, so was I.

"We got ourselves a what?" Pete barked.

"A mummy, sir. Hidden down in the apples. Looks like we got ourselves a mummy."

Twenty

By the time we reached the storage building, the place was in utter chaos. One man was vomiting in some bushes near the door, while Danny stood next to him, shivering, white as a sheet. Two other men were at the forklift, cursing as they studied its grisly cargo.

The only person who seemed to be keeping it together, besides me, was Pete. The picture of calm, he looked down inside the four-foot-high wooden box and then took control of the situation.

"Sam, your brother-in-law's a cop, right?" he said to one of the workers.

"Yeah."

"Call and tell him what's happened and see if they can come out here without drawing a lot of attention, would you? No sirens. Please."

"Yes, sir. I'll see what I can do."

The man ran off toward another building while Zeb and I stepped closer to the apple bin and looked inside.

Sure enough, nestled down among a bunch of apples was what looked like a mummy—though not with any gauze wrappings or other horror-movie trappings. Instead, it was simply a dried and shriveled-up human body, the skin yellowish-brown and papery and wrinkled like dried fruit. Though the hair seemed like normal hair, the face wasn't really recognizable as a human face. The body was buried in apples up to its chest, so all we could see was the top half, which sported a ragged gray T-shirt with some kind of faded animal imprint on it.

Zeb let out a low whistle, looking a little green himself.

"Man, Pete, I guess you'll have to write off the whole room. There goes a couple hundred thou worth of apples."

Pete cleared his throat.

"I'm not jumping to any conclusions," Pete said. "For all we know, this is some kind of practical joke or something."

Of course, having studied a bit about dead bodies, I knew it was no joke. Given the right conditions, a body could easily mummify during decomposition. If this body had just spent the winter in cold storage in a room that had almost no oxygen, then it must've slowly dried out as it decomposed, turning into the mummified shell that remained.

"It stinks," one of the men said.

"Not as much as you'd expect for a dead body," Zeb added, bending over the bin to look closely. "I found one in the woods once. A man had shot himself hunting. Shoot, that body stank so bad it burned the inside of my nose. I couldn't get rid of the smell for days."

He reached out one hand toward the mummy's face.

"Don't touch anything!" I said quickly.

"I wasn't gonna hurt it," he replied. "I just wanted to feel it."

"You need to step back," I said. "Nobody touch anything."

"She's right," Pete said, pulling a cell phone from his pocket. "Y'all move away from the bin."

"What happened, exactly?" Danny asked, still looking quite shaken as everyone followed Pete's directive and backed up. "How did you know it was there?"

One of the men shook his head.

"It was the smell," he said. "Soon as I lowered the bin down off the stacks and pulled it out, I said, uh-oh, we got ourselves a dead animal. I didn't want to scare the ladies in the packing house, so I drove the forklift out here, thinking it was a dead cat or something, and I could just dig it out and toss it over in the bushes. But that's no cat, I'll tell you what. That's a *person*."

I wondered if anyone else was thinking what I was thinking, that this person might be the body of Enrique Morales. I listened to the nervous chatter around me and didn't hear his name come up. Instead, the men were mostly talking about horror movies and mummies and Egyptian tombs. I supposed to them, this shriveled-up creature looked more like something out of Hollywood than the dried-out remains of a man they had once known.

Pete dialed on his cell phone, and I listened as he spoke somberly and softly into it.

"Lowell, it's Pete. I'm sorry to bother you, but I wanted to let you know we have a situation over at the storage...no, sir...well, yes, if you're up to it."

He ran a hand through his thick dark blond hair and exhaled slowly.

"Well, it's a...a dead body, actually. In one of the apple bins...Yes, sir...No, though I think I may have an idea...Okay. We did. They should be here soon...All right. Bye."

He clicked off the phone and slid it into his pocket. I stepped closer and asked as softly as I could, "Pete, do you think that's the body of Enrique Morales?"

Pete's eyes met mine for a long moment, and then he nodded.

"I recognize the shirt," he whispered. "And that looks like his color hair, though who's to say by that face if it's him or not?"

"They have ways they can find out," I said, knowing that the medical examiner would most likely start with dental records, and if they couldn't be found or didn't show anything conclusive, then there was a method for rehydrating the fingerprints to plump up the tips and get the prints. If all else failed, of course, there was DNA testing.

"Do you think it was an accident?" I asked.

Pete shook his head.

"I don't know," he replied. "I suppose it's possible, though how a man could've gotten buried in a bin of apples, I just don't have a clue."

A few more people came running as word spread through the various buildings about the mummy in the apples. One by one, they crowded around the bin and looked inside, an odd sort of excitement infusing most of their reactions. With all of these people milling around, I was very worried about the integrity of the scene.

"Pete, you need to get everyone to back off," I said, hoping he would understand the importance of preserving things exactly as they were. "At least until the police get here and they can secure everything."

"Yeah," he said, then louder again, "yeah, yeah, come on, people. Step back, step back. I don't want to see anybody within five feet of this bin."

He glanced at me for confirmation, and I held up ten fingers.

"Ten feet!" he amended loudly. "Nobody within ten feet of the box!"

They all did as he said, stepping back and forming a sort of circle. Now there were at least 20 people, and the murmur of the crowd was at a fevered pitch. I hoped the police would arrive soon. It would take only one person breaking the rules to get everyone else moving forward again.

Pete seemed concerned about the unattended machines inside the other buildings, and I watched as he pulled out several supervisors from the crowd and instructed them to get their people back on the lines. No one seemed to be cooperating, however, and finally Pete whistled loudly for everyone to give him their attention. Lacking a better choice, he climbed up and stood on the seat of the very forklift that held the bin in question.

"All right, folks," he yelled, holding on to the metal frame as he leaned outward. Slowly, the noise of the crowd died down until there was silence. "Listen up," he said a bit less loudly. "This situation is unprecedented around here, so I understand your confusion. But standing around and staring at it isn't going to make things better."

"Did you call the police?" someone asked.

"Looks like they're here now," Pete replied, pointing down the hill. Everyone turned and looked, and in the distance, a row of white police cars was just turning into the long driveway, with lights flashing but, as requested, no sirens. "The police are going to have a lot of questions," Pete continued. "And I want everyone to feel free to answer anything they ask. But please do not get on the phone and start calling all your friends and neighbors. We've got enough people here as it is. Is that understood?"

He looked from face to face, a sea of nodding heads. One woman sheepishly lowered a cell phone from her ear.

"Now, I don't know if having a dead body in there managed to contaminate the entire room or not," Pete continued. "We'll find out. But it sure as heck will contaminate the integrity of Tinsdale Orchards if we're not careful. I don't want to hear any rumors, I don't want to hear any jokes, and for goodness sakes, I don't want to hear anyone talking about this to any reporters."

He looked around and, again, most of the people nodded.

"We can't stop the news of what's happened here," he said finally, "but the best thing you can do to protect Tinsdale Orchards—to protect your jobs—is to keep your mouth shut and do your job. Now get back to work."

He stepped down from the forklift just as the police cars reached the parking lot. A shower-capped woman leaned over and whispered something in Pete's ear, so he made another announcement.

"One more thing," he said quickly before the people walked away. "If anyone suffers any, uh, mental or emotional distress because of what they've seen here today, I'm sure we can arrange for some counseling. Thank you."

The crowd dispersed a bit, though many people simply stood back and watched to see what was going to happen next. I, too, wanted to listen and learn, so I found an unobtrusive spot near the wall and sat down, hoping no one would notice me for a while.

And there was plenty going on to see and hear. I listened as the police were brought up to speed on the situation, watched them put up work lights and rope off the area with yellow Caution tape, even held my tongue when one young officer put both hands down on the rim of the bin as he looked inside. Fortunately, the chief saw what was happening, reprimanded him, and sent him off to some other duty on the fringe of the situation.

After a while Danny came and sat next to me, ostensibly to check on my well-being, but really, I think, to find some comfort himself.

"Man, I've been wondering if I'm cut out for this apple business," he said after a while, shaking his head. "After this, I'm thinking maybe not."

"I'm sure this isn't exactly commonplace," I said. "I don't know a lot about apples, but I know they don't usually come with a mummy in the box."

"Like Cracker Jacks?" he whispered, and for some reason it caught us both as funny. Hands over our mouths, we giggled silently, thinking of Pete's edict not to make jokes but unable to resist the emotional release of laughter.

"Danny was supposed to be driving it!" we heard someone yell, and we looked up, sobering instantly as a worker pointed toward the two of us. I recognized the yelling man as the one who discovered the body, the forklift driver who thought he was smelling a dead cat. Now he seemed to be on the defensive with Pete and Detective Sweetwater. "Danny was supposed to be on forklift today, but when we unsealed the room he wasn't anywhere around. So I did it instead."

"Pete sent me off to fix the tractor," Danny said, standing. "Besides, I didn't think we were opening the room up until tomorrow."

"He's right," Pete said. "I did send him to fix the tractor. And SR3 leveled out much more rapidly than any of us expected."

"Look, nobody's making any accusations here," Detective Sweetwater said. "I'm just trying to get my facts straight. So you're the one who drove the forklift and brought the bin out here, right?"

The man nodded and the volume of their voices dropped back to normal.

"I'm glad I was out working on the tractor," Danny said softly to me, after he sat back down. "It was hard enough seeing that without being the first one to discover it."

"Not easy to look at death, is it?" I said, wondering how it was that Danny had come to work on an apple orchard. He didn't really seem suited to the harsh realities of farm life at all.

"Oh, man, do you know if anyone has called Karen?" he asked. "I'd hate for her to hear about this on the news."

Without waiting for an answer, Danny stood and headed toward one of the buildings. I realized that as the orchard liaison, he might have some rather unpleasant duties coming up in the days ahead—particularly if that was a dead migrant worker in the box.

I needed to make a few phone calls myself, starting with Harriet. She didn't answer her cell phone, but I left a message on her voice mail that something big had come up and I would be a while. My hope was that she had already given up on me and gone to dinner with the Webbers. The poor woman had worked hard all day, but I hadn't yet given her a key to the cabin or shown her where it was, so she couldn't even go home and put up her feet.

I was just trying Dean's cell phone when I realized that a man had come up and was standing nearby, just on the outside of the boundary of police tape. I hung up the phone and slipped it into my pocket.

"Is that the body, over there?" the man asked.

I glanced around to see whom he was addressing, and I decided it must be me, since no one else was in earshot.

"Yes," I said. "In that wooden box."

He nodded.

"They figure out who it is yet?"

"I think they have some ideas."

"Wonder how long before they get it out of there. Looks like they brought enough police cars to fill a parade."

"I suppose so."

I looked at the man, at the back of his bald head, at his stooped posture, and thought he was very old. When he turned and faced me, however, I realized that he was probably only in his late 60's, but he looked older than that because he was ill. His face was pale and sunken, and in his hands he held an aluminum cane with a three-pronged base.

"Who are you, by the way?" he demanded, as if resenting my appraising gaze.

"I'm Callie Webber," I replied. "I was touring the orchard when the body turned up."

He harrumphed and tapped his cane into the ground.

"Callie Webber?" he repeated. "Don't know you, never heard of you. Do you work here?"

"No, sir," I said, "I was just visiting."

He gave another grunt. Then, as if dismissing me, he turned his back to me and faced the scene. I stood, feeling vaguely offended.

"Who are you?" I asked, stepping closer.

"Name's Tinsdale," he said, not bothering to look my way as he answered. "Lowell Tinsdale. This is my orchard."

Twenty-One

My conversation with Lowell Tinsdale ended up being fairly brief, since the police retrieved him for questioning as soon as they saw him standing there. But from our short exchange, I learned that the orchard had been in his family for generations and that he grew up, as he put it, "living, breathing, and sleeping apples," though he'd never seen anything like this. He seemed like a nice enough fellow if you looked past the gruffness, but I felt certain he was in very poor health. He had the sunken cheeks and dark eyes of a man struggling with a serious illness.

I hung around the scene a bit longer, but the place was becoming a circus, packed with curious townspeople, reporters, and soon to arrive, according to rumor, a news crew out of Charlotte. June Sweetwater interviewed me briefly as a matter of course, just getting on record how it was that I happened to be here for all of this. Once the coroner began issuing instructions to remove the body from the bin, however, I decided to leave. While I had managed to keep a sort of professional detachment about the whole mummy thing, I didn't know if I could handle seeing the body in its entirety.

I was just pulling out of the parking lot when yet another car came speeding up the driveway. When I realized who was inside, however, I pulled back into my parking place, turned off the car and climbed out.

It was Karen and Luisa. They jumped from their vehicle, but I had to stop them before they could get around the corner and see the horrible sight of the mummy being removed from the apples. If it was indeed Enrique, I knew Luisa would never be able to erase that image from her mind.

"Stop!" I called, and both women hesitated, looking at me. "Please, don't go over there yet!"

To my surprise, they both waited as I ran toward them. I took Luisa's ice-cold hand in mind and looked into her face.

"Is it him?" she whispered, her body trembling with fear and dread.

"What was he wearing the day he disappeared?" I asked.

"Jeans. A gray T-shirt."

"Tell me what the T-shirt looked like," I said.

A sob caught in her throat.

"It was…it was torn a bit, at the collar, here. I think it had a face of a bull on it, but the picture was faded…"

My heart sank. That was the shirt, all right.

"It may be him," I said finally, tightening my grip on her hand. "But you don't want to see him like this. Trust me, Luisa. You don't."

She tried to pull away from me, but then Karen grabbed her other arm and held on as well.

"Luisa, wait," Karen said. "Callie's right. Not here. Not like this."

"I have to know!" Luisa yelled, jerking free.

She turned and ran. A moment later we heard her bloodcurdling scream.

"NO!"

"No," Karen echoed, whispering, her face white, her hands to her mouth. She began sobbing, and then she closed her eyes and shook her head back and forth. "No. No. No."

I didn't know quite what to do. I thought I ought to go to Luisa, but I knew she was already surrounded by other people, and I didn't want to leave Karen alone in such a state. Finally, I took a step closer and pulled her into an awkward embrace. She didn't resist but instead broke down, sobbing against my shoulder. After a few minutes, she moved away and tried to pull herself together.

"He was a good man, such a good man," she cried. "He worked so hard. He wanted so much for his children."

"Where are the children now?"

"We couldn't find Pepe," she said, folding and refolding a tissue, "but Adriana is with Natalie."

"Good."

"Adriana doesn't know anything's going on yet, and Natalie said she wouldn't turn on the TV or the radio until she heard back from us. Oh, Callie, is it really him?"

"The shirt Luisa described is certainly the shirt that's on the body."

"Danny said the body was mummified," she whispered.

"Yeah. Looks like it spent the winter in an apple storage room." She looked dizzy, and I grabbed her arm for support.

"Do you know how those rooms work?" she cried. "They caulk and bolt the door and then they start sucking out the oxygen. What if he died like that, Callie? What if he died by having the oxygen sucked out of him?"

Before I could reply, a big van with giant letters on the side came barreling into the parking lot. Every conceivable spot was already taken, so the vehicle simply pulled onto the grass and parked near a mound of dirt. Moments later, several of the orchard workers came running around the corner, headed by Pete. He was yelling at the van driver, and from what I could tell, the man had driven right over some important new apple seedlings.

Karen and I watched the entire exchange, including the repositioning of the van. Then the reporters and the camera crew all got out of the vehicle and headed for the center of the action.

"We should probably go over there too, for Luisa's sake," I said. Beside me, I could feel Karen stiffen.

"No," she said. "I can't."

I understood, thinking she was talking about not wanting to see the body. But then as Pete walked past, he saw us there in the parking lot and froze. His eyes met Karen's. She stared back at him intently.

Finally, after maybe ten full seconds, he changed course and came walking toward us.

"Karen," he said, his voice sounding strained.

"Pete."

Feeling very self-conscious, I wished for a moment that I could simply evaporate into thin air.

"How is he?" Karen asked, surprising me. *How is he? He's a mummy is how he is!*

"Not good," Pete replied. "Not good at all. And now this…"

The three of us stood there awkwardly, and I began to wonder what I was missing. These two obviously had a history of some sort. For a brief moment, the air was so thick with tension that I wondered if perhaps Pete was Karen's ex-husband.

"I'll go check on Luisa," I said finally, just wanting to get away.

"No," Pete and Karen both said simultaneously.

"She's with the police right now," Pete said, turning to leave. "But I'll go look in on her just to make sure."

"Take care," Karen said to Pete.

He looked at her, started to speak, and then he simply closed his mouth, shook his head, and walked away.

"How do you know Pete?" I asked once he was gone.

She didn't answer but simply pursed her lips and shook her head. I waited a beat and then I told her I needed to be on my way.

"Okay. See you," she said vaguely. Then she walked over to her car and sat on the hood, staring off into the distance, her posture that of someone who has settled in to wait.

Walking to my car, I couldn't help but feel miffed. Karen was a bit reserved, but I thought the least she could do was answer an honest question.

As I drove away, my mind turned to the sight of what was probably Enrique Morales, four months dead and shriveled up inside a bin filled with apples. Many people had misjudged the situation, picturing him as a deadbeat dad on the run. In fact, the only place Enrique had run was straight into the arms of death. Once the mummy's identity was confirmed as him, then one question remained.

Was it an accident, or was it murder?

Twenty-Two

Poor Harriet. By the time I finally drove out of Tinsdale Orchards, it was nearly 8:30 P.M., and I had no idea where she was or what she was doing. My best guess was that she was either at the Webbers' house or at a hotel or a restaurant in town. Unfortunately, Greenbriar didn't have a line dancing club, or I'd know to look for her there.

I finally got through to her by the time I reached town. Yes, she was at the Webbers' house, and Natalie had just invited her to unpack her car and stay the night.

"I'm so sorry!" I said. "You can't imagine what's been going on."

"Don't worry about it. We know what's been going on," Harriet said. "We've all just been waiting to hear from you."

I told her to leave her things in the car and I would come there to lead her up the mountain to the cabin.

"Up the mountain?" Harriet asked a little nervously. "It's not too high, is it?"

"Just a steady incline," I said, knowing that in the dark she wouldn't realize exactly how high we were.

My cell phone battery was running low, so we hung up and I drove the rest of the way in silence. Despite not having done anything athletic today, I felt as though I had run a marathon. Every muscle ached and every joint throbbed. More than anything, I just wanted to get back to the cabin, get into my nightgown, and curl up on the couch with the telephone. Tom didn't have any idea of what had been going on here, I realized guiltily. I needed to go back to square one and fill him in.

Of course, once I got to the Webbers', I had to give them a play-by-play of the entire afternoon. Adriana was engrossed in a Veggie Tales video in the back bedroom, so we were free to talk. I explained the sequence of events from my point of view, and when I was done I suggested that they plan on having Luisa and her children spend the night there, since I had a feeling they would be in no condition to be on their own.

"What about Pepe?" I asked. "Where is he?"

"Dean and Ken are out looking for him," Natalie said. "They've checked all of his usual hangouts, but so far they've come up with nothing."

"That kid has too much freedom for a fifteen-year-old," I said.

"Luisa's been on her own, Callie," Natalie replied. "I'm sure she's doing the best she can."

By the time we left, I really felt as though I had just enough energy to drive to the cabin and crawl into the house. It started to drizzle halfway up the mountain, and I glanced in my rearview mirror to see Harriet's windshield wipers springing to life.

I flipped the switch for my own wipers, but after about 30 seconds, smoke suddenly started pouring out from under the hood! Blinker on, I drove to the narrow shoulder and Harriet pulled in behind me.

"Is your car on fire?" she cried as she ran up to me in the rain.

"I don't know!" I said, debating whether or not I should try and get the hood open. I had seen one too many movies of exploding cars to be comfortable doing that.

Finally, steeling my nerve, I ran to the front, felt for the latch, and got the hood up. Billows of smoke came rolling out into the night, and Harriet and I held on to each other as we stood a few feet away, wondering what to do now.

"You shoulda rented a Mustang, like me," Harriet said through the rain. "You're always cutting corners, trying to economize, and now look where it's gotten you."

Harriet screamed and jumped back as I stepped forward, ready to defend us. A man was standing beside the car, wearing only the bottoms of a pair of pajamas.

"That's my house there," he said, pointing across the street.

We looked to see a woman in a babydoll nightgown standing the doorway. She gave us a small wave and Harriet waved back.

"I didn't mean to scare you," the man continued. "I jes' came out here to see what smelled so bad. I thought maybe my house was on fire."

"No, I'm sorry," I said. "It's my car."

Now that he mentioned, it *did* smell bad!

"Want me to take a look?" he asked. The rain was coming down harder, and we were getting soaked.

"Do you know anything about cars?" I asked.

"A little," he said. By now most of the smoke had dissipated, and he leaned down to look but almost immediately stood back up straight. "Don't need to know much to figure out the problem here, though."

I stepped forward to see what he was talking about, and what I saw sent a chill down my spine. There, wired to the wiper motor, was the charred remains of something that looked very familiar.

"Somebody's playing a trick on you," he said. "Look here. They had your windshield wipers rigged to ignite this thing when you turned 'em on."

"Is it a stink bomb?" I asked, swallowing hard.

"Yep, that'd be my guess." He stood up straight and called to the woman. "Hey, honey, what'd we hear about stink bombs in the news?"

"At the church concert," the woman called back. "Where that guy was killed."

"Oh, yeah," the man said, and he began to tell us the story as it had been reported in the news. When he was finished, Harriet's eyes were wide, but I wasn't even listening. My cell phone was dead, and I asked Harriet if I could borrow hers.

"Who are you calling?" she asked as she handed it to me.

"The police," I said. "I'm calling the police."

Twenty-Three

I was glad that, in the end, the police didn't impound my rental car. Not that it would've mattered, really, but it would've been an inconvenience. Instead, they took a few photos and filled out a report, and then, just before they left, I was glad to see June Sweetwater pull to a stop and get out of her car to make sure the situation was being handled properly.

"From what I understand," she said to me from under an umbrella, "this stink bomb could've been placed there either at the orchard or at the Webbers' house?"

"Those were the times the car was unattended this evening. But the windshield wipers kicked it off, and it hasn't rained all week. How do I know it wasn't set up long before now?"

She asked me to think if I had turned on my wipers at any point since the stink bomb incident Sunday night. I closed my eyes and thought hard and finally decided that I was fairly certain I had used them for at least a few swipes this morning, when the windshield fogged up just a bit as the car was first warming up.

"All right, then," June said, patting me on the shoulder. "You be careful. I'm sure I don't have to tell you, but I think this was a message, loud and clear."

"Oh, I know it was," I said, my chin set. "But guess what? They sent that message to the wrong person."

When I finally reached the cabin and pulled into the driveway, I thought I could very well put my head down on the steering wheel and go to sleep right there. As Harriet pulled in next to me, I decided she wasn't looking much better, as her trademark pile of red curls was now sitting in a big damp wad on her head.

As I climbed from the car, I thought that the very first thing on my agenda in the morning was going to be getting down to the lake and out in a canoe. I didn't care how much work I needed to do or who or what was depending on me. If I didn't hit some open water and paddle out some of this tension, I thought I might explode!

Harriet said she needed a few minutes to pull her stuff together, so while she sorted through the luggage in her car, I climbed up the front steps in the dark, wishing I had thought to leave the porch light on. It wasn't until I was flipping through my keychain looking for the door key that I realized someone was already on the porch.

A sound, almost like a snort, came up from the other end. *Bear!* was my first thought, but then I realized it sounded more human than animal. Ears prickling, I could hear someone breathing, heavy and even.

Instinctively, I stepped in the other direction, toward the mound of firewood stacked next to the front door. I looked out toward Harriet, but she was oblivious, still rooting through her things, bent over to work in the circle of light from her trunk.

Silently, I slipped my keys in my pocket, grabbed a piece of firewood off the top of the pile, and held it in my hands like a baseball bat.

As my eyes adjusted to the darkness, I decided that I could just make out the shape of a person at the far end of the porch.

"Who's there?" I demanded loudly, taking one step forward. There was a rustle of noise from that end, then silence.

"What'd you say?" Harriet called.

My heart pounding, I didn't answer her, and again I thought of a bear. I knew I could take on a person, but a wild animal? No way! If that were the case, then my only hope was to either get into the house or down the front steps and back inside my car. More importantly, somehow I had to warn Harriet.

"Did you say something to me?" she asked again, clattering up the walk with a suitcase in each hand.

Suddenly, the figure on the porch sprung to life. With a great snort, it jumped up and knocked a rocking chair toward me.

"Run, Harriet!" I screamed at the top of my lungs. "Call nine one one!"

"Aaargh!" Harriet screamed, dropping her bags and running to her car.

"What is it? What is it?" a voice cried. "Who is that?"

The figure froze, and I strengthened my grip on the wood.

"What do you want?" I demanded.

"Mrs. Webber?" a boy's voice echoed across the black porch.

"Who is it?" I demanded.

"Pepe Morales. It's me, Pepe."

Heart pounding so loudly I was sure he could hear it, I lowered the wood as I realized the figure on my porch wasn't a bear after all.

It was, in fact, my new young friend, Pepe.

"What are you doing here?" I said weakly.

"I...I needed to talk to someone," he said. "I didn't know where else to go."

"Why did you scare me like that?"

"You scared *me*. I must've fallen asleep waiting for you."

He stepped closer, and I could see that it was, indeed, him. I blew out the breath I had been holding.

"How did you get here?" I asked.

He shrugged.

"I heard what was going on, so I caught a ride with someone to the orchard," he said. "But then when I saw...when I saw all the cops and people and everything, I freaked."

"Oh, Pepe."

"I remembered where you said you were staying and all, so I walked here."

I shook my head, trying to picture this boy running uphill, away from the confusion of the orchard. No wonder he had fallen asleep—he must be exhausted!

"Excuse me one minute," I said, setting down the wood and then rushing down the steps to Harriet's car. She was sitting inside, locked up tight, the phone to her ear. I convinced her to roll down the window, which she did just a crack.

"False alarm," I said. "It's a friend of mine. Tell the police we're okay after all."

She shut the window, spoke a bit longer into the phone, and then hung up.

"I don't know why," she said, getting out of the car, "I ever let you talk me into doing anything. I like my life calm. I like my life simple. But it seems like every single time—"

I cut her off by placing my hand on her forearm.

"It's Pepe Morales," I said softly. "Luisa's son."

While Harriet shut up and hung back, I went up the steps to find the boy and gave him a hug. I was afraid he might resist, but instead he gripped me tightly, and I was surprised to find that his body was shivering.

"Let's get you inside," I said. "Then you can tell me what's going on."

In the house, under the light, I got a better look at Pepe. His black hair was a tangled mess, and there were dark circles under his eyes.

Before we even spoke, I brought him a blanket and wrapped it around him and sat him on the couch. Harriet asked if he was hungry and he nodded, so she set about making some chicken noodle soup and hot tea as she familiarized herself with my kitchen. I told Pepe I needed to change into dry clothes but I would be right back. Once I was in the bedroom with the door closed, I called Natalie and told her he was here, but not to come for him yet.

"Oh, thank you for calling, Callie," she said. "I was really starting to worry."

"I'll call back when he's ready to go home," I said.

After hanging up, I changed into sweatpants, sweatshirt, and some very warm socks. When I came back out, I told Harriet she should do the same.

"Your room is at the top of the stairs," I said. "Please, just make yourself at home."

"Soon as I get the boy something warm to eat," she said, and suddenly I felt a surge of relief and happiness that she was here with me. Sometimes I got so tired of being alone, of handling crises all by myself!

I found Pepe where I had left him, curled in blankets on the couch, only now I saw that he had fallen asleep again. Lying like that, his head tilted down on the arm rest, he looked so young, so innocent. I closed my eyes and prayed that God would fill me with the wisdom and good counsel that the boy would need.

To that end, I retrieved my Bible and began looking for verses about death and eternal life—not that I planned to preach at him, but I thought I might find a verse or two that could give him some hope and comfort now that he knew his father was dead. Harriet put a bowl of soup and a cup of tea on the table, adding some crackers on a side plate. Then she picked up her bags from near the door and carried them up the stairs.

"Swanky," she whispered to me from the top of the stairs.

"Thanks," I whispered back.

I could hear her moving around, probably unpacking her bags and changing into dry clothes. She and I still hadn't had a chance to talk, so I was glad when she finally came back down the stairs, dressed in a nightgown, housecoat, and a pair of purple fuzzy slippers.

"What a cute place this is, Callie," Harriet whispered, smiling. "You kept calling it your little cabin, but it's really spacious and quite comfortable."

"Thanks."

"Is he still asleep?" she whispered.

"Yeah."

"Poor kid. I used to fall asleep when I was upset too. My mother thought it was the strangest thing. I got lost once in a department store, and I finally went to sleep under a clothing rack. That's where they finally found me, hours later!"

I put my Bible on a side table and gestured for Harriet to follow me into my bedroom. Leaving the door cracked so I could hear if Pepe awakened, I gestured for her to sit on one of the beds while I sat down on the other.

"I'm so glad you're here," I said, meaning it. "This has been a very long day."

"From what I've heard," she replied, "things have been pretty wild since you got to town."

Reluctantly, I told her the full story. I started with the stabbing victim and his death, and continued through the fire at Luisa's trailer to the mummy that was found today at the orchard. I had really hoped to avoid some of this stuff with her, because Harriet was very skittish when it came to things like murder and violence. It was usually easier to let her simply do her job while I did mine. But apparently she had already heard some things, so I thought it best to lay it all out for her straight.

"Sorry for getting you into this," I said.

"It's all right. I should have known going on location with you would get me into more than just debits and credits."

"Speaking of that, how do the books look to you?" I asked.

"Oh, the place looks great," she said. "Clean as a whistle so far."

"Good. I hope you're still as impressed by the end of the week when you finish your audit."

"Me too. Especially because the people there are so nice."

She talked about the Webbers, which then led to the inevitable discussion of Bryan and what it was like for me to be here in the midst of all these memories.

"I'm doing great," I said. "In fact, I think this trip was probably just what I needed. Things will be changing for me soon, and I guess it's good for me to see, finally, that I really am ready to move on."

"What?" Harriet asked, her eyes wide. "You're not moving, are you?"

"No," I said. "I meant moving on emotionally. I'm in a new relationship now, and things are starting to get serious."

"I knew it!" she said. "It's that gorgeous neighbor of yours, isn't it? Ooo, honey, you have landed yourself a hunk."

"No," I said, smiling, "it isn't Kirby. He and I are just friends."

"Who, then? You spend so much time working, I don't see how you have time to get out and meet—" She stopped, midsentence, and stared hard at me, as if she were working to form her thoughts. "Please tell me this isn't about you and Tom again. I already explained to you—"

"Tom came to see me," I said.

She blinked, silent for once.

"Last November," I continued, "after the whole mess with the smugglers and the INS and everything. He found out I had been in the hospital, and so he came to see how I was doing."

"He was in Singapore then," she said skeptically.

"Yes, he was. But he flew to Baltimore, rented a car, and showed up at my house. We spent about twelve hours together, and then he left again and went back to Singapore. In less than a week, he's coming home, and he's coming home to me."

"He came to see you as a friend," she said uncertainly.

"Well, sure," I said, "if friends hold hands and talk about their future and kiss each other like there's no tomorrow."

"Did he say 'I love you'?"

"No," I told her. "But I think he does. And I think that I love him."

I wasn't sure what her reaction would be, but she surprised me by jumping up, grabbing a pillow, and throwing it at me.

"You're lying!" she cried angrily, and I shushed her, pointing toward the other room. "You're lying," she said again, in a sharp whisper this time.

"Harriet, I'm sorry I didn't tell you sooner," I said. "But it was all so new, so private. Then the more time that passed, the harder it was to say anything. I hope you can forgive me."

She paced the floor for a few minutes and then stopped, hands on hips, and glared at me.

"What are we to each other, Callie?" she asked. "You and me. Acquaintances? Coworkers?"

"You know we're more than that," I said. "You're one of my best friends."

She nodded.

"That's what I thought too," she said, and then she turned on her heel and walked from the room. I could hear her clunk her way up the stairs, then back down to brush her teeth and use the bathroom, then back up to her room, where I heard the creak as she climbed into bed.

I decided to let her sleep on it, thinking that perhaps in the morning she would've cooled down a bit and we could talk some more. While I felt bad for keeping her in the dark all this time, I knew that if I had to do it all over again, I'd probably do it the same way. For some reason, talking about my relationship with Tom did not come easily to me.

Putting Harriet out of my mind for now, I walked back into the living room, where Pepe was still sound asleep on the couch. Exhausted myself, I put a hand on his arm and shook him awake. I knew there were people who were worried about him. And the sooner we could talk, the sooner he could get back with his family where he belonged.

Twenty-Four

~

Pepe sat at the table while I reheated his soup and tea in the microwave. Since I had woken him up, he seemed almost embarrassed to be here, and I tried to think of some way to break the ice with him and let him know that I was a friend and was glad he had thought to come to me when he needed someone to talk to.

"I bet if life had an 'Undo' function," I said, using computer-speak, "then you'd click on this day and make it so that it had never happened."

I set his food in front of him and watched as he dug in.

"No," he said finally. "I'd click on that day last fall, when my dad got killed. That's what I would undo."

Sitting across from him at the table, I told him we still didn't know for sure if the man found today at the orchard was his father or not.

"I heard what people were saying," he told me. "We both know it probably is."

I nodded, thinking we would know for sure tomorrow anyway, once the identification had been made by the medical examiner.

"I'm so sorry, Pepe," I said. "I wish I had some wise words or something, but the truth is, the whole situation is just really, really sad. I hope you and your family can look to God to find comfort."

He nodded.

"I've been praying for months for my dad to come home," he said. "Now I find out he was here all along."

"And that hurts," I said gently.

"It sucks," he replied.

He let me share with him a few verses of comfort from the Bible, but as he finished his meal, he pushed away from the table, looking as though he bore the weight of the world on his shoulders.

"So was my dad murdered," he asked me, "or was it an accident?"

I took a deep breath and let it out slowly.

"We won't know that," I answered, "until a forensic pathologist examines the body."

He nodded and then seemed to grow visibly agitated. Finally, he stood and began pacing.

"What if there was something," he said, "something I knew that I had never told anybody?"

My pulse surged.

"Then you should probably tell someone now," I said evenly.

He nodded, paced some more, and then came back to sit across from me.

"Mr. Pete wasn't the last person to see my dad alive that day, like everybody thinks."

"He wasn't?"

"No," Pepe said. "I was. I saw my dad last on the day he disappeared."

"Why didn't you tell someone before now?"

"Because I didn't think it was important." He waited a beat, lowering his head. "And I was afraid I would get in trouble."

Though I wanted to lean forward and pull the words from his mouth, I forced my body language into a nonthreatening stance, my back relaxed against the chair, one elbow on the table.

"Tell me about it," I said.

Nervously, he launched into the tale of how he had cut school that day, something he did frequently during the harvest season when there were so many kids at Go the Distance that no one noticed when one was missing.

"See, during harvest, Mom and Dad usually leave the dorms at six o'clock in the morning, but the bus doesn't pick up Adriana and me for school until six-fifty. That day, once my parents left for work, I got Adriana ready for school and sent her out with the other kids, and then I went back to bed."

"Were you sick?"

"Nah. I just like to play hooky sometimes, you know? I'm always surrounded by people. Skipping school during harvest means I get the apartment all to myself. Heck, I get the whole compound to myself. Just peace and quiet. Room to think. It's great."

"I understand," I said, and I did. In fact, I was thinking that if I had to give up my solitude for the communal life of a migrant worker, I wouldn't be able to stand it.

"Anyway, that day I was just lying around, and about noon my dad all of a sudden shows up at the apartment."

"That was unusual?"

"Yeah. Nobody ever came back there until quitting time. But there he was. He caught me."

"Was he mad?"

"That was the weird thing. Instead of yelling at me like I would've expected, he just sat down and talked to me for a minute. He seemed like he really had something on his mind."

"What did he say?"

"At first, he was like, 'Son, you shouldn't ever skip school.' He never had an education, you know, so it was important to him that his kids did."

"I'm sure it was," I said.

Pepe stood and began pacing again.

"Then he started talking about being poor but honorable, and that a man's honor was the most valuable thing he could have. 'You can't put a price on honor,' he told me."

"Okay."

"I thought he was just talking about me and skipping school, but after a while I realized he was really talking about himself. I don't know what about, but it was a weird conversation."

"Then what happened?" I asked.

"I asked him if he was okay, and he said something like, 'No, not really. I think I know something I shouldn't know. I've got to talk to someone.' I was thinking maybe he saw one of the other migrants stealing or cheating or something. I go, 'Why don't you talk to the priest?' and he goes, 'No, it's not the Padre I need. Maybe I should speak to Mr. Tinsdale.'"

"Did he talk to Mr. Tinsdale often?" I asked.

"Never," said Pepe. "None of the migrants ever saw Mr. Tinsdale."

"So it had to have been something very important."

"Yeah, " Pepe nodded. "But the last thing he said to me was the weirdest. I thought we were finished, 'cause he got his lunch from the fridge and told me I was grounded. Then, just as he was leaving, he turned back to me and said, 'I'm not sure who I can trust.'"

Pepe and I looked at each other, and I felt sure we were thinking the same thing: Whomever Enrique had trusted, it must've been the wrong choice.

Twenty-Five

It was well after 1:00 A.M. when I finally climbed into bed, my body beyond exhausted. Dean had come to pick up Pepe and was taking him back home with him, where the Moraleses were spending the night. Upstairs, Harriet was lightly snoring, and I wanted nothing more than to close my eyes and drift into sleep as well. First, however, I needed to hear the sound of Tom's voice. So much had happened today, and though I didn't feel like explaining it all to him now, I just wanted to know that he was out there, that he was missing me as much as I was missing him.

Fortunately, the time difference was in our favor for a change. Using the phone beside the bed, I dialed the numbers that would connect me to him in the middle of his workday half a world away.

"Callie?" he asked when he realized it was me. "You're up late. It's almost two-thirty here!"

"Yeah, I'm about to go to sleep," I said. "But I wanted to hear your voice first."

"Perfect timing. You caught me in the limo, on my way to a meeting."

"Busy day?" I asked.

"We're wrapping things up right and left," he said. "It's really very exciting. I'm anxious to come home."

"Do you miss me, Tom?"

I guess he could hear something in my voice, because he answered my question with a question.

"What's the matter, Callie? You sound very down."

"Things aren't going well here," I said, draping one arm across my eyes. "There are problems with the investigation, and then tonight Harriet and I got into a big fight…"

"You got in a fight with Harriet?" he laughed. "That must've been something to see! Between the two of you, I'm not sure who I'd put my money on."

"Not a fist fight," I chuckled. "An argument. I told her about us."

He was silent for a moment.

"About you and me?" he asked finally. "Do you think that was wise?"

"She's my friend, Tom," I said. "She deserved to know."

"It's just that we have an odd sort of situation," he said, "with me as the boss and you two as coworkers…"

"The whole boss-employee thing hasn't been an issue for us so far."

"No, but I think it might be hard for someone else to understand. So what started the argument? Is she convinced I'm not good enough for you?"

"I think it hurt her feelings that I didn't tell her before now. She and I used to talk about you all the time, you know, wondering what you looked like, what your life was like. Once things started changing between you and me, I wasn't sure how to tell her. Then you and I finally met, and our time together was so special I kept it all to myself."

He was quiet for a while, and I was starting to wish I hadn't called. It wasn't going the way I had intended.

"Am I really such a mystery man," he asked, "that the people who work for me use me as fodder for conversation?"

"Oh, Tom! Of course you're a mystery man," I said. "Who gives away millions of dollars and doesn't take credit for it? Who has a foundation and never steps inside its doors except at night, when no one's there? I even once asked Eli if you were horribly disfigured, like the beast in *Beauty and the Beast*."

"What did he say?"

"He told me you were a good-looking guy and to mind my own business."

Tom laughed.

"Fine," he said. "At least you and I have moved beyond all of that now."

"Yes and no," I said. "As close as we are, Tom, sometimes I feel as though I still haven't solved the mystery of who you are."

"Ah, Callie," he said, and I could hear sadness in his voice. "I'm afraid much of it has to stay a mystery. There are things about me, about my work, that you can never know."

"I know how I feel about you," I whispered.

"I know how I feel about you," he replied. "And yes. The answer is a thousand times yes. I do miss you. Of course I miss you."

"That's all I really wanted to hear," I said. "I can go to sleep now, mysteries and all."

"Call me back tomorrow when you're more awake," he said. "I want to hear about the problems you're having with the investigation."

"Have you got a couple of hours? That might be enough to get us started."

"Is there anything I need to know? Anything I can help facilitate from over here?"

"No," I said. "But thanks for asking. We can go into it the next time we talk."

We said our goodbyes, and then I hung up the phone and clicked off the light. I was asleep within minutes. In my dreams, Tom took my hand, and we went flying into the sky, the clouds mere puffs of cotton brushing our faces as we flew past.

Twenty-Six

It wasn't until I got up the next morning that I really thought about what Tom had said the night before.

What was the big secret about his work?

As I stood in front of the mirror and put concealer on the dark circles under my eyes, I thought about everything he had ever said to me regarding his job, and I had to admit that I didn't know much. He had invented something that was pivotal to the internet infrastructure, his invention had made him a multimillionaire in the private sector, and now he worked primarily for the government.

Beyond that, I had no idea what branch of government he worked for or what he did for them. My hunch had always been that he was some sort of programmer for the FBI or the CIA—or the Department of Defense. Certainly, he was connected at the highest levels. I supposed the biggest question I had to as myself at this point wasn't "What's the big secret?" but "Can I live with not knowing what it is?"

Deciding to put it out of my mind for now, I finished applying my makeup and then got dressed, pulling on a pair of DKNY slacks, a gray cotton twinset, and pearls. My head was muddled this morning, but I was going to stay true to my promise to myself and begin the day in a canoe. Unfortunately, that meant having to go to the Webbers and interact—something I just wasn't in the mood for yet. Perhaps, I decided, I could wait until they had left work and then show up once they were gone.

When I came out of my room, Harriet was sitting at the kitchen table, sipping a cup of coffee. She looked up at me, and I gave her a tentative smile.

"Good morning," I said.

"Omelet on the stove," she replied. I looked in the pan and, sure enough, half an omelet was there waiting for me.

I scooped it onto a plate and warmed it in the microwave while pouring myself some juice, and then I joined her at the table.

"All right," she said the moment I sat down. "Here's the thing. I am happy for you. I could not be more excited if you told me you had eloped with Santa Claus on Christmas Eve. I'm just hurt that you didn't tell me."

"I know," I said. "I'm sorry. I value your friendship more than you can imagine."

"Good," she said, and then she pointed a finger at me. "So don't ever keep a secret like that from me again! I feel like an idiot!"

"Why?"

"All my talk about 'I know what Tom looks like,' and 'Tom has a girlfriend.' How stupid could I be?"

I took a bite of my omelet, which was a bit tough. Harriet had many skills, but cooking wasn't necessarily one of them.

"I tried to tell you yesterday morning," I reminded her.

"I know you did," she replied. "Good grief. Let's just forget that entire conversation."

"You got it," I said. "Except the part where Tom chose me over a beauty queen."

"Fine," she said. "Except the part about the beauty queen."

"So am I forgiven?" I asked.

"On one condition," she said. "Details. I want lots and lots of details."

Of course, I wasn't about to give her a play-by-play of my entire evening with Tom. But I told her enough to make her happy, and she seemed especially pleased to learn he was even more handsome and more wonderful than either of us had ever imagined.

I eventually steered the conversation toward the day ahead of us and what each of us hoped to accomplish. I needed to spend some time with my database, loading in the information I had gathered the day before. Now that Enrique was most likely dead, it changed my investigation. Instead of trying to find his whereabouts, I needed to look through my interviews to see if there were any clues as to how this may have happened.

Overall, it was Pepe's story that provided the most promising lead. I decided I would have to get back to Tinsdale Orchards to see if Enrique ever talked to Lowell Tinsdale that day as he had planned. Also, I needed to pass along to the police the information Pepe had given me last night.

Though part of my day would be spent learning about the autopsy of the mummy, Harriet planned to do nothing more exciting than sit in front of a computer at MORE and crunch some numbers, and I knew that was how she wanted it. When it came to any of my dangerous, scary, or irregular activities, her motto was always "Don't ask, don't tell."

The drive down the mountain was a bit dicey with the wet roads from the rain the night before. I could see Harriet in my rearview mirror, and most of the way down her face looked as pale and frightened as if she were on a roller-coaster ride. I thought it must be awful to have a fear of heights, and I was glad I couldn't quite make out the choice words her lips were forming on the other side of her windshield.

At the bottom of the hill, I turned left and she followed suit, but when I came to the right turn for the Webbers' house, I motioned for her to keep going straight. I had already told her that the office would be up about a mile on the left, and I had given her a key to the cabin so that she could come and go during the day, if needed.

When I got the Webbers' house, I was quite relieved to see there were no cars in the driveway. I pulled to a stop and peeked into the garage, but it was empty as well.

Pocketing my car keys, I changed into sneakers and then nearly skipped around the house and down the lawn to where the canoe rested on a low wooden rack near the water. The canoe was big and heavy, but with a lot of pushing and pulling I was able to get it off the rack. Fortunately, the shed wasn't locked, so I stepped inside and chose a paddle from the ones that were hanging there on the wall. I grabbed a nice, lightweight aluminum one and then ran back to the canoe, put one foot inside, and pushed off from the shore. I settled down onto the metal seat, used the paddle to straighten myself out, and then, finally, I was off!

I started slowly at first, knowing that my muscles needed to be treated gently. Though I had managed to get in some laps in the hotel pool in California, I hadn't been able to paddle since I left Maryland nearly a week and a half ago.

After I warmed up, I continued at a pace fast enough to get my heart rate up, though not so fast to risk a pulled muscle. It felt so good! I let the wind whip at my hair as I went, feeling the familiar pull in my shoulders, the wonderful ache in my forearms.

There was a difference between lake paddling, which I was doing now, and river paddling, which I did at home. I had forgotten how good it felt to get out into a large body of water—particularly one this beautiful. In many places, the mountains loomed right up out of the water, their mirror images reflecting on the surface. The lake itself was clear but greenish blue, a color peculiar to the area and due to the various minerals in the water. All I knew was that in some ways this place felt more like home to me than my real home did.

I pressed onward, paying no attention to time or space but simply paddling, stroke after stroke. Heart pounding in my chest, I finally eased up, letting myself coast, letting the boat carry me forward through the water. Truly, there was nothing in the world like that feeling.

Rather than make my usual U-turn at the end of my outbound paddling, this time I simply turned to the right and cut a wide, slow arc through the open water. This brought me near the shore, and as I went I recognized a familiar stretch of rock at the base of the mountain. Among the crags and crevices, if the light hit it just right, you could always make out what looked like a giant face: Two darkish depressions formed a crooked pair of eyes, a large piece jutting out between them made the nose, and underneath was a slash in the rock that gave a sort of straight-lined mouth. Years ago, Bryan and I had nicknamed the face in the rock "Old Gus," and whenever we paddled past, we always told him hello.

"Hello, Old Gus," I said now, smiling wistfully.

I knew that if I continued on around two more bends, I would come to Camp Greenbriar. I thought about paddling there now, but I didn't have much time, and that was an experience I didn't want to rush. Instead, I made a wide circle to turn myself around. I would go there later in the week.

For now, I still had an investigation to run. To that end, I overshot the Webbers' house just a bit so I could take a look at the new neighborhood that backed up to their land. As Dean had said, the houses were big and expensive looking, though I didn't think they were very pretty, and none of them had much in the way of landscaping. From my vantage point on the water, I could easily understand why everyone felt certain that the person I had spotted running through the woods was headed straight to that neighborhood. I was just sorry the police hadn't been able to catch the person—whoever he was—that night.

Back at the Webbers' house, I struggled to bring in the canoe and ended up getting my sneakers all wet. I finally had it on the rack when I heard someone calling my name. I looked up to see Natalie stepping from the house onto the deck, waving at me. I waved back, thinking how much she looked like Bryan at that moment.

"Do you need some help?" she called.

"No, I got it."

I put away the paddle and joined her on the deck.

"That's sure a familiar sight," she said, "to watch you out on the lake."

"Oh, Natalie," I said, feeling the warmth in my muscles and hands, "I had forgotten how absolutely gorgeous it is out there."

Natalie looked tired, and it occurred to me she had probably been up even later than I had last night.

"Are you okay?" I asked. "What are you doing home?"

"Harriet told me you'd be here," she said. "I decided to come back to the house to see if I could catch you."

"Is something wrong?"

"Just sit here on the deck with me for a few minutes. I feel like this week is going by so quickly, and that we're jumping from crisis to crisis without any time to really talk."

"A lot has happened this week," I agreed.

"A lot has been happening in your life before this week, from what I understand."

Uh-oh.

Judging from Natalie's expression, I realized that Harriet must've said something to her about me and Tom. *How could she?*

"Have a seat, Callie," Natalie said.

Heart pounding, I did as she asked. Though this conversation had been inevitable, I still couldn't help wishing I were anywhere but here at this moment.

"Something tells me my coworker has a big mouth," I said.

Natalie sat in a chair next to mine so that we were both facing the lake. The morning sun sparkled on the gentle waves, and for a moment I closed my eyes and listened to the familiar sound of distant birds.

"She didn't say it on purpose. I overheard her on the phone with someone from your office. 'Callie's got a boyfriend, and you'll never guess who it is,' something like that."

"She must've been talking to Margaret," I said, thinking of our receptionist and knowing that of course Harriet would have to run and tell her the news of me and Tom. It was simply too big of a story to keep all to herself. And I had never said it was a secret.

"Do you remember the last visit you and Bryan made here before he died?" Natalie asked.

I nodded, picturing a blur of boating and board games and big meals with the family. As always, it had been a fun trip; at the time, we hadn't known it would be Bryan's last.

"One morning the two of you came down to the house so that he could fix my kitchen faucet for me. While he worked on that, you took out the canoe for a ride."

"I remember that morning," I said. "Seems like I was trying out some new strokes with the paddle. I just went back and forth out there, practicing my Minnesota Switch."

"That's right," Natalie said. "I was watching you, and I commented to Bryan what a graceful wife he had. Do you know what he said to me?"

I shook my head, feeling a wave of sadness suddenly wash over me, though I didn't know where it had come from.

"He said, 'Mom, she might not be so graceful the next time you see her. We've started trying for a family.'"

I closed my eyes and leaned my head back, feeling the threat of tears.

"I didn't know he had told you that," I said finally.

"Considering that he died before you had a chance to conceive," she said, "I almost wished he hadn't told me. Believe me, I mourned the children my son would never have almost as much as I mourned him."

"Me too," I whispered.

"Since then," she continued, "my prayer for you has been that you would find someone else to love, someone else to marry, while you're still young enough to have children of your own."

I opened my eyes and looked at her.

"Natalie, I don't know where this relationship is going to take me," I said. "It's still very new."

"That doesn't matter," she said, and when she blinked, a tear rolled down her cheek. "What matters is that you've finally come out of hiding and started *living* again. You're so young, Callie. Life still holds so much for you."

I reached out and took her hand in mine and we sat there, side by side, looking at the lake.

"Sometimes I feel very old," I said.

In the yard a squirrel scampered up the pole of a bird feeder, reached inside, and pulled out some sunflower seeds. Nearby, a blue jay squawked from a tree, and eventually the squirrel ran away—though not before he had filled his mouth with the seeds.

"So what are you trying to say here?" I asked. "That I have your blessing on this new relationship?"

She squeezed my hand tightly and then let it go.

"Yes," she replied. "I'm trying to say that no matter where life takes you—and I know it's going to take you somewhere wonderful—you will always be my daughter, and you will always have my blessing."

Twenty-Seven

Inevitably Natalie and I moved on to the topic of the Morales family. I asked her what she thought might happen next, and she said that basically things would remain in limbo until the autopsy was finished later in the day, though fortunately the children would be leaving town soon. As I had already figured out, the body first had to be proven to be Enrique, and then it would have to be determined whether he was killed or had died in an accident.

I asked Natalie what kind of accident could leave a man buried in a bin of fruit. She said it didn't seem likely but supposed there was always a chance he had fallen off a ladder while picking apples and had either broken his neck or been knocked unconscious when he landed in the bin. Other pickers could've dumped their apples in on top of him without looking, and before anyone knew it, the bin would've been taken to storage and locked away, where the drop in oxygen would finish the job the knock on the head had started.

"Sounds like a pretty crazy theory to me," she said. "But, then again, a mummy in a box of apples is crazy enough all by itself."

"What does Luisa think happened?" I asked.

"She thinks someone killed Enrique and hid his body there on purpose. It wouldn't have been hard to do—there weren't many workers around on the day he died. A quick blow to the head out in the field, hide the body among the apples, and wait for the forklift to come by and load up the bin with all of the others. If that were the case, however, then that leads to a very strange question: Why would you hide a body somewhere you knew it would be found a few months later?"

We puzzled around that one for a while but couldn't come up with any logical conclusions. I reminded Natalie we were wasting our time on conjecture anyway, at least until the results of the autopsy came out.

"There is one thing I have been wondering," I said. "I witnessed a very strange encounter yesterday between Karen Weatherby and Pete Gibson. Is there some sort of history there? I thought maybe Pete was her ex-husband or something."

"Ex-husband?" Natalie said. "Goodness no, Callie. Pete is Karen's brother. Well, stepbrother, I guess."

"Stepbrother?" I asked, my eyes wide.

"Yes. Didn't you know? Lowell Tinsdale, the man who owns Tinsdale Orchards? Pete's stepfather? He's Karen Weatherby's father."

"Why didn't I know that?" I asked. "She never said anything. In fact, when I was with her at Go the Distance, she acted all weird about the orchard. I asked her if she wanted to go there with me, and she practically threw me out the door."

Natalie exhaled slowly.

"That's because Karen and her father are estranged," she said. "Karen's story is really quite sad."

Natalie seemed reluctant to indulge in what might be considered gossip, but I told her that as a part of my investigation of MORE I needed at least a general understanding of the ties that bound the head of one of the charities they supported with the owner of the biggest orchard in town.

"Karen's mother died in childbirth," Natalie explained. "Lowell was devastated when she passed away."

"How sad."

"He also didn't have a clue what to do with his new baby girl. He brought in a woman to take of her, and then he left the raising of Karen to her. He buried himself in his work and the orchard simply thrived. I heard he was putting in fifteen-hour days, seven days a week. Whatever it took to erase the pain, not to mention avoid the little girl who was growing up to look just like her mother."

Natalie looked out at the water silently for a moment.

"Of course, there's no substitute for parents," she continued, "and the hired help let poor little Karen simply run wild. I heard a rumor once that the day she started first grade, they had to send her home early because she smelled so bad. The other students called her 'Birdy' for years because her hair was so knotted. It looked just like a bird's nest."

"The poor thing," I said. "I bet she didn't have a friend in the world."

"Oh, she had plenty of friends—three or four months out of the year, at least. The migrant children."

"Ah," I said, picturing it all clearly in my mind. An orchard owner's lonely daughter probably would have found great solace among migrant workers' children.

"Back then, you know, there weren't all sorts of rules and regulations like there are now. The migrant kids either helped their parents in the fields or stayed out of the way at the migrant camp."

"The migrant camp?" I asked. "Down by the creek?"

"Yes. Karen used to spend every possible minute she could there, playing with the children who weren't working. She learned their games and taught them things like hide-and-seek. Lowell left that girl to her own devices for thirteen years. Is it any wonder..."

Her voice trailed off, and I looked at her, surprised to see her blushing.

"What?" I prodded.

She lowered her voice, even though we were the only ones home.

"Is it any wonder he eventually found her in a compromising position in one of the barns with a migrant boy?"

I closed my eyes, imagining both the pain and shame of the young Karen and the rage and confusion of her father.

"Needless to say," Natalie continued, clearing her throat, "that was probably the first time Lowell Tinsdale had paid a moment's attention to the girl in thirteen years."

"What happened?"

"Well, for starters, he forbade Karen to have anything else to do with any of the migrants ever again."

"Ouch."

"When he saw that wasn't going to hold, he sent her off to boarding school in California."

"Oh, Natalie," I said, shaking my head sadly. "That must've destroyed what was left of the poor girl's spirit."

Natalie sighed.

"I don't really know what happened to her after that. She managed to get through junior high and high school, and then she stayed out West for college. I do know that once she graduated from college she announced to her father she was going to be an activist for migrants—and then she severed all ties with him."

"Served him right, I guess," I said.

Natalie nodded.

"He was none too happy about it," she said, "but what could he do? Karen was a grown woman. She had her own life to live. She was even married for a time."

"So how did she end up back here?" I asked. "I assume she's been out of college for, what, maybe ten or twelve years now? Did she decide that the ties had been severed long enough?"

Natalie exhaled slowly.

"I don't know, Callie," she said. "When Karen first moved back last year, Dean and I made great overtures toward her, you know, bringing her food, helping her move in, inviting her to church. She would never talk about herself, her past, or her father at all, except to say that she had become a Christian a few years ago and that ever since she had felt the Lord leading her to return home and help the migrants here. I don't know much beyond that. If her intention was to reconcile with Lowell, that certainly hasn't taken place yet, as far as I know. Now with him so ill, I have to wonder if they'll ever make their peace."

"What's wrong with him?" I asked, anticipating the answer before she gave it.

"He has a lung disorder," she said. "COPD. Chronic Obstructive Pulmonary Disease. I doubt he'll live to see next year."

"He looked pretty awful when I met him yesterday."

"You met him?" Natalie asked. "At the orchard?"

"Yes, he came out when the police were there."

I described his hollow face, his stooped posture. Natalie told me a bit more about his condition and said that, as sick as he was, she was surprised he had come out of the house at all.

"What's with the house anyway?" I asked. "For such a thriving business, the mansion looks like it's falling apart."

"That's Lowell," Natalie said, nodding. "Since he got sick, he doesn't want people around, doesn't want the noise or the activity of maintenance or repairs. He putters around in that big old home with no one but his nurses and attendants to keep him company. Everyone else is off limits."

"Even his children?"

She thought about that.

"I don't know about Pete," she said finally. "I'm sure he has access. As for Karen, what can I say? Between her and her father, the two of them are like a pair of stubborn mules. But what neither one of them will admit is that the one commodity they don't have a lot of is time."

Twenty-Eight

Natalie stayed home to get some things done around the house, but I needed to get into the MORE office, see how things were going with Harriet, and get a good look at my own investigation. On the way, I called June Sweetwater at the police station. I got her voice mail, so I left a message describing my visit from Pepe last night and his revelations about the conversation he had with his father just before Enrique disappeared. I wasn't sure what Detective Sweetwater would do with that knowledge, but I knew it was relevant to the case—particularly if Enrique's death was ruled a homicide.

When I came into the office, Harriet didn't seem embarrassed or uncomfortable, and I decided she wasn't even aware that Natalie had overheard her conversation with Margaret about me and Tom. It was just as well, since my resulting talk with Natalie had been actually quite liberating. I was glad to know I had my mother-in-law's blessing to live my life fully, especially if that life ended up including a new husband and some children.

Trying not to picture a bunch of little Toms and Callies running around, I settled down with my computer in the conference room at the opposite end of the big table from Harriet. She was buried deep in her work, eyes glued to the screen, her fingers making a steady clack-clack-clack on her keyboard.

Despite my distracted mindset, I soon found myself absorbed with my own work as well. I spent about an hour updating my database, typing in all of the information I had gathered thus far, particularly the rave reviews and comments I had received yesterday as I made the rounds of the charities that were supported by MORE. When I finished updating my records, I stood and stretched, glad that I had taken the time to go canoeing earlier in the morning.

"You getting hungry for lunch?" Harriet asked, looking up at me.

"Not quite yet," I said. "How about you?"

She shrugged.

"Maybe in a while," she answered. "I have some things I need to go over with you first."

"Sure," I said. "What's up?"

I pulled a chair down to her end of the table and then sat, listening as she reviewed her findings with me. As she talked, she pulled up figures on the screen and referred to printouts on the table, giving me an in-depth analysis of what she had found thus far.

Fortunately, she had nothing but good things to say about the MORE finances. She was also ready to sign off on the dental clinic and the Head Start program.

"What about Go the Distance?"

"It checks out fine, with one exception."

"What's that?"

"I'm just a little concerned about an expense item. They purchased a single vehicle last summer from Green Valley Motors for forty-nine-thousand-and-something dollars. If that's a company car, that seems like a bit much for a nonprofit."

"Yes," I said, "it does."

I tried to think of the vehicle I had seen Karen driving the day before. I couldn't remember the make or model, but it hadn't struck me as being particularly luxurious. In any event, I would check it out. Expensive company cars were an area of potential abuse in unethical nonprofits. On paper, nonprofit executives could list fairly low salaries and then hide their chief income through expensive side benefits—

things like fancy cars, travel for their family, and houses. I thought of one company in Maine that I had exposed just last summer, a camp for kids with disabilities. Turns out, one of the $60,000 camp buses was actually the camp director's brand-new Porsche. Suffice it to say, after that, I took a close look at every vehicle purchase.

"How about Su Casa?" I asked, thinking of the charity that built the migrant dorms.

"Su Casa is a problem," she replied. "I'm definitely seeing some red flags there."

She had my attention.

"There seems to be something odd going on between Su Casa and Hooper Construction," she added.

"The same people are involved in both places," I said. "Zeb Hooper and his son, Butch."

"Well, I'm afraid that Zeb and Butch just might be up to a little funny business. Either that, or somebody is keeping some awfully sloppy records."

"What's the problem?" I asked. "Please don't tell me they're taking money from one and putting it in the other."

I thought back to a case I had worked last September. Tom sent me to deliver a grant to a friend of his who headed up a hunger relief organization based in Philadelphia. In the end, it turned out that money was being siphoned from the nonprofit side of the business and poured into the for-profit side, raising some serious issues of legalities and ethics. After that, we were more wary than ever of companies that tried to run both types of enterprises simultaneously. Now whenever we had a for-profit and a nonprofit headed by the same management, we required an independent audit of both places before we would even begin the grant approval process.

"Let me show you," Harriet said. "It's hard to explain, but the problem stems from some donations that Hooper Construction made to Su Casa."

"Donations?"

"Look at this," Harriet said, pulling Hooper Construction's records up on the screen. "Last July second, Hooper Construction wrote a check to Su Casa for five thousand dollars, marking it in the books as a 'Donation.' "

"Okay."

"Now here's the entry in Su Casa's books, recording that donation from Hooper Construction, but instead of five thousand dollars, they've got it listed as *twenty*-five thousand dollars."

"What?"

She showed me the line entry, and though the date and the check number were the same, the amount was not.

"They did it again, over here, the January before. Again, Hooper Construction donated five thousand dollars to Su Casa, but in that instance Su Casa recorded it as a donation of *sixty*-five thousand dollars!"

"What do you think is going on?" I asked. "Is Hooper Construction trying to get a tax deduction on a bigger gift than they actually gave?"

"No," Harriet said. "That's what's so weird. If they were faking the amounts of their donations, then the figures would be reversed. Hooper Construction would be showing the larger amount and Su Casa would be showing the smaller amount."

"I'm so confused," I said, sitting back in my chair. "Why would Su Casa want to record a bigger donation than they are actually getting?"

Harriet put the books down, pulled her reading glasses from her nose, and looked at me.

"I've only got one guess, and you're not gonna like it."

"Try me."

"Well, usually when you see something like this, it's a sign of potential money laundering."

Twenty-Nine

Harriet and I worked straight through lunch, finally asking one of the secretaries to order something in for us so we wouldn't have to take the time to go out and eat.

Our process of elimination was simple. Since Su Casa had only been in business for two years, we went back and looked at every single donation of more than a few thousand dollars that they had received. Then we called each donor to verify the amount that had actually been given. In two years' worth of records, we found six bogus donations, with the overstated amounts totaling nearly three hundred thousand dollars. I began to agree with Harriet's theory that there was some money laundering going on.

"I wonder where the extra cash is coming from," I said. "What on earth could they be collecting money for in the boonies of North Carolina?"

To my mind, money laundering was usually associated with drugs or prostitution or—as in a case I had worked last fall—human smuggling. But I doubted anything like that could be going on here, and I wondered aloud how we could find out more about the principals involved.

I then buzzed Dean and asked him to come to the conference room. When he got there, I said that we were a little concerned about some things we had found in the records from Hooper Construction and Su Casa, and we wondered if he could tell us a bit about Zeb and Butch Hooper.

"What would you like to know?" he asked, pulling out a chair to sit at the table. "They're both friends of mine. Good men. Butch in particular. He's a deacon in our church and a real stand-up kind of guy."

"What about Zeb?"

"Well…" Dean said, his voice trailing off. "Let's see. I don't know Zeb as well. He kind of keeps to himself. I do know he was born and raised here in Greenbriar. His family was poor—very poor, from what I've heard. I think he grew up in an old shack on top of the mountain, sort of back behind Tinsdale Orchards."

"Above the high block?" I asked.

"Yeah, I guess. From what I understand, it's not much more than a crude cabin. I think it's still there, though it's probably abandoned now."

I tried to imagine Zeb as a young man, living above the orchard, always looking down the mountain at the Tinsdale spread in front of him. That had to have been difficult.

"Zeb Hooper and Lowell Tinsdale are about the same age, aren't they?" I asked. "I would imagine there's some animosity there."

"Oh, on the contrary. They were always the best of friends. Still are, far as I know."

"If Zeb was so poor," I said now, "how'd he get the money to start Hooper Construction? He's certainly not poor anymore."

"Gosh, no. He's done very well for himself. He's got a successful business, and between him and Butch, I think they own more property than anyone in this town."

"So where did the money come from to start the business?"

Dean was silent for a moment, and I sensed an undercurrent in his hesitation.

"What is it?" I asked.

"I don't want to gossip, Callie."

"I'm doing an investigation, Dean. It's not called gossip. It's called digging out the truth."

"I only know what I've heard. And it's just rumors."

"Every little bit helps," I said. "I promise you, it won't leave my lips unless it turns out to be true."

He exhaled slowly.

"Rumor has it that Zeb Hooper had one great love of his life. No one around here ever met her, but her name was Tatiana, or something fancy like that."

"Tatiana?"

"More importantly, she was a princess or something."

"A *princess?*"

"Yep. When he was a young man, he supposedly ran away to be with this Princess Tatiana. He came back a few months later with a hundred thousand dollars in his pocket and no mention of her ever again."

"Dean, that's the strangest story I ever heard."

"Yeah, I know. The rumor was that the princess' father must've paid Zeb off. Gave him money to go away and leave his daughter alone."

I sat back, wondering how on earth I could ever get more information about this. That just sounded too strange to be true.

"Was Zeb sad about it?" I asked. "Did he seem to grieve?"

"No, he came back to town a happy man. This was years ago, back before we moved here, but a lot of people know the story about Zeb Hooper leaving town poor and coming back rich. He never gave any explanation, just came home, bought the little construction company he'd been working for since high school, and changed the name to Hooper Construction. He obviously had a good head for business, because the place has done nothing but thrive ever since."

"When did Butch come along?"

"Zeb married a local girl a few years later, and they started having kids. The wife has since passed and both daughters got married and moved away. Butch was the only son and the middle child, I believe. Now he seems as successful at running the business as his daddy was. Maybe even more so."

I stood and began pacing while Harriet remained silent, taking everything in.

"Dean," I said finally, "I'm sorry to tell you this, but there's something funny going on with Su Casa's books. Financially, I'm afraid they're not going to pass our screening process."

"Well, if Zeb Hooper is operating his nonprofit in a way that's less than ethical, then we don't want to be affiliated with them anyway."

"That's what I was hoping you'd say."

Though I didn't want to allege money laundering out loud to Dean, I needed to know that MORE would be willing to remove Su Casa from their list of supported charities if we indicated there was a violation. Beyond that, there wasn't much for me to do except turn the information over to the necessary authorities.

I thanked Dean for his help and asked him not to say anything to anyone until we had more facts. Once he left the room, I got out my address book and made a phone call that would initiate asset checks for Zeb Hooper, Butch Hooper, Trinksie Atkins, and—since there was an irregularity with one of her expenditures—Karen Weatherby. If any of them had any excessive income or bank accounts or properties or stocks or whatever, I wanted to know about it. I thought about adding Danny Stanford to the list, but then I remembered that he had only been living here for a few months.

"This may be another case," I said to Harriet as I hung up the phone, "where someone has forgotten the 'non' in 'nonprofit.'"

Thirty

Harriet and I decided to table the problems we had uncovered for now. The asset reports would come back within 24 hours, and they would probably shed much more light on the subject. In the meantime, she still had work to do, and so did I.

There were a few criteria on my list that I thought I might be able to clear off fairly easily, so I set about doing that, starting with the principle that MORE should "pay salaries and benefits on a par with nonprofit industry standards." Harriet had already calculated the true salary breakdowns, including pay and benefits, for everyone who worked at MORE. All I had to do, then, was compare them with the amounts that people earned at similar agencies in the region. Fortunately, as expected, MORE was right in line for every single category, which meant that they had passed the criterion.

Next, I looked at the edict that MORE should "have an independent board that accepts responsibility for activities." I wouldn't be able to get to a board meeting while I was in town, but at least I could review previous meetings' minutes to see if the board handled matters in a tough, decisive manner or if they were simply "rubber stamps" for management. That I did, though I nearly fell asleep twice while reviewing the tedious notes. Once I had given the board my seal of approval for their procedures, I turned the information over to Harriet, who would make sure that no one on the board was financially profiting from their affiliation with MORE in any way.

Finally, to get a look at MORE's fund-raising practices, I called in their director of development and talked with him extensively about every fund-raiser they had done in the last two years. Though he would still need to go over some of the financials with Harriet, I felt that MORE would pass this criterion, "follows standards of responsible and ethical fund-raising," as well.

By 4:00 I was going stir crazy. I really wanted nothing more than to run down to the police station and find out everything that was happening with the Enrique Morales investigation—not to mention the related case of the stranger I had watched die a few nights before. Though I hoped the police had been able to trace out the man's expensive shoes and his watch, I felt that we would've heard something by now if, indeed, the John Doe had been given a real identity.

Thinking that there was one thing I *could* do, I shut down my computer and told Harriet I had some errands to run and would meet her back at the cabin later. She gave me a dirty look, but before she could speak, I said that if she waited until dark to drive up the hill, she wouldn't have to worry about the heights since she wouldn't be able to see the view anyway.

Once I left, and against my better judgment, I drove straight to Su Casa. My intention was to have a friendly little chat with Zeb Hooper. I wanted to see if I could get a bead on who he really was and what he could possibly be laundering money from. I stopped and bought a crumb cake on the way and decided to say I was just stopping by on my way home and thought I would drop off a friendly snack.

Unfortunately, Trinksie seemed to be the only one in at the moment. She was delighted with the crumb cake, however, and I watched as she helped herself to a large piece and gobbled it down right in front of me. When I asked where the others were, she said that Snake had run to town to get some light bulbs, and that Mr. Zeb would probably be coming in anytime. Danny had stopped by for a visit earlier, but he had gone back to work in the orchard nearby.

Trinksie seemed eager to gossip and I let her talk, knowing that anything she said might lead to a break in my case. I could tell that the mummy in the apples had gotten her quite worked up, and it interested me to listen to her conjecture. Apparently, rumor had spread that the mummy was probably the body of Enrique Morales, the missing migrant man.

"He was such a nice fellow too," Trinksie said. "I'd hate to think he ended up that way."

"Did you have many dealings with him?" I asked.

"Not really," she replied. "But he was nice to Snake. Enrique always had a pack of Juicy Fruit on him, and whenever he ran into Snake, he would give him a piece."

Trinksie talked about Snake, about his physical and mental condition. He had a very low IQ, she said, which meant he could do odd jobs and read and even get a driver's license, though he would probably never live on his own and had trouble handling money and making important decisions.

"Oxygen deprivation," Trinksie pronounced matter-of-factly. "The cord was wrapped around his neck when he was born."

"I'm sorry," I said. "That must've been very difficult for you."

"Not really," she replied. "Heck, I got six kids. Snake's the youngest and the only one who's still around to keep me company. I'd say that counts for something in this crazy world."

"It sure does."

"And he's a good boy. Everyone sorta treats him like their little brother."

"I've noticed that."

"He's got a good life. He cleans the parking lot over at Ingels on Thursdays and Fridays, he goes to Sunday school on Sundays, and he's even in a bowling league every Wednesday night."

"That's great, Trinksie."

When it became apparent to me that Zeb wasn't coming into the office after all, I finally extricated myself from the office and told Trinksie I would see her around.

I pulled the door shut behind me and gave a little start to see Snake in the parking lot, leaning against his blue Impala, smoking a cigarette.

He was wearing a dark shirt and a baseball cap, and instantly I thought of the person I had seen running through the woods on Sunday night. Certainly, he was the right height and weight. But was he capable of stabbing someone? He seemed so sweet and innocent.

Chills running down my back, I stepped out further toward my car.

"Hi there," he called out to me with a wave. "Y-you have a nice day now."

I waved back and kept walking to my car. As I drove away, I picked up the phone and dialed Detective Sweetwater.

"It's Callie Webber," I said when my call went into her voice mail. "I'm not sure, but I think I may have figured out who the person was that I saw running through the woods on Sunday night."

Thirty-One

My phone rang almost immediately after I hung it up. I answered to find that it was Dean, calling to tell me that the preliminary autopsy report on the mummy was in, and that it was definitely Enrique Morales.

"Listen," he said, "the medical examiner is a friend of mine. I told him you were investigating things for us, and he said he's willing to talk to you about the full report, if you want."

"Are you kidding?" I said. "Let me pull over, and I'll take his name and number."

As I hung up with Dean and dialed the ME's number, I stayed where I was, idling on the side of the road. The call went to an auto-mated answering system, but by pressing the man's extension I was able to get through. He said his name was Dr. Grant, and he was an old friend of the Webbers.

"Dean wanted me to bring you up to speed on the autopsy of this mummy," he told me. "It'll all be in the autopsy protocol, but he seemed to think you might want a verbal report ASAP."

He went on to talk about the body and his examination, and as he spoke I realized Dean may have fudged a bit. Apparently, this man thought I had some legal right to this information, either as the lawyer of record or as some sort of official investigator. Feeling just a tad guilty, I kept my mouth shut and let him talk.

And what he had to say was quite informative. Yes, the body was that of Enrique Morales; the dental records proved it quite conclusively. The body had been in apple storage for approximately four months, as suspected, and the unusual conditions of the room had served to mummify the corpse as it decayed. Cause of death was fairly certain at this point, though there were some abnormalities that were of enough concern that the body was being sent to Quantico for further examination and testing.

"What kind of abnormalities?" I asked.

"To put it bluntly, parts of the esophagus, the lungs, and the stomach are gone."

"Gone? What do you mean?"

"I made the standard Y-shaped incision, and when I cut down to the heart, those things weren't fully there."

"Were they surgically removed?"

"No. There was no incision front or back, and no other sign of external entry, either through the chest, the back, or the throat."

"Could it be a deformity of some kind?" I asked, feeling stupid even as I said it.

The doctor chuckled.

"Darlin', I've seen my share of irregularities, but I don't think anybody could live without lungs."

"So what's your conclusion?"

"Best I can figure, everything sort of dissolved postmortem."

"Dissolved?"

"Yes. I've been puzzling on this all morning. There's a little tissue damage to the lips, the tongue, and the soft palate, then more extensive damage to the esophagus, lungs, and stomach. I'm thinking this man died after ingesting some sort of caustic fluid in his lungs. Over the course of time, the fluid dissolved tissue away as it evaporated. By now, of course, the fluid has all evaporated away."

"Incredible."

He went on to say that, preliminarily at least, the opinion would show manner of death as homicide.

"If he'd been found with his head in a bucket of Drano," he said, "I might be inclined to believe it was an accident or even self-inflicted. But this body was buried in a box of apples. If I can figure out a way that a man could suck up enough caustic fluid to kill himself and then hide away in a bunch of fruit, I might change my opinion."

"Do you have any idea what the fluid was?"

"Oh, gosh," he said, "the list is endless. Could be acid, insecticide, bleach, detergent, you name it. 'Course, the sparkles only add to my confusion."

"Sparkles?"

"I'm sorry, did I leave that out? In what's left of the lungs and stomach, there are tiny flecks of sparkles, almost like glitter. I'll be analyzing them, of course, but it sure does seem odd."

Glitter. I tried to think where I had recently seen glitter. *At Go the Distance,* I realized. *In the art room.*

"Is there any way to narrow down what the liquid might have been?" I asked.

"We're working on it. We should know in a few hours."

"Have you written the report up yet?"

"I'm almost done. Shall I read you the opinion?"

"Please."

I could hear the click of a few computer keys, and then he started reading.

"It is my opinion that Enrique Morales, a thirty-eight-year-old Hispanic male, died as a result of the inhalation and ingestion of a caustic fluid. The cause of death was drowning. The mechanism of death was asphyxiation. The manner of death was homicide."

"Unbelievable," I said. "He drowned in something that ate away his insides."

"I have to say, this has been one of the most intriguing cases I've handled in a long time."

I thanked the doctor for his help, hung up the phone, and looked out the window at the gathering darkness. *Poor Enrique,* I thought sadly. *What a way to go.*

Thirty-Two

Lost in thought, I pulled back out onto the road and tried to decide what to do next. I remembered what Pepe had told me last night, that on the day his father disappeared, he had talked about going to speak with Lowell Tinsdale about something important. I decided to follow through on that and talk to Tinsdale myself. I toyed with the idea of talking to Pete Gibson instead, but something told me to go straight to the main man.

Enrique didn't know whom he could trust?

Well, neither did I.

It wasn't easy getting in to see Lowell Tinsdale. I had to stand my ground with a very stubborn nurse who insisted that the man had been worn out by the stream of police and reporters and other interested parties related to the processing of the crime scene and that my seeing him now was out of the question.

"Tell him I'm a friend of Karen's," I said, hoping that might do the trick.

With a huff, the woman told me to wait. A few minutes later she returned, much more subdued, and said simply, "He'll see you in the study now. Come this way."

I followed the nurse to a dark room with heavy furniture and drawn blinds. The only light came from a single lamp next to a low chair. In the chair was Lowell Tinsdale, his eyes closed, his head resting back against the seat. Strapped to his face, under his nose, was a clear plastic tube connected to an oxygen tank next to his chair. I sat across from him on a stiff leather bench and waited until the nurse left us alone.

"Can I help you?" he asked in a tired voice.

"Yes, sir," I said. "My name is Callie Webber, and we met yesterday, out by the storage—"

"Yeah, yeah, I know all of that. What do you want?"

"I have a question about the day that Enrique Morales disappeared. I need to know—"

"What does that have to do with Karen?"

I blinked, embarrassed.

"Nothing, sir. I said I was a friend of Karen's. I didn't say that had anything to do with why I wanted to see you."

He grunted but knew that, technically, I was correct.

"Are you a cop or something?" he demanded. "A reporter?"

"No," I said, hesitating. "I'm an investigator. A private investigator."

"A private investigator?" he said. "Who's paying you?"

"It's kind of complicated," I said. "I came here to research an organization, but my investigation ended up overlapping with this murder."

He opened one eye, peered at me for a moment, and then closed it again.

"Murder, huh?"

"Yes, sir," I replied. "I just got off the phone with the medical examiner. He's definitely calling the death a homicide."

I cleared my throat, trying to compose my first question. Before I could speak, however, he started talking.

"First of all the name's Lowell, not Mr. Tinsdale. Secondly, I've spent my whole day answering questions about Enrique Morales. What do you want me to say? He was a hard worker. He came back here year after year, always did the job, always stayed till the very end. Do I know why someone would want him dead? No. Have I got a clue how he ended up in storage? No. Do I know who killed him? No."

I scooted forward in my seat, wishing Mr. Tinsdale would sit up and look at me.

"Sir, some new information has come to light about Enrique's last day. As far as we know, the last person to see him alive was his son, Pepe. According to Pepe, when his father left him at lunchtime on that day, he was on his way over here to talk to you."

His eyes popped open.

"Me?"

"Yes, sir. Enrique was upset about something. He said he knew 'something he wasn't supposed to know' and that he was coming here to talk to you about it. The last thing he said to his son was, 'I'm not sure who I can trust.'"

"Well, I'll be."

Lowell seemed genuinely surprised.

"So did he? Did he come and talk to you that day?"

Lowell closed his eyes again.

"I can only tell you what I told the police. I was in respiratory failure at the time. I wouldn't have been willing or able to talk to anyone. Especially not one of the workers. I very nearly didn't make it through that bout alive."

I thought about that, decided to verify it, but assumed also that he was speaking the truth. Closing my own eyes, I tried to envision Enrique coming here to talk to Lowell and getting turned away at the door. Where would he have gone next? To see the foreman, Pete?

"I just never thought it would come to this," Lowell said softly. "Poor Enrique, murdered on my own property. When I kicked him out of here at thirteen, I should've told him not to come back ever."

"Sir?"

"Twenty years ago, when I found that boy kissing my daughter in the barn, I sent him packing. But he and his family showed up the next year for harvest, and he swore he'd stay away from her, so I let him stay. She was gone by then anyway. But he's been coming back every year since."

My head was spinning. The boy, the migrant that Lowell caught in the barn with Karen so many years ago, was *Enrique Morales?*

"I'm sorry," I said, shaking my head. "I knew that you caught Karen in a compromising position with a migrant. But I didn't realize it was *him*."

"Compromising position? Who told you that?"

"Excuse me?"

"They were just two kids. Fooling around. It's not like they had their clothes off or anything. Just innocent kisses behind the hay."

"Then why did you react the way you did?"

He thought about that for a moment.

"I was seeing red," he said finally. "Back then things were different. It wasn't considered proper for a white girl and a Mexican boy to be together…"

He let his voice trail off.

"You were afraid of what other people might think?"

"Hey, I'm not proud of it," he said. "But people weren't very open-minded, to say the least. Whites, blacks, Hispanics, there was no mixing. Especially not with my daughter on my property. It was one thing for her to play with those children and quite another for her to start some kind of romance."

"So you kicked him out and sent her off to boarding school."

"Don't think I haven't come to regret it over time. She would've gotten over that boy soon enough if I'd just let things take their natural course. Instead, I overreacted, jumped the gun, and lost my daughter in the process."

He looked into my eyes, and I realized he was speaking the truth. Judging from the pain and misery I saw in his face, this was a man who lived with a lot of regret.

Mustering what looked like the last bit of strength he possessed, he sat up, leaned forward, and pulled aside the curtain to look out at the sun setting over his apple trees. I could hear him breathing, even and hard, sucking the oxygen from the tube as if his very life depended on it—which it did.

"Zeb Hooper's been trying to buy this place from me for years," he said finally, dropping the curtain and falling back in his chair. "If I'd had any sense, I would have sold it to him and been done with it a long time ago."

Thirty-Three

A wave of exhaustion washed over me as I opened the door and stepped outside into the fresh air. Poor Lowell was so sick, it hung in the air around him like a damp, thick cloud. I had said goodnight and seen myself out, and now I simply stood on the stoop, taking in the last tiny glimmer of the sunset and trying to pull myself together.

Truth was, I liked the old guy. Despite his crankiness, despite his misguided past, I thought he had a sharp wit and a way of cutting through to the core that probably cost him a few friends but made for a straight-from-the-hip kind of fellow.

Taking a deep breath, I headed for my car, but before I got there, I heard a strange noise coming from the side of the house. Glancing around, I realized that the place was deserted, though a big spotlight mounted under the eaves kept the driveway from being too dark.

Whoosh! There it was again—an odd sound, like the breathing of a mechanical dragon. Senses alert, I took a few steps toward the noise to see if I could figure out what it was.

I didn't have to go far. Beside the house, next to the broken-down tractor, a man was standing in a circle of artificial light, welding a piece of metal with a blow torch. I couldn't see the man's face because of the dark protective face gear he wore, but I had a feeling it was the orchard foreman, Pete Gibson. I hesitated, wanting to speak with him but fearing he might in some way be dangerous.

"Callie?"

The torch fire disappeared as he flipped back the protective cover to reveal a red, sweaty face.

"Hey, Pete," I said, stepping closer. "You fixing the tractor?"

"Trying to," he said. "This has ended up being a major ordeal."

He put down the torch and removed the headgear completely.

"Were you in the house?" he asked. "With Lowell?"

"Yes."

"How is he?"

"Tired. Very tired."

He nodded, looking upset.

"How about a cold drink?" he asked. "I know I could use one."

Without waiting for my reply, he started walking away. Confused, I wasn't sure where he was going or if I should follow. I wanted to talk to him, but I had had something a little less isolated in mind—for example, in the middle of the day, surrounded by other workers. Here, we seemed to be the only ones anywhere around. Twilight had settled over the farm, and beyond the bright lights on the side of the house, it was getting quite dark.

Fortunately, I soon saw where Pete was going. There was a big white building about 50 feet away, some kind of oversized shed with a long, low porch across the front. On the porch, against the wall, was a red "Coca Cola" cooler the size and shape of a top-loading freezer. Glancing back at the house, I headed toward the cooler, getting there in time to make my selection while Pete held the heavy lid open.

"Wow, this brings back memories," I said, using the bottle opener mounted on the side of the cooler to flip off the top of my bottle.

"Yeah, it's a classic," he said. "'Course, these bottle tops can be twisted off nowadays, but I still like to do it the old-fashioned way."

He slammed the lid shut and surprised me by hoisting himself up onto it and sliding into a sitting position, his back against the wall.

"Join me," he said, so I turned around and did the same, ending up next to him on top of the cooler, looking back out at the driveway and the house. "I've had a heck of a day," he said. "It's nice to take a break and relax for a minute."

"Working late again?" I asked.

He took a long sip of his soda.

"I guess tonight I just didn't feel like going home."

"Where do you live?"

"Here at the orchard," he said. "I've got an apartment up over the main garage."

"That's convenient."

"Yep. It's mine for now, anyway."

We were companionably quiet, though my mind was full of questions. I wanted so much to ask him about Enrique and that last day, yet I wasn't quite sure how to approach the subject.

And actually, as I tried to think things through, I realized that just sitting there on the porch was kind of pleasant. The evening was cool but not cold, and fireflies lit the gathering darkness like tiny twinkling night-lights. There was a scent to the mountains I had always loved, an earthy, loamy smell that seemed to seep out of the ground and hover in the air every night at dusk. I rested my head against the rough wooden wall behind me and inhaled deeply, looking up at the black sky, trying to make out the silhouettes of the mountains against the backdrop of stars.

"You know," Pete said from his perch beside me, "before we found Enrique's body yesterday, my biggest worry was who you really were and why Karen sent you here. Now everything's changed. Life's too short. If she wants it, she can have it."

He took a long draw from his bottle, gulping the liquid down.

"I'm sorry, Pete," I said, "but I don't know what you're talking about."

He wiped his mouth with the back of his hand and stared out into the distance.

"Yeah, well, you'd have to say that, now wouldn't you? Don't worry, Callie. I'm not going to make trouble. If Karen's looking for a fight, she's going to be disappointed. That's what I told my lawyer this afternoon. Just let it go."

I let that sit between us for a minute, my mind racing. What did Karen want? Who did Pete think I was?

"Look, I'm afraid you have the wrong impression of me," I said. "I'm not sure what's going on here—"

"Yeah, right. I had my lawyer check you out, just to find out what you really were. A surveyor? An appraiser? Turns out you're an attorney. Big surprise."

"You had your lawyer check me out? Why? I told you who I was yesterday. My late husband was Bryan Webber, son of Dean and Natalie Webber."

He hopped down off the of the cooler and strolled to an open trash can filled almost to the top with empty bottles. He set his down on top of the pile and then looked at me, hands on his hips.

"Why did you come here to the orchard? Why did you ask Danny to give you a tour?"

"Because I'm interested in the migrants. I wanted to see what the migrants' work is like, how an orchard functions."

"Hah!" he said loudly. "So what does she plan to do? Wait until he's dead or start legal proceedings now?"

I swallowed hard, trying to get a handle on the situation.

"Pete, just tell me what you think is going on," I said. "Obviously, somebody, somewhere, has gotten their lines crossed."

"Do we have to play games on top of everything else? The will, Callie! Lowell's will! Karen's been gone for all these years, and now she's back, swooping in for the kill. Never mind that I've run this place single-handedly since he got sick. Never mind that I've been a good son to him since the day he took me in. Never mind—" his voice cracked, and I was surprised to realize that he was crying. "Never mind that I love him, and it breaks my heart that he's dying. He's the only father I ever knew, and he put me in the will because he loves me like I'm his own son. If she wants to fight me on it, then fine. Let her have it. Once he's dead, maybe I don't want to stick around here anyway."

He finished his speech and sat on the porch rail, his back to me. I felt strangely moved, and I had to fight the urge to go to him and put a comforting hand on his shoulder.

"It took staring death in the face, I guess," he continued softly. "Made me realize that there are things more important than owning a big house, owning some land. I'd rather spend what little time Lowell has left taking care of stuff around here and making him comfortable. The rest doesn't really matter, in the end."

I slid down off of the cooler and set my bottle on the recycle pile. Then I joined Pete at the porch rail and looked out over the driveway, exhaling slowly.

"Pete, if your lawyer had done a good job when he checked me out, he would've seen that my status as a lawyer has nothing to do with you. I work for a philanthropist. I investigate charities."

As clearly as I could, I explained to him I was an investigator for the J.O.S.H.U.A. Foundation, and we were hoping to make a substantial donation to MORE.

"I came to Greenbriar to verify their qualifications," I said. "Part of that includes getting a better understanding of the population they serve. That's why I needed a tour of the orchard. It had nothing to do with you or Karen. If your lawyer were really thorough, he would've realized that I don't even have a license to practice law in North Carolina."

He walked to the end of the porch and back, seeming to work things through in his mind.

"Is that the truth?"

"It is. I promise."

He went to the cooler and pulled out two more drinks, popped the tops on both, and handed one to me.

"Whew," he said, slipping up onto the cooler again. "I gotta have another one. Maybe Karen's not plotting against me after all."

I joined him back on the cooler and asked about the whole situation. According to Pete, he was very suspicious of Karen's motives in moving to town after ten years of being away, mainly because her return just happened to come several weeks after the changing of Lowell's will where he made Pete his sole heir.

"And don't think I didn't fight him on it," he said. "She's his daughter! No matter what's happened between them, she deserves some inheritance. I told Lowell to split everything down the middle, but he wouldn't hear of it. Now, with him trying to leave me everything, I'm afraid she'll contest the will and then I'll end up with nothing."

I suggested that perhaps she didn't even know about the will, that perhaps she had simply come back home in order to mend fences and make peace with her father. But Pete said that if that were the case, then why had she made no attempts to see the man since she moved back?

"Were you aware of Karen's past connection to Enrique Morales?" I asked, trying to guide the conversation into the area of the murder.

"What, that they were friends as children?" he asked.

"Well, yeah, and the whole barn incident."

"Oh, that. Sure. Lowell told me about it years ago."

"Then let me ask you a question," I said. "Do you think there's any way Enrique and Karen might have been having a relationship in the present day?"

He thought about that.

"No," he said finally, shaking his head. "Enrique was a real family man. He and Luisa were together all the time. Even if he'd wanted to have an affair, which I doubt, I can't imagine how he might have squeezed it in."

"Couldn't he have slipped away from the fields once in a while?"

Pete chuckled.

"Enrique had the highest picking quotas of any migrant worker we had. If he were taking time out for hanky-panky, then how'd he manage to pick so many apples? No, there's just no way."

I took a sip of my soda, feeling the carbonation tickle my throat.

"Tell me about Enrique's final day," I said. "Weren't you one of the last people to see him alive?"

"Apparently."

"So what happened?"

He sighed and settled a little more into the wall, his shoulder lightly brushing against mine.

"I've been over this with the police about a hundred times today," he said wearily. "The day Enrique disappeared, he and couple of the others were picking stragglers. We had finished picking the last of the apples in the high block the day before, and I needed him to go up there and do some clean-up work. I pulled Enrique from the line and told him what I needed him to do."

"Is that the last you saw of him?"

"No. Just before lunch, he asked if he could borrow the truck. He was real agitated. Said he'd left his lunch back at the dorms and Luisa had their car."

"Did you let him take the truck?"

"Yeah. Fifteen minutes later, I saw him coming back with his lunch."

"Did you speak to him?"

"He brought the keys into the office and tossed them on the desk. But we didn't speak. He seemed lost in thought, and I was busy straightening out a distribution problem."

"What then?"

"As far as I knew, he went back up to the high block to finish the job. The truck went around in the afternoon to gather the last of the apple bins. We put the bins straight into storage, never thinking there might be something funny about one of them. At quitting time, Luisa came and asked me where Enrique was. Turns out, no one had seen him since noon. She was concerned, but what could she do? When he still hadn't shown up a few hours later, we organized a search. The next morning, the police came and searched again. But we never found him, and no one ever saw anything suspicious."

"What did you think happened to him?" I asked.

Pete shook his head, holding his bottle with both hands.

"I didn't have any idea. I knew he loved Luisa and the kids, but the life of a migrant is a difficult thing. It has to get to them sometimes. I figured he skipped town. When that letter came a few weeks later, that confirmed it for me."

"I think the letter threw off a lot of people. The police included."

Pete nodded.

"So what do you think happened?" I asked softly. "Who killed him?"

"I have no idea," he said. "He was a nice guy, a hard worker. My best guess is that something happened by accident, and then someone tried to cover it up by hiding the body. People can do some mighty stupid things when their backs are against the wall."

I took a sip of my drink, thinking about the autopsy report and the missing lungs. It wasn't likely that Enrique's drowning in a caustic fluid had happened by accident.

Pete hoisted himself off the cooler and paced a bit in front of me.

"The thing that gets me," he said, "is why did I assume the worst about him? This hardworking, God-fearing family man, why was I so ready to believe that he would desert his wife and children? Do you know how many times in the last four months I've walked past that storage room door? Maybe a hundred. And it never occurred to me, not once, that his dead body was right there on the other side all along."

"You feel bad for doubting him," I affirmed.

"Yeah, I do. I feel bad for thinking the worst of a good man."

I finished my drink and climbed down from the cooler as well.

"You seem to do that a lot," I said. "Suspect the worst in folks. Me, Karen, Enrique. I'm surprised you haven't already tracked down the killer."

"Don't think I'm not looking at every single employee I've got, wondering, 'Could it be him? Could it be her?'"

I smiled.

"And?"

"And, so far, nothing."

"What about Danny?" I asked.

"What about him?"

"He seems an odd fit for an orchard. Maybe there's more to him than meets the eye."

"Danny's a good kid with a sad story," Pete said. "If you heard it, you'd understand why he is the way he is."

"Hmm."

"Plus, remember," Pete added, "he wasn't here back then. He never knew Enrique."

"What about Snake Atkins?"

"Snake? As the *killer?* That sweet kid wouldn't hurt a fly!"

"It was just a thought."

"No. No way. That's really grasping at straws."

"Ah, well," I said, taking my bottle to the recycle bucket. "It never hurts to explore every possibility."

I brushed my hands together before reaching into my pocket for my car keys.

"But on that note," I said, "I think I need to get going."

Pete nodded, taking a step back so that I could pass by.

"Well, speaking of exploring possibilities," he said, looking just a tad shy, "what would you think if I happened to ask you out on a date?"

My eyes widened.

"A date with the Fonz?" I cried, unable to help myself. "My inner preteen thanks you for this moment more than you could ever know!"

"That sounds like a thanks but."

"A thanks but?"

"Yeah, as in 'Thanks, but…'"

"Ah," I said, smiling at him, thinking he was even more handsome now than he had been at 19. "Thanks, but I'm involved with someone. I'm sorry. But I'm very flattered that you asked."

"That's okay," he said, leaning back against the porch rail and flashing me his million-dollar smile. "The best ones are always taken."

Thirty-Four

It was raining by the time I got to my car, a mist just heavy enough to require the use of the windshield wipers. Just to be safe, I popped the hood and looked inside, but there were no stink bombs or anything else unusual wired up inside. I closed the hood and got into the car.

"A date with P.J. the soda jerk," I said out loud to myself, grinning, as I drove away. A part of me wished I could call up my whole gang from way back when and let them know that he was still a hunk, he was still single, and he had actually asked me out. They'd all be green with envy, I felt sure.

Deep in thought about all that had transpired this evening, I drove up the mountain past rows and rows of apple trees, my car lights casting odd shadows in the tangles of leaves and branches. Just before the last rows of trees, I could see the parking lot for Su Casa, and then I drove up over the highest point on the mountain and started back down the other side. I was nearly to my house when I saw something along the side of the road to my left, and I instinctively braked, afraid it was a deer. What I saw, instead, left me startled and confused. I drove on, my mind racing, wondering what on earth Zeb

Hooper was doing at this hour walking up the mountain in the dark! I wouldn't have known it was him if not for the walking stick. The rain jacket he wore had a hood that obscured his face and shock of white hair.

I thought back to the other time I had seen him walking. He had been headed down the mountain yesterday morning. Now he was walking up, at night? I pulled into my driveway, parked the car next to Harriet's, and quickly got out. I thought if I went fast enough, I might be able to follow him.

Ignoring the drizzle, I ran out to the road and up the hill. I couldn't see Zeb up ahead, so I ran faster. Finally, as I reached the crest, I came to a stop, knowing it was no use. Bending over, gasping for breath, I thought that somehow the man had simply disappeared.

Disheartened, I walked back down the mountain, across my drive, and up the steps. As I swung open the front door, I was met with wonderful smells of tomato and oregano and garlic. Harriet stood at the stove, wearing an apron, stirring a big pot of spaghetti sauce.

"You're all wet!" she cried. "You didn't have another stink bomb, did you?"

"No," I said, "just a wild goose chase."

Harriet had already set the table, so I grabbed a towel from the bathroom and went on into the bedroom to change into dry clothes. Once I was dressed, I came back and took my place at the table. My mind was swirling with all of the events of the day, my brain simply overwhelmed.

What was Zeb doing going up the mountain in the rain, in the dark?

"This is so nice, Harriet," I said. "Do you know how long it's been since someone cooked for me?"

"Well, I'm no Betty Crocker," she replied. "But I do make a mean spaghetti sauce."

She said grace and then we ate, and I was glad to find that she was correct; despite her usual fare the spaghetti sauce was delicious.

"So what have you been out doing since you left the office?" Harriet asked. "Or do I really not want to know?"

"Nothing too shocking," I said, smiling. I told her about my talk with Lowell Tinsdale and then my conversation with Pete. Finally, I mentioned the strange comings and goings of Zeb Hooper up and down the mountain.

"Can you imagine what that's about?" I asked.

"Maybe he's a health nut and goes for a walk twice a day."

"Up a winding mountain road in the dark? I don't think so."

Harriet retrieved the telephone book and flipped through it until she found a listing for Zebulon Hooper.

"Okay, here he is," she said. "What's your address here?"

"Twenty-nine Mountain View Road."

"He lives at twenty-five. I guess that's below here? I'd be willing to bet he's got himself a lady friend. If he lives just below here and she lives above here, then what you're seeing is old Mr. Zeb taking himself a walk up to spend the night."

"That may be it," I said. "But you know as well as I do that the man's up to something."

"You mean the money laundering."

"Yes. He's got cash coming in from somewhere he needs to wash. We've just got to figure out what he's doing to generate that cash."

We tossed out ideas for illegal activities, but none of them seemed to fit the person or the area.

"Maybe he's an art thief," she said, "like a cat burglar. He goes out and steals—"

"Harriet," I interrupted. "We're talking about an older man. I don't think he's out doing anything very physical."

She continued to throw out other ideas, each more implausible than the next, while my mind worked with a conundrum that had been on my mind all day. Finally, at a break in her brainstorming, I brought it up.

"There is one thing about Zeb that's really been bothering me," I said.

"What's that?"

"The day I toured the orchard, he came there in his truck to buy a bin of apples, something he apparently had never done before."

"So?"

"So, who's to say he wasn't coming there to buy the bin that had the body in it?"

Harriet sat back, wiping her mouth with her napkin.

"Did he say why he wanted the apples?"

"To make apple wine," I replied. "I didn't even know there was such a thing."

"I think wine can be made from a lot of different fruits. Hey, maybe he has a still, out in the woods. He spends his nights up there, tending to it. Maybe he makes so much money selling hooch that he has to launder it through his charity!"

"Hooch, Harriet? Nobody makes hooch anymore, at least not illegally, for profit. I seem to recall that Prohibition ended about eighty years ago."

I gathered our dirty dishes and carried them to the sink.

"It was just a suggestion."

"I know," I said as I turned on the faucet and squirted soap into the dishpan. "We'll figure it out sooner or later."

I plunged a plate into the hot sudsy water. Sometimes my mind worked best when I was concentrating on other things.

"Hey, why don't we go do something fun tonight?" Harriet said, getting up from the table to put away the food.

"I'm not going line dancing," I said.

"There's no place to do that in town anyway," she said, sticking her tongue out at me. "But I saw a bowling alley. Or I bet we could find a movie theater."

"Sorry, Harriet," I said, "but I've got more work to do."

I also wanted to spend some time on the phone with Tom, though I didn't tell her that.

"What kind of work can you possibly do at this hour that would accomplish anything?"

"Internet research. It's time to hit some more of the criteria. I have some phone calls I need to make, too."

"Fine," she said. "But I'm tired of working. I guess I can watch a movie or something. You've got a pretty good collection here."

"I do?"

"Yeah, a whole cabinet full."

She crossed the room to swing open a door on the entertainment center, revealing several shelves of videos. I realized that they must've been bought and put there by the realtor in her efforts to make this place a more appealing rental unit.

"Well, there you go."

Harriet came back and finished putting away the food, and then she grabbed a towel to dry the dishes I had washed. We worked side by side in companionable silence and, again, I thought how pleasant it was to have someone with me. I loved my job enormously, but all the time I spent alone on the road was starting to take its toll.

"So, Callie," she said casually, and by the tone of her voice I could tell there was nothing casual about it, "now that you're dating Tom, has he told you what J.O.S.H.U.A. stands for?"

"No," I laughed. "That one's still a mystery."

"I think about it all the time," she said. "My best guess is that it's Just Our Secret Hidden Undercover Anonymous Foundation."

"Don't think so, Harriet."

"How about Jelly On Spaghetti Has Untold Aromas? Janie's Oversized Shoes Have Unusual Arches?"

"Hey, you're pretty good at this."

"Well? What do you think it is?"

"I don't know," I said. "I figure it's something religious, like Jesus Our Savior Hears Us Ask."

"Whatever it is, it's bound to be pretty cheesy. No wonder he doesn't publicize it."

While Harriet went back to the video cabinet and picked out a movie, I dumped the dishwater down the sink and wiped the table clean to set it up for my internet work. I figured it would take at least two hours to do all I had to do, but if I were successful, then I could scratch several more criteria off my list.

I tried calling Detective Sweetwater but got her voice mail again. I left another message and then went online. I was surprised to see an e-mail waiting for me from Tom, with the subject line "Call me." I clicked the letter open.

```
┌──────────────────────────────────────────────────────────────┐
│ □              Call me. - Message                        ▣ ▤ │
├──────────────────────────────────────────────────────────────┤
│ Reply   Reply All   Forward   Delete   << Previous   Next >>  │
├──────────────────────────────────────────────────────────────┤
│   From: Tom                                              ✉    │
│     To: Callie                                               │
│     Cc:                                                      │
│   Sent:                                                      │
│ Subject: Call me.                                            │
├──────────────────────────────────────────────────────────────┤
```

Hey, Callie, more phone problems here. I don't seem to be able to get through to you. Try calling me if you can. We need to touch base.

I'm happy to say I managed to wrap things up a day early, so I'm flying out in the morning. In the miracle that is the International Date Line, I will leave here, fly for many hours, and arrive in L.A. exactly one hour after I left Singapore on the same day! This time-change stuff never ceases to amaze me.

Since I have the extra time, I think I will stop at home and take care of a few things there, not to mention get some sleep and try getting over my jet lag. In any event, I should be heading your way by Sunday. As for where and how we will meet, watch for another e-mail between now and then, or I'll call you from California. I haven't quite worked out all the details.

In the meantime, try to finish up the case if you can, and be sure to make arrangements for Sal's care, since you won't be going straight home. Hope that's not a problem.

If you are not able to reach me by phone before I leave, just know I can't wait to see you and I am counting the minutes until we can be together. Work hard, get finished, and I'll call you from California.

Missing You,
Tom

I sat back in my chair, a slow smile curving my lips. No matter the problems and confusion here, he was still coming. We would finally be together in four days!

I got offline and headed for the bedroom to call him. Harriet was so absorbed in her movie that she didn't even notice. Hopefully, I would be able to reach him and hear the wonderful, calming sound of his voice.

Thirty-Five

Fortunately, I was able to get through without a problem. Tom said he was packing up some important files and papers in his office, and he would be leaving for the airport momentarily. I had no idea what kind of work he had been doing in Singapore, only that it involved a close-knit team of computer people and that the project was highly classified. He couldn't have told me about it even if he wanted to, though I doubt he would've wanted to. Talking about himself didn't exactly come naturally to him.

Today, however, he seemed a bit more introspective than usual. He sounded tired, and he said that he was so homesick right now he couldn't stand it.

"The problem is the idea of where home is," he told me. "Because I miss so many conflicting things. I miss my condo in California, where I have all of my stuff and where I can just relax and kick back. But I miss my family in Louisiana, and I miss the food there and my nieces and my mom. I miss the foundation in Washington and being involved with people there, going to meetings, helping the power brokers do their thing. Most of all, Callie, I miss you. I know we were only together that one time, but I miss seeing you, I miss being with you.

How do I roll all of this into one logical solution? Going 'home' means all of those things to me, but mostly it means going back to you."

"Then get back here to me. The rest we can do together."

I held my breath, knowing that was probably the boldest statement I had made to him yet. I wanted to be "home" to him, wanted to be the center point to which all of the other details of his life were secondary.

"That's kind of what I had in mind," he said. "I think it's time to lay the groundwork for our future."

"You do?"

"Yes," he said. "I do. I've been giving it a lot of thought, and I've decided that it might be best if you and I spent some time alone together first, really getting to know each other. I've been working out the details, and I think you'll be pleased with what I've lined up. Just have your bags packed by Sunday and await further instructions. I plan to whisk you away to somewhere very special."

"Ooo, now you've got me intrigued. Tell me about it."

"Nope, it's a surprise," he said, and I could hear the smile in his voice. "But you won't be disappointed."

"Tom, you could show up here wearing a burlap sack and carrying a box of pimento cheese sandwiches and I wouldn't be disappointed."

"Oh, darn!" he exclaimed. "How did you figure out my plan? Now I'll have to come up with something else!"

We laughed, but he refused to reveal anything no matter how hard I pleaded. I worried aloud that I might not have the proper clothes to wear, but he assured me that we could buy anything I lacked. As we talked, images filled my mind of the two of us in some glorious Hawaiian paradise: days basking in warm tropical breezes, sunset walks on the beach, dark nights under the stars…

It sounded wonderful, although those dark nights under the stars had me just a tad concerned. I was all for getting away alone, but I hoped he didn't assume my assent meant one room, one bed.

"I just…" I began, not knowing how to put it. "I don't want you to think that I, that we…"

"Say no more," he responded quickly. "I know where you're headed, Callie, and you don't need to worry. My intentions are honorable. Though that's not to say I don't fight thoughts of us…" He cleared his throat. "Its difficult not to think about it."

"I know," I whispered. "It is for me too."

"But this relationship is important to me," he continued, "and it needs to be worked out in accordance with God's Word. That's just how it is."

I closed my eyes, thanking the Lord for sending me such an amazing man. Bryan and I had shared a deep and passionate intimacy in our marriage, but I believed without question that sex was meant *only* for marriage and not outside of it—not even with the man of my dreams.

"For now, my dear, I've got to go. The airport awaits."

I told him to have a good flight and that I would try to wrap things up by Sunday. Once we hung up the phone, I realized that I never had told him about the investigation, the murders, or anything else that was going on.

Still, I felt good about the conversation that had transpired, and by the time I walked back out to the living room, my heart was soaring.

Thirty-Six

There was still a lot of work to do. Back at the computer, I pulled up my database and reviewed our progress thus far. Except for the problems with Su Casa, and of course the issue of the security violations that had gotten Luisa fired, I felt the investigation of MORE overall was winding down. Harriet still had some financial work to do, but basically between the two of us we had managed to satisfactorily cover every criteria except two: "is well rated by outside reporting sources" and "has a good reputation among its peers."

Considering MORE's black eye with the county, I expected to have a few problems with that last one. Nevertheless, I hoped to get enough good opinions to balance out the bad, and to that end I went online and worked on the last two criteria.

Ignoring the sound of Harriet's movie on the TV, I worked through every one of my reporting sources, from Guidestar and the Better Business Bureau Wise Giving Guide, to ECFA and Dunn and Bradstreet. MORE came out smelling like a rose, and I was especially pleased to see that the American Institute of Philanthropy Charity Rating Guide gave them a grade of "A."

For the final criterion, I sent out a number of e-mails to contacts in the industry, asking for references on MORE and any personal input they might be willing to give. In the morning, I would interview someone at the County Migrant Bureau, just to get their official opinion on record.

Before I went offline, I saw that the asset reports had already come in. I downloaded them to my hard drive, signed off the internet, and opened up the files.

I always loved asset reports, probably because they satisfied the snoop in me. I usually used an agency out of Tampa, and the profiles they put together for people I had an interest in were almost always dead-on accurate. I wasn't sure how they got some of their data, but there was no crime in my possessing the information, so I continued to depend on them to help me do my job—and tried not think of what it took for them to do theirs.

I looked at Karen Weatherby's profile first. According to the information in front of me, she had reported an annual salary of approximately $35,000 on her tax returns for the last three years. She owned no property, though she did have a small IRA, one savings account with $11,249 in it, and an excellent credit rating. There was a trust in her name, established at the age of 21 by her father, though it didn't look as though she had touched the money, which now totaled more than $500,000. Otherwise, she had no assets except her car, listed here as a 1999 Intrepid. This did not answer the question of the $49,000 vehicle, so I still had some work to do.

Trinksie Atkins seemed to be a study in near-poverty. Apparently, she had filed for bankruptcy last December, and now she had exactly $329.42 in her checking account. She had no savings account and did not own a home. She paid insurance on two vehicles—an old Toyota and Snake's ancient Impala.

Turning to Butch Hooper, I saw that his financial picture was a bit more complicated. He reported an annual income in the low six figures, and he seemed to own an enormous amount of rental properties in and around Greenbriar. Add to that his CDs, IRAs, a good bit of stock, and about $20,000 in savings bonds, and he was quite comfortable. There was nothing wrong with that, as long as it had all come from his for-profit business.

Butch's father, Zeb, presented a much more confusing picture. Though he seemed to own a lot of property as well, most of his was completely undeveloped and therefore generated no income. And though by all rights he should be as wealthy as his son—he was the one who founded Hooper Construction, after all—according to this he had a checking account with a few thousand dollars in it, a savings account with a few thousand more, and not another single asset except his home and his land. It made no sense. Unless he had a gambling problem or something, Zeb Hooper should be much more well-off than this record showed.

Of course, I thought, sitting forward, *there are always offshore accounts. Maybe he's stashing his money in Switzerland or something.* On a hunch, I dug out my address book and called one of my more unscrupulous contacts, a young computer hacker I knew in Seattle who was willing to provide almost any kind of information for a price. His particular specialty was unearthing credit card records.

"All I want to know," I said once I had gotten him on the phone and given him Zeb's information, "is if this guy has been taking any trips. I'm especially looking for trips overseas."

He agreed to see what he could find out and said for me to call him back in an hour or so for the results. As soon as I hung up the phone it rang, and I answered it thinking it was my hacker friend calling me back with a question.

Instead, it was Detective Sweetwater, following up on my voice mail messages from earlier, when I told her about Pepe's information regarding his father's comments on the day he was killed and also that I had a feeling I knew who the person was I had seen running through the woods. I switched to the phone in the bedroom, where we could talk.

"I'm sorry to call you so late," she said, "but with information that important, you should've asked someone to radio out for me."

"It was just a hunch, though," I said. "Based on a dark shirt and a baseball cap."

I described seeing Snake in the parking lot at Su Casa, and the feeling I had gotten when I looked at him.

"I'm sorry I can't be more certain that it was him," I said. "But I just wanted to suggest that you might want to look in his direction."

"All right," she said. "Thanks for the tip."

"Have you gotten an ID on your John Doe yet?" I asked.

"Not yet," she replied. "And now things are complicated by the Morales murder."

"How is that going?"

"Not well. It's a little hard to follow a trail that's four months old."

"I might have some relevant information for you," I said. "Though I was hoping to wait until I had my proof a little better organized."

"By all means, jump right in," she said. "I can use all the help I can get."

I explained to her that our financial investigation of MORE had turned up some irregularities with Su Casa. It appeared as if someone there might be using the organization as a front for laundering money.

"I don't know what that might have to do with Enrique's murder," I said, "except that their building is located near where he disappeared. Also, Snake works there part time. Tenuous connections I know, but still."

"You have proof of this money laundering?"

"Sort of. To really investigate, you would need to pull cancelled checks, bank records, and all of that. But we have enough information to justify an investigation. The authorities would have to take it from there."

She was quiet for a moment, obviously mulling that over.

"There's a guy in Asheville who handles white-collar crime," she said. "I think I might defer to him in this. Could you meet with him tomorrow and show him what you have?"

"He'd do better to sit down with my associate, Harriet. She's the financial whiz on my end who uncovered this."

The detective took Harriet's cell phone number and said she would be putting her man in touch. When we hung up the phone, I went back into the living room, joined Harriet wearily on the couch, and told her to expect the man's call.

Thirty-Seven

How I found myself at the Greenbriar Lanes Bowling Alley a half hour later is another story. Somehow, in my conversation with Harriet, I realized I could do something the cops couldn't do without a warrant—I could poke around a bit for further proof that Snake was tied in with the vandalism on Luisa.

Consequently, Harriet and I ended up cruising the bowling alley parking lot, looking for Snake's car. On the one hand, Harriet was not at all happy about being involved with the physical part of my investigation. On the other hand, she was feeling wired up and glad to get out of the house.

She was driving, and we both rolled down our windows, peering through a misty nighttime fog for the vehicle in question.

"You said it's a light blue Impala?"

"Yeah. You see it?"

We drove slowly up the parking aisle and passed directly behind Snake's car. There was no question it was his. The bobble-headed Chihuahua peered out at us from the back dash.

"Circle around again," I said softly, pulling on a pair of gloves.

She did as I instructed, but this time I had her stop before we got to the car. I hopped out and then she slowly drove on past, using her car to provide cover as I walked to the Impala and easily jimmied the trunk. I leaned inside for less than a minute before slamming the trunk and jumping back into Harriet's car.

"Okay, go, go," I said, and so she increased her speed just a bit and went back around the parking lot one more time.

"Well?" she asked.

"Well," I said excitedly, pulling off my gloves. "I was right. He has an emergency auto kit in the trunk, and the kit contains flares."

"And?"

"And it has slots for four flares."

"And?"

"And one of the flares is missing. My guess is that was the flare that was used to start the fire at Luisa's trailer."

We gave each other a high five and then she found a parking spot at the end of the row and pulled to a stop.

"Okay, Callie," she said, grinning. "I gotta admit, in a way it's kind of fun doing things just a little bit outside of the law."

"I'll make a real detective out of you yet, girlfriend," I said, giving her another high five.

"So tell me again," she asked, "why are we going inside?"

"Because I want to know the 'why' behind the 'what,'" I said.

"Okay," she replied, rolling her eyes. "That explains everything."

We went into the bowling alley, surprised to see that it was nearly full even at 11:00 on a Wednesday night. Smells of popcorn and musty carpet and dirty feet permeated the air, that odd odor unique to all bowling alleys. Beyond the smells were the sounds, the thunderlike roll of the balls down the lanes, the ping of the pinball machines along the wall, the electronic beeping of the digital scorecards.

"Hey, it looks like ol' Greenbriar has kept up with the times," Harriet said, admiring the computerized setup that complemented each lane. We walked over to the front counter and started untying our shoes.

"League play only, until midnight," the bored girl behind the counter informed us. Harriet and I looked at each other.

"Is the snack bar open?" I asked.

"'Til we close at one," she said.

We tied our own shoes back on and strolled along the backs of the lanes to the snack bar, where we purchased two sodas and an order of fries that neither of us wanted.

Fortunately, the eating counter inside the snack bar looked out over the bowling lanes. We sat, ate, and observed the whole place, which was definitely hopping.

Every lane was filled with a team, and each team member was wearing a matching shirt with a company logo on the back. It didn't take long to find the group we were looking for: Hooper Construction, all in yellow.

They were in the second-to-last lane on the left, and the team members were Butch Hooper, Snake Atkins, and two other men I didn't recognize. Zeb Hooper was not among them.

From what I could tell, they were all pretty good bowlers except for Snake, whose every third or fourth roll went into the gutter. Still, they all seemed to be having a good time, and it looked as though Snake was a welcome, accepted member of the group despite his lack of proficiency with a bowling ball.

"So how do we do this?" Harriet asked once our fries were gone and we had drained the last of our sodas. "Should we stroll over there and say hello?"

"Give it another minute," I said. "It looks like they're about to take a break."

Sure enough, soon three of the four men began heading toward the snack bar.

"Well, hello, Callie!" Butch said when he saw me. "I'm surprised to see you here tonight."

"Yep, we were out looking for something to do, and this was the only place that seemed to be jumping."

"Oh, yeah," he laughed. "Bowling is big in Greenbriar."

I introduced Harriet, and then Butch introduced Snake and the other men.

"I thought you needed five to make a team," I said.

"Yeah, Pete couldn't make it tonight, so we're bowling blind."

"Bowling blind?"

"When you're short one but you don't wanna forfeit the game, you put the missing guy's name down and he gets an automatic hundred and fifteen points."

"What's Pete's usual score?"

"Around two hundred, so his not being here really hurts us."

"Pete didn't come because he's sad about Enrique," Snake told us. "He said it's 'cause he wasn't feeling well, but that's not true. I know the real reason. He's just sad."

The other men looked embarrassed, but I smiled at Snake encouragingly.

"I think everybody's sad about Enrique," I said. "So I guess we can't blame Pete one bit, can we?"

I managed to give Harriet a quick glance, and she knew what I wanted her to do. She needed to distract Butch and the other man so I could speak to Snake by myself.

"So, what's your shirt say?" Harriet asked Butch, turning on the charm. "Hooper Construction? Is that your company? Because I'm thinking about building a little vacation house…"

"Hey, I think I'll get more soda," I said to Snake. "You want some too?"

The two of us went to the counter and I asked for a refill. I pulled out my wallet and flashed my cash so that Snake would see it.

"Can I buy you something to eat?" I asked. "Something to drink?"

"Sure!"

He ordered a chicken basket, a side of onion rings, and an extra large Coke.

"Too bad you can't bring food out to the lanes," I said, hoping he and I would able to sit in the snack bar and talk while the rest of his team played their next round.

"They got a little table right behind every lane, so you can eat and bowl at the same time."

"Oh. Good."

We made small talk while we waited for his food, though with Snake it was rather like making conversation with a young teenager.

"So tell me more about Enrique," I said as we stood at the counter. "Your mom told me you were friends."

"He always gave me Juicy Fruit," Snake agreed, nodding.

"Are you friends with his whole family?"

Snake grew visibly agitated, playing with the leather thong of beads that hung from his belt.

"I don't…I don't really know his wife or his little girl."

"What about Pepe?"

"Pepe and his friends used to pay me," Snake said mischievously, looking around and lowering his voice. "To do something they couldn't do."

I leaned in close.

"What's that?" I whispered.

"I bought cigarettes for them. 'C-cause they were minors but I'm not. I'm legal."

"I bet you buy cigarettes for a lot of the boys in town."

"No, but sometimes they get me to buy their beer. They say, Snake, old buddy, could you buy us some beer?"

"Do you do it?"

"Nah, 'cause I got caught. I got in big trouble. So now I don't do that no more."

"Aren't you afraid you'll get in trouble for buying cigarettes?"

"No, 'c-cause I smoke too. So everybody just thinks I'm buying them for me."

I nodded, wondering how to take this conversation where I wanted it to go.

"You know," I told him softly, leaning toward him, "I know a secret about Pepe's trailer."

"What?" he asked, coming in even closer.

"You know the fire they had there the other day? Well, you're not going to believe it, but somebody set that fire on purpose."

He jerked up straight, looking as guilty as if I had caught him with the gasoline can in his hands.

"So why do you think someone would do something like that?" I asked.

"Dunno."

"Starting a fire is a dangerous thing. But whoever set this fire did it very, very carefully."

"Very carefully so they wouldn't get burned. Just like they were told."

"That's right. My problem is, I just can't imagine why someone would do something like that. It's so *mean*."

"It's not mean if it's a prank."

"Setting a fire isn't a prank, Snake. It's serious."

He stepped away from me, his body nearly vibrating from the tension.

"It's a prank if they have to do it for their initiation," he said finally.

"Initiation?" I asked. "Like, a club?"

"Yeah, I guess setting fires and lighting stink bombs and things doesn't really hurt anybody. And then they can earn their beads. Or…or whatever."

I looked at him. He was still nervously fiddling with the thong on his belt. I remembered it from before—single strip of leather about six inches long, and at the end hung about eight plastic beads.

Snake's rattler.

The noises of the bowling alley pinged and rumbled all around us, and from across the kitchen I could see the counter person headed our way with Snake's food. My mind raced, wondering what to do with these last few seconds of conversation.

"How about if someone gets stabbed?" I said. "That's not a prank."

"I don't know anything about that!" he cried. "Just do your job and shut up. Just do your job and keep quiet."

"Who told you to keep quiet, Snake?"

He shook his head.

"Who gives out the beads?" I asked, trying again.

"I can't tell you," he said. "If I tell, I'll get stabbed too, just like that guy."

"Here you go," the waitress said, sliding the tray to Snake. I paid for the food and told her to keep the change, eager for her to leave.

"This is none of your business, okay?" Snake said, on the verge of tears. "Leave me alone."

He stomped off like a terrified child, carrying his food to the table near the lane.

I watched him go, wondering what to do next. I didn't want to push him too far, but there was more to say.

Harriet was already down by the lane, deep in conversation with Butch about her imaginary vacation house. I walked down there myself, watching as the men seemed to wrap up their conversation so they could start their next game.

"I'm gonna bowl an outhouse!" Snake cried, biting into an onion ring, seeming to already have forgotten our conversation. "Gonna bowl an outhouse!"

I looked questioningly at Butch, who smiled.

"A score of one hundred eleven is called an outhouse. It's Snake's favorite score."

Butch picked up his ball from the queue and stepped onto the shiny wood floor of the lane. As he prepared to roll, I leaned down next to Snake and spoke in his ear.

"Why would you want to be in a club," I whispered, "with someone who threatened to kill you?"

He glanced at me and then shoved his mouth full of onion rings. When he couldn't shove in any more, he simply started shaking his head. Then he put both hands to his mouth, held it tight, and shook his head back and forth, back and forth as fast as he could.

"Okay, buddy," I said, one hand on his shoulder, patting him until he calmed down. "That's okay. You don't have to tell me right now if you don't want to."

Thirty-Eight

I called the police station from the car as Harriet drove us home, and despite the late hour, I insisted that Detective Sweetwater would want to talk to me. She called me back just a few minutes later, sounding as if they had roused her from a deep sleep on my behalf.

"What is it Callie?" she asked.

"I just had a conversation with Snake Atkins," I said. "You need to bring him in—both for questioning and for his own safety."

"Give me a reason," she said, sounding much more awake. "What have you got?"

I explained to her what I had learned, that someone had created a "club" and told Snake that if he performed certain "pranks" he would be initiated into that club.

"The club symbol," I said, "is a leather thong he wears on his belt. My best guess is that every time Snake pulls one of these pranks, he gets a bead to put on that thong. Apparently, once he's earned enough beads, he'll become a full member of the club."

"Do you think there is such a club?"

"No. I think someone took advantage of the whole 'snake' angle and invented it just for him. I mean, what could be more appealing to that kid than to earn his own 'rattler'? He's easily duped, apparently, but I'm afraid he's in way over his head on this one."

"Did he stab our John Doe as one of his pranks?" she asked.

"No, but the person who did told him if he said a word about it to anyone, he would be stabbed too. I feel certain he was a material witness to that crime."

The detective thanked me for the information, and I told her there was one more thing, that they would probably want to get a warrant for Snake's car because in his trunk they would find some road flares that might match the one that started the fire at Luisa's trailer.

"I'm not even going to ask you how you know that," the detective said.

She thanked me again for my help, and I hung up the phone.

Though I ought to be exhausted by now, I was running on a second wind. When we got home, I called back my hacker friend in Seattle and asked him if he had been able to come up with anything on Zeb Hooper's travels.

"I'm sorry, Callie," he said. "I found some pretty good credit card records, but as far as I can tell, he hasn't been out of the country—or if he has, he didn't pay for it with plastic."

"Not even the Caribbean?" I asked, thinking of the Bahamas or the Caymans.

"Nope. The only tickets I've seen are flights from Asheville, North Carolina, to Laguardia."

"New York?" I asked. "Can you give me dates?"

He read off what he had, and my heart was pounding as I hung up the phone.

"Harriet!" I said, interrupting her as she was brushing her teeth.

"What?"

"Do you have the Su Casa records here with you?"

"No," she replied, pausing to spit toothpaste into the sink. "They're down at the office."

"Can you remember the dates of any of those big cash deposits?"

She finished brushing her teeth, thought for a minute, and then said, "Just two: January tenth and July second of last year."

I looked at the dates I had written on the pad in front of me: Zeb Hooper had gone to New York City on January 8 and July 1 of last year. My guess was that he was either delivering something or selling something and then coming back home and depositing the money in the bank, laundering it through Su Casa.

The question was, what on earth could that something be?

Thirty-Nine

After a night spent tossing and turning, I was up by six the next morning. Sitting up in bed, I decided it was just as well. There was some exploring I wanted to do, and I'd be better off doing it early in the morning before anyone else might be around to see me.

I threw on some clothes, left a note for Harriet, who was still asleep, and headed out to my car. The morning was chilly, and I was glad I had worn a sweater. I had the key in the ignition, ready to turn, when a movement in the rearview mirror caught my eye. Snapping my head up, I realized that someone was just walking by on the road, whistling softly to himself as he went.

It was Zeb Hooper! I froze, feeling fairly confident he wouldn't notice me unless he specifically turned to look inside my car. Sure enough, he walked on by, his gate slow and steady. Once he was past, I quietly opened my car door and climbed out. Then I stuck to the tree line and crept across the muddy ground to the road, watching his back as he continued down the hill to his own home. As he went, I noticed that his clothes were filthy. Once he turned into his driveway, I knew there was nothing more to see. The mud under my feet gave me an idea, however.

Sure enough, along the shoulder of the road, right where he had been walking, his footprints remained, deep indentations in the mud. Without hesitating, I decided to take a little walk myself, in the opposite direction of the footprints, to see where they had come from.

The prints led me up past two more houses and around a curve toward the crest of the hill. When I was nearly to the top, I was surprised to see that the prints simply veered off into the brush beside the road.

They led to an empty lot filled with bushes, weeds, and kudzu blocked by a barbed wire fence and posted with several bright yellow "No Trespassing" signs. Bending over, I studied the footprints in the mud, noting that it looked almost as though he had simply walked right through the fence! I stepped closer and studied the wire, and I soon realized there was a latch on the fence post. By unhooking it, I was able to swing the wire in easily, step forward, and then close it behind me. Looking around to make sure I wasn't being observed, I carefully continued to track the prints on the ground. To avoid leaving prints of my own, I tried stepping on leaves and grass.

Soon, however, I lost the trail. The ground was higher here, and a bit rocky, and there just wasn't enough mud to make tracks. I stood where I was, looking ahead and side to side. As far as I could tell, I was in the middle of nothing, a bit of woods along the road with absolutely no indication of a home, a trail, a stream, or anything else except kudzu and rocks and trees.

Disappointed, I let myself out of the fence and walked all the way back down to my car. I decided that tonight, when Zeb Hooper took his walk again, I would be ready for him. I was going to track him in person this time and see which way he went once he reached this point.

Eager to keep moving, I got in my car, drove over the top of the mountain and just a little bit back down the other side. From what I remembered, there should be a street coming up on the left, a gravel road.

I turned onto it and drove a short ways, bouncing in the ruts and the mud. Afraid I might get stuck, I finally pulled over to the side and turned off the car. The rest I could do by foot. I got out and set off at a slight jog down the road, hoping I didn't have far to go. Eventually, the house showed up on the left, a tiny run-down shack that definitely looked deserted.

Zeb Hooper's boyhood home.

I wasn't sure what I was looking for, but my suspicion was that Enrique might've been murdered in that house. It was back behind the high block, and though the police had given it a cursory going-over during their initial search for Enrique, I wanted to take a second look. I had to wonder if someone had lured Enrique in there, killed him, and then brought the body back down the hill just a short ways to where a bin sat full of apples, waiting to be picked up by the truck. There, the killer or killers hid the dead body down in the apples, and later that same day it was moved into storage, no one the wiser.

I stepped from the road onto the overgrown lawn, but as soon as I did, three wild dogs flew out from under the porch and started racing toward me, yelping and snarling. Heart pounding, I moved backward, my mind racing for some sort of defense. I thought the dogs were being territorial and that they might stop when I reached the road. But they kept coming, teeth bared, barking furiously. I scooped up a handful of gravel and threw it at them, but they didn't stop.

Finally, I turned and began running, the smallest and nastiest of them nearly latching onto my ankle as I went. I knew I couldn't outrun them to my car, so I angled across the road to the woods on the other side and then simply jumped into the trees, grabbing for a branch and trying to swing myself up onto a limb. It didn't work. My hands slipped and I fell—but I fell far and hard, because the ground slanted steeply down at the base of the trees. When I hit the ground, I rolled another ten feet down, grabbing for something to hold on to, ripping kudzu vines as I went. I came to a stop beside a pile of stones, sat up, and began throwing the rocks up at the dogs, who were standing on the edge of the precipice, barking and growling down at me.

When a rock connected with one of them, its growling turned into yelps of pain. I kept throwing and they kept growling, but then finally, slowly, one by one they gave up and went away. When I knew they were gone, I collapsed fully onto the ground, and only then did I begin to tremble.

Gingerly, I ran my shaking hands along my legs and then my arms, checking for injuries. Though I had some nasty cuts and scratches, none of them were bleeding very badly, and I didn't think anything was broken. Knees wobbling, I slowly stood and got my bearings, brushing leaves and twigs and vines from my clothing. I turned and looked around to see that I was on the high block of Tinsdale Orchards, at the very back. I decided to call Harriet and have her pick me up at the road and drive me back to my car. With those dogs still up there, I wasn't taking any chances. Fortunately, Harriet was still at the cabin, just putting on her makeup, and she said she could come as soon as she got dressed.

I reached the highway before she did, so I found a big rock near the trees and sat, still feeling jumpy and growing more achy by the minute. As I waited there beside the road, I looked at the neatly tiered farmland in front of me, the endless rows of apple trees broken only by the sloping black roof of the small Su Casa building that jutted away from the hillside on the next tier down.

Su Casa.

Rubbing a sore elbow, I thought of all I knew about Su Casa. Like a bunch of tiny threads weaving through an ugly tapestry, it kept appearing throughout all of the bad things that had happened here. Snake—who was being duped into vandalism—worked at Su Casa. Zeb Hooper—who was probably laundering money—was doing it through Su Casa. Enrique—who was found dead in a box of apples—disappeared somewhere neared Su Casa. I sat up, the hairs on arms rising.

Enrique must've seen something, I realized. Whatever Zeb Hooper was doing to bring in money, Enrique must've stumbled across it. His cryptic conversation with his son, Pepe, must've been about that, about what a man should do when he knows something he's not supposed to know and can't decide whether to tell or figure out whom to trust.

I stood and looked at the building below me, wondering what secrets it held inside. Did Zeb Hooper kill Enrique Morales? If so, what was it that had been worth killing for?

Harriet showed up then, pulling to a stop with her eyes wide.

"Callie!" she exclaimed. "What happened to you? You look like you went to the mat with a rabid squirrel—and the squirrel won!"

I got in and directed her to my car, explaining as we went. Feeling bruised and frustrated and itchy, I climbed into my vehicle, turned it around, and drove back home, theories bouncing around in my head like popcorn.

Once there, I called the Webbers' house, and Dean answered the phone.

"I have a quick question about last fall," I said to him. "I know when Enrique disappeared, a search was made of the orchard. Can you remember if anyone looked inside the Su Casa building?"

"They couldn't look inside," he said. "It wasn't built yet."

"What do you mean?"

"Well, it was under construction at the time. It was just going up."

"Just going up? Su Casa isn't a new charity, Dean. We've been going through several years of records for them."

"No, the charity isn't new, but the facility is. Su Casa used to operate as a separate business right out of the Hooper Construction building. But last year Butch talked Lowell Tinsdale into donating some land so that they could build a separate facility just for Su Casa. As I said, at the time when Enrique died, that building was just being built."

"Can you recall how far along the construction was at that point? I mean, was it just a cement slab or had it been framed out or what?"

He hesitated for a moment.

"Oh, goodness, Callie, I don't remember exactly. Hold on."

I could hear him talking with Natalie about it, and then he came back on the line.

"From what we can recall," he said, "the cement foundation was definitely in and a little of the framework was up, but not much. The materials were all there, though, because I can remember we spent some time checking behind stacks of plywood and bales of shingles and things when we were first searching for Enrique. Seems like the back wall was built already. The building sits right against the hill there, you know, so that whole section was done with cinderblocks, if I'm not mistaken. But the rest of it wasn't up yet, except maybe for the main beams."

"Okay," I said. "That's what I needed to know."

We got off of the phone, and I was glad I had a clearer picture now of the lay of the land when Enrique was killed. I decided to keep playing with the idea that he had seen or heard something he shouldn't have, and that was why he was killed.

I climbed under the pounding water of a hot shower, thinking that it didn't matter how many credible—or incredible—theories I could come up with. There was only one real truth about what had happened to the man. The hard part was digging through all of the lies to get to it.

Forty

My head seemed clearer once I was clean and dry. I treated my cuts and scrapes from the first aid kit I found in the medicine cabinet, grateful that at least my face had been spared. Once I was dressed for the day, my injuries barely showed.

Harriet had wanted to get an early start and had already left for the office. In the quiet of the cabin, I made myself a simple breakfast of poached eggs, whole wheat toast, and hot tea. As I sat at the kitchen table and ate, I thought about my plans for the day. My first stop would be the County Migrant Bureau over in Marwick, where I would interview the director and get his opinion of MORE. I already expected it to be unflattering, considering the snafus that had happened last fall with Luisa.

From there I needed to drop in on Karen Weatherby at Go the Distance. My reason for going was to find out about the expensive vehicle she purchased from the car dealer. But I also hoped to broach the subject of her and Enrique and their entangled past while I was there.

Finally, I was most eager to talk again with the medical examiner, since some of his tests should be back today. Between the corrosive chemical and the sparkles in the lungs, I was dying to know what new conclusions he had been able to draw about Enrique Morales' body.

When I finished eating, I put my plate and cup into the sink and hit the road, driving down the mountain and out of town so that I reached the County Migrant Bureau by 9:30. The interview went along about as I had expected. Yes, they had worked closely with MORE, but no, the agency did not have a clear record with them.

"We weren't too happy with the incidents that happened last fall," the county agent said to me. "But it wasn't enough to pull the plug. And they are serving a vital function over there."

I took notes from our conversation, writing "vital function" and underlining it several times.

"It all boils down to shoddy controls," the man said several times. "If you've got shoddy controls, all kinds of bad things can happen."

Of course, a part of my investigation had taken into account the office's controls, and—except for Ellen Mack putting the passwords in her Palm Pilot—I knew they weren't shoddy at all. At least no other, unexpected problems had popped up; except for the two blights on their record from last fall, the agency was clean. Unfortunately, it would take a while for Dean and Natalie to rebuild MORE's reputation with this man and his office. Hopefully, solving the crimes related to Luisa would help repair the damage that had been done.

Glad to get that over with, I turned up the radio loudly and sang along as I drove back through the mountains, back toward Greenbriar. Despite everything that had been going on, I felt myself slipping into a wonderful mood. I had a feeling it had to do with the breathtaking scenery that surrounded me on every side. Once I reached the lake, I felt as though I had died and gone to heaven. Oh, how I had missed the Smokies! Looking out at the deep green of the hills and the sparkling blue of the water, I tried to compare the beauty of this place to my home on the Chesapeake. The two were very different, yet I loved them equally.

Since I was driving back to town along the lake highway, on a whim I decided to make one quick detour before arriving at Go the Distance. I found the road to Camp Greenbriar easily, turned into the camp, and drove about a quarter of a mile. As I had expected, the place was closed up for the season, and I pulled to a stop at a chain that blocked the road. I decided to leave my car there and get out and walk the rest of the way, though I was still feeling a bit edgy from the morning's encounter with the dogs. I unzipped the bottom compartment in my purse and retrieved a small bottle of mace that I kept there. I clutched it in one hand, and with the other I grabbed a big stick from the side of the road. Thus armed, I felt more confident as I walked into the deserted camp.

When I reached the main compound, I was surprised to see that a number of things had been changed, and I remembered Natalie telling me the place had been bought out by a management company a few years ago and that it had undergone some extensive renovations. From what I could see, the improvements included a big new main building, some tennis courts, and even a swimming pool. Peering through the trees, it looked as though they had added some extra cabins as well.

I headed for the lake, which was pulling at me like a magnet. The walkway was covered with dry, dead leaves, and I crunched through them toward the water.

I reached the small sandy beach area first, and I walked down to the edge of the lake and bent over to dip my fingers in it. Despite the warm March day, the water was still quite cold. Standing, I looked around to see, on the other side of the dock, the empty racks where the canoes would go once the camp opened back up for the summer.

The dock had been rebuilt and improved since my Camp Greenbriar days, but it was still in the same location, halfway between the beach and the boats, jutting about 30 feet into the water. I walked out and stood at the end, gazing at the gorgeous scenery in front of me. Then I turned around to look back at the shore. This was the very spot where Bryan and I had said goodbye to each other at the end of our first summer together, the year that we were 16. Smiling now, I thought back to the dramatics of it all. After six weeks of being together almost every single day, I didn't think I would be able to survive a whole year without him. How I thought my heart would break as we said our final farewell! I could remember sobbing, holding tightly to him, promising him I wouldn't forget a single moment of our time together. As my father honked the horn from the parking lot, Bryan took my hands in his, and we looked each other deeply in the eyes.

"You won't forget me?" I asked tearfully.

"How could I forget you?" Bryan had replied simply. "You're the great love of my life." Amazingly, even at the tender age of 16, he had been right. I *was* the great love of his life.

We just didn't know that his life would be cut so short.

Shaking my head, I walked up the dock and tried to focus on other memories: the relay races, the campfire songs, the arts and crafts. As I walked around the main area and saw how many things had changed under the new management, it struck me that "Camp Greenbriar" as I had known it didn't really exist anymore except in memories. I found that sad, in a way, but it was also kind of a relief. The place had moved on, just as I, too, was moving on.

Forty-One

When I reached Go the Distance, I wasn't sure whether to walk in or knock. It was a place of business, of course, but with Karen living right upstairs, it was also someone's home. Preferring to err to the side of caution, I rang the bell and waited, and after a while I could hear the footsteps of someone coming.

Karen peeked out of the curtain and then opened the door.

"Callie? What are you doing here?"

To my surprise, I saw that she had been crying. Her eyes were red and swollen, and in her hand she clutched a tissue.

"I wanted to ask you a few questions," I said. "Are you okay? You look upset."

"I was thinking about Enrique," she said, looking down. "I just heard the results of the autopsy. It turns out he was *murdered*."

"Oh, Karen," I said. "No wonder you've been crying. Why don't I come in and make some tea and you can tell me about it?"

We were sitting in the break room 15 minutes later, our tea turning cold in front of us, the entire story of Enrique's autopsy laid out for me by Karen. Though it was a gruesome death, and the thought of murder was incredibly disquieting, I was intrigued by her extreme distress. A part of me still wondered if she and Enrique had been closer than they should've been.

"You know, Karen," I said gently, "I'm a little confused about your relationship to Enrique. It seems as though you knew him well, but I don't quite understand why. Did he come here a lot with the children or something?"

She looked at some point over my shoulder, sighed heavily, and then looked me in the eye.

"It's a long story," she said. "Why don't we go back to what I was doing when you got here? Then we can work as we talk."

"No kids here today?" I asked.

She shook her head.

"Pepe and Adriana have gone to Texas to stay with Luisa's sister. I really miss them, though of course I'm glad they're safe now."

I nodded, feeling sorry I hadn't had a chance to say goodbye.

Karen had been in the midst of cleaning out the giant closet in the art room. I followed her down to the sunny space where the closet doors were propped open and various art supplies littered the table and counters and floor.

"If you want, you can sort these things while I wipe off the shelves," she said, not waiting for a reply. There was a bucket of soapy water on the floor inside the closet, and she reached in and took out a big sponge, squeezing out the excess over the bucket. Then she climbed the stepladder and began wiping the shelves, starting at the very top, the lemony smell of cleaner filling the room.

"My maiden name is Tinsdale," she said as she worked. "My family owns Tinsdale Orchards."

As I divided crayons from colored pencils and markers, she went on to tell me her story, which was basically a more elaborate version of what Natalie had already told me. Hearing Karen explain it, however, made the thoughts and feelings of that poor little neglected rich girl come alive. At one point, Karen climbed off of her ladder for emphasis, gesticulating wildly as she described the life of the migrants.

"As adults, we can look at the squalor of how they lived," she said, "and we're repulsed by it. But for a kid, Callie, it was like a magical wonderland. They lived in their cars! They had tents down by the creek! To me, it was like a four-month-long camping trip, and I was fascinated by everything about it."

She rinsed the sponge in the bucket and started wiping again.

"But beyond the logistics of how they lived, I was drawn most of all to the dramatics of how they *lived*. I came from a silent, sterile house where there was no noise, no mess, no love, and enough distance between people and rooms to make it seem like an endless, empty castle. By contrast, these people were so crammed together, so noisy, so angry, so happy, so alive! And they loved each other! Even the food they cooked was alive, rich with the smells of onions and tomatoes and peppers, and when you'd bite into it your eyes would burn because it was so strong. The mothers yelled at their children and the parents kissed each other right out in front of everybody, and if you wandered into the wrong campsite you might be swatted and yelled at or your might be pulled in for a giant, smelly embrace and handed more food, another tamale, another fajita. I know those people were poor and unhappy and tired and in every way disadvantaged, and I don't kid myself that I would've been better off as one of them. I'm just saying that to a child, I couldn't see all that was wrong there. I could only see that the people connected to each other, that they were real, that they were like a giant family. And a family was the one thing I didn't have. I was speaking fluent Spanish by the time I was ten, and every night I prayed that God might turn my skin brown and my hair black and let me go with them when they left."

"When did you meet Enrique?" I asked.

"I couldn't even tell you, except to say that he was always there, always a part of the group that returned every year. I spent November through July like a hermit, creeping around my big old house, going to school in town but living inside my own little shell. No one could get inside, not that anyone ever tried. By the time summer came, I was crossing the days off on my calendar, wishing them away, living for the moment when those first few trucks and cars full of migrants would come rattling up the hill."

She chuckled as she described how she spent the first half of every summer reading on a blanket in the yard, toasting her skin in the sun, trying to get herself as dark as they were.

"It never worked, of course, so by the time they got there I was always a red, splotchy, peeling mess. They didn't care. They didn't care that my hair was always in tangles or that I had no mother or that my clothes were stained and torn. They were outcasts too, and they pulled me into their world and made me one of them as quickly and simply as if I were a part of it year-round. We always had the fall together, the glorious harvest, when the parents would head into the fields and the children were left to their own devices back at the camp. All year long I worked on my handwriting so that in the fall I could write intelligent, grown-up sounding excuse letters to my teachers so I wouldn't have to go to school. 'Karen cannot come to school next week, for she has developed a ventricular aberration of the patella.' The stupid teachers never knew the difference. I doubt I made it to my classes even half the time during harvest."

"That's so sad."

"What's sad was when slowly the migrants would start to leave. That's when Enrique and I grew close, because his family was one of the ones that stayed through to the end. By October there were maybe half a dozen kids left, and Enrique was always my favorite. He was funny and adventurous and between the two of us we were forever building bridges out of twigs or damming the creek with stones or creating playhouses in the kudzu. For several years there, he was my very best friend in the world, and when the end came and his family would load their car and drive away until the next time, I was utterly inconsolable. Those were the times when the housekeeper would write my excuse notes for school for me, real notes that couldn't begin to touch on what was wrong: 'Karen could not come to school last week because she was ill,' when in fact I was locked in my dark bedroom, moaning and crying like the mad wife out of *Jane Eyre*. Sooner or later I would emerge and everyone would pretend that there was nothing wrong, and I would go back to school, dead inside, until the following summer when my friends would return and I could come back to life again."

My heart was heavy for her as I continued to work, and I felt a surge of anger toward Lowell Tinsdale for allowing his daughter to suffer so.

"The year I was thirteen," Karen said softly, not looking at me, "wasn't nearly as much fun for me as previous years, since the migrant kids my age weren't free to play anymore. They were working the fields now with their parents, and only the younger ones stayed back at camp. I still hung out with them, but it wasn't the same, and half the time I felt like a mother or a baby-sitter rather than a friend. I actually made it to school a lot that year, because my days with my buddies didn't really begin until the end of the workday, when they came in from the fields. The nights were still great fun, of course, because then everyone was around and busy and noisy, cooking over their fires and laughing and talking and fighting. But for the first time I started feeling that there was a difference there. My skin wasn't brown. My hair wasn't black. Most importantly, I didn't work hard all day in the sun until my hands bled. I was just the rich white kid who lived in the big house. Suddenly, I didn't blend in so well anymore."

Karen got down on her hands and knees and starting scrubbing the floor of the closet.

"Maybe that's why the relationship between me and Enrique changed. Because I was trying to hold on to something? Because I wanted to keep him close to me, one way or another? All I know is that we went for a walk through the camp late one night and accidentally happened upon a couple making out under the stars. We left right away, of course, but it changed something between us. It put something there that hadn't been there before."

"I can imagine."

"A few days later, we finally got up the nerve to talk about it. Enrique told me he'd never kissed a girl before, but he had thought about it a lot. Of course, I had been thinking about it as well. So we met in the barn and agreed to try kissing each other."

"I think that's sweet."

"We were so innocent, Callie. I didn't love him or even really like him that way, but he was thirteen and he was a boy and he was my friend. So we did it. We kissed."

"And?"

"And it was scary and fun and tingly and exciting and all those things that a first kiss is. We were trying it again a second time when my father walked into the barn and caught us."

"Oh, Karen."

Though I had already known what she was going to say, I could still feel her surprise. I could still feel her pain.

"I can't even describe for you what happened after that," she said, and I could see tears filling her eyes as she talked. "My father kicked me out, basically. He sent me to an exclusive all-girls school in Santa Barbara, California—about as far away from North Carolina as you can go and still be in the continental United States. I felt like my world had ended and I had been banished to some far-off kingdom made up of nuns and rules and little girls in plaid uniforms. I came home every Christmas, of course, but in the summers my father always had to find some way to get me out of here before the migrants came. I was usually sent away to summer camp for the month of August, and then it would be time for school to start again in September."

She rinsed the sponge in the bucket, the water dripping noisily.

"Of course," she said, "if I hadn't missed my migrant friends so much, I might even have given the school half a chance, for it really wasn't such a bad place. At least there was structure there, and adults who inquired after my health and seemed to care that I was smart and mature for my age and a bit talented as well. They did the best they could with me, in any event. By the time I graduated from high school five and a half years later, I had made a home for myself there, of sorts."

"What happened after graduation?"

She shrugged, dropping the sponge into the water and drying her hands on a nearby towel.

"At that point, there was no reason to come home. I wasn't a little girl anymore, eager to play with the Mexicans down by the creek. I had no way of knowing what had happened to any of them, though I assumed they were still coming back, year after year, still working their way through harvest. But that part of my life was over. I went to UCLA and ended up falling for one of my professors, a man twenty years my senior."

She gave me a sardonic smile.

"No psych degree required to figure out that one," she said. "We were married the day after I graduated from college and stayed together until I finished graduate school. I'd like to say the divorce was painful, but the truth was that it was the best thing that ever happened to me, because it got me going back to church and into therapy. I was finally able to confront some of the truths of my past and make peace with myself."

"You had a lot of strikes against you," I said.

"Well, I suppose it's true what they say, 'that which doesn't kill us makes us stronger.'"

She came over to the table and began going through a stack of construction paper, sorting it by color.

"So how'd you end up back here?" I asked.

She was quiet for a long moment, making piles of red, piles of blue, piles of green.

"I worked with the migrant population in Washington state for a couple of years, developing programs, working out solutions for education and health care and housing. But I missed home. I missed the mountains. I missed, believe it or not, my stupid father. He had remarried when I was in high school, but when I heard she passed away and then that he had such bad lung problems, it was almost like the Lord was telling me to come home and make my peace. So I came back and started Go the Distance."

"But you haven't made your peace."

"Not yet," she said evenly. "I'll get to it."

"I saw him the other day," I told her. "And, frankly, Karen, he doesn't look well."

She bit her lip and nodded, not replying.

"What about Enrique?" I asked, changing the subject. "Did he remember you when you came back?"

She smiled, and this time it was a warm and genuine smile.

"The day I opened for enrollment here, one of the migrants—one of my old friends—recognized me. Word spread that Karen Tinsdale was back, and by that night about fifteen people showed up at my door. It was probably one of the most special nights of my life. We ate

Mexican food and reminisced, and I got to know their spouses and children. I especially liked Enrique's wife, Luisa, and of course his kids were adorable. Except for the fact that my father and I haven't yet reconciled, coming back here was the single best decision I have ever made in my life."

"Did you and Enrique ever acknowledge what had gone on between you?"

"The kiss?" she asked. "Oh, Callie, it was such an unimportant part of our past together. We had years of fun and friendship. The only important thing about the night we kissed was the impact it had on my father and on my life. Enrique and I were just friends. Now my friend is dead, and they're saying it was murder."

Karen began putting everything back in the closet. As she did, I couldn't help picturing her as a sad and lost little girl, spending three-fourths of the year without a single friend. Her story seemed genuine, her relationship with Enrique aboveboard.

Once she had cleared the table, I decided to wipe it off for her. I picked up the bucket and carried it over. It wasn't until I plunged the sponge into the water, however, that I realized what was there right in front of me: a bucket of cleanser, with tiny pieces of glitter floating on the surface.

Forty-Two

I was out of there by 12:30, confused and frustrated and wondering what to do next. Karen's story seemed so genuine, so sincere, and yet the physical evidence threw a monkey wrench into the whole thing.

It wasn't until I was several blocks away, however, that I realized I had never gotten around to asking her about the expensive car purchase that Go the Distance had made. I turned around and drove to the car dealer that had made the sale, figuring I could finesse the answer that way.

It didn't take long. There were only three salesmen on the floor, and when I asked for the same person who usually dealt with Karen Weatherby at Go the Distance, one of them raised his hand and said, "Guilty as charged!"

For some reason, the three of them thought that was hilarious, so I laughed along with them, waiting until the other two disappeared back into their offices before launching into my tale.

"Karen's a friend of mine," I said, "and I know she's happy with the vehicle that she purchased here. I thought I might see if you have any more like that."

"On the lot?" he asked, blinking so excessively that I had a feeling it was either a nervous tic or this was his first day with contact lenses. "No, that was a special order."

"It was," I said. "Do you have the details on it? Because I may want to buy exactly the same thing."

His eyes stopped blinking and instead lit up, and I could almost picture little cartoon cash registers going off inside his pupils. Reluctantly, I followed him into his office, where he went through a drawer until he found what he was looking for. Slapping some papers down on the desk in front of me, he asked if I would be wanting the 21-foot model, or if the 18-foot would do.

As we talked and I tried not to sound stupid, I slowly figured out what he was telling me. The $49,000 purchase hadn't been a car at all, but a mobile unit for the education center. Custom-fitted with desks, computers, special wiring and phones, it was basically a second Go the Distance on wheels. I felt fairly ignorant that I hadn't figured that out myself, especially since Karen had talked about her mobile branch. What did I *think* she was using—a bicycle?

Specs in hand, I thanked the salesman and cut the conversation short, saying I would get back to him once a decision had been made.

"It takes a long time to get those in from the company," he called after me. "And then the custom work takes a while as well. So don't delay!"

"I've got time," I told him, giving a wave and then getting into my car. As I drove away, I set the papers on the empty seat, planning to add them to the case file at MORE.

I headed there now, wanting to touch base with Harriet—not to mention Dean and Natalie—and then use the phone to call the medical examiner. I wanted to find out if the sparkles in Enrique's lungs were ordinary glitter and if the chemical that had eaten away his insides had yet been determined.

On the way, I called in to see if anyone wanted me to pick up some lunch. I reached Harriet, who sounded as if she were flying.

"I did it, Callie!" she whispered excitedly into the phone. "I *detected.*"

"You detected what?"

"I did something a detective would do. My heart's still fluttering like a hummingbird's wings in a sugar factory."

"What happened, Harriet?"

"Well, it all sort of came together by accident. I got a hankering for a barbecue sandwich for lunch, see, and Dean told me the best barbecue in town was at a little place called the Pig Stop on Chester Lane."

"The Pig Stop?"

"I know. It sounds disgusting, but he was right. It was the best barbecue I've had since Podner's, and it came with really good cole slaw too. Anyway, while I was there waiting for my sandwich, who should walk in but Butch Hooper."

Why didn't I like the sound of where this was going?

"What'd you do, Harriet?"

"After he ordered his sandwich, he came over and said hello, and I invited him to share my table while he waited for his food."

"Okay."

"Once he sat down, he asked me if I had thought any more about the vacation house I wanted to build here—"

"What vacation house?"

"The one I told him about at the bowling alley last night, when I was trying to distract him from you and Snake."

"All right, go ahead."

"Okay, so anyway, he asked me if I had thought any more about my vacation house, and all of a sudden I got an idea from a detective show I saw once. I think it was Matlock, or maybe Jessica Fletcher, who said that the best way to see if someone is honest is to give them an opportunity to be dishonest."

"Oh, Harriet—"

"No, Callie, it went perfectly! I've been wondering if all this sneaky stuff at Su Casa with Zeb Hooper involved Butch Hooper as well. But now I feel sure that Butch is an honest man. He turned my proposition down flat."

"And what, exactly, did you propose?" I asked, a part of me not wanting to know.

"I threw a deal on the table. For my vacation house. I had already told him last night that I wanted to do the floors in this incredibly expensive Italian marble. Today, I simple elaborated on that. I said that I have a friend who drives a delivery truck for the marble company. I said we place the order, the guy delivers it, but then we say it never showed up. The company's insurance covers the lost load, and we get a second shipment for free. I said he and I could split the difference."

"Harriet!" I said. "That's crazy."

"I don't know, Callie. I got exactly the reaction I was hoping to get: I made him an offer he couldn't refuse—and then he refused it!"

"What did he say?"

"He got kind of mad and disgusted. He said he really didn't think we could do business together, and that he would appreciate it if I would look elsewhere for a construction company."

"How do you know he wasn't onto you?" I asked. "I mean, he knows you're here with me. Don't you think he's smart enough to have figured out you might be testing him?"

"Oh, I'm positive he didn't suspect a thing. I saw his gut reaction, Callie, and it confirmed for me that he is a man of character."

I turned into a small roadside fruit stand and wrapped up the phone call. I would have to have a serious talk with Harriet later about "detecting." By taking her along to the bowling alley last night, I realized now that I had created a monster. I only hoped I could nip this new proclivity of hers in the bud. Just as you wouldn't operate on someone unless you'd been to medical school, I would tell her, you shouldn't go out detecting unless you have the training and a license.

Forty-Three

My lunch ended up being a wonderful assortment of vegetables and fruits. I bought a tomato, a cucumber, and two plums, and when I got to the office I washed them, sliced them, and ate each one in turn.

Though I was eager to touch base with Dean and Natalie, they were currently out of the office. It was just as well, because the thing I wanted most to do was to get on the phone with the medical examiner and find out what new information had been uncovered about the body of Enrique Morales.

When I got Dr. Grant on the phone, he remembered who I was and pulled the file on Enrique so he could give me the information without error. Fortunately, he still assumed I was somehow entitled to this information, so I didn't disabuse him of that notion.

"Let's see… All right, the chemical that ate him up was a combination of sodium hydrosulfite and sodium bisulfite."

"What is that?"

"They're both reducing agents, and they're used in a variety of ways, primarily in manufacturing."

"Manufacturing? Are you telling me he was drowned in a vat at some production plant?"

"It's possible. Though it's just as likely that he drowned in a water treatment facility or in a bucket of stain remover. These chemicals are very versatile."

"What about the glitter?"

"Also versatile. The glittery substance is actually small flecks of mica."

"What's mica?"

"The micas are an important group of minerals. There are more than thirty different kinds, and they're used for a lot of industrial purposes: as a lubricant, in paints, in roofing shingles, and in insulation. I think years ago the pioneers used mica to make windows. In the rough, it's very pretty and shiny. It can come in big sheets, or in much smaller chunks and flakes. It is often ground up for industrial purposes. Nowadays, you can find mica in all sorts of products. I think they even use it sometimes to put the sparkles in ladies makeup."

He went on to describe the mica mining process, but I was only half listening. I was still stuck on his list of products that contained mica: paint, shingles, insulation.

In other words, construction materials.

"So if I theorized that he died at a construction site," I said when he paused to take a breath, "that wouldn't be an unreasonable assumption?"

"A construction site? Well, yes and no. The chemicals could be used in a variety of ways in a construction setting. But the mica… hmm…I'm not sure."

"But you just said they put mica in shingles and paint and insulation. The man disappeared near a construction site where there were pallets of shingles, not to mention other building materials."

"Yes, *ground* mica. But the mica in the subject's lungs wasn't ground up at all. It was in flakes, the way that it comes in its original state."

"What about glitter?" I asked, thinking of Go the Distance. "Could he have drowned in a bucket of cleanser that had flecks of glitter in it, like the kind you'd find in a school?"

"Again, mica is used to make glitter sometimes, but these flecks were unprocessed. So, no, it's not glitter."

"Then what are you saying?" I pressed. "Given the chemicals and the mica, where do *you* think he was killed?"

"If I had to make an educated guess, I'd say it happened at a mica processing plant."

"Are there such things in the area?"

"There aren't any in Greenbriar, of course, but there's one in Asheville, and probably ten more within a sixty mile radius. The hills around here are full of mica, so it stands to reason that it would be processed nearby."

"So you think he was killed at a processing plant and then brought back to the orchard and put into the apples?"

"Doesn't sound likely, does it? Yet I don't know how else you could account for all three elements to be present at once—sodium hydrosulfite, sodium bisulfite, and mica flakes."

I took a deep breath and let it out, wondering when, exactly, this case got so complicated.

"So what have you concluded about the manner of drowning?" I asked finally.

"Only that the body wasn't fully immersed. As far as I can tell, only his head was submerged. My guess is that someone grabbed him by the hair and shoved his face into a vat or some kind of container that had the chemicals and the mica in it. It wouldn't have taken long for him to die, so while it wasn't a pleasant end by any means, at least it would've been mercifully brief."

I thanked the doctor for his help, gave him my numbers in case he came up with anything further, and concluded the call.

After entering all of the information in my database, I went online and did a search for "mica." Right away it was obvious that I would need to be a bit more specific. I checked out a few websites, but they were mostly filled with processing specifications, so finally I gave up and went into my e-mail.

Sadly, there was nothing there from Tom, but I was glad to see that the e-mails I had sent out for references on MORE the day before had come pouring back in. I went through them one by one and entered them into my database. I was thrilled that every single contact had returned a glowing review. When I finished assembling the data, I began typing up my report, summarizing some of my conclusions. Harriet was in with the director of development, but I hoped that when she came back to the conference room we could review the entire investigation.

The phone rang while I was waiting for her; it was the medical examiner, and he sounded excited.

"Ms. Webber," he said, "I hope you don't mind that I called you back. I just thought of something."

"Yes?"

"It was your questions, actually, that led to me it. After we hung up, I was trying to imagine a situation other than a processing plant in which sodium hydrosulfite, sodium bisulfite, and raw mica might all be found in the same place. And then it hit me."

"Yes?"

"Gem mining."

"Gem mining?"

"Yes! In its natural state, mica is often found in a cluster with other gemstones. Rubies, sapphires, quartz, aquamarine—you name it. I won't go into the geology of it, but the fact remains that many different kinds of gems are often found together with mica. And an old gemhunter's trick is to soak the stones in iron remover. It gets some of the marks and stains off, and then they can get a better idea of the quality of the gems."

"I'm afraid you've lost me," I admitted.

"If you went panning for rubies," he said, "the first thing you might do once you got home would be to take a bucket, fill it with a solution of iron remover—in other words, sodium hydrosulfite mixed with sodium bisulfite and water—and then soak your stones in it. Chances are, there would be some mica in those stones. And, chances are, some mica flakes would break off and float in the water."

"You're saying that Enrique Morales could've been drowned in a bucket of soaking gemstones?"

"It's quite possible," he said. "At least that would explain the presence of all three elements at once. And since a bucket of rocks and stain remover could be found almost anywhere, he could've been killed right on the premises there and then easily hidden in the apples. No trip to a mica processing plant necessary."

"Can you think of any reason why someone would be soaking their gems right out in the open at an orchard?"

"Well, now you're really getting into conjecture, which isn't my area. I deal in physical analysis."

"Oh, come on, Doc," I urged. "Your job's not as cut and dried as all that. If you didn't like conjecture, you wouldn't be a forensic pathologist."

He laughed.

"Fine, then," he said. "I'll give it my best shot. You said something earlier about a construction site? In these mountains, it's not all that unusual for stones to turn up—sometimes valuable stones—right on the ground. Right in the dirt. You hear stories all the time about people walking through the woods and picking up a rock that turns out to be an emerald worth a thousand dollars."

"Really?" I asked, my heart pounding as many pieces of the puzzle began to click into place.

"Sure. I know the stories get exaggerated, but there's no question that the mountains are filled with important rocks and minerals. I would imagine that a little construction could stir things up, maybe unearth some precious gems. Who's to say that the workers didn't find some stones and set them to soaking right there on the site? It's hard to know what you've got, really, until it's been cleaned. Maybe our man was caught stealing valuable rocks from somebody's bucket."

"He wasn't that kind of guy," I said quickly. "More likely, he saw the gemstones and threatened to tell the landowner. By all rights, the stones would've belonged to him, wouldn't they?"

We threw around several different scenarios, but I didn't want to hold the doctor up any longer, so I let him go with a request that he contact the police with the same theory. As we hung up, I had to resist the urge to jump up and dance around the room, just from the relief of finally understanding what was going on. Gem mining! Of course!

Zeb Hooper was mining gemstones, traveling to New York to sell them, and coming back home to launder the profits through Su Casa! I thought about the kudzu-laden field where I had tracked his footprints this morning. I had to wonder if somewhere up there, hidden by the vines, was an entrance to a mine.

I thought of Zeb's asset report, and I realize that was why he owned so much undeveloped property in the area. He must've bought it all for the mineral rights!

How Enrique had stumbled across what Zeb was doing, I could only imagine. But, as the medical examiner said, there was probably a bucket with soaking stones right there at the Su Casa work site.

I felt sad for poor Luisa, for poor Enrique, and for all of the migrants. Despite Karen's rosy descriptions of life in the migrant camps, one of the driving forces in their lives was pure poverty. I thought back to Enrique's last day, to the conversation he'd had with his son. He had talked about being poor but honorable, saying that a man's honor was the most valuable thing he could have. "You can't put a price on honor" he'd said to Pepe.

Perhaps he had been trying to decide whether it was worth trading his honor for some gemstones.

Forty-Four

Feeling antsy, I checked my watch and tried to calculate where Tom might be at that moment, but "somewhere over the Pacific" was the best I could figure. For some reason, knowing I couldn't contact him by phone made me want to talk to him a thousand times more! Soon we would be together, I told myself, and that's all that really mattered.

But if our reunion was to come together seamlessly, this investigation had to be brought to a close before then. Fortunately, Harriet finished her session with the fund-raising person, and she and I were finally able to get down to brass tacks in the conference room. We pulled out the list of ten criteria for judging a nonprofit and went down one item at a time, looking at my data and her records as we wrote out our conclusions.

This part of the job was always very painstaking, but I still enjoyed it immensely. There was such closure in slowly going down a list and tying up all of the loose ends that we had been working with all week.

By the time we got to the bottom of the list, we knew we were almost finished. Harriet still needed to look into a few things that related to the board of directors, and I still needed to sit down with

Dean and Natalie and talk about their future plans for
of the criterion was "plans and spends wisely," and though Harrie.
I had already verified that they spent their money very wisely, I still
needed to know where they planned to take this place in the future.

Of course, "plans wisely" was a fairly subjective guideline. I gen-
erally tried to watch for two danger signs: underplanning, where a
company simply let their development unfold willy-nilly, and over-
planning, where they had an unrealistic expectation for the things they
would be able to accomplish in the immediate future. As long as a
company fell between those two extremes, I was fairly generous with
my approval. Dean and Natalie were such level-headed people that I
felt certain this criterion would give us no problem.

All that was left, then, was for Harriet and me to write our list of
contingencies for approval. We had three: sever ties with the prob-
lematic Su Casa, take steps to mend relations with the County Migrant
Bureau, and implement better protections and procedures regarding
passwords. If MORE could do those things, then we were going to recommend that they receive the grant of 1 million dollars.

Dean had already said he was willing to break off from Su Casa if
there were some unethical goings on there. But I didn't see how the
relationship with the County Migrant Bureau could be mended until
the events of last fall had fully come to light. The agent at the bureau
was convinced that the problems had happened because MORE suf-
fered from "shoddy controls," but that simply wasn't true. If we could
prove to him that the two security violations were actual cases of criminal mischief and malicious intent, then perhaps he would revise his
rating of MORE.

Of course, in order to do that, more of the questions surrounding
the death of Enrique Morales needed to be answered. My hope was
that I could close out the final part of the charity investigation and
then dedicate my efforts solely toward identifying Enrique's killer.

Luckily, the local police were working to achieve the same goal, and
Detective Sweetwater was a nice woman who was willing to share in
a fairly open exchange of information. Needing some of that information now, I dialed her number and was surprised to get through
to her in person.

"I don't believe it," I said. "You're actually at your desk?"

"I'm staying close to the office today," she said. "We've got plenty going on right here."

"Can you tell me what happened with Snake?" I asked. "I've been worried about him since I talked to you last night."

"We've been questioning him for quite a while," she said, "but so far he won't name names. Somebody has him good and scared."

"I guess I'd be scared too if I watched someone get stabbed right in front of me."

"I suppose you're right. Part of the problem, of course, is that we can't exactly go at him like we would a normal adult. I don't want any problems down the line when it comes time to prosecute, so we're treating Snake as a juvenile. In other words, nobody's screaming in his face. We're just trying to gently wear him down."

"Has he admitted to any wrongdoing?"

She hesitated, and I knew we were walking a thin line here between the sharing of information and the violation of confidentiality.

"We've managed to get some details of a few incidents, yes," she said vaguely.

"Then I have to ask you about two specific ones. Just tell me what you can."

I went on to remind her of the files that had been stolen from the MORE office and the database that was erased. Though I doubted Snake was intelligent enough to handle the computer side of things, I felt certain that he had stolen Ellen Mack's PalmPilot and given it to someone who was smart enough to take it from there.

"Actually, Callie," the detective said, "those were both on our list of suspected crimes, and he did talk about them. He admitted to taking the files but said he didn't break into the office to do it. Apparently, his mother was working in the building at the time, and all he had to do was walk over to Luisa's desk and take them. We believe that's how he earned his first bead. Putting the files in the laundromat later that night probably earned him the second."

I sat back and thought about that, feeling very stupid. The day we met, Trinksie mentioned that last fall she was trying to start up a non-profit fund-raising business. Was it really too big of a leap for me to realize that she had been doing it in one of the "starter offices" at MORE? With a great flash of clarity, I understood that the county agent had a point. If all of the outside people who took advantage of those offices had access to confidential information within the building, then MORE *did* have shoddy controls. Quickly, I pulled out my list of contingencies for approval and added one more: Construct a physical barrier between the starter offices and the rest of the MORE facility.

"So tell me this," I said to the detective. "Has he admitted to stealing a PalmPilot?"

"Actually," she laughed, "he confessed to taking a 'little baby computer' from someone's drawer. We weren't sure what he meant, but I bet that's it. According to him, he put it back the very next morning."

"What did he do with it while he had it?"

"That's the big question, Callie. He gave it to someone, but he will not tell us who that someone is."

I thought of Zeb Hooper, and I wondered if he had the computer knowledge to break into a mainframe and wipe out a database. Somehow, the picture didn't quite fit.

"Pretty soon," the detective said, "whether he names names or not, we're going to have to book Snake for aiding and abetting."

"I was afraid of that. How about his mother? Is she there at the station, freaking out on you?"

"You're a very perceptive person, Callie. Let's just say one of her other children has taken her to the doctor so that she can get a sedative."

"Poor thing."

"So tell me quickly and then I have to go, did our white-collar crime investigator get in touch with your coworker?"

"I'm not sure," I said, and then I asked Harriet, who was absorbed in her own work across the room.

"He's meeting me here in the morning," Harriet replied, and I repeated that back to Detective Sweetwater.

"Good," she said. "Because I'm not moving on Zeb Hooper or Su Casa until our guy has had a chance to see what you've got."

"I assume the medical examiner called you today with his theory about the gemstones and the iron remover?"

The detective was quiet for a moment.

"You sure do manage to find things out," she said. "I suppose I should've asked this a lot sooner, but are you by any chance licensed to investigate in the state of North Carolina?"

"Yes," I laughed. "I am. Since I travel for my job, I've kept current in a number of states. There's also some reciprocity. I can fax you copies of my papers, if you need."

"Are you a bounty hunter too?"

"No. Just a private investigator."

"Do you have a permit to carry?"

"Nope. I don't even own a gun."

"All right, then," she said, "I guess we're on the same page. But I think you need to step back a bit and let us do our jobs."

"Aw, come on, Detective," I said. "You're doing your job, and I'm just doing mine."

Forty-Five

After I hung up the phone, I entered a few notes in my database and then went to see if Dean and Natalie had returned yet to the building. I was glad to see that they were both in Dean's office. I knocked on the door and asked if they had a few minutes to meet with me.

"Of course, Callie," Natalie said. "We're at your disposal."

She looked tired and upset, and I learned that they had just come from the funeral home, where they helped Luisa make arrangements to ship Enrique's body to Mexico for his funeral and burial next week.

"There will be a small memorial service here on Saturday," she said. "But come Monday morning Luisa will be leaving Greenbriar for good."

"What's going to happen to her?" I asked. "Is she okay?"

"In a way," Dean said, "I think Luisa is just relieved that her questions have finally been answered."

"Answered?" I asked. "But we still don't know who killed her husband."

"No," he said, "but at least she knows that he's not somewhere out there suffering. It's been a long, horrible four months for her, and now at least the waiting and wondering are over."

"I understand."

We talked about Luisa and the children for a few minutes, but finally Natalie asked what I had come there to talk about.

"Tell me something happy," she told me, pinching the bridge of her nose. "It's been a very difficult day."

"Happy," I said. "Okay, how does this sound? My investigation is almost over, and your agency is looking very, very good."

Natalie gasped and Dean grinned, and they both stood and hugged me.

"It's not over yet," I said, "and I'm afraid we do have a short list of contingencies that would have to be taken care of pending approval. But overall you've scored very well. If we could just get to the truth about those two acts of vandalism last fall, then I think we'd be ready to close things up."

"I know the police are working very hard on it," Natalie said. "I'm going to pray that the truth will come to light very soon."

"I hope so," I said. "In the meantime, we need to cover one last area that we haven't really touched on yet. I wonder if you could share with me your future plans for MORE? I know you put on your grant request that you hope to expand, assist more charities, and start working with the migrants before and after they are actually in the area. But I'd like to hear some concrete ideas about how you're going to make those hopes a reality."

They seemed eager to talk about the future, and I took notes as they laid out their plans and ideas and dreams. As I had expected, they seemed to have a good grasp of how their agency was going to grow and change, and they were well within my guidelines to pass this particular criterion.

When we finished talking, I added the info to my database and then told Harriet I had something to do but that perhaps she and I could meet for dinner in town later.

"You've been working so hard," I said, "I think you deserve a break."

"I think we both do," she said.

We arranged to meet downtown at Sparky's Restaurant at 5:30. My fruit-and-vegetable lunch wasn't exactly sticking to my ribs, and I knew I'd be quite hungry by then.

In the meantime, I had some serious thinking to do, and so I drove to the Webbers' house and took out the canoe and treated myself to an afternoon paddle.

It was exactly what I needed to clear my head. The day was warm and sunny, and I paddled slowly, not looking for exercise but merely some mental clarity. Somehow, I always seemed to think better with a paddle in my hands.

I spent the first ten minutes or so in prayer, asking God to provide me with wisdom and strength. When my prayer was over, I let my mind go back over the sequence of events and the facts I knew thus far. Once I had reviewed the timeline, I tried to isolate the names of the people who were involved with the case and then considered what sort of motive each of them might've had for killing Enrique Morales.

Of course, the most obvious choice was Zeb Hooper, considering all that we now knew about his nefarious doings with Su Casa. But the man wasn't exactly computer literate, which meant he couldn't have done it entirely on his own.

I thought perhaps his son Butch could've helped him, though everyone seemed to feel Butch was the very salt of the earth. I couldn't rule out the possibility that Karen or Pete might've been involved. For Karen, I knew she could have one of several different motives. Did she blame Enrique for the teenage kiss that had destroyed her life? Perhaps she wanted a relationship with the man now, but he had turned her down? I had to admit that neither motive seemed to make much sense, but I had to throw everything out on the table in order to process it through.

Pete didn't seem to have a motive for the murder, though he struck me as a passionate man. Perhaps he would be capable of killing someone in an argument, say, in the heat of the moment.

Danny, too, was a consideration. But I couldn't really count him among my suspects because he hadn't even moved to Greenbriar until long after Enrique disappeared.

Lowell Tinsdale I ruled out simply because he was too ill at the time. That left Snake or his mother Trinksie, neither of whom were capable of murder or computer tinkering, I felt sure.

Paddling toward the distant shore, I thought about the mysterious John Doe, the man who came here one night and ended up getting stabbed to death in a church parking lot. In my mind, when I tried to imagine how that had come to pass, I saw a group of three: John Doe, Snake, and the person—whoever it was—who was manipulating Snake to commit acts of vandalism. While Snake lit the stink bombs and tossed them into Luisa's car, perhaps the other two men had argued, and it ended with the stabbing. To get away, Snake had run through the woods behind the Webbers' house, where I had seen him. The person who did the stabbing must've simply driven away, out of the church parking lot, leaving the stabbed victim on the ground to die.

What did we know about John Doe? Judging from the way he was dressed, he was wealthy. He was also connected to Enrique's murder somehow, since his fingerprints were on the letter that had been sent to Luisa four months before from New York City, ostensibly from Enrique, telling her he didn't love her anymore.

But there was one other connection to New York City, I realized, and when I put it all together, it seemed to make sense. If John Doe had sent the letter from New York, then that meant he might live in New York, which meant that when Zeb Hooper flew off to New York, John Doe could've been the man he was going to see. Was John Doe a gem dealer? If so, for some reason, the dealer had come to Greenbriar and had ended up getting himself killed. Chances are, he was here looking for money. Was it blackmail, perhaps?

I paddled myself in a wide curve so that I was slowly headed back toward the shore. There was one question I couldn't figure out, and that had to do with the money laundering through Su Casa. Basically, I wondered why it was necessary. As far as I knew, there was nothing illegal about possessing, buying, or selling gemstones in the United States. I didn't understand at all why Zeb had to hide his profits through some tricky bookkeeping. My best guess was that by passing them through Su Casa, a nonprofit, he was saved from having to pay taxes on them.

I thought back to that night in the parking lot, when the man lay dying on the ground. What had he whispered as his final word? "Jim" or "Jim's"?

I said it out loud now, listening to the sound it made on my lips. "Jim's."

I didn't know of any Jim who was connected with this case.

Paddling toward shore, I said it again, and then suddenly I realized what the man had meant. The truth had been there all along! His final word hadn't been "Jim's."

His final word had been "gems."

Forty-Six

I reached the restaurant a few minutes early. Inside it was dark but roomy, with flickering candles on the tables and wooden booths lining the walls. The hostess seated me in a booth at my request, and then I perused the menu, hoping Harriet would get here soon because I was starving.

There was a bar adjoining the restaurant, and I could tell that it was a popular place. As the clock crept past 5:30, people began crowding into the bar area until they were more than two deep. The restaurant, however, was still only about half full when I finally gave up on Harriet and ordered a homemade bowl of vegetable soup for myself. Sure enough, Harriet called me a few minutes later, saying that she had been delayed but that she would be here soon.

"Eating alone?" a man asked as I hung up my phone.

I glanced up to see Danny Stanford, all brown curls and dimples, dressed in the jeans and work shirt of the orchard.

"Hey, Danny," I said. "I'm waiting on a friend, but she's been delayed. Would you care to join me?"

"I'm just having a drink," he said. "But sure. The bar's kind of crowded tonight anyway."

"Looks like a popular place."

"Only on Thursdays," he replied. "Free catfish buffet until seven."

He sat across from me, flashing me that dimpled grin. I realized we hadn't really had a chance to speak since we were together at the orchard, trying not to laugh at our maudlin joke about the mummy.

"Hey, look, I'm sorry about what happened the other day at the orchard, the way Pete just kind of took over your tour and everything," Danny said. "I don't know what came over him. I've never seen him like that before."

I nodded, taking a sip of my water.

"I think it was a case of mistaken identity," I said. "He thought I was someone else. We got it straightened out."

"Oh. Well, I'm glad you got a good tour at least. Though of course I'm sorrier still about the way it had to end. What a mess, huh?"

"Yeah, that was really something. I'm curious. What are the people at the orchard saying about the death?"

"You mean who killed the migrant? Everybody's got a different idea, and everybody suspects everybody else. Most of them just go on and on about what a nice man he was and a hard worker and all of that. Have you ever noticed, once somebody's dead, all you hear are the good things?"

I sat up straight.

"What do you mean?" I asked. "Were there things about Enrique that weren't so good?"

He took a sip of his drink and shook his head.

"Oh, I don't know, I just mean in general. Nobody's all good or all bad, but once they're dead, all you hear is how wonderful they were. I find it ironic, I guess. Some of the people who work there hate migrants. They probably weren't giving that guy the time of day when he was alive. But now that he's dead, they're all like, 'Oh, we'll miss his smiling face! He always had a kind word!' Give me a break."

"I guess it is kind of hypocritical."

"Please. To most folks these migrants are just a dime a dozen, nameless, faceless, quantities of people who show up, do their job, and leave. Cheap labor, almost interchangeable. Now that one of them is dead—and dead in such an exotic way, I might add—they want to pretend that he mattered. I'm sure he never mattered to them before."

"What's Pete saying about all of this?" I asked. "I imagine the death has had some repercussions in the workplace."

"Pete's so focused on his precious apple trees, I don't think he's even noticed. You saw what I'm talking about from your tour. He's like a walking apple encyclopedia."

"That's the truth," I chuckled. "I know more about apples now than I ever dreamed I'd want to know."

"Yeah, well," he laughed, "I guess you could say apples are his passion."

I took a sip of my water and then set it on the napkin in front of me.

"So what's *your* passion, Danny?" I asked.

"Excuse me?"

"You seem a little out of place at the orchard," I explained. "I just wondered, why are you there? What are you doing?"

He set down his drink as well and stared at a point somewhere beyond my right shoulder. When he spoke again, his voice was low and soft.

"I grew up in apple country," he explained. "A little bit northeast of here."

"Really? But you don't have a Southern accent at all."

"That's because we moved away when I was ten. My dad got a job in Detroit, working for a recording studio."

"Impressive."

"Not really," he said sheepishly. "He was an accountant. Not exactly a glamour job."

"That must've been quite a culture shock for you, Southern country boy moves to a Northern city?"

He nodded.

"At first, yeah. Eventually, I learned to fit in. But I never lost that yearning to come back home. I guess you could say the Smokies were in my blood."

I didn't tell him that I knew exactly what he meant, that I had spent nearly every moment since I got here thinking that very same thing.

"After college, I went into accounting too. But my heart wasn't in it."

"So let me guess," I said with a grin. "You were sitting in a traffic jam one day in your suit and tie, chewing Tums and honking your horn, when you finally realized you didn't want that life anymore. You decided to chuck it all and move back to the mountains. Get back to nature."

"Well, not exactly."

My soup came at that moment, and I waited until the waitress had left before speaking again.

"What, then?" I said as I unrolled my silverware and put my napkin in my lap. "That's a pretty brave move. Leaving the big city for the country life."

Danny downed the last of his drink, set the glass softly on the table, and met my eyes with his own.

"A few months ago, my parents were driving home in the snow from a party. They hit some black ice and skidded into the path of an oncoming truck. They were killed instantly."

I put my hand to my mouth.

"At their funeral," he continued, "I realized that life's too short, too fragile, to waste even a moment. I closed up the house, quit my job, and headed to the mountains. The position at Tinsdale Orchards was the first opening I found where they were willing to hire someone without experience."

To cover my embarrassment, I ate a spoonful of soup, letting the silence sit between us.

"I'm sorry, Danny," I said finally. "I didn't know."

"Yeah, well, it's not like I tell this story to everyone I meet."

He waved to the waitress to bring him another drink. I felt a surge of sadness for him, and I wondered if his time in the mountains would end up being his salvation or merely his escape.

"But enough of my sob story," he said. "I didn't mean to be such a downer."

"My fault," I said. "I shouldn't have asked."

He made an attempt at small talk, launching into a humorous tale about a machine malfunction at the orchard. I let him talk, eating my soup and making the occasional comment. The waitress brought him a fresh drink, and then he moved on to the subject of Karen. Just from the way he spoke, I could tell that he was smitten with her and eager to take their relationship to another level.

"She's pretty single-minded right now, with her charity and all," he said. "But I can be fairly tenacious when I put my mind to it. I'll wear her down eventually."

I wondered how much he knew about Karen's connection to the orchard.

"Is that uncomfortable for you," I asked, "working for her father with them being estranged and everything?"

"Nah. I've only seen the old man once or twice. I work for Pete, really. He calls the shots around there."

"I wonder if Karen and her dad will ever reconcile."

He shrugged.

"She hopes so. But that first step is always the hardest. I keep telling her he may not be around much longer and she'd better make her move while she can."

"I wonder what Karen will do with such a big inheritance," I said innocently, remembering my conversation with Pete. I wasn't sure if Karen knew about the change to the will—or, if she did, whether she would've shared her thoughts on the matter with Danny. But it was worth doing a little fishing to find out.

"To be honest," Danny said, lowering his voice, "I think she has big ideas for the place. It'll remain a working orchard, of course, but she wants to turn the house into a migrant resource center."

"Really?"

I listened to him talk about Karen's plans, feeling fairly certain that she had no clue that she wasn't in line to inherit after all. Poor Pete, he may have been right. By leaving everything to him, Lowell may well have set Pete up for a long court battle where, in the end, he would come out with nothing.

Harriet finally appeared just as I was finishing my soup. I introduced her to Danny, and after chatting for a moment, he excused himself and returned to the bar. Harriet slid into the booth across from me and apologized for being so late.

"So what's that cutie pie's story?" she asked.

"He works at Tinsdale Orchards."

"Does he pick apples?" she asked. "'Cause I can change my name to 'Apple' if it means he'll pick me!"

Harriet was disappointed to learn that Danny was already spoken for, but we settled down and enjoyed our meal nonetheless. North Carolina was known for down-home cooking, and I treated myself to a true indulgence: chicken-fried steak and mashed potatoes smothered in white gravy. I could feel my arteries hardening with every delicious bite.

When we finished eating, Harriet and I took a stroll through downtown Greenbriar, and I shared with her some of my memories from coming here over the years. She asked how it was that the boy I met at summer camp at 16 could end up becoming my husband.

"I know what those summer camp flings are like," she said. "You fall head over heels for a guy and become an instant couple, think you'll die of agony once you have to go your separate ways, and then within a few weeks you've forgotten all about him."

"It was different," I replied, wondering how to explain it. "The next summer, the year I was seventeen, we both just knew somehow. It wasn't a fling. It was a forever kind of love. That was the year we were applying to colleges, so we found one that was a good fit for both of us, and everything else just sort of fell into place."

Harriet shook her head slowly from side to side.

"Why do I get the impression that you've always been like a sixty-year-old woman, even inside a seventeen-year-old body?"

I laughed out loud.

"My mother used to say that!" I told her. "She called me 'the old lady' when I was a kid because I was always so logical and methodical."

"Well, hey, I guess it's paid off in the long run. Now you have a career that requires you to be logical and methodical."

"I suppose so."

We walked along together quietly in the cool night air, each lost in our own separate thoughts.

"So what do you think will happen with you and Tom?" she asked finally. "Is he a forever kind of love too?"

I smiled.

"I'm not sure," I said. "I hope so. But there's still an awful lot about him that I don't know."

"He's a very private guy," she agreed. "I don't know if I could deal with all that as patiently as you have. I think at some point when he's going on and on about 'that's not relevant' or 'let's not go there,' I'd just hog-tie the man and drag him through some manure."

"Is that how you deal with problems in your love life, Harriet?" I asked, chuckling.

"You better believe it," she said. "When a fellow gives me any guff, I say hog-tying is the way to go."

Forty-Seven

Back at the cabin, I dressed warmly in a sweater, jacket, and gloves, even though the night wasn't all that chilly. I thought it better to be safe than sorry, since I wasn't sure how long I'd be outside.

I left Harriet settled in front of the television, and I was relieved that her urge to "detect" seemed to have passed, particularly since one of her favorite shows was on. I told her I was going for a walk, and though I don't think she believed me, she seemed too engrossed in her show to put up much of a fuss.

Unfortunately, I thought as I stepped outside and pulled the door shut behind me, I didn't have my night-vision goggles with me on this job. But as my eyes adjusted to the darkness, I thought I would be able to see enough to get by. Walking as quickly and quietly as possible, I started the climb up the road, keeping near to the tree line.

Once I reached the spot where Zeb's footsteps had disappeared into the brush this morning, I scoped things out and found myself a nice hiding place, across the road and up a bit behind a tree. Again I wished for my goggles, but at least the moon was bright, nearly three-quarter full.

I only had to wait about an hour. Just when I was starting to feel chilled, I heard the distinct sound of footsteps on the pavement. I froze, hoping my cover was as good from a lower angle as it was from in front. I needn't have worried. One glance at Zeb as he walked by showed me that he was totally absorbed in his own mission, and that he wouldn't have noticed me if I had been standing in the middle of the road, waving a flag.

Nearly duplicating his earlier footprints, he stepped from the road and into the brush across the street. As I watched through the branches of the tree, he used the hidden latch to get through the fence and then kept going. Afraid I might lose him in the dark, I quietly extricated myself from my hiding place and dashed across the street just as he disappeared into some trees. I quickly let myself through the fence and then made my way in the same direction that he had gone until I caught sight of him and hid myself behind another tree.

As I watched, he walked around to the far side of a mound that was covered with kudzu vines. Then, much as I had expected, he reached into the kudzu and simply opened it like a door. He clicked on a flashlight, stepped forward, and then let the door close behind him.

It was all I could do not to leap out from behind the tree and run directly to the spot where he had disappeared. Instead, I forced myself to wait ten minutes and then proceed slowly and carefully.

Heart pounding, I made my way across the brush and up to the mound. Silently, I reached through the vines and felt the solid hardness of a door. My fingers found a handle and, holding my breath, I pulled, just as I had seen Zeb do. Sure enough, the door came open, revealing a space so black there was no way for me to know what was inside.

It smelled of dirt and mold, and I took a tentative step forward, reaching out to feel the walls and ceiling with my hands. From what I could tell, they were made of dirt, reinforced with wood beams. Incredible.

It was definitely the entrance to some kind of mine. I was desperate to explore it, but I couldn't do that while Zeb was still inside. If he was staying true to his pattern, he would be here all night and go back

down the hill in the morning. I'd simply have to force myself to wait
until then and come back to explore once I knew he was safely home.

I'd never sleep tonight! Reluctantly, I stepped out through the
kudzu, silently shut the door, and retraced my steps back to the road,
making sure I hadn't left any telltale footprints. I jogged all the way
back to my house, my heart pounding as much from the excitement
as from the exertion.

Once I got home, I went onto the internet and did some searches
for North Carolina and mines. Sure enough, as I read I realized that
this area was loaded with precious and semi-precious gems, not to
mention metals and marble and even gold. According to one website,
western North Carolina had more minerals per square mile than any
other place on earth! While I had known gem mining was a popular
tourist attraction around here, I had no idea how much the world
depended on North Carolina's supplies of iron and copper and, yes,
even mica for its mineral supply. By the time I had finished reading,
my brain was spinning with all that I had learned.

I doubt I slept more than a few hours the whole night.

I was up at daybreak, dressed and waiting by the front window,
my eyes glued to the road. Zeb finally appeared around 7:00 A.M.,
looking dirty and exhausted. After he had gone past, I waited a full
five minutes before stepping outside and quietly shutting the door.

It was a cool morning, and I was dressed for warmth, knowing I
might be heading down into subterranean temperatures. I crept to
the end of the driveway and peered around the bushes toward Zeb's
house. As expected, there was no sign of him. I felt pretty safe in
assuming that he had gone inside his house and would soon be
headed for bed. No wonder he worked at Su Casa in the late afternoons—he was mining all night and then sleeping all morning!

I stuffed two flashlights into one pocket and my camera into the
other, zipped them shut, and started up the mountain. I didn't have
far to go, but by the time I got there I was breathless—partly because
of the altitude and partly from nervous excitement. Though this venture was necessary to my investigation, I was about to trespass in a
very big way.

And I could only imagine what I might find when I did!

Even in broad daylight, the door wasn't visible. But I reached confidently through the thick green vines, found the handle, and pulled. As before, the portal simply came open in my hand, revealing a dark tunnel inside. Looking from side to side, I unzipped my jacket pocket, pulled out a flashlight, and turned it on. Then, taking a deep breath, I stepped into the tunnel and let the door shut behind me.

It was dark. Dark and dank and creepy. I played the light around on the walls, ceiling, and floor, but as I had assumed last night, they were simply made of packed dirt, reinforced by rough wood beams. Gingerly, I stepped forward. The ground under my feet was slightly sloped, but solid.

Heart pounding, I started inching forward, praying mightily that I wouldn't encounter anyone—either in front of me or behind me. I checked my pocket for the spare flashlight just to be sure, and then I pressed onward, trying to tell myself to walk faster, *walk faster.*

As I went, the light from my flashlight lit the way, revealing the ceiling as it sloped downward, eventually nearly touching my head. The ground was wet in places, with wide, mucky puddles, and the walls were oozing moisture like sweat. I wondered if I would encounter any snakes and, if I did, what kind they might be. Remembering back to my hiking days with Bryan, I tried to recall the varieties of snakes that were found in the Smoky Mountains.

Yuck. Concentrating on my progress, it felt as though the tunnel went straight back under the road. The slope leveled out after a while, and then the ceiling dipped even lower. I now had to bend as I walked, though I was no longer headed downhill. Still, the tunnel was so long!

The further I went into the mountain, the more uneasy I became. What if someone caught me in here? How would anyone ever know? No one would hear my screams. Worse, though, was the thought that the tunnel might not be stable.

The ceiling became so low I nearly had to crawl, and at that point I stopped and assessed the situation. Crouching on the ground, I shined the light behind me and in front of me. Nothing but empty tunnel in either direction.

I crawled forward, my knees sinking in the muck, the flashlight clinched in my teeth. I was wishing I had a hard hat with a built-in light when I hit my head on something—and then I wished I had a hard hat for protection from myself.

"Ouch!" I whispered, putting a hand to my forehead.

Stopping, I leaned back on my knees and looked up. In front of me was a hard, solid rock wall.

The tunnel had come to an end.

I knelt there in the mud, a surge of tears stinging my eyes. To have come all this way and end up finding *nothing?* I had visions of caves, mines, miles of tunnels, mountains of glittering jewels. Instead, I was sitting in the muck, at a dead end in front of a rock wall. In frustration, I pushed at the rock with an angry groan.

Much to my surprise, it gave way.

Forty-Eight

Crouching in the tunnel, I looked at the opening where the rock had been. Slowly, carefully, I inched forward to put my head through the hole.

I was at the entrance to a mine.

I played my flashlight around on the walls and ceiling of the large chamber. Though these walls were of dirt just like the tunnel, there was something different here. As I scooted through the hole, stood up, and moved closer, I realized there was some sort of shiny substance in the dirt, like little flecks of glitter. That, I realized, must be the mica.

I tried to stretch out the pains in my back from bending over for so long, and then I turned my attention back to the big rock that had blocked my way at the end of the tunnel. It was now in the mud on the ground, and I realized that it was just a big, flat piece of slate. It had been used to cap the tunnel on purpose, though I didn't know why. It was probably there to serve as a diversion in case someone happened upon the tunnel and tried to explore it.

Heart pounding, I wanted to look around, but at this point I knew I was in grave danger. If anyone came down that tunnel, I would be trapped deep in the heart of the mountain with no one to hear my cries. I checked my cell phone, but as I expected the screen said "no service." If I were to explore, I'd be doing it without backup of any kind.

Still, I was here. There was no way I was going to turn around and go back home without at least poking around just a bit. I shined the flashlight on my watch and decided to give myself exactly ten minutes. I had to choose whether to go right or left, and I went left.

In those ten minutes, I methodically wandered through the mine, moving from wide chambers like the one I had come in on to narrow passageways and then back to larger areas again. There was a lot of debris cast about—broken shovels and picks, chunks of wood, empty bottles and cans. Nowhere did I see gleaming jewels clustered on the walls, but I had to remind myself that gems in the rough weren't always easy to spot. Eventually, I came to a small dented bucket, and I looked inside to see some rocks soaking in a liquid. Nearby was a dirty pair of rubber gloves. Steeling my nerve, I pulled on one of the gloves, reached into the bucket and took out a rock.

It was sort of gray and brown and white, with shiny pieces of mica jutting out from the sides. One end was an odd shade of blue, and as I held the rock in my hand, I realized that it was a lot heavier than a rock that size would normally be.

Looking around, I saw that this same type of rock was protruding from the walls here and there throughout the mine. Whatever kind of gem this was, there was certainly plenty of it here.

Pulse surging, I pulled out my camera and took a picture of the rock, the flash blinding me momentarily as I did. I set the rock back into the bucket, pulled off the glove, and then snapped a picture of the bucket. Though I didn't see how a grown man could be drowned in a container that size, I supposed it was possible.

It wasn't until I entered the next chamber that I realized my mistake. There, beside a group of wide wooden beams that ran floor to ceiling, was a much larger bucket. This bucket was also lined on the bottom with rocks and filled with a clear liquid that smelled kind of like detergent. Nearby were discarded bottles of iron remover.

I felt certain this was where Enrique had been drowned.

Knees wobbly, I stepped closer to the bucket, and then I saw that behind the beams was what looked like wooden stairs. I had a feeling they led the way up and out of the mine at a location far removed from where I had entered. I tried to get closer to the stairs and shine my flashlight up them, but the beams blocked the way.

I debated taking a picture of the bucket and the stairs, but I was afraid that the flash might alert someone to my presence, just in case the stairs did lead to another exit and there might be someone on the other side. My time ticking to an end, I turned and left, making my way through the weaving and winding passageways back to the tunnel. I didn't look forward to climbing through the claustrophobic muck and mud, but since it was the only way out for me, I gritted my teeth and climbed inside.

Getting the big piece of slate into place wasn't as difficult as I had thought it would be, as there seemed to be handholds carved into the rock. Taking a deep breath, I started out on hands and knees, reminding myself that the passageway would get wider as I went.

Once I had crawled about ten feet, I stopped to get a photo of this part of the passageway. I set my flashlight in my lap and was just digging for my camera when I heard the noise.

It sounded like whistling, and it sounded like it was coming my way!

Frantically, I turned off my flashlight and sat there in absolute darkness, heart pounding in my throat. Someone was headed down the tunnel toward the mine. Judging by the whistling, I assumed it was Zeb Hooper.

As quickly and as silently as possible, I shoved my flashlight into my pocket and scooted backwards, kicking out the slate with my foot.

Blindly, I slithered out of the tunnel into the mine, tripping on the slate and scraping my already-scraped knees. Looking into the tunnel, I could see a dim glow in the distance, and I knew the person was getting closer.

On hands and knees, I lifted the slate and pressed it into place, capping the tunnel. I knew I had only a minute, maybe two, before the cap would be coming back off.

I had to make a quick decision. My first inclination was to hide nearby, wait until the person came through, and then slip out of the tunnel behind them. But as I clicked on my flashlight, I saw that there really wasn't anywhere to hide, since I couldn't know whether this person was going to turn right or left once they got into the mine.

There was no other choice. Breathing heavily, I ran along the passageway until I reached the chamber with the buckets, the beams, and the stairs. I had no choice but to go up and out, no matter what was on the other side.

Forty-Nine

It wasn't easy. First I had get to the stairs, which meant wedging myself between the beams. As I did, dirt began raining down on my head. I realized the beams must be there to support a ceiling that wanted to give way. I closed my eyes and forced myself through. Once I got on the other side of the beams, I climbed up the stairs. They did indeed lead to a door. There was no doorknob, so when I reached it I simply pressed and pressed until I could feel it start to give way.

Something was providing resistance from the other side. I pushed harder. With a scrape and a big thud, the door finally swung open. As it did, my flashlight slipped from my hand and clattered down the stairs, and more dirt began crumbling down from overhead. Shielding my eyes from the falling debris, I stepped on through into a dark room. The dirt stopped falling and I shut the thick, heavy door, collapsing against it. I had made it.

I wiped mud from my eyes and looked around, trying to figure out where I was. Light was coming in from under another door, but otherwise the room was dark, and there were no windows. A box of papers had spilled out across the floor, and I realized that must've been what caused the thud.

Heart pounding, I knew I wasn't out of danger yet. If the person in the mine had heard the thud or the falling dirt, they would come looking. When they got there, they would find a flashlight lying on the ground, still turned on. They would know someone was in here.

I went toward the other door, toward the light. Cautiously, I inched it open, to see what looked like a storage room. It was empty, so I stepped through, vaguely recognizing it. Then I realized where I was.

Su Casa.

The tunnel that led to the mine had led all the way to underneath Tinsdale Orchards. In a flash, I understood why Zeb had to launder his income from the gemstones: *They weren't his gemstones!* He was slant mining onto Tinsdale property and stealing the gems from there.

The door I had come through to get into the building was a door from the mine into Zeb's office at Su Casa. I turned and looked at that door now, but it didn't even show. From this viewpoint, it just looked like a cinderblock wall. Zeb had fashioned himself a hidden door out of wood and cinderblocks, another secret entrance to the mine.

That must've been what Enrique Morales found that had gotten him killed. This building was under construction the day Enrique disappeared. I was willing to bet he somehow stumbled upon the secret door, and his discovery had cost him his life.

I wasn't going to let that happen to me. Without pausing to think, I stepped back into Zeb's windowless office, clicked on the light, and began pushing his desk along the wall to block the door. The desk was heavy, but slowly it began to move. With a great groan, I slid it into place. It would be nearly impossible for someone to open the door from inside the mine now.

That done, I ran out into the front office, startling Trinksie so badly that she screamed and dropped the files she was carrying. Danny Stanford was there too, and though he didn't scream, he also looked shocked.

"Callie!" Trinksie yelled. "Where did you come from?"

"What happened to you?" Danny echoed, and I realized that I was covered, head to toe, in mud.

"Trinksie, call nine one one," I said, but she just stood there, stunned.

"I'll do it," Danny offered, stepping toward the phone. "What's wrong? Are you hurt?"

"You're not going to believe this," I said breathlessly, "but I've been down inside a mine."

"A mine?" asked Trinksie.

"A gem mine. Like rubies, emeralds? This building sits atop an entire mine, and there's an entrance to it right from Zeb's office."

They stared at me like I was crazy.

"Yeah, hold on just a second," Danny said into the phone, and then he looked at me skeptically. "What do you want me to tell them?"

"Just say they need to send the police out here right away. But no sirens, because we've got to get the other exit covered before he tries to come out."

"He who?"

"Zeb Hooper. He's in the mine now, and he may have realized I'm onto him."

Trinksie started fanning her face with her hands.

"This just isn't happening," she said. "You're nuts."

Charging past me, she headed straight for Zeb's office. I followed along behind as Danny tried to explain the situation to the authorities over the phone.

In the office, Trinksie saw the moved desk and the spilled box and demanded to know what I had done. Just then, the door from the mine began rattling, and I knew that Zeb was on the other side, trying to come through. Trinksie screamed.

"I'll handle this," Danny said, squeezing past us and going to the desk.

Even as the door continued to rattle, Danny rifled through various drawers.

"What are you trying to do?" I said.

He found what he was looking for in the back of the top left drawer. As he pulled out his hand, I saw that he was holding a gun. Pointing it at the door to the mine, he squeezed the trigger. A bullet blasted through the cinderblock, leaving a smoking hole the size of a fist.

Instantly, the rattling stopped. From inside, we could hear the sound of Zeb's body falling down the stairs.

Danny turned toward us, the gun still clutched in his fist. Trinksie and I stared at him, open-mouthed.

"Move the desk away from the door," he commanded, gesturing with the gun.

Maybe I was a little slow, but it took me a good 30 seconds to realize that he was now pointing the gun at us.

I wanted to do something quick and simple to disarm him. But Trinksie stood between me and him, and there was nothing I could do that wouldn't put her in even more danger.

Danny held us at gunpoint while Trinksie and I struggled to move the desk away from the door. Once we succeeded, he ordered me to stand with my hands against the wall, then he pointed the gun at my head and told Trinksie to go into the storage room and get a roll of duct tape. She did as he said, and then he ordered her to tape my hands together behind my back.

"I'm sorry, Callie," she sobbed as she did so. I didn't reply but merely kept my eyes, unblinking, on Danny.

When she finished with me, he had Trinksie turn off the office light, pull the door shut, and then open the door to the mine. Gun to our backs, he forced us to go down the stairs as he brought up the rear, pulling the door shut behind him.

Zeb was lying at the bottom of the stairs, his right shoulder covered in blood. Trinksie ran to him, still crying, and I was surprised that he was alive. I was also surprised to see that there were lights on inside the mine, a string of bare bulbs along the ceiling, wired from a plug near the door.

We crowded at the bottom of the stairs, blocked by the heavy beams. Danny pointed to one of the beams and told Trinksie to kick it out of place. As she did so, the beam fell to the ground and a shower of dirt rained down on all of us.

"Pull him through," Danny barked.

She tried dragging Zeb between the beams but he was too heavy. Finally, Zeb used his legs to push himself while Trinksie pulled on his good arm, and they managed to make their way past the beams to the center of the room. At Danny's command, I followed until we were all to the far wall of the chamber. He threw the roll of duct tape at Trinksie and told her to tape Zeb's hands. Zeb moaned as she did so, in terrible pain from his wound.

"The police will be here any minute," Trinksie said as she worked.

"The police aren't coming, you idiot," Danny said. "Did you really think I dialed nine one one?"

Once Zeb was taped, Danny frisked him and came up with a pocketknife. After tossing it to one side, he ordered Trinksie to sit down with her back to me, and then he managed to duct tape the two of us together using one hand and his teeth while he held the gun steady with the other. When he was finished, he stepped back and admired his handiwork.

"Well," he said, breathing heavily from the exertion. "What do you think of this? Callie, thanks to you, we're all here together."

"What's going on?" Trinksie whimpered.

"What's going on is that Zeb and Danny are illegally mining on Tinsdale land," I explained. "I was trying to explore the mine after Zeb had left for the day, but for some reason he came back."

Zeb stirred and then rasped, "I needed the sump pump. My basement's taking on water."

I looked from Zeb to Danny, who was watching us with a bemused expression on his face.

"Why don't you let us go, Danny?" I said. "Zeb's still alive. It's not too late to save this situation."

"Oh, this situation has dragged on way too long already. Zeb, I do believe it's time we parted ways."

Except for Trinksie's sniffling, the three of us on the ground were silent. Danny seemed to catch his breath and calm down, and then he pocketed the gun and methodically went about doing something with the beams near the stairs. At one point, he stopped and went deeper into the mine.

"Zeb," I whispered when Danny was out of earshot. "That's your gun he's got. How many bullets are in it?"

"From my desk?" Zeb asked in a weak voice.

"Yeah."

"Six. Well, five now."

That was still five too many.

Danny came back into the room, humming, carrying a small ladder. I watched as he propped it against the wall near the beams, checked it for steadiness, and climbed with what looked like a pick in his hand.

"Danny, don't," Zeb said. "You'll bring the roof down and kill us all."

"Hmm," Danny said sarcastically as he climbed. "Well, I think it's worth the risk, and you folks are going to die anyway."

When he reached the top of the ladder, he braced himself against it with his legs, then he swung the pick at the ceiling. Dirt poured down on him as he did so, but he didn't seem to care; he just kept working.

"What is he doing?" I asked.

"He's taking out the queen," Zeb replied.

"The queen?"

"I stopped him from working on it weeks ago when I realized he was compromising the integrity of the ceiling. If he brings that stone out, I believe the whole area will cave in."

I leaned forward and looked, and from what I could see, Danny was chipping away at the dirt around a giant rock that protruded from the ceiling. The white-and-blue color of the rock was the same as the one I had pulled from the bucket earlier, except it was about a hundred times bigger. At least.

"What kind of stone is that?" I asked.

"Sapphire," Zeb said. "The whole mine is sapphires."

"You wanna talk about sapphires," Danny called out to us as he worked. "This queen is gonna top your Princess Tatiana at least four times over."

Princess Tatiana. I thought back to where I had heard that name, remembering that Princess Tatiana was the woman Zeb Hooper was rumored to have run away with in his youth, when he later came back wealthy enough to buy a construction company.

"Who is Princess Tatiana?" I asked.

"Not who, *what*," Danny said. "It's a sapphire. One of the biggest ever found. Until now."

Of course! Zeb didn't leave town with a woman way back then. He left town with a big, valuable stone. He took it to a gem dealer, sold it, and came home with the profits. Princess Tatiana was a *sapphire*, not a person.

"Is that how long you've been stealing from this mine, Zeb? Since you were a young man?"

"When I was a young man, this was a working mica mine. They didn't even care about the sapphires back then."

"The story goes that Zeb used that big, ugly rock as a doorstop in his house for about ten years," Danny said, chipping away. "Then one day he realized what he might have, so he took it to a dealer and sold it for a small fortune."

"What happened between then and now, Zeb?"

He exhaled slowly, and though I knew he must've been in con- siderable pain, he seemed willing to talk.

"I just wanted to buy the mine," he said. "I tried to come by things legitimately. I've bought property all over this town, looking for gems. But there's never been any vein like this one, and Lowell wouldn't sell it to me."

"So you tunneled your way in from the other side of the moun- tain?"

"That tunnel worked fine for years. But I'm getting older. I thought there was an easier way. When I found out Lowell was donating land to Su Casa, I made sure we built right where we did. I gave myself a new entrance, straight from my own office. What could be simpler? Or so I thought, until my gem dealer came down here from New York and tried to blackmail his way into my source."

"Your gem dealer?" I asked, thinking of the man who was stabbed behind the church on Sunday night.

"That's me!" Danny said loudly, taking an extra big swing at the ceiling. As the pick connected with the dirt, an entire chunk came flying down and almost knocked him off the ladder.

"Wait a minute," I said. "Danny, you're a gem dealer? What about Detroit and your job as an accountant?"

"What about your parents' accident?" Trinksie added.

He paused in his work and looked at us.

"People are so gullible," he said. "Give 'em a good sob story, and they'll believe anything."

"Danny's from New York," Zeb said. "Everything he's said or done since he got here has been a lie. Now he's gonna kill us all, just the way he killed Morales and just the way he killed Roy."

"Roy?"

"His old business partner. The man who got stabbed Sunday night? Roy came here looking for a sweet deal himself, but nobody blackmails the blackmailer. Danny simply did him in."

"Danny stabbed that man in the parking lot?" Trinksie asked angrily. "Danny, you're the one Snake was trying to protect?"

"Snake is the best flunky I ever found," Danny said. "That kid would do almost anything to become a member of the club." He laughed, his voice echoing against the rock. "A club. Best idea I ever had."

I took a deep breath in the dusty air, trying to clear my mind.

"Wait a minute," I said to Zeb. "How could Danny have killed Enrique Morales? Danny wasn't even living here back then."

Danny laughed.

"I was visiting," he said. "I came here to call on my buddy Zeb, to see where he was getting such sweet stones. I knew there was something funny about his situation, but I never guessed he was building himself a secret entrance to somebody else's mine."

"Danny only stayed in town a few days that time," Zeb explained. "And he kept a very low profile while he was here—he was either in the mine or at my house. I don't think anyone else ever saw him. When Enrique discovered the hidden door, Danny tricked me into luring him down here, and then he killed him."

"Hey," Danny said, swinging his pick. "It's a tough job, but somebody had to do it."

"You never said you were going to *kill* him," Zeb said. "I just thought you would rough him up a bit. Convince him to keep his mouth shut."

"I don't understand," Trinksie said. "Why did you put Enrique's body in the apples?"

Danny gave a sharp laugh.

"That was just supposed to be temporary," Zeb said. "We hid the body there 'cause we needed to stash it somewhere in a hurry. We weren't sure if Enrique had told anyone about the mine, so we couldn't leave the body down here, in case someone came looking."

"We were gonna come back and get the body out of the apples that night, after dark," Danny continued, "maybe throw it in the lake or bury it in the woods. But by then, the apple bin was gone. The truck had come and picked it up, and that migrant had already been sealed tight in the apple storage, with no way to get him out until springtime."

"So the day that the room was unsealed," I said, "Danny was supposed to be driving the forklift, and the bin of apples you came to pick up in your truck was the bin with the body in it?"

"If all had gone according to plan," Zeb said. "Though we knew it might be a bit tricky."

Trinksie shifted her weight, causing the duct tape to cut into my side.

"What about that letter from New York?" I asked. "How did Roy's fingerprints get on it?"

"I wrote that letter and sent it to Roy," Danny snapped. "He was just supposed to put it in an envelope and mail it back down to Luisa. But the idiot had to go and read it first. That got him curious enough to eventually come down here and see what was going on for himself."

Trinksie shook her head.

"I still don't get it," she said. "Danny, why did you move here and take a job on the farm? Why did you pretend to be someone that you're not?"

He paused in his work to consider her question.

"I haven't seen a vein this rich with sapphires in my entire life," he said. "I knew a job on the orchard would give me a good cover for sapphire mining—plus it would give me the chance to get that migrant's body out of the apple storage before anyone else saw it."

"Why did it matter, after all that time?" I asked.

"Because of how he died!" Danny said. "The chemicals, the mica. We knew if they did an autopsy, somebody would put two and two together eventually."

"But then why the position with Go the Distance?" I asked. "The whole orchard liaison thing?"

"Because Karen Weatherby is set to inherit this entire place. Duh. Maybe Tinsdale wouldn't sell this property to Zeb, but I was gonna give it my best shot to marry into it. The old guy was supposed to die long before now."

I thought of Karen and Pete and Lowell's will, and I realized that Danny had no real interest in Karen. He only wanted her for her inheritance—an inheritance she didn't even know she wasn't going to get! I had let myself get sidetracked by their issues. They had nothing to do with any of this.

The real issue was that Danny Stanford was a sociopath, willing to manipulate, lie, steal, and kill just to get what he wanted.

"You said it couldn't be done," Danny cried exuberantly. He swung the pick with a mighty blow, and then we all watched as the big rock broke loose from the ceiling. Like a giant pendulum, it hung there for a moment, and then it came completely free and crashed to the ground with a deep, heavy thud.

I braced myself for what would come next, closing my eyes and bending my head. The roof held, however, and after a moment, Danny cheered with glee.

"I told you, Zeb!" he said, tossing the pick. "I told you it would hold!"

He ran to the big bucket of soaking gemstones and dumped the liquid out onto the ground. Then he started going around the room and collecting sapphires from various piles, throwing them all into the bucket. Apparently, if this was the last looting of the mine, he was going to do a thorough job of it.

Finally, he took off into the cave, laughing.

"Where is he going?" I asked Zeb.

"He's probably collecting the stones from all of the buckets," Zeb replied.

"Is he gone?" a voice asked from the top of the stairs.

"Snake?" Trinksie whispered. "Is that you?"

"I thought Snake was in jail!" I said.

"I bailed him out this morning," Trinksie replied.

We heard the door open, and a moment later Snake appeared at the bottom of the stairs.

"I-I been listening through the hole in the door," he said softly. "Is he gone now?"

"Snake!" I whispered sharply. "Grab that knife by the wall and come cut us loose!"

He did as I directed, grabbing Zeb's pocketknife that Danny had confiscated, running over to us, and quickly slicing through our bonds. My hands were numb, and I flexed my fingers in front of me as I ran for the pick that Danny had tossed to the wall. Snake helped Trinksie to her feet, and then she tended to Zeb.

"All right, folks!" Danny cried, coming into the room with two bucket handles in each hand. "It won't be long now."

When he entered the room, he hesitated, momentarily surprised when he saw we weren't still taped together on the ground. He recovered quickly, however, dropping the buckets and reaching for his gun.

Just as quickly, I swung back the pickax to throw at him, but then Snake decided to be brave and make a run at Danny. With Snake in the way, I had to hold off from throwing the sharp tool. In an instant, Danny gained the upper hand.

"Stop!" Danny cried, pointing the gun as the boy froze in front of him. Still looking at Snake, Danny said, "Callie, put the pickax down and come back over with the rest."

Reluctantly, I dropped the tool into the mud and rejoined the group.

"Snake, buddy," Danny said, forcing a smile. "I'm so glad you're here. I've got some heavy things I could use your help with."

"I-I'm not your buddy," Snake said loudly. "You tricked me."

"Tricked you?" Danny asked. "Tricked you how? You finally made it, dude. You're in the clubhouse!"

"Th-this isn't a clubhouse," Snake said. "You tricked me."

Danny motioned with the gun for Snake to back up, and then he herded us all tightly together against the wall.

Gun still pointed at us, Danny walked over to the gigantic sapphire on the ground and looked down at, as if he were trying to decide how to handle it by himself. Finally, he knelt down and in one quick motion hoisted it onto his shoulder with a groan.

"All right, then," Danny said, still pointing the gun at us, straightening his legs with the weight. "I've got four people and five bullets. Who wants to die first?"

Smiling, he pointed the gun at me. Before he could squeeze the trigger, however, I leaped toward him in a low tackle, hoping to take him down at the knees before he could get off a clean shot. Unfortunately, he lost his grip on the big rock, and it fell, breaking my force and scraping my shoulder as I hit the ground.

"Uh-oh!" Danny cried, stepping back out of my reach. "Looks like we have ourselves a hero here. Don't you know, girl? Heroes are the first to go."

From the ground, I looked up into the barrel of his pistol as he cocked it with his thumb. He was going to shoot me, and there was nothing I could do about it.

"Wait!" I said, trying to stand, my mind racing. "If you shoot me right here, I'll get blood all over your stones."

He laughed.

"Blood from a stone," he said. "Get it?"

He reached down and grabbed my arm, lifting me the rest of the way up, spinning me around, and pinning my arm behind my back. It hurt like heck, but I remained silent, hoping that by fighting him I could distract him long enough for the others to get away.

Unfortunately, I felt the cold steel of the gun barrel against my temple. He had me in a tight armlock, with no way for me to get out.

Before he could squeeze the trigger, however, a clump of dirt fell onto his forehead. Distracted, he looked up, and I seized the moment to stomp on his instep and then twist around and free my arm. More dirt fell, and Trinksie screamed. I ran toward her just as the roof caved in, dirt and mud crashing down on top of Danny, the booming thunk of tons of earth echoing throughout the mine. As if in slow motion, I reached my arms out and swept Snake and Trinksie forward, throwing them toward the passageway. The three of us landed on the ground, and clutched each other tightly, covered our faces, coughing and gagging through the dust. When things cleared somewhat, we looked back to see that the entire chamber had caved in. Instead of a dirt ceiling, now the dirt formed a giant mound on the ground and above it was only wide-open blue sky.

Danny and Zeb were no more.

Fifty

The hospital room was dark, the shades drawn. I tapped lightly on the door and walked in to find Lowell Tinsdale awake and staring at the ceiling.

"Lowell?" I said softly, stepping toward the bed.

He looked over at me and then turned away. I walked over to the bed anyway and pulled up a chair and sat beside him.

There were wires and tubes everywhere, particularly the ever-present oxygen tube that ran under his nose. One of his machines made a steady whoosh, in and out, and I focused on the sound of that as I sat and waited patiently for him to acknowledge that I was there.

"What do you want?" he said finally, turning toward me. "I told the nurse no visitors."

"I broke the rules," I said. "So sue me."

He raised one gnarled finger and pointed it at me.

"You…" he said, shaking his finger. "You are a pip."

"A pip?"

"Yeah. I like you. You can stay."

"I was staying anyway."

"See?" he laughed and then he started to cough and then he began to choke. Finally, he recovered and breathed in and out, in and out. "Like I said," he whispered. "You're a pip."

In my hand, I had my Bible, and in the quiet of the room, I turned to the book of First John. It was so dark in there that I had to squint, but once I found the verse I wanted—the fifth verse of the first chapter—I began to read aloud.

"This is the message we have heard from him and declare to you: God is light; in him there is no darkness at all…"

I continued to read until I got to the ninth verse, and then I spoke a bit more loudly.

"If we confess our sins, he is faithful and just and will forgive us our sins and purify us from all unrighteousness."

I stopped reading and closed the book, holding it in my lap.

"You don't have much time left, Lowell," I said bluntly. "Are you right with God? Have you given your heart to the Lord and asked for forgiveness of your sins?"

"My sins are too big to be forgiven."

I placed my hand on top of the Bible and prayed silently for God to give me the words that would reach this man's' heart.

"God promised us the He would purify us from *all* unrighteousness,'" I said. "That means He will forgive *all* our sins, Lowell. Even the sin you committed the day you first turned your back on your daughter."

"I have begged God for mercy on my soul," he said wearily.

"Then God has already given you that mercy. All you had to do was ask for it. Now you just have to ask your daughter for forgiveness as well."

He closed his eyes and shook his head.

"It's too late now," he said. "I can't make it up to her."

"Yes, you can," I said. "You can hold her by the hand. You can say 'I love you, Karen.'"

"She doesn't want to hear that from me," he whispered.

I heard a fluttering noise, and I looked up to see Karen standing there in the doorway, tears streaming down her face.

"Yes, I do, Daddy," she told him. "Yes, I do."

I left the two of them there in the room, patting Karen on the shoulder as I went. Hopefully, with what little time he had left, they would be able to make their peace.

Out in the waiting room, I saw Pete sitting in a chair, and I went to him and gave him a hug.

"Karen's in there with him now," I said, taking the seat across from him.

"I know," he replied. "We came here together."

"Together?"

He nodded.

"I went to her last night and told her about the will. We met with the lawyer this morning and drew up some papers that laid out how things will be distributed once I inherit. We split things right down the middle. She gets the house and I get the orchard."

"Who gets the sapphires?" I asked.

He grinned.

"Any money from those will go into a trust, with the interest to be used to support Go the Distance."

I nodded, feeling a surge of emotion.

"You're a good man, Pete," I said. "I wish you the best."

We shook hands and then said goodbye.

"Hey, Callie," he said, calling after me. "If you ever want a date with a soda jerk, the offer stands."

His twinkling eyes and handsome grin made for an enticing invitation indeed. But I wasn't interested, and with a smile and a wave I turned and walked away. I already had someone, and in less than 24 hours, he and I would be face-to-face.

I found my car in the parking lot, thinking about the cryptic e-mail, I had received from Tom this morning. It had said, simply, "See Skytop for further instructions." I wasn't sure what his message meant, but I would be going to the rental company in the morning to turn in the keys to the cabin, so I assumed I would find out then.

For now, I drove to the church for Enrique's memorial service, though I knew I would be getting there just a little bit early. Natalie and Luisa had planned a simple ceremony, to be followed by some food back at the house.

When I pulled into the parking lot, I couldn't help thinking of all that had happened in the past week, starting with the man I had watched die not 50 feet from where I was now. I turned into a space and shut off my car, sitting there for a moment in the quiet and getting my thoughts together.

This had been one of the most complicated cases I'd ever worked—made infinitely more difficult by the crimes that had been committed. Though it would be a few weeks before MORE would get the actual check, I had recommended that they be approved for the million-dollar grant, providing they followed our contingencies.

As for Harriet, she had left early this morning to drive home to DC. She was taking with her a newfound love of the Smoky Mountains, several jars of barbecue sauce from the Pig Stop, and the telephone number and e-mail address of a certain white-collar crime specialist who seemed to have found her particularly engaging.

I had already said my goodbyes to June Sweetwater, the detective who had presided over the crime scene at the mine yesterday with the utmost of compassion and professionalism. Zeb Hooper and Danny Stanford were indeed both dead, killed by the impact of the collapse.

The "aiding and abetting" charge against Snake Atkins had been dropped, given that he had had no involvement with the stabbing in the parking lot except as a witness—and then he had been threatened into silence by Danny Stanford afterward. He would still face charges of "criminal mischief" for the petty vandalism he had committed against Luisa, but given Danny's coercion and manipulation that had tricked Snake into committing the acts in the first place, his lawyer hoped that he could work out his sentence through probation and community service.

Snake didn't know this yet, but the mayor was also planning to award him a medal for bravery, citing his heroic efforts in coming into the mine and cutting us all loose from our duct tape. Trinksie also looked at me with something near hero worship, claiming I had saved her and her son's life by throwing them free of the collapse.

Sadly, I wouldn't be seeing the Morales kids again, but I walked into the church and hugged Luisa before taking a seat in the pew. As a young widow, I knew the road she had in front of her. It wouldn't be easy, but at least she was going back home now where she would find comfort and fellowship from her friends and relatives.

The service for Enrique was lovely, with some Bible passages read, a few songs sung, and then a brief eulogy given by Dean. There were many praises you could give a person, Dean said, but the highest praise he knew was what he could say of Enrique Morales: He was a good husband. He was a good father. He was a good man.

When the service was over, we adjourned to the Webbers' house, where we mingled about and nibbled on comfort food and relaxed in the afternoon sun that sparkled on the lake. Luisa didn't stay long, and as she said her goodbyes, she gave me an extra-long hug.

"There are no words for what you have done for me and my children," she said. "Only *gracias*. From the bottom of my heart, *gracias*."

After she left, the somber gathering grew a little more lighthearted. I had an opportunity to see several of the relatives one more time, including Ken Webber and his lovely wife and their two sons. I thanked Ken for his help this week. It was always a pleasure to work with someone intelligent who knew how to get a job done.

I ended the afternoon sitting on the deck, looking out at the mountains and the water. Dean and Natalie joined me there, and we talked a bit about all that had taken place since I first arrived only six nights before.

"I always knew you were good at your job," Natalie told me. "But I have to say, Callie, this week you have simply astounded me."

"Me too," Dean said, patting my arm. "If I ever need a superhero to sweep in and save the day in every way, I sure know who to call."

"Aw, shucks, guys," I said. "You're going to make my head swell."

Once the guests had all gone home, I took out the canoe and paddled into the lake to enjoy the sunset. It had been a long week, filled with unexpected trials and tribulations. In the past seven days, it seemed as if the theme of death had run through everything I did, from watching a man die and then seeing a man who had long been dead to bringing comfort to a man who was going to die soon. Strangely, death was the one thing that had made me apprehensive about coming here in the first place, where I knew my relationships and my memories would lead me to think about the death of my husband.

Yet, in spite of the memories here, this had been a good week for me emotionally, a good time for me to see how far I had come in the healing process. Tomorrow I would take a bold step of faith toward a deeper, more serious relationship with Tom. I knew that I was ready. And with the blessing of my friend Harriet and of Bryan's parents, I was looking at my future head-on, eager to embrace it.

For now, I would close this chapter of my life in prayer, remembering especially Luisa and Pepe and Adriana and all of the migrant workers all over the country. Danny Stanford had said that the migrants were "a dime a dozen," worthless and replaceable. I knew that wasn't true. I knew God's Word said that every single person on His earth mattered. Every single one was precious to Him.

Eventually, I found myself drifting past the face in the rocks, Old Gus, and the moment was so sharp and so clear and so filled with déjà vu that I fully expected to be able to turn around and see Bryan there in the back of the canoe.

"Hello, Old Gus," I said as I paddled past.

Hello, Old Gus, I could almost hear Bryan echo behind me.

As the last rays of sunlight disappeared from the sky, I brought the canoe back to the shore, praying as I paddled that God would keep His hand on all of the people I had met during this past week. I prayed, too, that He would be with me and Tom as we embarked on a new adventure together.

Fifty-One

The adventure began the next day at noon, when I showed up at the Skytop Vacation Rentals office to turn in the keys to the cabin. I had enjoyed a final breakfast on my deck early in the morning and then had closed the place up and joined the Webbers for their 10:00 Sunday church service. We said our final farewells in the parking lot afterward, and now I was dropping off my keys and hopefully getting some kind of instruction from the people at Skytop as to what I should do next.

The woman who signed me out had a funny look on her face, and when she handed me my receipt, she reached under the counter and gave me a small white box, breaking into a big smile.

"This is for you," she said.

I opened the box to find a cupcake inside, topped with pink icing and decorated with a bunch of tiny plastic balloons. There were words written on the inside of the lid: "See Regina at the Marwick Country Club for further instructions."

Smiling, I thanked the woman, went out to my car, and made the 20-minute drive to the Marwick Country Club, eating the yummy cupcake on the way. Once there, I went inside to the front desk and asked for Regina. A woman came out, grinning, and handed me a little heart-shaped Mylar balloon on a stick. A tag hung from the stick and it said, simply: "See Sarah at the Hertz counter in the Asheville airport for further instructions."

That was an hour's drive away, so I settled in and drove there, imagining the possibilities of what Tom had in store. When I reached the airport, I had a feeling I would be turning in the car, so I gathered up my things and brought them inside to the rental counter. I asked for Sarah.

She knew who I was. She told me that she would be taking back the car, and after giving me the receipt, she excused herself to go into the back room. A moment later, she emerged with a balloon bouquet and handed it to me with a smile. I took the bouquet and pulled out the card that was attached, fully expecting to be given a gate and flight number. Instead, I was directed to "See Andrew at the limousine pickup area for further instructions."

I found the fellow named Andrew, who immediately escorted me to a waiting Rolls Royce limousine. Laughing, I climbed inside. The limo was empty except for a gigantic silver balloon, as big as a widescreen TV, emblazoned with the words "See Tom for further instructions."

My heart pounded with excitement as Andrew drove away from the airport on the interstate, and several times I checked my hair and makeup in the mirror. We rode along for about 15 minutes before he took an exit, and I watched curiously out the window as we seemed to be heading into the middle of nowhere. He finally pulled to a stop on the side of the road next to a big field. Then he jumped out of the car and opened my door to let me out.

"Where are we?" I asked.

"You'll see," he replied.

Carrying my luggage, he escorted me to the middle of the field and then stood there with me, smiling like a Cheshire cat. No matter how many questions I asked him, his answer was the same: "You'll see."

And soon I did see.

Actually, I heard it first, a odd sort of blowing sound. I heard it again, and I looked up in the sky to see a giant hot air balloon. A basket hung from underneath, and leaning over one side, looking down, was Tom.

It seemed to take forever for the balloon to land so that he could climb out and come to me. When he finally did, I was smiling and laughing, and he swept me into his arms, lifting me from the ground and spinning me around.

Oh, how wonderful he looked to me! The broad shoulders, the dark hair, the gorgeous eyes—they were as familiar to me as if I had seen him only yesterday. He set me down and then firmly placed his hands on each side of my face. He kissed me hungrily, his lips demanding against mine. I kissed back just as strongly, trying to meld together with him, trying to erase every moment of every day we had spent apart.

When the kiss was over, he finally spoke.

"Your chariot awaits, my dear."

He loaded in my luggage, helped me into the basket, then climbed in himself as the limo driver tossed the ropes to the man who was in the basket working the controls. Suddenly, there was a whoosh of air, and the balloon lifted from the ground. We were aloft!

Waving goodbye, my heart was in my throat as we quickly pulled upwards into the sky. Tom and I held onto each other and looked out at the incredible view, the mountains that spread before us in endless chains of blue and green among the smoky puffs of clouds. It was almost as if Tom were giving this place to me, as if he were wrapping up all of my beloved mountains and handing them to me with a bow.

I was enraptured.

In retrospect, I don't know how long the balloon ride lasted. I do know that it must've gone on for at least an hour, possibly two. We never left the beauty of the mountains, though we drifted past the famous Biltmore House and Gardens, and then past lakes and valleys and rivers and streams and even a city or two. When we finally began to land, I didn't know where we were. It was another field, another limo was waiting, and then we were escorted to the comfort of the massive vehicle and whisked away down the road. This time I didn't look out the window. I simply wrapped myself in Tom's arms, my head against his shoulder, my eyes closed tight.

"Thank you for that," I whispered. "Thank you more than you'll ever know."

I tilted my chin up and kissed him again, much more gently and sweetly this time. As we kissed, I thought about how I loved the feel of him, the very taste of him. Though he was here and he was real, there was something about the entire day that was so *un*real, probably because we had waited for it for so long.

I didn't know what our destination would be, but finally we slowed and turned onto a driveway of shells, crunching along as we pulled through overgrown oak trees and up a gentle incline. It looked like a farm of sorts. We drove along a white wooden split rail fence, passing a small pond with two ducks floating on the surface. As we climbed, the driveway curved to the right, and up ahead I could see a house, lined on one whole side with giant picture windows. A weeping willow tree blew gently in the breeze next to a stone terrace.

We drove around the far side of the house, where I saw three buildings that were each connected with a covered walkway lined with hanging flower pots.

"Where are we?" I asked.

The car came to a stop, and a man and a woman appeared from the smallest of the three buildings, let us out, introduced themselves, and began unloading our things from the trunk. I watched as the man carried my suitcases toward what I assumed was the guest house.

Holding my hand, Tom led me into the main house, up the steps and into the room with the massive picture windows. From there we looked out over a long, sweeping lawn, the pond down below, and more mountains visible in the distance. In a side pasture, I spotted several horses grazing among giant oak trees. Tom gave me a tour of the elegantly furnished home, taking me full circle through the entire place, ending on the terrace outside.

"You'll be in the guest house," he said, "and you have the services of the live-in couple from over there if you need anything."

I took it all in, wondering how I could tell him that while all of this was wonderful, none of it really mattered. I didn't need the *things*. I just needed him.

"Where are we?" I asked again. "This place is beautiful."

"It is, isn't it? It belongs to a friend of mine. He said we're welcome to use it while he's out on tour."

"On tour?"

"With his little band."

He winked and hummed a few bars of a familiar country song. I gasped as I recognized it. Leave it to Tom to be on house-sharing terms with one of the biggest stars in the world of country music!

We went out to the pasture to meet the horses, and we fed them green apples from a tree on our side of the fence.

"This is Lucille," Tom said, introducing me to a chestnut mare. "And that one's Gambler."

I held out apples to both, and they took them greedily from my hands.

"As I told you on the phone," Tom said, "my greatest hope is that we can spend some time just hanging out. I need to rest, and I'm sure you do too. I don't want to think about anything but each other."

I looked up at him, and in his eyes I thought I could see so much. I could see his sweetness. I could see the future. I could see love.

"Are you scared?" I asked, reaching out to pat the horse's flank.

Tom gazed at me for a long moment before looking away.

"I'm scared I might disappoint you," he said. "I'm scared you might decide you want nothing more to do with me once you know everything there is to know."

I laughed.

"I can't imagine that."

"Callie, things aren't quite as simple as they seem. As you get to know me better, there might be elements of my job, of my past, that are difficult for you to hear."

I held out another apple to Lucille, and she grabbed it from my hand, crunching it loudly with big square teeth.

"We're not kids, Tom," I said softly. "We both come to this with full, rich histories of our own. I look forward to learning about you—to learning *everything* about you, in time. Your past has made you who you are. That's all."

He nodded and reached out for Gambler, who stepped forward and nuzzled his chin against Tom's hand. Beside me, I thought I could feel Tom's muscles slowly relax.

"So how about you?" he asked. "Are you scared?"

"Sure I am," I said, glancing at him and then turning my gaze back to the horses. "Most of all, I'm scared I won't ever hear the words you're thinking, the words I know you're just dying to say."

Now it was his turn to laugh.

"Oh, yeah? How do you know what I'm dying to say?"

"I just know," I told him. "I know because it shows in everything you do."

Growing serious, he turned to face me and took my hands in his.

"You're right," he said simply. "There is one thing I have been wanting to say. I love you, Callie."

To my surprise, tears filled his eyes. I reached up and touched the side of his face. He was no longer some far and distant dream but a reality, standing in front of me, needing to hear the words I also longed to say.

"Ah, Tom," I replied. "Don't you know? I love you too."

Mindy Starns Clark's plays and musicals have been featured in schools and churches across the United States. Originally from Hammond, Louisiana, Mindy now lives with her husband and two daughters near Valley Forge, Pennsylvania. Visit Mindy's website at www.mindystarnsclark.com.

Mindy's fast-paced and suspenseful inspirational writing—with a hint of romance and a strong heroine—are sure to make this exciting mystery series one that will delight readers everywhere.

Coming next in the fourth book in the series *A Quarter for a Kiss:* A frantic call for help from Florida—where Callie's dear friend and mentor, Eli Gold, has barely survived an attempt on his life—plunges Callie and Tom headlong into a mystery, working together to unravel the threads of an old case. As they do, Callie uncovers other secrets that reveal more about Tom's work—more, perhaps, than she was ready to know. Look for this new addition to the Million Dollar Mysteries soon at a local Christian bookstore near you.